Tiger's Trek

Books by Colleen Houck

The Tiger's Curse Series

Tiger's Curse

Tiger's Quest

Tiger's Voyage

Tiger's Destiny

Tiger's Promise

Tiger's Dream

Tiger's Tale

Tiger's Trek

Reawakened Series

Reawakened

Recreated

Reunited

Standalone Novels

The Lantern's Ember

Terraformer

Tiger's Trek

COLLEEN HOUCK

BLACK STONE PUBLISHING

Published in 2025 by Blackstone Publishing
Cover and book design by James Egan of Bookfly Design

Printed in the United States of America

First edition: 2025
ISBN 979-8-212-22173-3
Adult Fiction / Fantasy / Epic

Version 1

Blackstone Publishing
31 Mistletoe Rd.
Ashland, OR 97520

www.BlackstonePublishing.com

For Brad
If I had to head out on a crazy trek
through the Siberian wilderness,
there's no one else I'd want to suffer with more.

Storm-clouds hurtle, storm-clouds hover;
Flying snow is set alight
By the moon whose form they cover;
Blurred the heavens, blurred the night.
On and on our coach advances,
Little bell goes din-din-din . . .
Round are vast, unknown expanses;
Terror, terror is within.

—Faster, coachman! "Can't, sir, sorry:
Horses, sir, are nearly dead.
I am blinded, all is blurry,
All snowed up; can't see ahead.
Sir, I tell you on the level:
We have strayed, we've lost the trail.
What can WE do, when a devil
Drives us, whirls us round the vale?

"There, look, there he's playing, jolly!
Huffing, puffing in my course;
There, you see, into the gully
Pushing the hysteric horse;
Now in front of me his figure
Looms up as a queer mile-mark—
Coming closer, growing bigger,
Sparking, melting in the dark."

Storm-clouds hurtle, storm-clouds hover;
Flying snow is set alight
By the moon whose form they cover;
Blurred the heavens, blurred the night.
We can't whirl so any longer!
Suddenly, the bell has ceased,

Horses halted . . .—Hey, what's wrong there?
"Who can tell!—a stump? a beast? . . ."

Blizzard's raging, blizzard's crying,
Horses panting, seized by fear;
Far away his shape is flying;
Still in haze the eyeballs glare;
Horses pull us back in motion,
Little bell goes din-din-din . . .
I behold a strange commotion:
Evil spirits gather in—

Sundry, ugly devils, whirling
In the moonlight's milky haze:
Swaying, flittering and swirling
Like the leaves in autumn days . . .
What a crowd! Where are they car-
ried?
What's the plaintive song I hear?
Is a goblin being buried,
Or a sorceress married there?

Storm-clouds hurtle, storm-clouds hover;
Flying snow is set alight
By the moon whose form they cover;
Blurred the heavens, blurred the night.
Swarms of devils come to rally,
Hurtle in the boundless height;
Howling fills the whitening valley,
Plaintive screeching rends my heart . . .

—"Devils" by Aleksandr Pushkin,
translated by Genia Gurarie

Contents

Once upon a time, a hunter, a priest, a soldier, and an outcast were asked to escort two tsarevnas on a long journey. If they accepted the responsibility to care for the royal twins, guide them to the Dreaming Mountain, and protect them from harm, the men would be gifted with more riches than they could carry, and they'd each earn a boon from the empire.

The men agreed to render aid, even when they discovered the tsarevnas were cursed by magic to roam the earth as fierce tigers.

Together, the unlikely heroes accomplished many difficult tasks, battled fierce beasts, and eventually made their way to the cave of the White Shaman, only to discover . . . everything they'd been told was a lie.

Prologue

What Falls off a Cart Is as Good as Gone

The first thing she became aware of was the sound of wind rustling the leaves in the trees and the feeling of warm rays of sunshine bathing her cheeks, neck, and arms. It had been so long since she'd felt that warm. Straightening her toes, then her legs, she stretched languidly, curling her back and wriggling as if trying to nestle deeper into the soft grass, not even bothering to blink open her eyes, fully intending to sleep longer. Then wisps of soft hair tickled Veru's nose.

Irritated, she brushed her fingers against her face and stretched an arm out, patting around for her travel blanket. Not finding it easily, she grunted and mumbled, "Nik, did you steal my blanket again? Give it back. Or go and find me another one, won't you? There's a good man." She yawned deeply, smacking her lips a few times, before snorting loud enough to startle herself awake more fully.

When she didn't hear a response or Nik's telltale scrambling to obey her orders, the tsarevna finally cracked open an eye and blearily studied her surroundings. "Nikolai?" she called out. "Where can that blasted, nikudyshnyi have run off to?" she mumbled. Then Veru used her palm to rub the sleep from her eyes and shouted for her sister. "Stacia?"

Almost in an instant, as the specter of sleep departed, awareness returned.

Something was very, very wrong. She was in a meadow. A green meadow. Alone. And she was . . . human. And . . . clean. Had it all been a dream? A strange nightmare? Veru quickly scrambled to her feet, teetering on legs she hadn't used to stand upright in months, and discovered to her shock that she was wearing a dress, not her typical fur-lined travel clothing or even her armor. Her upper lip curled in disdain when she plucked at the thin, gossamer-like skirt. Quickly, she searched the sides of the fabric, hoping for a belt with a knife or a sword or at least a pocket with some type of tool, but found only a wide ribbon cinching her middle. The pinching she felt came not from a weapon but from a corset.

Almost instinctively, she shook her whole body and felt the tiny hairs on her arms and the back of her neck stand up. *Is that the trigger*? She waited. Breathing deeply. Expecting the tiger to explode from her body and take over at any second.

She'd lived with the cat for so long that her human body felt almost unnatural. She couldn't have dreamed something so vivid. So real. Her mouth even watered at the thought of catching and devouring a raw fish. Veru touched her thumb to her lip to wipe away a drop of saliva as she told her stomach to stop rumbling.

She was surprised to find she missed her claws and teeth and ran her tongue across her smooth canines. For a moment, she thought about her situation. She was alone. She possessed no weapons. No armor. And she was in a strange, unknown place. There was nothing she and her sister had wanted more than to regain their humanity, but Veru was practical. Survival was key. As a tiger, she'd have natural defenses. *Not to mention a coat*, she thought as she rubbed her arms.

Decision made, she closed her eyes and tried to wish herself back into her tiger form. Nothing happened. "Come on. Come on!" she shouted at the sky. She felt vulnerable in her human skin and cursed again the fact that she didn't at least have her armor. But even begging and rubbing her fingers over the amulet that hung around her neck did nothing to help the situation.

Pacing, she bit her lip and tried speaking to her inner animal, but it was strangely silent. In fact, for the first time since her transformation, she felt as if she were completely alone, stripped of everything that made her feel . . . safe. "I guess she's really gone," Veru whispered, not sure if she meant her tiger or her sister or both.

"It's all up to me now," she said softly as she wiped away a hot tear that fell to her cheek.

With no other options, she yanked the ribbon from her waist and went to work on the laces at the back of her dress. It took some rather extraordinary feats of stretching and balancing on her part, but eventually she managed to get the top half of the sky-blue confection of a gown off so she could start working on the corset, which was laced even tighter than the dress had been. Veru figured if she could pry some of the boning out of the fabric, she could use it as a weapon or a tool that would help her hunt or start a fire.

So intent on her work was she that Veru didn't hear the noise of someone approaching until the whistle finally caught her attention. Veru recognized the musical sound and who it belonged to immediately.

"Danik?" she cried out, a wide grin on her face as she stood and rushed forward to find her friend, bunching the folds of billowing fabric in her arms to cover her chest.

She saw him as she rounded a tree, but, like her, he was dressed differently. Instead of his hunter's attire, he was clad in clothing more befitting a traveling musician. His hair was a bit longer, and he still had the blond stubble on his chin and cheeks. White loose-cut trousers were tucked into tall black leather boots, and he wore a beautifully patterned tunic tied at the waist with a belt. Instead of his hunter's pack, he carried only his domra, with a small bag tied to the instrument.

Veru grabbed hold of his arm. "Please tell me you have food or at least a knife in there. I'm starving."

Gently, Danik took hold of Veru's hand and stepped back, a look of deep concern on his face.

"My good lady. Of course I am more than willing to share with you whatever victuals I have at my disposal. It is clear to me by your present state that you've been brutalized."

He clucked and tsked at her torn and bleeding fingers, something she'd done to herself while trying to tear the stitches from her corset using bits of stone and twigs. Hissing, she snatched her fingers from his, more of an involuntary response than because she actually felt any offense. Over the years, she'd become accustomed to treating men who touched her without permission in that manner. It was a way of protecting herself from unwanted attention.

In truth, she trusted Danik and even thought on occasion she might enjoy being close to him. She certainly did as a tiger, or at least, she'd learned to like being with him when there was no pressure. Still, at this point there was no reason to let things go too far. Friend or not, Veru was unwilling to let him know she'd actually liked his fussing over her.

Nonplussed, Danik placed his hand back on his bundle and gave her a kind smile despite her scornful expression. "Dobryy vecher. Though I'm a stranger in this land, I'll do my best to see you back to your hearth and home. I've no cloak to offer you, but perhaps I may be of service in helping you repair your . . . er . . . abused garment?"

"My hearth and . . . ?" Veru blinked, confusion replacing the ire. Then she laughed. "Oh, I believe I understand. You just don't recognize me as a person." She squared her shoulders, hoping he'd somehow recognize the fierce and powerful soul he knew inside the beautiful package who stood before him now. "Danik, I'm Veru, the tiger you've traveled with all these months."

"The . . . tiger. Yes." He nodded dumbly. "I see. I'm think I'm starting to understand."

When Danik's eyes melted in pity, she threw up her hands and shook a fist at the sky, which caused her loose dress to slide even lower. Only a thin slip of material above her ruined corset kept her from exposing herself. Danik shifted away from her uncomfortably, looking everywhere but at Veru's face or bosom, and Veru stomped off and let out a frustrated bark. "Unbelievable! You have no idea at all who I am, do you? Or is it you just can't see past my . . . you know . . . all this," she finished, indicating her face and form.

The poor man simply shook his head while avoiding eye contact. "I'm not sure I . . . I take your meaning, good lady."

Veru mumbled curses about men and their eyes while shrugging back into the sleeves and bodice of her dress. Of course he couldn't think with her half dressed. Most men were so taken with her beauty that they stopped and stared, even when she was fully encased in armor and sweat poured off her body. It was the reason she covered her hair whenever possible and wore the heaviest of helmets. What was she thinking? Once she'd shrugged back into her bodice as best she could, she snapped her fingers to regain his attention. "What about Stacia, Nik, Zakhar, or Iriko? Do you recall them? Or have your brains disappeared into your nether regions?"

"Z-Zakhar? Oh. Yes. I know him. I believe he's the man I met along the trail. Nice fellow."

With her dress still gaping in the back where she'd torn her laces, Veru grabbed hold of Danik's shoulder and shook him. "Zakhar's here? Show me."

Chapter 1

There Is Plenty of Sound in an Empty Barrel

"You . . . you wish me to take you to the young man I found earlier?"

"Exactly. Yes," Veru said, spinning and heading off in the direction from which Danik had appeared.

"I'm not certain I can find the young man you seek," he said, trailing behind her.

"What? What do you mean you can't find him?"

Danik cupped the back of his neck. "The sun will be going down in an hour or two, and without knowing where *I* am, how do you expect me to find your young man?"

Veru let out an exasperated sigh and turned. "I don't know. How about *tracking* him?"

"That sounds good. Do you know how to do that?"

"I know a little, but you're much better at it than I am. Of course, when I was a tiger, I was excellent at doing such things, but I seem to have lost that ability, for some reason."

"A tiger . . . yes. And may I ask, when did the two of us meet, exactly? I'm afraid I can't quite recall."

"You must have hit your head somewhere. Hopefully, Zakhar will be able to come up with something that can help you remember."

"I see." Danik began walking beside her almost hesitantly. "If—if it's not too forward, might I inquire as to the lady's name? I think you said it before . . ."

His walking companion snorted. "Sure. The full name is Verusha Irena Vasilia Stepanov. But you can call me Veru. And to answer your question, we met when you caught me in a trap."

"Stepanov . . . that seems familiar. I feel like I should know that."

"Yes. Yes. You should. But it's not important now."

"It isn't?"

"No."

"A trap? Why were you in a trap? And what do you mean when you say I was the one who 'caught' you?"

"I was a tiger, and you're a hunter. Do you see the connection?"

"Oh no, you are mistaken there." Danik laughed. "I could never be a hunter. I'm a musician. You must have confused me with one of my cousins. Some of us do look alike, though, so I can see how you could get it wrong."

"No, I'm not wrong, Danik. It was *you* who caught me. You caught me and then you freed me, and after that I saved your life when the wolves came for you. Truly you remember *nothing*? What of your parents?"

"My parents? Funny you should mention them. That's why I'm out here, you see. I'm searching for them. We've become separated somehow. But I know they're here somewhere. I just need to find them. If I think hard enough, I'll recall my home's direction. The songs help me. My mother taught me a remembering song when I was just a boy. It always helped me find my way when I was lost. When I don't sing, I fear I forget nearly everything."

"That's interesting. Perhaps this is a part of your trial."

"My trial?"

"Stacia, she's my sister, in case you've forgotten her too. Anyway, she mentioned that the voice told her we'd all be facing further trials before going home. Perhaps this is what was meant."

Danik peered at her for a moment, his brow furrowed in

concentration, but then his features relaxed and he fixed his gaze ahead. His eyes had that lost, dreamy look again. He seemed almost surprised to have a traveling companion. "Privet," he said. "Have we met?"

"Ugh!" Veru could almost wrench her hair out in frustration. *What good is Danik in this state?* she thought. Then she tripped over the hem of her skirt and mumbled something under her breath about her trial being cursed by filmy, useless dresses and brain-fogged men.

Veru yanked her skirt free and straightened, throwing her shoulders back and promptly snagging her long hair in a tree branch. To his credit, Danik didn't laugh as she unwound her locks from a thorny briar and began pulling seeds from her tangles. Instead, he stopped her, took a torn section of her dress, ripped it into two long strips, and deftly gathered all her hair at the nape of her neck, securing it with one strip of ribbon, then wove the other through her hair in loops and secured it at the end.

"Spasibo," she murmured after introducing herself again. "How did you learn to do that?" Veru asked. "You don't have any siblings."

"No. I don't," he said, screwing up his face in deep thought. "I do have many nieces though. And I've strung many instruments in my day. It's not a difficult thing when you're working with fine material."

Danik hadn't called her hair beautiful or compared it to the sun like other men or prospective suitors, and somehow that made the compliment feel deeper and more genuine. She also liked the fact that he didn't stand there mooning over her afterward to see if his words had any effect. He simply turned away and continued on as if he had no interest whatsoever in the result. Such a thing made her respect him all the more.

Of course, there was another possibility . . . she mused. There was a chance he didn't mean it to be a compliment at all. Perhaps he was referencing the fabric of her dress and not her hair. Or it was more likely that he'd just simply forgotten she existed again. But Veru didn't think so. She had felt the slight hesitation as he drew his fingertips away from her hair, and she was very familiar with the fine quality of it, having used it to her advantage many times in the past, despite her frequent threats to her sister to hack it off with her knives.

Despite his memory loss, it was clear Danik felt comfortable with her. His shoulders were relaxed, and he seemed like himself even if he couldn't recall certain details of his life. He also seemed to retain his tracking skills. When she pointed out signs of a trail, he knelt and easily picked up the path someone had made through the trees, spotting broken twigs, slight impressions, or plucked berries she would have missed.

At least he possessed something useful. Without her knives, claws, or armor, what good was having a memory? She was almost jealous of his constant mind resets.

When he again asked her who she was, which she calculated happened about once every twenty minutes or so, she wondered if there was a trigger or if it was happening automatically. She began paying attention to verbal cues in the conversation and wondered if singing would indeed help him retain more information.

"I miss my home too," Veru admitted, after a few moments of silent tracking.

"You do?" he asked, turning to her. "Are you lost like me?"

"I am."

"What's your name?"

"Veru."

Danik smiled and bowed. "A pretty name for a pretty girl."

"Thank you." Veru grinned this time instead of taking her usual offense, especially knowing he would forget her in the next few moments anyway. "Since we're both lost, you can sing, if you like. It might help us find our way."

"All right."

As the pair walked on, Danik began to hum and then sing. It was a haunting song of passing, one Veru remembered he'd written for his own parents. It reminded her of the loss of her own mother. Tears pricked her eyes. When Danik noticed, he stopped abruptly. "There now, kotenok. I didn't mean to cause you pain."

Taking her arm, Danik turned Veru toward him gently and swept a tear from her cheek. The gesture was tender and sweet, not at all groping and needy like the men who'd tried to touch her before. Veru didn't feel the need to swipe at him this time. Instead, she looked into his ocean-blue eyes and felt like she wanted to sink into their mysterious depths and discover what secrets dwelled behind them.

The song *had* helped him remember. He'd called her kotenok, *little kitten*. There must be a part of him that remembered. But then his eyes fogged again, and Veru sighed and stepped back.

Danik cleared his throat, and only then did she realize those very eyes had drifted down her face to the gaping neckline of her dress. With her corset gone, her bosom was dangerously close to spilling out over the top of the now-too-small bodice. She could feel the heat in her cheeks. It slid down her neck until her pulse quickened as it did before battle. Her skin felt tight and warm.

"Perhaps I can help with this," Danik said gently. "If you'll allow me?"

Veru hesitated. It was interesting. This was the first time she ever recalled wanting a man to touch her, and yet she knew somehow that allowing it was dangerous. Not that she thought he'd hurt her. She had no fear of Danik in that way. No. What she feared was letting her guard down. Letting a man know her. As a tiger, she didn't need to worry about it. But as a woman . . .

She felt vulnerable. Exposed. As if an enemy was circling, but she stood weaponless, bathed in an orb of light, unable to see him. She felt the warning thump in the uptick of her pulse and the hitch in her breath telling her to run or reach for her knives. The sensation of Danik's presence, his offer, had suddenly changed their relationship. No longer were they friends, companions, colleagues. Now she was facing off against him, an opponent in battle. It was two warriors taking the measure of each other, scanning for strengths and weaknesses.

She was about to say no, but before she could protest, Danik spun her around and began deftly tugging at the torn laces of her dress, tying the sections one by one. Each touch was a brand, a fiery lash on her skin. The bodice tightened until it resembled something like a decent piece of clothing. Only then did she remember the carefully stitched rabbits he'd thrown down to her when she'd been stuck in the pit. He'd filled them with sleeping herbs.

"Who taught you to sew?" she managed to say, trying to distract herself as he worked at her back.

"My . . . my uncle," he said after a moment.

Was that a quickening of his own breathing she heard, or was he forgetting again? "But isn't he a hunter?" she questioned.

"Yes. But his father was a bootmaker. I apprenticed with him for a time. He always brought my family the best sinews to make strings for our instruments."

Danik began to hum but paused when he reached the top of her dress, his fingertips resting for just a moment at the place the fabric kissed her bare skin. She could feel the fine hairs along the base of her scalp rise as if trying to reach out and touch him. Veru froze in place, wishing for the first time in her life that a man *would* draw her closer. She longed to feel Danik wrap his arms around her waist and pull her body tightly against his, or press his lips against her neck, but just as she wished it, he was gone and walking beside her again, once more her good-natured friend.

Peeking at him from the corner of her eye, Veru could see no reflection of the inner struggle that she felt at being near him in her human form. He was still humming—a sweet, happy tune that turned into a whistle—but she couldn't tell by his posture or his eyes if he remembered their recent encounter. Perhaps he'd already forgotten it. That was probably for the best. If she knew what was good for her, she'd forget it too.

What a curse it was, feeling an unfulfilled desire and being unable to act upon it. She suddenly felt great pity for all the men who had looked at her with lovelorn expressions over the years and her exploitation of them. It was a cruel thing she had done.

They walked for what seemed like an hour before they finally came across a small stream. Stopping, they drank deeply, and Danik agreed that it would be wise to stay close to the source of water to continue searching for her friend. Veru was surprised that he remembered they were looking for someone. Perhaps the humming helped. Danik told her that not only would they need the water, but it was logical to assume that her friend would want to stay close to it as well.

In fact, they were about to make camp as best they could without food or fire when they spotted a sign of smoke not far from where they were.

"Should we go investigate?" Danik asked. "He could be the one you're searching for."

"It's probably him," she agreed, biting her lip and glancing at the quickly darkening sky. "Do you think we can make it?"

"If your feet can take it in those shoes, I'd say yes."

Truthfully, Veru hadn't given the shoes a thought. She glanced down at her slippers and smiled. "My paws are tougher than you think," she teased.

"Let's press on, then, if your, um, *paws* can take it."

They ended up crossing the stream three times in an attempt to avoid the worst of the brambles, which made the trek to the source of the fire a much longer process than it should have been. Veru missed her tiger eyes as well as the stamina she used to have. Her body was weary. She couldn't recall ever feeling as weak as she did now—even when she'd been human before. It was like all her muscles had turned into the wet noodles her nurse fed her with broth when she felt ill.

Perhaps that was the trouble. All the trekking through the cold and damp had made her sick. She wondered if Stacia and Iriko were facing the same thing. Perhaps it was a malady that affected only those with a tiger nature. Danik certainly looked like his normal, hardy self. They continued walking long past sunset, peering into the dark, searching for signs of the smoke, and stopped often to listen intently for animals that might be hunting them.

Both were grateful when the full moon rose, bathing the trees with dim light, and Veru swallowed her pride and stifled her nerves when Danik reached for her hand. Despite his denial of hunting ability, he appeared to possess a keen sense of direction, much more so than Veru herself. This both impressed the tsarevna and made her inwardly chafe at the same time. Never in her life had she been dependent upon a man before. She loathed the very idea of it, and yet there was a sort of comfort in letting go and allowing him to bear the weight of responsibility.

She knew, if she had to, she could get them to the fire as well, but there was freedom in letting him take the lead. Veru trusted Danik, even if the musician didn't quite trust himself. Perhaps he only guided her out of a sense of chivalry or duty, but she knew better. She knew him. The tsarevna had traveled with him long enough to know that he was equally happy allowing others to take charge. Danik wasn't a glory hound, that was certain.

"You . . . you trust this man, I take it?" Danik asked. "Is he your brother, or a husband perhaps?"

Veru stared at the side of Danik's head in the darkness, studying his profile by moonlight, wondering why he asked. As he waited for her answer, his fingers squeezed hers as if he were worrying a knot, anxious and tense.

"Yes," she said softly. "I trust this man. And no. He's not my husband or my brother. He's a friend. Your friend, actually. He's a priest."

"Oh, a priest. That makes sense."

Tension melted away from his shoulders. "Still. Stay behind me. We don't know if all is well or if he's alone."

The pair crouched behind a copse of bushes, trying to make out the camp near the fire. It had taken them the better part of an hour after moonrise to find the camp. Once there, they finally spotted a lone man and studied his movements, watching him feed sticks into the crackling flames. The man hummed a little song as he worked, then sat back and rubbed his hands together.

"That's not him," Veru hissed quietly.

"No. He's not the one I met before," Danik admitted.

"Are you sure?" Veru asked. "You know you can't remember well."

"The man I met before was younger. At least I think he was."

"You two are welcome to come over and warm yourselves," the man by the fire said, keeping his back turned to them. "I promise I mean you no harm."

Danik and Veru glanced at one another, and though Veru meant to caution him and hold him back, Danik just shrugged and stepped out of the bushes, saying, "Thank you for your kind offer. I'm afraid we have nothing to trade. We're strangers in this land who just stumbled into one another."

"I'm new to this land myself. But I did manage to make some tea, and I do have some meager provisions to share, if you'd like."

"I'm not sure I enjoy tea anymore," Veru said, finally emerging from the shadows.

The man laughed, and Veru liked it. There was something about him that put her immediately at ease. She didn't trust it. Circling the fire, she kept the flames between herself and the stranger, attempting to tug Danik close to her. He followed her amiably enough but didn't have a natural sense of danger like she did.

Perching on a log, Veru studied the man. His hair was short and white, and his accent was like nothing she'd ever heard before. He stumbled over his words often and paused frequently as if searching for just the right word.

He handed her a steaming mug. It smelled sweet and warm, and there was something different floating on top.

"It's called lemon," the man said. "They don't grow where you're from. But I think you'll like it."

"It's good," she admitted, not tasting it at all, then closed her eyes and cursed under her breath as Danik gulped down his entire cup in three great swallows, then reached for her cup. She'd have to keep a careful eye on him. "But how do you know where I'm from?" she asked the stranger.

"I know a lot about you. I've been watching the two of you for some time. I . . . I'm something of a guide for those with a tiger nature, you see."

Danik spluttered his tea.

"There now, son. Don't waste it. It's a good brew." Leaning over, the man refilled Danik's cup and gestured that Veru should commence drinking her own. She sipped carefully and found the beverage delightful. Still suspicious, but delightful.

"So you're saying she's a tiger?" Danik asked, confused.

"Oh yes. Indeed she is. Not at the moment, of course."

"Not at all, apparently," Veru countered.

"Really?" the man said. "That's terribly interesting. You're saying you can't even change for a short time?"

Veru shook her head. "Not at all."

"And do you possess the tiger's abilities?"

"Not as far as I can tell."

"How fascinating."

Danik spoke up. "I don't understand. What's fascinating? Who are you, and what's going on?"

"Ah yes." The man set down his own cup on a nearby rock. When he leaned over, Veru noticed an amulet hanging around his neck. It looked similar to her own, but not quite. "Allow me to introduce myself. My name is Anik Kadam."

"You're a tiger too!" Veru exclaimed.

The man looked at her quizzically. "Why would you assume so?"

"The charm you wear. It's like ours."

"Hmm. Very astute."

Anik pulled the charm out to show them. "Do you see the writing on the edge?"

"Yes," they echoed, peering at it in the firelight. "It's a different language," Veru said.

"Exactly. This charm was loaned to me. I wear it for safekeeping and for protection, but the tiger remains with the owner."

"Then there are tigers in your part of the world as well?"

The man paused. "Yes. I suppose that is the best explanation for the moment."

Veru snapped her fingers. "It's the scroll prophecy. It said something about learning from our elders."

"Right. Well, I suppose you could call me an elder, though technically speaking—"

Veru stretched out her legs, crossing them at the ankles, and interrupted the man. "So teach us. What do we need to do to get out of here, get home, and get rid of the tigers permanently? That is why we're here, right?" She jerked her thumb at Danik. "Also, he needs his memory back. He must've been thumped on the head during the transition. He has no idea what's going on."

"I *can* speak for myself, you know," Danik groused.

Anik Kadam held up his hands. "Keep in mind, I am here as your guide, not as your fix-it man. I'm not the Wizard of Oz, young lady, here to give him a brain and you a trip home to Kansas. You young people have a set number of tasks ahead of you. How—or if—you complete your journey will determine the course of your life. This is true of all of us, of course. In your case, the process is simply accelerated. Trust me when I say it's for your own good. It's no small thing either. And definitely not something you want to face on an empty stomach or without a good night's rest. I insist. Questions will wait. I'll set you on your path in the morning. The others are being told the same thing."

"Hold on. You know where the others are?"

"Yes. We are the ones who created this dream, after all."

CHAPTER 2

When Leading a Tiger About by the Nose, One Must Be Careful

Iriko was completely accustomed to opening his eyes and seeing nothing, so most mornings he didn't bother trying to understand the world through vision. Instead, he'd honed his other senses, or rather, the abilities the tiger inside afforded him. He typically just listened to all the sounds around him—the scuffling of rodents under the snow, the cry of birds of prey far overhead, or the snorting of larger animals he might hunt for breakfast.

Then he might wrinkle his nose and taste the air or let his fingers touch the tiny particles brought to him on the wind. Finally, he'd use his nose. He'd always believed scent to be the most powerful tool an animal possessed—other than teeth and claws, of course. Many times he'd study the village dogs and watch how they'd use their noses to search for prey that burrowed deep inside the snow.

But Iriko had learned through experience that wasn't the case at all for a tiger. Touch and hearing were what a tiger depended on the most, not their noses, though, to be fair, his sense of smell was incredibly keen now. Much more advanced than when he'd been simply human. His heightened senses and exceptional strength were the reasons he was still alive.

It was the tiger who'd blinded him. His mother might have believed Iriko's disability was due to his being an outcast from his people, or the result of some sort of curse related to the death of his sister, but that wasn't the reason. Well, at least not in an immediate sense. Iriko could see just fine for many years after he left his home.

No. He knew his eyesight had been taken by the animal caged within. It was desperate to escape the human prison he'd locked it in. Each time Iriko had felt the pull to change, he'd resisted. It was difficult at first. Nearly impossible, in fact. But over time it became easier, until, for a while, he'd thought he tamed the beast.

Then the tiger began haunting his dreams. It wasn't frightening at first. He couldn't even see the monster, only sensed its presence in the dark shadows at the edge of sleep. Iriko then began napping in short bursts, practicing dream defenses, but the tiger was clever. When the boy created mental images of thickly laced huts with no doors, the tiger pierced it with wicked claws, not entering but leaving the quivering young man with no misunderstanding that he could cross the threshold whenever he liked.

If the boy created a dream where he sat inside a ring of blazing fire, then the tiger leaped up onto the highest tree branch and looked down on him from the shadows with glacier-blue eyes that glowed in the dark. Iriko knew the tiger could leap over the flames and devour him if it chose. It teased him, lounging in the branches until he went mad and dared the beast to come and take him. The tiger only yawned, rolled over, and slept. The boy never could.

Sometimes Iriko tried conjuring a weapon, aiming it at the beast's heart, but he could almost hear the snort of laughter as it slunk through the bushes, evading him easily. When he tried to ignore the tiger, turning his back to it and keeping his eyes tightly shut, the monster actually sat down beside or behind him, pressed its back against him, and made a sort of chuffing sound. Once it even licked him. Iriko thought it was probably tasting him in anticipation.

Still, Iriko fought. Years passed, and as they did, the tiger became more and more aggressive. It began pacing and snarling in irritation. Iriko told it to just leave, that it didn't belong to him, that it had all been a mistake, but the tiger came to him again and again, night after night, roaring, demanding he acknowledge its presence.

He tried to build walls between them, but it did no good. Every mental barrier, every door he slammed in his dreams, crashed down with the swipe of a heavy paw. This continued month after month, and year after year. Each night the tiger stalked him, challenged him, broke down whatever barrier he constructed, until at last Iriko lay prone at its feet as the cat breathed hot, fetid breath across his face.

There it stood waiting—watching him, studying him, trying to break him—but Iriko was nothing if not stubborn. He'd rather die. And the tiger knew it. When Iriko didn't flinch before the massive jaws, the beast roared and went into a frenzy, raking sharp claws on either side of Iriko. Still frustrated, it tore apart everything in the dream until there was nothing left but bits and pieces of shadow and dust.

Then one day the attacks ceased. The tiger was quiet. That was the day Iriko opened his eyes and saw nothing.

For a long time, the tiger lay dormant, allowing Iriko to use the cat's power, but asking nothing in return beyond his vision. Then recently the beast had begun to stir once more. In the last few months, Iriko's dreams had been haunted again. First it was the roar, then the shadow. One that grew brighter until Iriko understood he was once again seeing, but not through his own eyes. This time he was the monster in his dreams. Iriko didn't try to put up barriers. He knew what was coming.

The tiger would soon appear again. It would ask, and the answer would be the same. There was nothing that would make Iriko give in. The young man knew it was only a matter of time before he lost something else. Something important. But Iriko didn't care. He was ready to die. He deserved it. After all, why should he get to live when his sister didn't?

At least in his dreams he could see. He almost looked forward to them. It had been years since he'd seen the sun or the rise of the moon on the snow—that is, until he saw the world again through the eyes of the others.

He knew they were coming before they arrived. The tigers visited his dreams. His tiger met theirs. Iriko watched them play together. They greeted one another. They seemed happy. He almost felt happy watching them. His tiger paced, but not in anger. It anticipated their arrival. The air changed. The tiger didn't push Iriko to shift. Not anymore. But the young man felt its desperation. It wanted, needed, to be with the others.

When Iriko joined them, it felt right. Not only for the tiger but for himself. For a while, the tiger was at peace. Then, the last night, it pushed in again, harder than he ever had before. Sweat broke out on Iriko's forehead. He almost changed. The tiger roared, and Iriko knew there would be another reckoning. More than his eyesight would be taken this time.

Then he woke, and all seemed well, until they entered the shaman's cave and drank the elixir. He knew something was wrong when he couldn't taste anything. For just a moment, before sleep overcame him, he thought the tiger had taken his sense of taste. Iriko thought that was a punishment for both of them and decided it was something he could live with if it meant walking on two legs. Then sleep came, and he gave in to the dreamworld.

But the tiger didn't come to him in his dreams this time. Iriko listened. His ears worked. He could still hear the scuffling of rodents. In fact, he could even hear the chittering of their young as they cried for the warmth of their mother when she scurried out of their den. He let out a breath. The exhale was deep and heavy. It sounded different. It felt different. The air on his skin felt . . . strange, as did the ground beneath him. He shifted. *Whoa. That's . . . definitely new.*

Iriko's sense of balance was off. His body wasn't right. *No. It can't be.* But a part of him knew it was. *Please. No. No!*

Curling his upper lip, he inhaled, and scents hit the roof of his mouth, tickling his brain with information. The fresh, crisp tang of rain on mildewing leaves told him it was late fall. A sharp, sickly, musty odor implied a small animal had recently died nearby. The blood was old and made his stomach turn. He heard something move below, and the new scents translated for him. Two humans—one he knew, one he didn't. A bird landed nearby, and seeing him, it took off screeching, causing a flock of others to soar. He attempted to stand and confirmed his suspicions. He was in a tree.

For a moment, he teetered precariously, clinging to the branch and having absolutely no idea how he'd gotten there or how high up he was. Then instinct kicked in. He dug in his claws and used his tail for balance and found a place where he could drape his body comfortably until he could figure out what to do next. In the meantime . . . he roared.

Nik and Stacia woke to the roar of a tiger, and both of them assumed it was Veru. Nik came to attention immediately, shouting the tsarevna's name as he ran headlong into the trees. Stacia groaned and rolled over. "Just let me sleep a bit longer, will you, Veru?"

It's not Veru, a voice in her mind said.

Stacia blinked, rubbed her eyes, and sat up, looking around, confused. "Who said that?"

I did. And who are you?

"What do you mean who am I? Who are you? Are you playing at invisible again, Nik? I don't think it's funny."

It's so strange. I think . . . I think I'm seeing from your eyes. But that can't be! Are you . . . are you Stacia?

Just then Nik returned. "I don't see Veru anywhere. Is she here somewhere?" Then his eyes widened. He reached down and plucked Stacia to her feet. "Hold on! You're yourself again! How did you do it? What happened? When did it happen? Is Veru with you? Veru? Veru!"

"No, Nik. Veru's not here. I don't know how it happened. But . . . but I think Iriko is talking to me."

"Iriko? Where is he?"

I'm not sure where I am. I'm still blind. But I know I'm in a tree. Look up, Stacia. Can you see me?

"It's definitely him," Stacia announced. "He said he's in a tree. Do you see him?"

They began scanning the trees, but they couldn't make out Iriko's form—a task that should have been easy, Nik thought, considering the man was huge and nearly naked.

It's odd trying to look for yourself through the eyes of another, Iriko mused as Nik and Stacia continued walking back and forth in the forest, searching for any sign of him. Then, finally, it was Iriko who said, *Stop! There. The tall tree with the broken limb hanging from the top. Do you see me? I'm halfway up, near the trunk.*

Iriko had suspected he was a tiger, based on the fact he had claws and pads where fingers should be, and when he ran his tongue in his mouth, he could feel the sharp points of fangs. But seeing his old enemy looking back at him through Stacia's eyes and knowing that was him nearly made him sick. *How had this happened?* he wondered. Had he inadvertently given the tiger control? Would he be forever stuck in this form just as Veru and Stacia had been?

"Where?" Nik asked, shading his eyes.

"I see him," Stacia said, then gasped, covering her mouth. "Incredible! Iriko, you're . . . a tiger!"

And by your conversation with Nik, and the fact that I can see feet and hands when you look down, I'm assuming you're human.

"Yes, I . . ." Stacia squeezed her arms, then touched her face. "It appears that I am."

Then I'm happy for you. Iriko was surprised to find he truly was happy for her. His mother had been right. The tigers were not something to be trifled with. A person should be prepared to take on the responsibility of such a weighty calling. Stacia and Veru had enough to worry about already. They didn't need to bear the mantle of protector of his people too.

"Thank you, Iriko."

You're welcome.

Iriko thought he could hear the words she didn't say. Words like, "I'm sorry about *you*," or "I wish I knew how to help," and "I don't like seeing others shouldering a burden while I am relieved of such."

He understood. When he'd first met the tsarevnas, he'd felt an immediate kinship. Like him, they were stuck. They just wanted to be rid of the burden, of the responsibility. The others couldn't possibly grasp what the three of them were going through.

If it wouldn't be too much trouble, would you mind helping me find my way down? Iriko asked.

"Of course," Stacia answered, with a quick nod of the head. Iriko wondered then how long the two of them had been staring silently at each other, lost in thought.

Well, he amended, *I suppose the two of us were just staring at me. What an odd thing.*

Iriko was surprised when instead of simply standing below the tree and looking up at him, Stacia actually placed her hands on the trunk and began to climb. Nik watched from below and shook his head, as if knowing he couldn't have stopped her if he tried. There were a few times Iriko worried when she chose handholds that he wouldn't have selected for himself, but then he guessed that her weight was much lighter than his own. She only slipped once, though, and soon she was by his side. That's when he got a really good look at what he'd turned into.

Iriko's tiger form was not nearly as frightening through Stacia's eyes as it had been through his own, especially now, when it wasn't attacking. Stacia reached out a hand as if to place it on his shoulder, then hesitated. "May I?" she asked politely.

If you like, Iriko answered.

"He's a beauty," she said as she patted his shoulder.

I suppose. The tiger didn't look at all like the one possessed by his mother or sister. Apparently, the form changed with each owner. If he recalled, his sister's tiger had been a sort of fawn color. Iriko's tiger had a moon mist–silver coat overlaid with midnight-black stripes. It was a strange thing staring into his own glacier-blue eyes in a tiger's face. Even when he shifted his head and closed his eyes, he could still see that Stacia was taking his measure. She studied him from the tops of his ears to his whiskers to his flicking tail.

When you're finished . . . he stated sulkily.

"Sorry," Stacia said. "I've just never seen one of us from a human's perspective before. We're quite deadly, you know."

Iriko turned his head back. She was bracing herself by putting one arm on a branch on either side of his body, almost as if she were hugging him. Her face was very close to his.

We're deadly when human as well. The tigers inside us lend us their power. There's quite a lot we can do, even in human form. Maybe I can teach you.

"I'd like that," she said.

Iriko couldn't tell if she meant it or not. She sounded like she did. He cursed his blindness. It wasn't the first time he had done so, but it was the first time in a long while he wanted to see the face of someone else.

"Now, what will be the best way for me to help you down?" she asked.

Stay close. And show me the distance from branch to branch.

"Okay. We'll go slow."

They made it down from the tree with relative ease, and Iriko suddenly wished it might have taken a bit longer. Nik regrouped with them at the base.

"Right. Now that we're together, let's figure out where we are and then find the others, shall we?"

Doesn't matter where we are, Iriko said. *Why don't we just start looking?*

"I agree," Stacia said. "Iriko said we should just find them. Who cares where we are."

"Not so," Nik said. "I've learned from some pretty awful experiences that where you are matters. It can lead to death if you're not careful. First, we need to take stock of our surroundings, determine our resources, fend for ourselves, then we seek our companions." He ticked off a list on his fingers. "We need water, food, and shelter. Once we are safe, we can worry about other problems."

Stacia raised her hands. "Okay, agreed. Resources." She cocked her head, considering Nik. "You know, I have to say, I'm shocked you're not wanting to run headlong into danger to look for my sister, especially knowing your"—she waved a hand in the air—"special connection."

Nik frowned. "It's not that I'm not concerned about Veru. If I knew her whereabouts, I'd certainly begin looking, but you can't save someone if you aren't standing on solid ground yourself, can you?"

"That much is true," Stacia admitted. "Very well." Turning around, she spotted a knapsack by a tree and picked it up. Inside, she found Nik's magic boots and tunic.

When she handed it to him, the relief was evident on his face. "Thank the skies," he said.

Water's not far, Iriko said. *Game should be easy enough to hunt near that.*

"Iriko knows where to find water, and he can hunt for us."

"Good enough for me," Nik said as he rummaged through the bag. "Hold on. There's something else in here."

He pulled out a piece of parchment and unrolled it. When the tiger didn't bother trying to look, he simply held it out for Stacia.

"It looks like a map," she said.

"Yes. But to where?"

They studied the different sections until Nik's stomach growled, then he rolled it up and carefully put it back into the knapsack. "We'll figure that out later. Let's find water and food first. If you'll lead on, Iriko?"

The gray tiger with the unseeing glacier-blue eyes lifted his nose in the air and tasted the wind, then flicked his ears, listening. *This way*, he said.

Stacia slid her fingertips into the ruff of his neck and walked beside him, falling into an easy rhythm. The two of them began a one-sided conversation, which often led to Stacia laughing at something or another that Iriko said.

It wasn't that Nik cared in particular. He wasn't jealous of the half man, half tiger or his connection to Stacia. He just didn't like the ease with which the big man had come into their lives and assumed the position of confidant and protector for his tsarevnas. That was his role. He'd worked hard to earn their trust. It was something that had taken years to develop, and it chafed that all Iriko had to do was show up with his big muscles and twitching whiskers, and they were eating right out of his hand.

Nothing ever came easily for Nik. It wasn't fair or right. He deserved better. Someday he'd be given the opportunity to show his worth, and then everyone would see just what he was capable of. No one would laugh at him then or call him a coward. They'd know he was good and strong and brave and that he was a man who could do hard things.

The trio walked for the better part of an hour, when Iriko suddenly stopped.

"What is it?" Stacia asked.

I smell another person . . . and . . . and meat cooking.

"Is it Zakhar? Danik? Veru?" she asked excitedly.

No. It's . . . he's familiar, but . . . I'm not sure. Maybe we should keep heading toward the water.

Stacia turned to Nik. "He smells a person ahead, and whoever it is seems familiar to him. They're cooking meat. What do you want to do?"

Nikolai liked that Stacia asked him. It meant she trusted him to make weighty decisions.

"Which direction?" he asked.

The tiger and the tsarevna conferred. "He believes it's ahead—straight for one thousand paces and then left for another four hundred, give or take." To Iriko, she murmured, "That's how you measure everything? What about distance or direction? North or northwest?" She paused. "Huh. I suppose you're right. That would make it difficult. But what if there was a mountain in your way?"

Nik rolled his eyes. "While the two of you talk about it, I'm going to put on my boots and zip over there and scope out the area. If I don't come back, we'll meet at the fire."

"Right, but what about—" Stacia's hair blew back as Nik breezed past them and disappeared into the trees. "Huh. He left us."

Does he often do that? I thought he was supposed to follow your orders, not go off on his own.

"Yeah. He's more Veru's friend than he is a soldier these days."

Are you saying they're intimate?

Stacia snorted. "No." She quirked her head and considered. "At least

I don't believe so. Veru doesn't let any man come close to her except Nik. I'm not sure she even considers him a man, truth be told. At least not in that way. He's more of a younger brother."

Interesting. I don't think he thinks of the two of you in a brotherly way.

That comment caught Stacia by surprise. She knew, of course, that Nik had feelings for Veru, but her? That wasn't possible. And yet . . .

Iriko interrupted her thoughts. *And what about you? I don't know the word in your language. Are you . . . beholden?*

Throwing her head back, Stacia laughed. It was something she rarely did, and she found she liked it. Usually she was wound as tightly as her hair, trying to prove to herself and everyone else that she was as good a leader as her father had been. There was something about being around Iriko that made her feel reckless, like it was okay to abandon the pressing duties that weighed on her and leave them on the floor like ruined garments for someone else to pick up.

"No. I'm not *beholden*. Nor do I have any suitors at the moment."

Why not? You must be quite wealthy. And there's an entire empire to be won along with your hand. Surely you can't be that *unattractive.*

The tsarevna stiffened at that, removed her hand from Iriko's neck, and took a step away. "That's none of your business," she answered curtly.

Apologies. I didn't mean any insult. Beauty isn't as prized among my people. Don't misunderstand me—it's nice, but when your days are spent following herds and your body is exposed to the wind, snow, and ice, even the most beautiful women age quickly, their skin becoming a map of experience and trial. When we select a life's companion, we are lucky to find someone we laugh with as we work together, a person who is kindhearted and quick of mind, a good teacher and storyteller. Strength of character and resilience. This is what is important to us. Beauty is temporary. A trifle.

"I see. Then . . . it sounds as if I might fit in well with your people."

Perhaps. Perhaps not.

"You don't think so?" Stacia asked, placing her hand back on the ruff of his neck. They continued forward, walking at their own pace, figuring Nik would discover them easily enough. "I'll have you know I'm an excellent general. I've studied with all the best fighters. I'm a master of every weapon in the empire. Certainly I can fight off a reindeer."

The tiger snorted. *You don't fight a reindeer. You herd them, preserve their meat and skin. For us, life isn't about war, at least not most of the time. It's about day-to-day survival.*

They walked quietly for a moment. Then Stacia said, "You must think of me as a pampered, spoiled thing compared to your women."

You forget I've seen your hands. You have scars and calluses caused by pain and lessons only you learned. Those hands don't belong to someone pampered and spoiled. But you're right. I don't think it would be a good idea for you to live with my people.

Stacia could feel the prick of hot tears at the back of her eyes. She'd never felt the sting of rejection hit her in such a way before. She supposed she'd never let herself care about a man's opinion of her until now. She wished above all else that she was wearing her armor and that she had a weapon in her hands.

The thin, flowery peasant's dress she'd woken up in was nothing like the heavy clothing she was used to wearing in the castle. And she never left her hair hanging down her back. She might as well be dressed in her nightclothes. No wonder he thought of her as useless. Stacia clenched her fists and stiffened her back. Iriko was wrong about her, and she could prove it. She'd like to show him exactly what kinds of lessons she'd learned the hard way as a young woman. Then her shoulders sank. He was right. No matter what she did, she'd never be as brave or as clever or as strong as others needed her to be.

Almost unable to choke out the words, she asked stiffly, "Why? Why would you consider me not good enough for your people?"

One simple reason: You're far too white to fit in with us.

"I'm . . . I'm too white?" Stacia spluttered.

That's right, Iriko said coolly. *A girl that white? We'd lose you too easily in a blizzard.*

Stacia snorted with shock and then began laughing.

Besides, a redheaded tsarevna with absolutely no experience with reindeer migration is a liability. There's simply too much to teach you.

"Is that right? I'm a quick study, I'll have you know. Hey, wait a minute. How do you know I have red hair?"

I'm a quick study too. And if you think you're so capable, then let's begin your first lesson. You should be able to smell the cooking meat by now. Try to find it yourself.

Stacia closed her eyes and inhaled, then frowned and tried again.

What is it? Iriko asked.

"Something's wrong. I think . . . I think my tiger is missing."

CHAPTER 3

When Leaving for a Day, Take a Week's Supply of Bread

Zakhar couldn't believe his luck. Not only had he woken in a strange place with his full faculties—unlike Danik, who he'd run into on one of the trails and tried to convince to come with him—but he had retained his bag with all his inks and parchment, including the scroll and their bits of food and supplies, a few traps, and a skein of water.

Then, to top things off, the young priest-in-training had stumbled into a clearing where he'd found a campfire already built, meat cooking on a spit, and bags full of supplies. As he rummaged through them, compiling mental lists, he believed such items would last him weeks if not months—that is, assuming, of course, there was no prior claim to them.

He called out, over and over again, but there didn't seem to be any owner, so he sat down cheerfully to wait for the return of the traveler, knowing that most people, when they saw a man of the cloth, were very happy to share. After an hour or two of the most patient waiting, and offering the charitable service of monitoring the meat, not wanting it to burn, turning it every so often, he gave in to temptation and began pulling off little charred pieces, popping them into his mouth, rationalizing that most individuals wouldn't mind sharing a bit, especially the overcooked sections. After all, he had put in a fair amount of labor and would indeed continue to do so to serve his fellow man.

Zakhar chewed with great satisfaction and continued the process of turning, pulling off pieces, justifying to himself that it wasn't his fault if some of the most juicy and tender bites just happened to come with the charred sections, and he ate until he was well filled, or maybe even a little more than full. Then he sat back with his shoulders against a large rock and fetched out his parchment for some quiet study. He was busy marking translations onto new paper when, to his surprise, Nik zoomed into the clearing.

It took the young man a moment to slow down and turn around. While he did, Zakhar rose to his feet, stoppering his inks carefully before doing so, and cheerfully greeted his friend. "Nikolai! It's good to see you. Have you come across the others?"

"Are you alone? How long have you been here?" Nik asked immediately.

"A few hours, I'd say. What about you? How do you fare?"

"I'm with Iriko and Stacia. They're coming, but not as fast. Obviously."

"Obviously," Zakhar agreed with a grin.

"But you haven't seen Veru?"

"No. I have seen Danik though."

"Danik? Where?"

Zakhar frowned and spun, then shrugged. "I've never been very good with direction. It was at least a half a day ago by my reckoning. He seems to have had a mental lapse of some kind. He didn't recognize me at all and said he's searching for his family. What's strange is that I know his parents died quite some time ago. It's the reason he became a hunter in the first place."

Nik froze. "Did you say he lost his memory?"

"Yes. I tried to convince him to follow me, but he wouldn't have it. He's much more of a strapping fellow than myself, so there would be no forcing him, would there? Besides, I'm no fighter. I mean, look at me. Then I made an attempt to follow *him*, but he quickly outpaced me, and I'm no tracker, so I found a good spot, and . . . well, here I am."

"No. I understand," Nik replied without really looking at Zakhar. Instead, he was staring intently at the camp and the roasting meat. "What is that, Zakhar? Did you catch it? Roast it?"

"Well, no," Zakhar admitted. "I found it. I'm not quite certain who it belongs to. I haven't seen anyone, though I've been here for some time."

"No. No. No," Nik groaned, walking around the meat as if it were an enemy he needed to fight. "You ate some, didn't you?"

"Yes. I did. What's wrong, Nik?" Zakhar asked. "There's plenty left for you and the others, if that's what you're getting at."

Running a hand through his hair, making it stand on end, Nik said, "No! I'm not worried about eating. There's magic in this place. I can sense it. It's just like the boots. With magic, you have to be very, very careful. It's quite possible that Danik ate some of this, too, and that's what caused his memory lapse. In a few moments, you might not be able to remember your own name."

Crouching down, Nik inspected the fire. He picked up some of the ash and rubbed it between his fingers, then smelled it.

Zakhar swallowed, his mouth suddenly dry. "M-magic, you say?"

Though Zakhar was a priest, he knew very well that magic was real. He'd seen it with his own eyes. There was no denying it. Still any talk of such things might result in excommunication, exorcism, or worse! There was simply no place for it in the church. No room for overlap. But Zakhar didn't ascribe to the old folktales, superstitions, and lore in quite the same way.

He didn't think of magic as being evil like most of the clergy did. At least not all of it. He just thought of it as something one might want to consider cautiously and possibly avoid. Ignoring it was folly. Knowledge was key. Magic was simply about understanding the rules and respecting the power. It was much like how Danik described learning about a wild animal or being careful when walking on too-thin ice. Zakhar was certain that if he could document the various tools, types, or abilities, and find patterns, then he might be able to make such things work in their favor.

"Yes." Nik rose, dusting his hands together. "Magic. How much did you eat? Let me see your eyes. Stick out your tongue."

Zakhar complied. "Thome," he mumbled while Nik squeezed his jaw and stared into his mouth, looking for who-knew-what.

"Huh? What did you say?" Nik asked, releasing Zakhar's face.

"I said I ate some."

Nikolai didn't notice the blush that colored Zakhar's cheeks. "Some" was a bit of an understatement. In truth, he'd eaten more than enough to fill his belly. In fact, the young priest-in-training was feeling slightly queasy from having eaten too much. Zakhar decided to come clean and thus avoid the confession box upon his return.

"Actually, I ate quite a bit. Is it going to kill me?"

Letting out a disappointed sigh, Nikolai replied, "Well, I doubt it. If it was magic meant to kill, you'd already be dead."

"That's good at least," Zakhar said, trying to offer a positive note to temper his sour choice.

"Not really. Sometimes dead is the better option."

"Oh."

Now Zakhar felt utterly useless. "I beg your forgiveness. I'm a simpleminded cretin."

Nik put his hand on his friend's shoulder. "There's nothing to forgive. Wisdom comes with experience. That's all."

As for Nikolai, he was now desperate to find Veru. If she was lost like Danik and had forgotten who she was, there was no telling what might happen to her, especially if she was back in her human form like Stacia. He squeezed Zakhar's shoulder. "Look, Stacia and Iriko will be here soon. They can track you on their own, thanks to the tiger thing. But think now. Tell me where you saw Danik. I'm going to look for him. There's only a bit of daylight left. I've got to find him and then hope that Veru is with him. If she isn't, well . . . we'll cross that bridge when we have to. But if Danik isn't far, I should be able to find him quickly enough, and we'll regroup. When they arrive, tell them where I've gone. Do you understand?"

Zakhar nodded and then pointed in the vague direction from which he'd arrived at the clearing. Nik again instructed him to wait by the fire for Stacia and Iriko to appear, then departed with a whoosh of his magic boots.

Now that Zakhar knew about the possibility that he'd eaten magic-laced meat, he was extremely nervous. He wrung his hands and could no longer concentrate on his work. He constantly wondered what he might be forgetting and if his lack of focus could be blamed on a new diminution of knowledge. Deciding the best thing to do was recite the things he knew and record them so he wouldn't forget, he set about making a list of everything he could remember, starting with the most important details—those things pertaining to himself.

He wrote about his family—his very, very large family—and how there was always a lack of food. Then Zakhar dipped his quill and recorded the day he'd decided to join the priesthood. That day, a traveling priest had come to their small village to perform various baptisms, marriages, visits to the sick and elderly, and other rites.

Such a thing happened around once a year, as their village wasn't large enough to fund a church. When the cleric was finished with his various engagements, he conducted a service in their small schoolhouse, and all the townspeople crowded in to take part. His family had a very lean harvest that year, and the older children were going without some things so the younger kids could eat.

That day, their mother had made them scrub and wash up to look their best for Sunday services. Zakhar knew she was embarrassed to have her family seen in worn clothing with unpolished shoes, but she'd seen to it that their faces were scrubbed until they were shiny and red, and their fingernails were clean. His sisters' hair was brushed and braided in various crowns and tied with little bits of twine and ribbon his mother had saved or traded eggs to acquire.

Then they'd crowded into a pew together, twitching and pinching one another until the service was finally over. Afterward, Zakhar watched his quiet father press a precious coin into the collection box while the fat priest watched intently, his eyes fixed on the meager coin that probably meant so very little to the clergyman but was so very important to Zakhar's family. Even as a young man, Zakhar could see the priest's smug shrewdness hidden just below the surface.

The man took the offering, jiggling the box slightly, as if to show all in the schoolhouse how little his large family had contributed, then smiled at his family piously and extended a trite blessing before moving on. It was that day that Zakhar told his family he wasn't going to be a farmer. He was leaving them to study to be a priest.

It wasn't that he was impressed with the man or his calling. No. Zakhar was simply determined to never be hungry again. The idea that he could enter any town and expect the people to hand over food and money to earn his nod of approval was almost intoxicating to him. Then there was also the fact that he couldn't get the image of his parents out of his mind. He knew he could never be the type of man who would take money from poor families and withhold blessings from them if they refused to pay.

Why should money feed fat priests while children went hungry? It didn't make sense to Zakhar then, and now that he'd read the Scriptures for himself, it still didn't. Gluttony was a sin. But there was a tiny voice in Zakhar's mind that said leaving his family was a sin too. Sometimes his heart burned over the shame of it.

He'd tried to justify his decision over the years by telling himself he'd left them to protect others, but the truth was, he never went back to visit them. Not once did he return to his little town to see if his younger brothers and sisters were still alive. Never did he try to rescue any of his siblings or his mother or father. There were some days when the guilt of his actions overwhelmed him.

Other times he had sat in the warm church by the fire, studying, and then ate a full plate of food, and asked himself, *Why weren't they smart enough to do what I did?* Then he'd go back to his little cot in the church and cry until he fell asleep. He'd wake up the next morning and fast, determined to be a better man, a better servant of the Lord.

Round and round it went. He never seemed to find absolution. *How can I ever hope to guide others when I feel so lost myself?*

Zakhar was writing about the adventures of meeting the tigers, when Iriko and Stacia appeared. He was grateful for their arrival, not only because it served to lift him from his doldrums, but because it was a relief for him to realize he still remembered who they were. The meat had not made him forget.

What was even more surprising was to find Stacia and Iriko had switched places. Now the young man was in tiger form, and the young lady was . . . well, a young lady—and she was striking. Zakhar rose immediately, his quill dropping carelessly from his fingers to the page and the papers spilling across his lap to the dirt. Ink smeared and left a large well on the page he'd been writing.

"Oh no!" Stacia said, bending to help him gather his writing. "We're so sorry, Zakhar. We didn't mean to startle you."

Zakhar blinked. His mouth suddenly went dry. He tried to wet his lips, but nothing happened. He *was* a cretin.

When she pressed the papers into his hands, he swallowed, and to his shame, his voice squeaked. "Sp-sp-pasibo, Tsarevna," he mumbled and then quickly clicked his heels together as if he were a soldier on the battlefield and bowed, but the effect was lost, considering he wasn't wearing the polished boots of a royal soldier.

"Relax, Zakhar. It's me. I know I look different, but try to treat me the same."

"With respect, my lady. You . . . you're royal. I mean, your face is stamped on the coins in the church coffers."

Is that true? Iriko said.

"You hush," Stacia replied.

"Excuse me?" Zakhar responded, confused. He looked between her and the tiger, who made a sort of chuffing noise. He pointed between the two of them. "Is . . . is he talking to you?"

"Yes."

"And you understand him? Like he did when you were a tiger?"

"Yes. And he's still blind as well."

"How fascinating," Zakhar said. All former feelings of awkwardness vanished as he found a seat and pulled out a fresh piece of parchment. Indicating a spot next to him, he dipped his quill. "Please, tell me everything that's happened to the two of you thus far." He held up an ink-stained finger. "Oh, and before I forget, don't touch the meat. Nik thinks it's tainted with forgetting magic."

Is he serious? Iriko asked. His jaws were wide open right next to the meat, preparing to pull it away from the fire. *I'm starving!*

"Well, of course you are," a too-happy voice said from the darkening tree line. "And just so you know, there's nothing magically wrong with the meat. Is it magic? Technically, yes. But it will fill your bellies. And believe me—you'll need it where you're going."

"Who's there?" Stacia cried out bravely, placing herself in front of Zakhar, who squeaked again and began gathering his things should they need to hastily depart. She had no weapons, but she'd fought without them before. Of course, she'd never faced a magical being, but there was a first time for everything.

Iriko's heavy body slid along her leg until he stood next to her. She placed her hand on the ruff of his neck.

You be my eyes, and I'll be your claws and teeth.

Stacia nodded, though she knew he probably wouldn't get that. Still, she could feel the two of them beginning to move in sync. It reminded her of her army. She had trained a group of elite soldiers, and they'd worked together until they moved almost as one, anticipating each other's moves to the point where they only needed a few hand signals. Together they'd infiltrated enemy camps, sneaking in and out without a life lost. They'd been a secret tactical unit used on many occasions.

Then last year everything changed. Their mother announced it was time for Stacia and her sister to come out of hiding. They needed to be public figures. It was for the good of the empire, she'd said. The first thing their mother had done was make those prokljatyj coins. Stacia had tried to tell her it was a mistake to spread their images all over the empire. Enemies would recognize them.

It meant Stacia and Verusha wouldn't be able to function as warriors any longer. Stacia had tried to reason with the tsarina, but their mother wouldn't listen. It didn't make sense at the time. Of course, now Stacia understood why. Mila knew she was dying. The season for hiding was over.

Stacia couldn't blame her mother for doing the things she did. Mila was trying to preserve the legacy she and the twin's father, Andrey, had worked so hard to build. As their daughter, she could understand it, but that didn't mean it was easy to accept. The empire was their dream, not hers. She and her sister were too young, and their parents had left them too early. It wasn't fair. Why did life need to be so hard? Why was there only one path? Was a choice too much to ask for?

As for Zakhar, his eyes were riveted on the young woman standing in front of him. He'd been around young ladies in the past, of course, but none of them had looked like the tsarevna. She stood with such bravery, such authority, such power. He could see her leading an army on the battlefield, her sword held high as she shouted orders. Stacia was fascinating.

"Breathtaking." His mouth formed the word softly before he could stop himself. He didn't think she heard him, but the tiger's ears flicked backward, and his face colored. *What am I thinking?* He was a priest. He shouldn't have such feelings about a woman. Then again, was it wrong to appreciate beauty or art? *Yes*, Zakhar thought. *That must be all it is. I simply want to* draw *her. She is royalty, after all.*

Besides, even God, looking down on all His creations, felt right in pronouncing them "good," didn't He? There was nothing bad about admiring the lines of a horse. And how much closer to God was a woman than a horse? Men and women were made in His image, weren't they?

Of course, now that Zakhar was thinking of horses, he was envisioning the tsarevna, Stacia Stepanov, dressed in glistening armor as a goddess warrior astride a black horse, with a cape flying behind, ascending into a storm-filled sky to fight a horde of monsters. What an imposing image. The horse's mane a reflection of her glorious red hair, which would be the focus of the painting and would frame her face like the sun bursting through the cloud, shining light upon the darkness . . .

"Now, now," the voice said. "Put away those sharp claws and let's sit awhile, shall we? There is much to discuss."

Zakhar swallowed, attempting to shift his focus to the man speaking and record his words instead of imagining the heretical art his fingers and mind were desperate to create as his muse continued to inspire him with her every move. He closed his eyes and mentally rehearsed the Ten Commandments, even mumbling them nonverbally to regain focus.

There was a rustling in the bushes, and a bald man stepped out. His eyes sparkled shrewdly. Stacia always looked at the eyes. Most would have focused on the man's gap-toothed smile and dismissed him. Not Stacia. Her parents had trained both their daughters to look for details that might not be as obvious.

Every visiting diplomat was a test. Every soldier they faced had a tell, a weakness. Her father always said, "Battles are fought with the strength of your mind, not with the power of your arm," and "A true conquest is achieved only when there is no loss of life and both sides have gained something."

As brilliant as her father had been, it was her mother who was the keen observer of people. Mila never failed to notice things the rest of the family had missed. Immediately, just as she'd been trained, Stacia began to catalog details of the stranger. She took in his clothing, the color of his skin, his accent, the way he carried himself, and possible places he could conceal weapons.

Her mind spun in a million different ways as she sought patterns, but every time she thought she was narrowing in on a certain thing—like the way he was standing, for example—he'd suddenly straighten up and turn and wink at her, then she'd have to start all over again. It was disconcerting, to say the least.

The man carried a white walking stick taller than himself that was carved at the top to look like a roaring bear. "Like it?" he asked when he saw Zakhar inspecting the staff with the utmost concentration. "He's got quite a bite, this old bear."

The man pushed a hidden button, and the bear's mouth opened, revealing a hidden spearhead. It gleamed like polished stone, and when turned in the light of the fire, it shone in colors of purple, blue, and green. "Now if it's magic you're looking for, this old spear has it in spades. Get it? Spades?" He laughed uproariously at his own joke, then looked around. "Oh dear. I suppose that one didn't translate well."

He wiped a tear from his eye. "I've been spending too much time with Kadam. Anyway, this one is just on loan, my dear. I'm expecting it back, understand. And mind you, don't scratch yourself with it. I'd have a difficult time reattaching you to your body if you did."

"Reattaching me to my . . ." Stacia hadn't even suspected there'd been a weapon hidden inside the walking stick let alone imagined the man would readily hand it over to her. Taking the offered weapon with only a shadow of the diplomatic smile her mother would have preferred, Stacia quickly found the catch that hid the spear point. After practicing using it a few times and hefting its weight, shifting it from palm to palm, she recovered her manners and nodded. "Thank you."

"Take good care of it. You'll need it." The easy manner in which the stranger warned her caused her to frown anew.

"You're the man from the cave," Zakhar said. "You brought us here, didn't you?"

"Very astute. Yes. I did. It's my first time acting as a guide. How am I doing so far? Kadam thought it would be a good idea."

You're the White Shaman, Iriko said.

"I thought we went over that already. Don't you have any better questions than that?"

Stacia echoed, "The White Shaman? Where are we? Why have you brought us here?"

"That's a better question. You're in your dreamworld. The one Kadam and I created for you."

"*You* created?" Zakhar probed.

"Yes. Well, with the help of the tigers, of course."

The tiger kept coming to me in my dreams, Iriko replied.

"Of course he did. The tigers test you. Your job is to—"

"Pass their tests and wisely rule . . ." Zakhar interrupted as he hurriedly shuffled through papers.

"That's right," the shaman said gleefully, clapping the young priest on the back. "It sounds like you know what to do, so I'll just head on back to my cave. Best of luck to all of you. I hope you all survive."

"Hold on there," Stacia said, blocking the shaman's exit with his own staff. "You need to give us more information than that."

The old man sighed, shook out his robes, and sat down by a log. "Very well. At least bring me some of that nice venison, will you? I'm quite famished. Creating dreams this complicated takes quite a lot of energy, you know."

"I'm sure," Stacia said, flicking open the spear point and using it to carve off a nice hunk of meat. She tossed some to Iriko, who caught it and downed it in one swallow and then began hacking off another section.

"Hey!" the White Shaman groused. "That spear isn't a steak knife, I'll have you know. It's very sensitive. Take care of it, and it will take care of you."

"It is taking care of me. It's taking care of my hunger. Yours too, if I'm not mistaken. Here." Stacia handed the man a steaming portion of meat wrapped in a piece of Zakhar's precious parchment, knowing he, too, would complain about his resources being used in such a fashion. But when she swiped a piece of paper from under his inkpot, he not only said nothing, but he also didn't even make eye contact. In fact, when she handed him a piece of meat and thanked him for the use of his parchment, he only grunted his thanks, was obvious about avoiding physical contact with her, and only ate half his portion. Apparently, he'd already eaten plenty, as his not-hungry belly wasn't what was ailing him.

When they were all eating, or at least still nibbling on the delicious roasted meat, with only the fire to stave off the evening chill, the shaman began telling them about a dangerous quest. As he spoke, the night grew darker, clouds covered the moon, and the air grew thick with mist. The three young people weren't sure if it was the chill in the air or a sense of foreboding that made them draw closer together as they listened.

CHAPTER 4

The Horse of Hope May Gallop, But the Ass of Experience Walks Cautiously

Nik was in a near panic as he searched for Veru. He hadn't felt as desperate when she'd been lost and trapped in tiger form. At least then he knew she was unlikely to be mauled by wild beasts. If she woke up in human form like Stacia, without weapons or armor, she'd need him. It might even be possible she'd be stuck up in a tree like Iriko—helpless and blind. She'd need someone to lean on. Someone to be her eyes. She'd need her friend and longtime companion.

As his feet pounded the ground at blinding speed, his body swaying around obstacles, his eyes searching for something, anything that looked out of place in the trees, his mind stamped out the repeated chant: *She needs me, she needs me, she needs me.* The thought of seeing her again in human form, her arms open to embrace him, the tears of gratitude shining on her cheeks, thrust him over mountains and through valleys. He even ran across a wide lake without stopping or sinking. Such was his drive to find her.

When darkness fell, he ran by the light of the stars and the moon. Finally, finally, his body gave out. There was nothing left inside him to keep him going. He was hungry, drained. Even his fierce desire to be the one to save his tsarevna wasn't enough. As he slowed, the countryside, which had been nothing more than a blur of color around him, came into focus, and he stopped by a large tree and bent over with his hand against the trunk, trying to catch his breath.

Only then, when his own gasping quieted, did he realize he heard the steady breathing of someone else. Rounding the large tree trunk, he discovered a tiny man nestled between the great roots of the tree, his little hands pressed together, tucked against his cheek as he snored. Nik crouched down beside him and saw the man had a knapsack. He wondered if the man carried any food, and if he might be willing to share it with a stranger.

For a moment, Nik thought it would be smarter if he just left the man alone and kept looking for Veru, or at least began heading back to Zakhar, Stacia, and Iriko. He had a good sense for magic, and this man had something of magic about him. Nik was certain of it. He'd escaped death from magical beings enough times to know it was foolish, but his growling stomach told him he needed to press forward regardless.

Clearing his throat loudly, Nikolai Novikov said, "Excuse me, good sir. I was wondering if you might have some food to spare for a stranger. I can pay you back, if you'll let me. I have friends close by, and they have various skills in hunting and so forth. It's just that I have to find them, you see, and to do that, I need food."

The man kicked and groaned, then turned over, waving his hand as if trying to shoo Nik away.

Taking a step closer and speaking a bit louder this time, Nik said, "Hello? Again, I'm sorry to wake you, but I need help."

There was a loud protest and then a mighty thrust of both feet before the red-faced little man wrenched his body into an upright position. "What do you think you're doing? Can't you see the sun has set?"

Nik stepped back, his eyes wide as he stared into the man's one large eye set in the middle of his forehead.

"What are you staring at? Judging my size, are you? Wondering how someone with such short legs got himself so far out in the forest? Well, shame on you! You 'normal-sized' people go around constantly thinking you're better. Well, you're not. Now get out of here. Whatever you're peddling, I don't want any."

"No. No, you don't understand, sir. I'm not judging you. And I didn't want to disturb you," Nik added, trying desperately not to stare at the man's one large eye and failing. "I'm merely asking you for help."

"What? What is it you say? You want my help? *My* help? Did I hear you correctly?"

"Yes. Yes, you did."

He sighed and sat up straight, yanking his tunic into place. "Very well. Who do you want me to curse? And keep in mind the quality will depend on how much you can pay. And I charge double at this hour."

"Curse? Um . . . no one."

"No one? Son. Don't you know who I am?"

"Uh . . . no?"

"You're not a bright one, are you?"

"Well, I've always thought that—"

"Let me answer for you: *No.* You're not. And just to speed up this conversation so I can go back to sleep, I'm a likho."

"Oh. Nice to meet you, Likho."

"No, no, no. My *name* isn't Likho. I am *a* likho, as in the supernatural-creature-you-never-want-to-meet." He blinked, waiting for a reaction from Nik, and got nothing.

"Seriously? The Bringer of Misery? The Master of Temptation? The One-Eyed Demon of Disaster? The Ghoulish Gnome of Grotesquery?"

"I don't think *grotesquery* is a word."

"Don't talk back to your elders, son."

"Look, are you going to help me or not?"

The man pressed his hand over his one eye, then scrubbed his face. "This is what the younger generation is coming to. They lose all respect for their ancestors. You work and work to maintain a reputation, to develop a sense of fear and foreboding, and then what? They lose all interest. What's worse . . . they've never even heard of you. What's the point, I ask you. Maybe it's time to retire. They've all become desensitized anyway. Nobody stays long enough to hear the old stories. Short attention spans, that's the problem."

"Umm, are you just going to sit there talking to yourself?"

"Who said I was talking to myself? Weren't you listening?" He sighed loudly and got to his feet. "Never mind. What is it you want, kid? Just spit it out and leave," he said grumpily.

"I just wanted to know if you'd be willing to share some food. That's it."

"Share my . . . share my *food*?" The corners of the likho's mouth lifted, and then he began to chuckle. Soon the chuckle turned into a full belly laugh that caused actual tears to leak from the man's very large single eye. He wiped them away with both hands, as there seemed to be a tear duct on either side. Stepping forward, the man clapped Nik on his arm, which appeared to be as high as he could reach, and said, "Thanks for the laugh, kid. Just for that, I won't curse you for waking me. Just see to it that you don't do it again. I don't do favors twice."

Reaching down, he picked up his sack and flipped it over his shoulder, then rounded the tree.

"Wait!" Nik called out and attempted to follow, but when he stepped around the tree, the likho had vanished.

Stomach rumbling, Nik wandered through the forest for an hour, hearing nothing but the sound of hooting owls and the rustling in the underbrush of small things being hunted by larger things. He cursed himself for a fool. Why had he run off by himself and taken no note of where he was going and how far? Now he was no good to anyone. How could he save Veru when he wasn't even capable of saving himself?

Soon a thick mist covered the ground, and his feet began sinking in the mud. He'd come across a boggy area of the forest. The air stunk with rot and putrefaction, and instead of the rustling in the underbrush, he heard the sound of splashing and the guttural groaning of large creatures rattling the water as they called and moved. He felt the prickle of tiny things crawling on his neck, and he brushed furiously at his arms and face.

Sometimes it was sweat. Occasionally, it was something else. Fortunately, nothing bit or stung him as he made his way through the muck, praying for it to end and hoping he could find a scrap of food and not end up being food for something else. When the moon sank, so did his hopes. Why, oh why, didn't he stay with Stacia and Iriko? At least then he'd have a tiger on his side. What an idiot he'd been. He was so weak with hunger that his vision blurred. His thirst was a powerful thing, but he dared not drink the water he found pooled between the trees lest it make him sicker than he already felt.

His father was right about him. He *was* a durak. A nikudyshnyi. A useless, good-for-nothing boy trying to pretend he was a man. To his shame, tears formed in his eyes, both of them, and cascaded down his hot cheeks. He was without a friend, without a home, without a family. Perhaps it would be better if he ended up food for something in a swamp. His head felt as thick and foggy as the air. Then, despite his sobs, he thought he heard something.

"Pst!"

Nik wiped his eyes and nose on his sleeve and peered into the dark, trying to locate the source of the sound.

"Hey, kid. Up here!" the voice beckoned again.

He could just make out the figure of the same small man with the one large eye that he'd run into before. "What are you doing up there?" Nik asked.

The man managed to roll his one eye all the way around in its socket. "Not that it's any of your business, kid, but I was attempting to take a romantic moonlit stroll in a fetid swamp with my ladylove, who apparently feels I've been ignoring her far too much. Despite my skillful efforts at amour, it seems the lady in question still believes our courtship has taken a turn for the worst, and as vengeance for my poor treatment, she secured me to a tree, where I'm meant to be an offering to the local bolotnik."

Nik sucked in a breath. "Sorry about that. Sounds brutal."

"Brutal. Yes," he agreed flatly.

"So . . . he's going to kill you?"

"One would hope. I suppose it depends on if the bolotnik is a male or a female. For my sake, I hope it's a male."

Swallowing, Nik asked, "What—what would a female bolotnik do to you?"

The man shuddered. "You really don't want to know the answer to that question."

There was a loud sucking sound in the nearby swamp, followed by a guttural thumping noise that made all the other sounds in the forest go quiet.

"Is that it? I mean . . . her?" Nik asked in a hiss.

"Probably," the man said. "Look, kid. I think we got off to a bad start. What do you say? How about you help me, and I help you?"

"That's what I was asking you before," Nik replied.

"Yeah, yeah. No time for quibbling. You going to let me down or what?"

"Okay, fine. But I don't have a knife."

The man sighed with frustration. "You don't need a knife, son. Just use your magic."

"Magic? What magic?"

"Your boots."

"What? How? How do you know about that, anyway?"

"No time! Just do it. Tell your boots to get me down. They'll know what to do."

"I don't trust you."

"You don't trust anyone. But you've got to start somewhere, kid. Besides, it's not like you have a choice. Without me, you'll just keep running around aimlessly for the next decade, not using your magic to its full potential, assuming you even have what it takes in the first place."

Nik hesitated.

"Come on, boy. You know you want to. Curious minds. Killing cats and all that."

"Killing cats?"

Another scream shook the leaves on the tree.

"Tell you later. Just hurry!"

Nik sprang into action. "Fine!"

Nik told his boots to help him free the man. His stomach wrenched painfully in protest, but at least he wasn't running. It took a minute, but the laces responded to his command. They stretched upward and wrapped around the vines holding the man to the tree, then tightened until the vines broke as if they'd been cut. Next, the laces wrapped around the man and gently lowered him to the ground.

Once down, the man rubbed his wrists and twisted his neck until Nik heard the sound of popping. "Ah, much better," the man said.

Just then the trees near them parted, and Nik saw a swamp monster more terrifying than a leshi, more dangerous than a kikimora. Suddenly, he understood why the small man with powers of his own had been so very afraid. The two of them stared up into the gleaming yellow eyes of a female bolotnik.

CHAPTER 5

A Silver-Tongued Speaker Is Pleasing, But a Pinched-Lipped Listener Is Priceless

Veru couldn't sleep at all. The same wasn't true for her two companions. Danik was lightly snoring. That didn't bother her. She'd long since become used to his patterns of sleep. In fact, she found the sounds he made during slumber rather musical.

She'd always had trouble sleeping. Especially when on the road, out among her soldiers. Veru made it a habit of carefully vetting the men she allowed in her inner circle. Still, she never slept easily and kept her knives in ready reach. It was something she and Nik had in common. They both liked sleeping with their eyes on the tent door. It was only when Veru's back was pressed against her sister's that she allowed herself to sink into blissful oblivion.

Nik always tried to put her at ease. He knew when she was exhausted and when she was hiding it. And she could rest her eyes when he was near. At least, a little. But much as she valued Nikolai, the moment she stirred, he was at her side, checking to see if she needed anything. It was almost as if he'd been watching her while she slept. It was . . . disconcerting. As much as she trusted Nik, she never felt . . . settled or relaxed around him. At least not completely.

With Danik, it was different. He was so at ease with himself, so absolutely calm, even in the face of death, it helped quiet her stress as well.

She attributed it to the way he was able to create a bubble of music in his mind. Even when he didn't have an instrument in his hands, he could hum or sing or play something in the air with his fingertips. All he needed to do was close his eyes, and he'd get lost in a melody of his own making.

Veru doubted even the reanimated dead could wake Danik when he slept. He probably wouldn't fear them either. When the wolves attacked, he was more worried over sending the hungry animals to *their* deaths than of his own demise. His dreams seemed peaceful too. There were no specters to haunt him in the dark. He was a simple man with simple needs. Perhaps that was what she liked about him. The emotions he felt, he put to music. It told her all she needed to know.

The other man, the new stranger, was quiet. She suspected he was sleeping now as well, but she really couldn't tell by any sounds he made. His breathing was steady and rhythmic, but not as deep as Danik's. Lying there on a mat provided by the stranger, her head cushioned on her arm, Veru stared at the embers of the banked fire and felt the chill of the night air tickle her exposed skin and penetrate the thin blanket and her even thinner gossamer dress.

She rolled over to warm her back and forced her eyes closed, surprised to find them wet with tears. At first she thought her emotions might be due to missing the companionship of her sister or perhaps the loss of her home and mother, but then she realized what she was really feeling was the disappearance of her tiger.

For the first time, Veru appreciated how the tiger's fur had kept her warm even in the bitter cold. It had felt like a warm blanket wrapped around her, and it had soothed her in a way that was difficult to describe. *Where had the cat gone?* Was she cured? If so, then why did she feel so . . . empty? Clutching the piece of amulet at her neck, she concentrated, trying to call the lost tiger. If she found her, perhaps she'd find her way home as well. *Come back to me*, she cried out in her mind, trying to sense the presence of her whiskered other half. But there was no answer. Veru finally gave up, her body shivering.

On cool evenings, all she needed to do was curl her body in a circle, tucking her head a bit, and it was like sleeping beneath a dozen plush blankets. Even when snow piled on top of her, she was never cold. She simply shook off the wet, fluffy stuff and her coat dried without the cold mush ever penetrating deep enough to cause a chill.

Having claws and teeth was like never being without a weapon. Veru was always prepared for a fight or to hunt. She never had to worry about being taken seriously or losing an important tool or weapon, because they were always with her. As a human, she'd sleep with her knives at the ready, endlessly working to keep them sharp and polished. Tigers didn't need to concern themselves with such things. A tiger's weapons were always ready.

Then there was the miraculous ability to heal that came with the magic. Veru had to admit that special gift often came in handy. Not once did she need to worry about infection or a cut. Even though Danik's trap might have proved deadly to a real tiger—and it certainly was painful enough—not long after it was removed, the broken bones and sinews in her foot were completely healed. She barely gave it a thought anymore.

Now that she was human again, she'd have to think twice about where she stepped—be wary of cuts, scrapes, and broken bones, especially as she didn't have her armor. What was worse, not only did she now need to take care of herself, but she'd also have to take care of Danik. Without weapons and proper clothing, they'd be vulnerable.

Though she knew that their original goal had been to figure out a way to rid themselves of the tigers, Veru was no longer certain she wanted to part with the cat. Now that she was gone, Veru could admit she missed her feline counterpart, and not just because she needed her as a weapon. The tsarevna felt the loss of the bond with the cat in a way that was surprising. *Maybe I just need to coax her out of hiding*, she thought. *Perhaps if I find just the right lure.*

The night passed slowly for her as Veru kept pondering what she might do, continually opening her eyes to check on the progress of the moon. When it finally sank, and she saw the first signs of sunrise, she wearily stretched and sat up, thinking she'd try to get the fire going again before the others woke, but when she turned around, her human joints aching and creaking in a way her tiger body hadn't, she found the fire was already crackling and a warm mug of tea had been placed on the rock beside her.

Danik was still snoring, sleeping soundly, but the stranger sat bright-eyed across the fire and lifted his mug, nodding to her before sipping.

"Dobroye utro," he said quietly. "Did I pronounce that correctly?"

"You did. Dobroye utro to you as well. Good morning. Have you not been speaking our language very long?"

"I suppose that depends on your definitions of *long* and *speaking*. Suffice it to say, this is my first time with your language, so please forgive me any errors and feel free to correct my mistakes. I promise you won't offend me."

"Konechno. I will."

"Spasibo."

"Are you now going to tell me what we're doing here? Who you are? And what is expected of us?"

"I'll tell you as much as I am able. Is that sufficient?"

Veru nodded, indicating he should do as he liked, but not verbally agreeing to anything at this point in the conversation. She could tell this one was wily. She'd have to tread carefully if she was to learn what she needed. Her parents had taught her well.

The man smiled. "You remind me . . . well . . . I suppose that's neither here nor there. I just find you quite a remarkable young lady, Verusha Stepanov."

Veru's brow knit together, the only indication that he'd surprised her. "Thank you, I think."

"You're welcome. Now, the first thing you'll need to know is that this 'land,' as it were, is a dreamworld. It has been fashioned by your White Shaman as a test. This is standard for your, er, tigers, from my understanding. If all goes according to plan, you will pass your tests, acquire your various gifts, and learn what you need to know to help you in your life's purpose along the journey."

"I see." Her mind reeled with questions. How she wished Zakhar was with them. At least he would have paper and ink so she could write down everything. "Before you continue," she said, "don't you think it might be best to wake Danik? This does pertain to him too, I'm assuming."

"Oh yes, it does, of course. But if you'd prefer to let him sleep, I don't mind visiting with you alone for a bit. Whatever you'd like me to repeat for him, I can. In his current state, he's unlikely to remember all the details, but it doesn't hurt, in any case. Is there anything pressing you'd like to know about before he wakes? Something you'd prefer to keep between the two of us, perhaps?"

"That's an interesting question, considering you're a perfect stranger to me."

"You're absolutely correct. It is rather forward. Maybe you'd be more comfortable if you knew me better first. I'm an open book about most things. Ask me whatever you like."

"Very well. Are you a shaman?"

"No. In my past, I was a military adviser. I trained the princes of my country in battle strategy and different forms of combat. Then I became something of a businessman."

Veru frowned. "You went from combat to a tradesman?"

Kadam smiled. "It does seem like something of a step down, to your way of thinking, doesn't it? But isn't that what emperors and kings do? It's all a game of chess, or you would better know it as a game of bezique. They just barter in politics, laws, armies, and borders rather than goods. When you think about it, there isn't much difference between two warlords moving soldiers on a battlefield, two kings moving armies across a city-state, or two merchants moving cargo ships filled with cloth, tea, or fish.

"All those scenarios are simply games of wit. Sometimes, yes, it's about strength and power."

"But more often the outcome depends on who is the cleverest rather than on the hand you're dealt," Veru finished.

Kadam laughed. "Precisely."

"And did you train your princes in strength, stealth, or smarts?"

He smiled. "Yes."

"So, did your young tiger princes on this other world successfully accomplish these tests as well?"

The man blinked. "Now, I never said—"

"You didn't have to. I may be young, but I've traveled much of the empire, and my parents have taught me to observe people and question them well. I've never seen the type of fabric you're wearing or heard your accent before."

"Perhaps, but that doesn't mean—"

Veru held up a hand. "There is also much to be learned in what a man doesn't say. When I ask certain questions, and you hesitate or choose your answers carefully, it tells me you are hiding information. Then I sort out the information you do tell me from the missing pieces and put together the puzzle. You don't belong here, do you, Anik Kadam?"

Veru was proud of herself for watching and choosing her words so carefully. She'd always been outspoken. Too much so, according to her mother. Perhaps being a tiger and not having a voice had been good for her. It had given the tsarevna the opportunity to observe rather than blurt out her first impression. She'd also learned the benefit of a second pair of eyes. There was great value in working with a partner, even if there was the occasional disagreement.

The man paused and sipped his tea, but his eyes were twinkling.

"It's all right if you don't want to tell me, you know. I don't need you to confirm it. You answered the way I would have."

He lowered his cup and smiled. "You are quite bright, my dear. What a leader you'll be."

The light in Veru's eyes dimmed at that comment, and she looked away. "I'm not meant to be the next tsarina. It needs to be Stacia."

The man cocked his head. "Why do you believe that?"

"No one will listen to me or take me seriously. They just want to marry me off and flounce me around in big dresses." Veru looked down, picking at the fabric of her skirt. "Much like this one," she said with a grimace. "All they want is a pretty doll to auction off to the most advantageous suitor. That's not who I want to be."

"And why do you think all they will see is your outward appearance?"

"It's all most people see."

"Maybe. But character runs deep. You can show them more."

"It's useless. The men just drool all over my skirts, and the women are so busy hating me or destroying me with gossip that they can't see the good I can do."

"That is a problem," he agreed.

"So you understand, then. It needs to be Stacia."

He grunted. "I think everything will be clearer once you finish the tasks you need to accomplish here. I find that if you let problems sit for a bit, just like tea, the leaves settle, and you can see to the bottom. Then you often discover it's not as difficult to sift through as you first believed. It's the constant stirring that's the issue with most things. Let's just worry about one thing at a time, shall we?"

Veru sighed. "Fine. Tell me what I need to do so I can get on with it."

"I can see you feel determined as to your future."

"I do, but that isn't really something you need concern yourself with."

"I disagree. My role is to help all of you become your best selves. The concern I feel for you is natural, I assure you."

"Just not as natural as it might be for your own princes."

"Perhaps not yet," he agreed. "But don't disregard my experience simply because I'm still learning about all of you and your world."

Veru gave the man a long look and sipped her tea. Then she took a several long gulps, draining the mug, and said, "It's no sbiten, but I suppose any man who grows these sour . . . what do you call them?"

"Lemons," Kadam said with a grin.

"Right, lemons, and pours enough sugar in the mug to sweeten them up knows enough about balance to teach me *something*." Veru dipped her finger into her mug and lifted out the slice of lemon, squeezing the remaining juice between her fingers and smelling the rind. "Do you have a knife?" she asked.

He reached into a bag and handed her a small knife with an ivory handle. She unclipped the sheath and slid it out. The blade was sharp and well cared for, and it fit in her hand as if it had been made for her. Veru twirled it around and between the fingers of her dominant hand, getting the balance of the blade. Then she set the slice of lemon on the edge of the mug and began flicking the knife back and forth between her hands, picking up her speed.

Though she favored her left hand, she'd long ago taught herself to use both hands with equal skill. Her father and various weapons masters had trained both sisters in how to shoot all manner of archery weapons and use various types of swords. Her sister preferred swords as her weapon of choice, but Veru had always favored daggers. She carried at least twelve on her person at all times, including a few hidden within her boots.

She even had specially made leather gloves that concealed small knives that she occasionally wore to state dinner parties. One never knew when a spy might slip in undetected. Of course, her mother always stationed guards, but there was nothing like the kiss of cold, hard steel against the vulnerable pulse point at the wrist to make a girl feel safe. Veru would always grin when a man would try to corner her and kiss her wrist, only to discover he was pressing his hot lips against sharp metal instead of her soft skin.

As she twirled the knife, lost in her thoughts, Kadam watched her practice her skill. His fascination with her technique soon turned to awe and then stunned appreciation. He knew she was only playing, but she was good. No, she was more than good. She was adept. Deadly, even. She might have even given Deschen a run for her money.

Before Kadam realized her full intentions, the knife was at his throat and she was behind him, her arm wrenching back his forehead to expose the length of his neck. He clicked his tongue, chiding himself for losing focus, for being too soft. Just because he instinctively knew she wouldn't hurt him didn't mean he should let his guard down. After all, even a caged tiger can scratch. He blamed his age. He needed to do better if he was going to mentor these young people and find a way back to his own. Closing his eyes, he centered himself and breathed in, then let out a long, slow breath.

Veru asked nothing, and Kadam said nothing. Instead, reflex took over. It had been a long time, but Kadam still possessed the basic skills he needed to overcome an enemy. Quickly, he maneuvered himself under her arm, disappearing before she even had a chance to tighten her hold. He grabbed her wrist and twisted it quickly, hard, so the knife flew from her grip.

Deftly, he plucked it from the air before it fell to the ground and tucked it into his belt, before flipping her by using her own wrist. Her feet flew over her head, but she managed to twist in the air, landing on one foot and kicking him in the head with the other. Kadam turned away in time, so the worst of the blow was deflected.

She bent to pick up a large stick and launched a new attack, which he easily deflected with his bare arms, eventually tossing her branch aside. When that was out of reach, she pulled a burning branch from the fire and brandished it at him.

"Why do you seek weapons instead of fighting hand to hand?" he asked. "I find it oddly curious. You're obviously capable. And yet you go out of your way to seek something to use against your attacker."

"And I find it curious that you'd rather talk than fight," Veru retorted.

Kadam knocked away the burning branch and grabbed her hand, easily shifting her weight and tossing her over his shoulder. She fell with a thump on top of a still-sleeping Danik, who spluttered awake with confusion.

"Hey, now. What's happening? Where's the fire? Don't step on my instrument."

He pushed Veru off and leaped on top of his domra, shielding it from harm.

"Nobody fell on your precious guitar," Veru said sulkily as she rose to her feet and patted away the dust from her skirt. When she tripped on a torn hem, she cursed under her breath, ripped off the offending edge, and wrenched up her hair into a ponytail, tying it with the torn fabric.

"It's not a guitar," Danik said, yawning while rubbing his chest where Veru had landed a moment before. "Why were you two fighting, anyway? Was it about breakfast? Did he not save me any? If not, then you have my permission to kick him again."

"It wasn't about your breakfast. We haven't even eaten yet."

"Indeed," Kadam replied, returning to his various bags. "We were about to start cooking when the tsarina offered to demonstrate her skill with knives."

"She did? And I missed it?" Danik said. "At least breakfast is still on the table—or rock, as it were."

"Exactly," Kadam replied with a chuckle. "Here, lad. You can help me with the porridge."

"You didn't miss anything," Veru said crossly, wrenching her skirts across her lap as she sat by the fire again. "And I'm a tsarevna, not a tsarina. You got the word wrong."

Kadam smiled over the pot as he poured in the dry porridge. "My mistake. I'll try to remember that."

Danik ate his entire bowlful and half of Veru's, then began inquiring about lunch. "Don't think I've ever been this hungry. I hope you brought enough to last awhile."

"Yes," Veru said, licking her spoon. "How long, exactly, do you expect us to stay in this dreamworld?"

"Dreamworld?" Danik replied, his brow knit together. Then his eyes cleared, and he turned to Kadam. "My friend, if you could part with enough supplies for a few days, I'm sure I'll find my parents' village. I just need to pick up the trail, you see. And then—"

Kadam put his hand on Danik's shoulder. "Son, I'm afraid you aren't here to find your parents."

"I'm not?"

"No."

"Your job is to protect this young lady."

Danik peered at Veru and swallowed, then jerked his thumb at her. "But she's—"

"I know," Kadam said soberly. "She's royalty, son. Can I rely on you to see her safely home?"

"Really?" Veru sneered. "We're going with that?"

"Hush now. Deep-seated memories rooted by emotion stay longer than anything else. It's why he searches for home. It means something. The heart doesn't forget. The mind may, but the heart never will. Trust me. I have some experience with this. The two of you will need each other."

"Okay, fine," Veru replied stiffly. "A forgetful minstrel blasting his trumpet to announce my victorious return to the empire it is."

Danik folded his arms. "I don't play the trumpet."

Veru waved an arm. "Doesn't matter. How do you expect us to get out of here, anyway? And what happens if we die in this place?"

"Let's hope it doesn't come to that, shall we?" Kadam hedged.

"I can die now, can't I? Without my tiger, I won't heal like before."

"I suspect you'll soon discover that."

"What?" Veru asked, now panicked. "The death or the healing?"

"None of this sounds like anything I want to be a part of," Danik said. "I appreciate the breakfast and all, but—"

"Son," Kadam said, stopping Danik by catching hold of his arm. "I know this place is strange and you don't remember this woman, but you've walked with her before. You know her heart. It's a good one. She's protected you, and you've watched over her. She knows your songs."

"She does?" Danik turned to Veru, who nodded to him and rose as well.

"I do. I quite enjoy listening to you sing at dusk when the fire burns down. My favorite is the song about the snow falling in the trees."

"That—that was my mother's favorite too!" he exclaimed.

"So you'll help her find her way?" Kadam asked.

Danik studied Veru's face as if looking for something he recognized. Then he nodded. "It's the right thing to do."

"It is," Kadam said. "Now that that's been decided on, let me give you your supplies."

"Wait a minute," Veru said quickly. "You're not coming with us?"

"Not at all. This is your journey. Not mine."

"But what about the others? Iriko? Stacia? Nik? Zakhar?"

"You'll run across them eventually. The various paths all lead to the same place. Now then, I believe I have cheese, honeycomb, porridge, bread, some stoppered bottles with which you can draw and store water, some blankets, and a bit of soap. I've placed the knife you seem to like so much in this pocket."

"Do you have a change of clothing in there?"

"Not as such, no. Your White Shaman didn't seem to believe you'd need that."

"Wonderful. Would you thank him for me?"

"Yes . . . well, sorry about that. He was rather insistent and gleeful regarding your attire. I'm afraid I couldn't talk him out of it. Nor could I convince him to provide either of you with a decent weapon other than the small knife. Very confusing. There is a fire starter, though, so you should be warm enough."

"Look, just give us the supplies and be on your way, then. I'm sure you did all you could. Tell him we think you're an excellent guide. We couldn't have asked for better," Veru said, turning away from Kadam as if in dismissal.

"Now, see here, young lady. I understand you're used to ordering others around—and I'd be a bit touchy myself, were I in your place—but vinegar never caught flies."

Veru frowned. "Why would I want to catch flies?"

"Don't they use that expression here?" Kadam asked. "Well, regardless, I will be monitoring your progress. Try to remember this is for your own good. You are to learn and be tested. Should you do well, I believe you will acquire various gifts."

"Did this happen with your tigers?"

"Actually, yes. Miss Kelsey was given weapons by the goddess Durga, and she won prizes—the Golden Mango, the Divine Scarf, and so forth."

"A scarf? What kind of a prize is that?"

"I'll have you know that scarf saved our lives many times over. When we wrapped it around ourselves, it changed our appearance. We could look like anyone. When she was chased from the world tree and fell, it carried her to safety."

Veru's mouth fell open. "Tell me more about these weapons given by the goddess," she demanded.

Kadam waved a hand. "I've already said too much about my world and my tigers. None of this applies to you anyway. Your tasks will be very different. Your gifts unique. Your challenges your own."

Rising, he handed Danik one knapsack and placed the recently cleaned pot in the top, then fastened it and tossed a second one to Veru.

"Just remember," Kadam said, parting a bush and indicating they should begin on the path near the stream, then placing his hands on each of their shoulders, "the strongest weapons you have will always be your minds and your friends. Learn to trust them."

The pair stepped through, and the bush snapped back to shape behind them. Veru turned and parted it again, saying, "But what about . . . ?"

When she looked past the greenery, she saw nothing there. The little camp where they'd been sitting a moment before had vanished. The fallen logs, campfire, collected firewood, and even their boot prints were missing. "Kadam?" she said.

The only reply was the wind rustling the leaves. A slight shiver went through her. Taking his hand, Veru said, "Come on, Danik. I guess we're on our own now."

CHAPTER 6

Brotherhood Is the Best Treasure

"Let me make sure I've got all this down," Zakhar said. "You want us to head out into this wilderness on our own, and you say that at some point we'll run into Nik, Danik, and Veru?"

"That's right," the White Shaman answered.

"And we're supposed to find, what, exactly?" Stacia asked.

"It will be different for each of you. But, like I said, you'll know it when you find it."

"Because it will speak to us . . . magically," Zakhar read from his notes.

"Yes. Yes. How many times must we go over it? I have to say, this rather seems like the long version of the dreamworld. I don't know how Kadam does it. He must sustain himself on more than mushrooms. As for me, I'm ready for a nap and perhaps another meal. You young people tire me with all your questions and your constant lack of faith."

Stacia folded her arms across her chest. "Right. It must be difficult, what with the constant dreaming and the unlimited power at your disposal. Not to mention the omniscience. That must be terrible for you."

"Sometimes it is, I'll admit. But such is my lot in life." The White Shaman missed the rolling of Stacia's eyes but did smoothly roll to his feet. "Now then," he said. "I believe I have checked all the boxes Kadam gave me. You have your supplies, your instructions, you are at your starting point, and you know your end point. How you get there, and if you choose to finish, is now up to you. I wish you all the best of luck."

"*If* we finish?" Stacia said. "What is that supposed to mean?"

"You always have free will. Some remain here and never return. Others . . . well . . ."

"Others . . . what?"

"Others simply don't remain."

"Do you mean to say we could perish in this place?" Zakhar asked.

"I wouldn't use the word *perish*," the wily shaman answered.

"Really?" Stacia said. "What word would you choose?"

"Oh, I don't know. I'd have to think on it for a time. I'll get back to you on that one. Farewell for now, young ones."

"But—but how do we contact you if we need you?" Zakhar asked, almost desperate.

"Ah, that's an easy one," the White Shaman answered. "You don't."

Stacia rose, putting her hands on her hips. "What kind of a guide doesn't stick around to direct anyone?"

"There are all sorts of guides, young lady. Some are more helpful than others. Some don't even help you at all. Ever heard of the Cheshire cat? Kadam told me the most delightful story about a cat, a rabbit, a tea party, a deranged hatmaker, and a mouse. Maybe he'll share it with you someday. I think I'd like to be a guide such as that cat. Good day to you, then."

With that, the White Shaman smiled widely, showing the gaps where some teeth were missing, and then he faded away. The last part of him that vanished was his strange smile and the sound of his laugh.

"I don't like him," Stacia said.

I do, Iriko replied. *He's funny. I can almost see him too. His smell is that strong. Musky. Like mildew. Almost like a reindeer during rutting season.*

Stacia laughed, and the sound of it surprised Zakhar. Not only because nothing funny had been said, but because she laughed with gusto. It wasn't the dainty feminine laugh his mother had trained his sisters to use—the type intended to trick men into marrying them with a coy, flirty sound that was supposed to make men go weak in the knees.

The tsarevna laughed like she meant it, and she didn't care who heard it. The sound wasn't exactly pretty. It was more like the kind of noise he'd expect to hear in a tavern, if he ever went to a place like that. Now that Zakhar thought of it, he didn't think he'd ever laughed like that. Sure, he'd experienced fun. Like the time the young men went outside to sled, and they'd all whooped in delight racing up the hill, but this was different.

He suspected the laugh had something to do with Iriko. He knew the young man had an easy way with the tigers when he was a man and the sisters were cats. It was interesting to him that a person with so severe a disability could develop such a joyful outlook. But with his mother, Iriko had been so . . . bitter and angry.

As for Zakhar, he had found Iriko's mother a perfectly congenial woman. She was certainly perhaps a bit stern-natured, but she appeared to care for her son a great deal. Most mothers did, he'd found as he practiced counseling sessions with those who attended church and listened to parishioners who wished to attend confessional.

Maybe the wide swing in emotions had something to do with the tiger nature. He made a mental note to ask more questions about it later, but when he did, he'd have to do so . . . delicately. The last thing he wanted to do was upset the tsarevna. Perhaps he could make some inquiries through her directed toward Iriko, and he'd learn more about her at the same time.

"So you were saying you don't like our guide?" Zakhar said.

"No. What are your impressions?" Stacia asked as she hefted two bags, one for each shoulder.

Zakhar shrugged. "I'm trying to stay open-minded about it. Perhaps more information will surface later."

"That's a wise course. My parents always cautioned against judging too rashly."

Making sure they had collected everything, Zakhar carefully knotted his large bag, and Stacia helped him secure it on his back. "Perhaps you'll tell me more about them at some point, now that you're in your human form. I'd love to make a record of them and the charms and what you know about how they were handed down."

"I'm happy to answer any questions you have," Stacia said. "It will help pass the time as we walk."

"Unless you'd rather talk to Iriko. I can keep quiet instead if you'd prefer," Zakhar offered.

Stacia clutched the straps of the bags and peered at him. "I'm not uncomfortable with conversation, if that's what you're asking me, Zakhar. I'm used to passing long journeys with my soldiers. We'd end up knowing a great deal about each other by the time we reached our destination. I'm sure it will be the same with the three of us."

Nodding a bit too hard, Zakhar agreed. "I'm also fine with conversation. Though it's not easy to take notes while walking. I do have a fairly good memory, so it's possible I can record things in the evening from our daily conversations, if that's agreeable to you. It will be largely based on my recollections and not verbatim, as it's been in the past, but—"

Holding up a hand, Stacia said, "I'm also used to working with scribes. I trust you. Do what you will with recordkeeping. I just ask that you allow me to read any notes that will be used for group records before sharing them with the others. Anything you want to keep personally is, of course, your own business. Is that agreeable?"

"Yes, Tsarevna."

"That's the first order of business. Call me Stacia."

"Very well. Stacia, it is."

That's not what I'm *calling you*, Iriko said, interrupting.

"Why? What are you planning on calling me?"

You'll know when I use it.

"Fine, don't tell me. I don't care. Now, Zakhar, I believe you have the map."

"I do." He shifted a leather tube held by a strap from one shoulder and slid out a coated parchment. "What do you think is protecting this?" he asked. "A wax of some type?"

Stacia shrugged. "Who knows? He said it came from Kadam's time. Maybe it's magic."

Zakhar grunted. "Sometimes what we think is magic is simply something we don't yet understand."

"That sounds pretty forward-thinking for a man of the cloth."

His face colored. "Yes. Well. Like I said . . . I prefer keeping an open mind. When you close it, you close the doors to learning, don't you?"

"That's true. I like that."

They found a large rock and set the map on top. Zakhar quickly found the campsite where they'd been and the creek he'd followed to find it. "He told us to head toward the sunrise and follow the stream until it split, then cross to the lower side, heading south for two days."

"Very good. I'm appointing you as a trail leader. Iriko will warn us if there are any predators in the area. Now that I have a weapon, I'll act as company guard, with Iriko as my teeth and claws. Agreed?"

Zakhar nodded, pleased she found his skills useful and would be relying on him. He knew he'd prove next to useless when it came to fighting. "I'm also a decent cook, if we can manage to catch anything."

"Good man," Stacia said, clapping him on the shoulder. "Then let's head out. Let me know when you get tired. We're going to be missing those boots Nik wears."

At least the two of you won't freeze here, Iriko added.

"That's true enough," Stacia agreed, then added for Zakhar's sake, "Iriko said at least we're warm here."

"Yes," Zakhar said.

The little group plunged down the trail, and for as many questions as Zakhar had for Stacia, he felt too shy around her to ask. It was obvious she was very comfortable on the trail, working with men. She also seemed to have no problem with taking charge and organizing the group. That was fine with Zakhar. Danik and Nik had taken charge before, and he was happy to let them.

Nik was a driven sort of leader. He knew where he wanted to go, and he was bound and determined to get there. The problem with him was that, as a follower, you weren't sure he had your best interests at heart. You got the feeling he'd just as soon sacrifice you for the greater good, meaning *his* good, if it suited his needs.

Danik was much easier to follow. He was happy and cheerful, and he got you where you wanted to go, but he took his time getting there. You might all arrive, but it probably wouldn't be on time, and he might have forgotten his purpose on the way.

As for the tsarevna, her leadership style was very different. She made a man feel seen and important, a vital member of her crew. Not only that, but she definitely had a sense of purpose and direction. It remained to be seen if that attitude would carry through over the next few days or not, but so far Zakhar was very impressed with her. He hoped it was merely admiration for her skills as a royal he was feeling, and all the other emotions that seemed to be accompanying that esteem would melt away into simple respect.

They made good time, and Stacia even complimented Zakhar on his pace. It was the tsarevna who called a halt and needed a rest at midday. Zakhar handed her some of the wrapped meat and gave a healthy portion to Iriko. They had been hiking near the stream, so they stopped to fill their bottles, and Stacia removed her shoes and dipped her feet in the icy water, hissing as she did.

"What's wrong?" Zakhar asked.

"I'll be fine," she said, rubbing her heels. "It's the footwear he created for me. I'd have preferred my hiking boots. And this skirt is slowing me down."

Zakhar crouched down to look at her feet. There were blisters on her delicate arches. That just wouldn't do. He frowned and removed the bag from his back.

"Here," he said. "There are extra changes of clothing in the bag. I saw leggings and tunics, and there's a pair of woolen socks and soft-soled boots. See if those will fit."

Stacia smiled up at him. "Wouldn't you prefer to change out of your priest's robes?"

He shrugged. "No. They help me remember my vows."

"Are you saying you forget?"

Heat crept up his neck. "Not forget, exactly. Let's just say all of us are tempted on occasion. My robes are simply another layer of protection. Like your armor in battle. We all fight our enemies in different ways."

"I suppose we do."

He pulled out the boots, clothing, and socks, and handed them to her. "There's a thick copse of trees over there. It would be a good place to change. I'll stay here with Iriko."

"Okay. Thanks again, Zakhar."

"You're welcome, Tsarev—I mean, Stacia."

He watched her disappear and then turned around, so his back was to the trees. He was going to say something to Iriko to make certain the tiger would avert his eyes as well, but then he remembered the tiger was blind, so it didn't matter which direction he was looking.

Just then the tiger made a chuffing sort of noise, and he looked over at the huge gray beast with black stripes. He heard Stacia yell out, "Well, can't you choose *not* to look?"

Zakhar's eyes widened.

She continued, "Fine! I'll close *my* eyes, but it makes it hard to get dressed, you know."

When the tsarevna emerged, she bumped the tiger's shoulder with her hip. "Ever heard of privacy? Can't you switch to looking out of Zakhar's eyes for a while?" There was a pause. "Well, that's a bit inconvenient then, isn't it?"

She sighed in resignation, then said, "Come on, Zakhar. Let's go. Oh, and Iriko has something he'd like to confess, by the way."

"He does?"

"Yes, you do," she said with irritation. "You *should* feel embarrassed."

Zakhar stared at the tiger, wondering what he would do or feel if he'd been in that position.

"Of course it's a sin. Don't you think it's a sin, Father?"

"Uh, technically, I'm not a—"

Stacia interrupted him, clearly still lecturing Iriko. "What do you mean you're not sorry? Well, if a priest can't make you sorry, and God can't do it, then I'll sure as hell give it a try!"

Zakhar held up his hands. "Okay now. I think this is getting—"

"You name the place and the weapon, whiskers. You want to go fang to fang and claw to claw? Fine! You think you can best me as a human? I don't think so."

"You know there's a great scripture about turning the other cheek," Zakhar began, trying to make peace.

Stacia finally turned to him, her face livid. "What do you think I'm so angry about? He was spying on my bare *cheeks*. That's the whole problem, isn't it?"

Spluttering, his own cheeks turning apple red, Zakhar said, "I'm not . . . Correct me if I'm wrong, but wouldn't you have had to turn completely around for him to—"

Stacia waved a hand. "Never mind. It was a metaphor."

"Right. Well, that's not exactly how metaphors—"

"Are you trying to pick a fight too? Because I'm happy to take both of you on at the same time."

"No. No. Not at all. If you say he saw your, um . . . backside, then I believe you."

"Thank you."

"Yes, well . . . if you'll be so good as to allow me to speak with Iriko, man-to-man, perhaps I can clear this up."

"Be my guest," she said, throwing up her hand and stalking away several paces.

Zakhar took a breath and said quietly, "Now, Iriko, I know that I won't understand you, but you can understand me, so here it goes." Zakhar clasped his hands behind his back and began pacing while the tiger sat and angled his head toward the priest. "I don't have much in the way of personal experience in relationships between men and women," he began, "but I have counseled many bitter, angry souls. I've found that most things can be fixed with apologies. Sometimes that requires swallowing pride, but it's worth it. I know you can't do anything about your . . . vision problem."

The tiger huffed softly in response, sending a small shiver down Zakhar's spine.

"Yes. Well, regardless, the girl's embarrassed. Would it be too much to say you're sorry? That no harm was meant? Now, most priests would say it's a sin to lie. But I say, on occasion, the good Lord Himself might tell a woman she's beautiful, when compared to others she might be found lacking"—he held up a finger—"and I would venture, even when she's angry. After all, He who created the cunning wolverine and the wild boar and pronounced them good can surely find joy and splendor in even a furious woman. I wouldn't consider such a thing a lie. I'd instead call it looking at someone with godly perspective.

"Your job, as I see it, is to speak to our Stacia using godly—or perhaps princely, if you can't bring yourself to do otherwise—language. Every woman, but this one in particular, who you depend upon so very much, must be treated with great care and consideration. Now, that's all I have to say on the subject. Unless you'd like me to go on?" Zakhar paused, waiting for a noise from the tiger.

When he heard none, he said, "Then, if you'll permit me, I'll do my best to guide you back to the stream."

Zakhar's hand was trembling as he placed it on Iriko's ruff, but when the tiger began walking beside him, he grew bolder and steadier.

When they approached Stacia, she turned, hands on hips, and said, "Well?"

After a moment of silence, Zakhar saw the corner of her lip quirk up. "Is that right?" she said. "Well . . . who would have thought? Spasibo." Stasia turned and picked up her pack. "I'm talking to you, Zakhar."

"What? Me?" he said, shouldering his own.

"Yes, you. Thank you for whatever it is you said to him. It helped." Stacia patted the tiger, and he rubbed his head against her palm, then dug it into her hip, nearly knocking her over.

"Oh. Yes," Zakhar sputtered in response. "Pozhaluysta. You're welcome. It was nothing."

"Oh no. It was something."

They had just begun walking again when they heard a rustling in the bushes. Stacia pressed the button on the walking stick, revealing the hidden blade. "Who's there?" she cried. "Come out at once, or my tiger will maul you and swallow you for supper!"

CHAPTER 7

Every Bolotnitsa Praises Her Own Swamp

"Now, now beastie," the little man said, holding up his hands. "There's nothing you'll be wanting here. It's all been a simple misunderstanding. I'm already spoken for, you see? Perhaps the lad might be interested?"

He turned back for just a moment to catch Nik's eye.

Panicked, Nik shook his head vehemently, saying, "What? *No!* I am *not* interested."

"Okay, son. Calm yourself. Don't want to be *offending* the pretty bolotnitsa now, do we?" he said with his one eye wide open and his teeth clenched for emphasis. Then hissing under his breath, he added, "Use your magic. Fashion a net to hold her while I distract her."

Nik nodded but stood rooted to the wet ground, gape mouthed as the bolotnitsa slid further out of the water, exposing her slime-covered torso.

Digging unnaturally long arms into the muck, she pushed her body into an upright position and smiled at the two of them as she wove back and forth in the air. That was when Nik realized the bottom half of her body was shaped like a snake's. Nik just so happened to be terrified of snakes.

The bolotnitsa opened her mouth, and her jaw unhinged, exposing a menacing set of sharp teeth with two protruding fangs that glistened in the moonlight. Moving closer, her hair flickered in the light, and the tips sprung to life with tiny white filaments. They were beautiful in a way, almost mesmerizing. Nik could see how in the dark water they might serve to lure prey closer to those deadly jaws. Even he had a difficult time looking away from her.

He shook his head and instructed the boots to weave a net to trap the creature. The laces went to work, creating a webbing that intersected between the trees. As he worked, the likho kept talking, making some sort of an attempt to woo the terrifying creature, but whatever he was doing didn't seem to be working.

"Faster, boy," the little man said. "Faster!"

Nik concentrated, widening the net and stretching it over the bolotnitsa's head. When he was ready, he cried out that it was time. "Okay!" Nik cried. "Whatever you're going to do, you'd better do it now!"

The likho rubbed his hands together, mumbled a few words, and then it was like powerful bursts of light exploded right in front of the bolotnitsa's eyes. She screamed and writhed, bringing her long limbs up to protect her head. Then they heard a hiss and a snarl. Nik let his net drop, picked up his magic boots, and ran. The likho, now free, grabbed his arm, telling him to move like his life depended on it.

Normally, Nik should have been able to outpace the other man, even without the boots. His legs were much longer, and he was younger and trained in such things. But his body was tired. He'd already used up most of his energy. "Faster, boy!" the likho warned. "You've got to run faster!"

The bolotnitsa was out of the trap before they'd gotten far and was soon crashing through the trees behind them. They could hear her quickly catching up to them. The swamp was her territory, and the boggy ground was thick and wet and didn't easily release its grip on their feet. Nik didn't think he could run much longer. If they split up, one of them might make it, but not both. He didn't know what to do. Then, suddenly, he did.

Reaching over, he grabbed the likho's arm. "Stop," he said. "I know how we can hide. You'll have to trust me and remain very still and quiet." Ever practical, Nik had long ago fashioned several pairs of breeches as well as shirts that were made to be worn inside out and backward but didn't appear as such to any but the most careful of observers. He now made it a habit to always wear his clothing in a such a way. He'd also learned that being butted and kicked by various animals wasn't nearly as important as the tunic created for him by the old kikimora—though it did help.

When he'd sewn his special breeches, he also included a secret pocket, and that's where he always kept his magic tunic. Quickly, he unbuttoned it and pulled it out. He told the likho to stand very close to him and then slid it over his head. Once he yanked it into place, it covered both of them.

The woods went silent around them as the magic did its work, making the two of them invisible. They moved together quietly, slowly, until they found the shadow of a great tree in which to hide; then they waited, hoping the magic would work on a creature of the dreamworld—a being of magic herself.

Sweat broke out on Nik's face as he heard the screams of the frustrated bolotnitsa. She hissed and slithered through the swamp, her claws and scales scraping and making a sucking sound as she moved. She came very close once, so close they could see her yellow eyes glance at the spot where they were hidden, but her reflective eyes passed over them, and she soon moved on, screeching and angry.

When they could hear her no more, they finally stepped out of the shadows, and Nik removed the tunic, carefully folded it, and placed it back inside the hidden pocket of his trousers. Then he flipped his shirt right side out and put it back on. The likho stared at him thoughtfully with his one eye, stroking his chin.

"I'm wondering how a lad such as yourself came by leshi and kikimora magic. They don't often bless wayward youths with gifts like that. Tell me, boy. Did you steal it?"

"What? No!" Nik said, offended. "They . . . they loved me in their own way."

The little man grunted. "Interesting. Very interesting. Well, seeing as how I owe you a boon myself, are you certain there's no one you'd like me to curse?"

"Is cursing all you can do?"

"It's mostly all I do."

"Can you help me find my friends?"

"Probably not. But I can help you find the nearest settlement and get you some grub."

"I suppose that'll do. What's your name, anyway? I can't call you the likho."

"Why not?"

"I usually know the given names of my friends, not just their, er, species or, I guess, kin."

"Is that so?"

"Yes."

"Well, I don't have any friends." He turned and began walking.

Nik followed. "I thought you said you were out tonight wooing a girl. Wouldn't you call her a friend?"

He snorted. "There's no such thing as a woman you can be friends with. Any woman claiming to be your friend has other plans for you, son."

"Really? I hope that's true."

The one-eyed man gave Nik a long glance. "I never said those plans included marriage. Lots of reasons a gal might have to keep a fellow on a chain. Could be she's got no one else better at the moment. Or maybe he's a good hunter or can fix up her house. You follow?"

"But she *could* intend to further the relationship, couldn't she?"

"Yes. I suppose that's true. But a woman who intends to do that lets the man know fairly quickly. If she doesn't, you can be certain she has another reason for keeping him around. Move on or move out. That's my motto. Never waste time being friends with someone of the feminine persuasion. Come to think of it, I don't much consider it worth my time consortin' with anyone, male or female, lest I'm looking for something permanent like. A friend, in my opinion, is just someone waiting around to ask favors of you. Borrow your favorite axe and then leave it out in the rain. That sort of thing. Don't need none of their kind hanging around, if you know what I mean. I prefer the solitary life, in most cases."

Nik nodded distractedly, thinking about his relationship with the tsarevna. *Could Veru have been using me all this time?* He didn't like to consider the possibility. Even the thought of it made him sick. But what the likho said made sense. It felt right.

Then he began mentally listing the reasons why he loved her. She was a kind person. Generous. She wouldn't hurt him in such a way. It wasn't in her nature. Also, Nik wasn't that naive. He'd seen abuse, experienced it personally. Veru cared about him. She was just careful. He understood careful. Her position made their relationship complicated. That was all.

Settled, Nik asked, "Well, you can consider me a friend, if you like. And I promise not to borrow your axe or leave it out in the rain. The only thing I ask is that you tell me your name."

The little man blew air out his nose. "Don't want to."

"Why not?"

"I hate it."

"Hate what? Your name? Why?"

"My mom thought it was cute, but it isn't. It's humiliating, is what it is."

"Is that why you prefer all those other names? The Bringer of Darkness and Doom and so forth?"

He sighed. "It's the Bringer of Misery, the Master of Temptation, the One-Eyed Demon of Disaster, and the Ghoulish Gnome of Grotesquery."

"Right. Right." Nik eyed the man, then snickered. "What's the Master of Temptation about? Do you tempt people to overindulge during mealtimes? That sort of thing?" Teasing, Nik gestured as if he were tempting someone at the dinner table. "Here, madam, taste this sweet corn cake with honey sauce. Isn't it delicious? Oh yes. Have another. And another! Ha, ha, ha!" He wrung his hands together and giggled in fiendish delight, then said with a deadpan expression, "That's just weird. I wouldn't brag about it, personally."

The likho blinked his one eye and said, "You are a foolish little man-child, and you know nothing of which you speak. I don't know why I bother saddling myself with an idiot such as you."

"Um, because I saved your life, that's why. That's a good reason to have a friend, by the way."

"That's not a good enough reason, and I'm regretting it already. The bolotnitsa is starting to look better and better as each moment passes, I assure you."

"You're trying to distract me, and it won't work. Just tell me your name and get it over with."

"Bah!" The likho wrinkled his nose and pursed his mouth as if he'd just bit into something sour. "It's Pasha. Pasha Odnoglazy Pogodin."

Nik stared at him dumbly. "What's wrong with that?"

"Don't you get it?" the man asked incredulously. "She cursed me. Pasha means small. My mother is the reason I'm the size I am. If it weren't for that name, I might have been a strapping large man. But look at me! And Odnoglazy? Do you know what that one means?"

Nik scratched his cheek. "I think it means bright or full of courage."

"Yeah. But it also means one-eyed," he shouted, using both index fingers to point at his eye.

Shaking his head, Nik said, "No, I don't think so. I think it means single-eyed, as in focused and purposeful."

Pasha, the short, one-eyed likho, dropped his arms and just stared at the boy, then mumbled under his breath, "You're an idiot, kid. There's no point arguing with you. Is there?"

They kept walking and fortunately came upon a berry bush with some just-ripening blackberries. Pasha let Nik eat most of them, which revived him well enough that he could soldier on for another hour. When they found a good place to camp, Pasha used a bit of his magic spark to create a fire, and they slept soundly until midday the following day.

Nik knew when he woke and studied his surroundings that he was well and truly lost. He had no idea where he might find Veru or Iriko or Zakhar or Stacia. His only hope was to find the nearest settlement and hope there was word of them there. In the meantime, he decided to find out if Pasha would teach him a bit of his magic. Unfortunately, the little man proved stubborn about sharing his gifts. That didn't stop Nik from asking. He'd worked with stubborn magicians in the past and managed to pry their secrets from them, and he was sure he could do so again.

"How far is it to the next town?" he asked when they resumed their journey.

"Another day's walk. Why?"

"We'd get there faster if we used my magic," Nik offered.

"We could. But you wouldn't last. Not enough energy," Pasha said.

"You see, that's what I don't understand. How do you know? You knew about my magic before I even showed it to you."

"Not all of it," Pasha admitted. "The cloak surprised me."

"Yes, well, they told me to keep it hidden for a reason, I suppose."

"They were wise to do so. That's some powerful magic they gave you, son. A kikimora's death shroud given with her blessing to the intended victim is a rare thing indeed."

"She's dead now. I don't know about the leshi. They were like grandparents to me, in a way."

"That explains it, then. If they loved you, they bestowed a blessing instead of a curse. It doesn't happen often, but it does happen."

"I suppose you think that makes me lucky, then. Is that right?"

"You tell me."

"Don't you dabble in luck?"

"Bad luck. And curses. I specialize in curses. Told you that, didn't I?"

"You did."

"Speaking of which, it might be a good time to tell you that you've got a sorrow riding on your back, kid."

"I've got a what now?"

"A sorrow."

"What does that mean?"

"It's a curse of sorts. Sometimes you bring it upon yourself. Sometimes it just finds you when you're vulnerable. But once they latch on, they're difficult to shake."

Nik spun in a circle, trying to see his back. "I don't see anything."

"Course you don't. You wouldn't. They're invisible to all 'cept ta those who do things like cursing others."

"Well, what's it doing to me?" Nik asked with a panicked expression, constantly wriggling his shoulders and flicking his hands at the back of his neck like he was trying to rid himself of a spider.

"Oh, you probably wouldn't feel much of the effects at this point. It's a bit like having a mosquito drawing on you or maybe one of those river leeches. They feed on sadness, you see. That and negative thoughts. It's like I said—once you have one, and they start getting plump off you, they tend to stay. This one looks nice and ripe. Not huge, mind you, but he's definitely not starving."

Nik darted up to Pasha and put his hands on the shorter man's shoulders, shaking him desperately. "What do I do? How do I get rid of it?" he demanded.

"Calm down, boy," he said. "The 'what' is easy. The 'how' is the problem. What you do is to turn around your thoughts. Think positive about yourself, your future, and your life. Simple, right? How you do that is complicated, especially as the sorrow gets bigger. You see, the more he feeds, the heavier he feels."

Nik stomped away, pulling at his hair and spinning in circles, trying to see the invisible creature clinging to his back. Eventually, he gave up and started walking again. Pasha, taking pity on the lad, tried to explain.

"Look . . . have you ever felt like you have the weight of the world on your shoulders? Well, that's him. Life dragging you down? Making your head feel heavy, your body slouch, your feet drag? That's him too. Feel like you have no energy? That's him sucking the life out of you. He wants you to feel that way, because that sadness—that going-nowhere feeling—is like a giant-roast-pig-with-an-apple-in-its-mouth buffet dinner to him.

"Turning all that around to joy—to effervescent, bubbly,

happy-go-lucky, fun-in-the-sun, nothing-weighs-me-down, free-as-a-bird bliss—is the only way to get rid of a sorrow for good. And that's as rare as golden Caspian osetra. Most people just find a way to live with it."

"And what happens if you can't?"

Pasha winced and reluctantly added, "Well, there are some. Not many, mind you, but some, who feed their sorrow so much that they can barely function, and the only way they can think to escape is by death. Of course, what they don't know is that even when they kill themselves, it doesn't kill a sorrow. If they drown, he just swims around, looking for another person to latch on to. If they hang themselves, it's not long before someone else comes along to see what happened, and he just hitches a ride." He patted Nik on the elbow. "Try to cheer up, kid. Most everyone has at least a little sorrow. The longer it lives with you, the better it gets at poking your little hurts, triggering its favorite brand of candy. It's the rare person who can shake him off for good. The key is in not overfeeding him."

"How . . . how common are these things? Does everyone have one?"

Pasha scratched his chin. "Depends, I suppose. They're more widespread after wars and during winter. They're a bit like the plague or influenza or maybe lice. They pop up when folks are at their weakest, downtrodden, and in pain."

"I see." Nik was silent for a moment and then asked, "Do you have a curse to cause happiness?"

He wasn't prepared for the knee-slamming, belly-ripping laughter that followed. When Pasha finally quieted, he answered Nik's query, but first he glanced at Nik's back. "It wouldn't be much of a curse to make someone happy now, would it, lad?"

"I suppose not," Nik replied with a dark expression, slumped shoulders, and tightened fists.

"Can I make a suggestion?"

"Might as well."

"It would do you some good to learn to laugh at yourself. You felt stupid just now, didn't you?"

"It was your fault. You laughed at me."

"The question was funny. I laughed. If you think about it for a minute, you'd see why it's funny too."

"You want to humiliate me."

"No, I don't. People do humiliating, stupid things all the time. All of us have things to learn. All of us screw up. Why do you think I have a job cursing people? I'm about the wealthiest person here. Why? People want revenge. All. The. Time. I say, learn to laugh at the stupid stuff. Let it go. Who cares? You think you're the only sensitive soul in the universe? Think again. You believe you're the only one who's ever been maligned, abused, targeted, unloved, or taken advantage of? Well, I have a client list that goes on for days that says otherwise. You assumed I wanted to humiliate you. You don't know why I laughed, just that I did. You want to blame me, assign fault for your feelings. The truth is, the only one responsible for how you feel is you."

"But you don't understand. My life hasn't been—"

"Hasn't been what? Fair? A bed of roses? Sunshine and buttercups? Well, cry me a river, son. That's true of everyone. Here's another piece of free advice: Life isn't about the cards you're dealt, and it isn't even about winning. It's about keeping your cool while seated at the table, behaving like a gentleman, leaving the game with your dignity intact. When you have done that, you've won. In the end, it doesn't matter how much you collect, how much you lose, or anything else. Leave the game with a handshake and a smile for everyone at the table, even those who disrespect you, and guess what, the game is yours. You've won."

"I don't think we're still talking about the same thing."

"Look, kid. I like you. You saved my life. I'm going to help you out. Here." Pasha reached into his coat. "Now, this is only on loan. I'm going to want it back, but seeing as how you believe the world is against you, I'm going to prove to you that having everything go your way isn't necessarily the key to happiness."

"What do you mean?" Nik said, eyeing the little man suspiciously.

Pasha pressed a deck of cards into Nik's hand. "This is my lucky deck. Use this and you'll never lose. It doesn't matter what game you play or how you play it. You can't lose. No matter what."

"Yeah?" Nik said, taking the cards. "And what's the catch?"

"No catch. It's just a lesson. You think the world is out to get you, and that's what's making you unhappy. Well, here you go. Now you'll beat the world at its own game every time. It can't get you. Will that make you happy? I don't think so. In fact, I think that sorrow on your back is going to get bigger. Tell you what—I'll make you a deal. If you can shrink that sorrow in a week's time, I'll figure out a way to reunite you with your friends. If not, well, maybe you do something for me instead. What do you say?"

"I'd say my part of the obligation sounds pretty vague."

Pasha laughed. "Not a trusting soul, are you?"

"Not really. Besides, what if I use these boots of mine and scarper off, taking your trick deck of cards with me?"

"First off, don't forget who I am. I can find you anywhere, boy. Second, those boots of yours won't do you any good for a bit more than a week anyway. Took near all their power to save our bacons back there. They'll need just a bit to recharge. And third, there's no other town within days of walking on any side. Trust me on this. Try to leave before I find you, and you'll be wanderin' this place for a long, long while."

Nik grunted. "Might've told me all that before I decided to save you."

The one-eyed man clapped Nik on the arm and said, "I might've. But I didn't. Good luck, son. Keep on down this trail for a few more hours, and you'll come across a little road. Follow it, and you'll find a small village. I'll meet up with you at the end of the week."

"But wait. What am I supposed to do about . . . ?"

Pasha ignored Nik's question, side winked with his one large eye, said, "See ya around, kid," then stepped behind a large tree and disappeared.

CHAPTER 8

A Bitter Truth Is Better Than Sweet Lies

Not knowing what else to do, Veru began to walk. Danik held her hand, letting her take the lead without question and didn't mention searching for his parents' home again, though he did frequently ask her if they were on the right path to her home. When she noticed he'd become distraught if her answer was, "I don't know," she began lying, assuring him that, "Yes, following the river is the right way."

He'd settle down then for a time, until he forgot he'd already asked and plied her with the same question again. It tested her patience after she answered him the tenth time, so Veru tried distracting him with music.

"How about you sing for me?" she suggested. "It might pass the time while we walk." Veru was proud that she managed to keep a kind smile on her face despite the pain in her feet caused by the too-thin slippers, and not for the first time, she gave silent thanks to her parents for their meticulous training not only in leadership and weapons but in how to remain calm and collected in tedious diplomatic affairs. Such drilling served her in times like the present, when her nerves were raw, and her patience was waning.

She remembered how Stacia always seemed to excel at the smiling and shaking hands and the endless lines of people wanting to pet and talk to them. Veru detested every moment and just knew that nearly every man looked at her lustfully and every woman's eyes gleamed with jealousy. When she couldn't threaten them with her knives, she'd cut them with her sharp tongue instead. As a cat, though, she'd learned that there were those who could appreciate her beauty without lust. It was something entirely new for her. So instead of attacking immediately, she was trying to wait and see what the person's intentions were first.

"I can, if you like," he said. "But wouldn't you prefer to rest for a while? You're limping," Danik added.

Veru half laughed, half hissed. "Noticed that, did you? I was trying to hide it."

"But why?" Danik asked with a confused expression.

She sighed, wondering how many times he was going to ask her about it and decided it might be better to just go ahead and sit down.

Finding a rock that would suit, she sat and hiked up her skirts enough to peel off her slippers and dip her feet into the frigid water. Under normal circumstances, she wouldn't dream of exposing so much leg to a man, but Danik was different somehow. It was hard to define their relationship. Perhaps it was due to spending her time with him as a tiger. She'd become so relaxed around the hunter that she didn't think of him as seeing her as a woman.

Veru chided herself, remembering she should be more careful, and shifted her skirts to cover her knees. Despite her comfort with Danik, he was still a man. And from her experience with them, they only treated her one way. It was the reason she covered herself in armor as often as possible. She felt safe. Then again, with his memory problem, he'd likely forget he ever saw her bare leg. Perhaps it didn't matter. She peered up at him and didn't see signs of the smitten, lovesick, or lustful expressions she was used to detecting in other men. Danik looked the same way he always did, albeit a bit confused.

Veru weighed her options and decided that as long as he wasn't acting giddy with love, she'd treat him like she would any traveling companion, just as she would Nik, for example. It would be a nice change actually, to have another friend, someone she could trust, other than Nikolai. True, there were some things she didn't feel comfortable sharing with Nik. Veru knew Nik had feelings for her, and she had to be careful with him.

Though she trusted her sister, her relationship with Stacia was complicated. As much as Veru loved her twin, she'd never felt she could truly confide in her. At least not since they were young. They'd been best friends once upon a time, but when her sister grew nearly a foot taller almost overnight and took to the sword as if it were a third arm, making their father oh-so-very proud, Veru grew jealous and withdrawn.

It didn't help when Veru's bosom became far too ample to hide. The young tsarevna had taken to wrapping her chest at first, ignoring the discomfort it caused. It was her father who noticed her stance had changed. It was something about the way she moved in training and how her arms could no longer cross her chest at the same place.

Her mother came in one evening to "talk" to her about it, dismissing the maid who'd prepared her bathing water. When their discussion was over, Veru felt humiliated. Even more so, when their father decided to separate the girls for different types of training exercises the next day. Veru was to report to different instructors after that, this time expert female assassins, and they knew about the way she'd been binding herself.

The first week, their mother supervised her training personally, keeping her sharp eyes on her daughter and making certain Veru understood the "gifts" that came with her new body. Mama took the opportunity to explain to her daughter that beauty was something men often exploited and used for themselves, but she would teach Veru how to use it against them for her own good and how to protect herself from those who would take advantage.

Veru was grateful for her mother's insights now and could see the practicality of what her mother had taught her. Indeed, there had been many, many times when her training had been of great importance, not only to her but to her family and to her country. And her skills had saved her from unwanted advances time and again.

But that didn't mean that she didn't feel great envy every time she saw the ease with which her sister moved about the courtyard, holding her shoulders back and her head high. The men slapped her on the back or clapped her arm as if she were one of them. Her confidence was born of skill and camaraderie. The men knew and trusted her.

Yes, she was a tsarevna, too, but if a man pledged devotion or love, she would see it in his eyes or feel it in his touch and know it was real. Such emotions would last because they weren't based on golden tresses, dimpled cheeks, or ample curves. Stacia wasn't destined, as Veru was, to see the light of fondness and affection in her husband's eyes fade, along with her beauty, as the years passed.

"My lady, Veru?" Danik said, lightly touching her shoulder. "Why would you attempt to keep your pain a secret?"

Sucking air between her teeth as she twisted her foot in the frigid water, she decided to answer him truthfully. "My family has a thing about hiding our weaknesses. We never like to let an enemy know if we're tired or hungry or hurting. It gives them an advantage over us. I suppose we are much like the animals you hunt in that way. We hide our pain, even when caught in a trap."

He stared at her for a moment, then crouched down and lifted her foot from the water. Gently, he touched the arch and pressed a fingertip to swollen blisters on the toe and heel. Without looking at her, he took hold of her torn skirt hem and ripped off a bit more fabric, then gently wrapped one layer around her big toe and another over the top of her foot and around the back of her heel, covering the raised swelling. As he carefully placed her shoe back on her foot, he said softly, "I may have forgotten many things, my lady. But know this: I do not seek to trap you, and if I could avoid doing so to any of God's other creatures, I would. And I hope you know—I am *not* your enemy."

Rising, he moved to her other foot and worked without speaking. Veru didn't quite know what to say. She'd never been taken care of by a man before, never let one touch her in such an intimate fashion. True, Nik was training as a medic and had tried to tend some superficial cuts, but she never let him do more than bind a broken finger. Veru wasn't sure she'd ever let him treat her for a real wound—that is, unless she was unconscious.

Their surgeon had listened to her lungs through her clothing, once bound her broken ribs, and given her various concoctions to help with her monthly pains. Luckily, she'd never suffered from anything truly serious.

As Danik ran a fingertip gently over the arch of her foot, she well recalled the risk he'd taken in trying to free her as a tiger. How he'd tried to ease her pain by feeding her rabbit with medicinal herbs sewn carefully into the carcass. Danik had done everything in his power to save her. And that was before he'd even known she was human. If it had been anyone else, she would have her hand in his hair and her knife against his throat, but his words rang in her mind again and again.

I am not your enemy, he'd said.

His calloused fingers didn't linger but moved deftly over her skin. He was quick and efficient, but his expression held great compassion and perhaps a hint of remorse, just as it did when he skinned an animal or removed one from a trap. It was almost as if her hurt caused him pain. Whatever Danik was, he was her friend, just as he had always been. She'd known that since he'd first looked down at her in the pit and took pity upon a suffering beast.

When he was finished, she put her hand on his shoulder. "Thank you," Veru said quietly. "I know you aren't my enemy, Danik."

He placed his hand on top of hers and squeezed. "You never need to hide the truth from me. I'd never use pain or hunger or any other thing you might perceive as weakness against you. I only want to help. Do you believe me?"

Danik's blue eyes locked on to her face, searching for something. It was as if he was seeking desperately for acceptance or understanding or . . . perhaps it was still a home—a place where he was known, where he could be himself, feel safe and at complete ease.

Veru had to admit she also craved such a place. She hadn't felt like she'd had that sense of security for many years. Her mother tried her best, but without their father, the palace never felt the same. He was their anchor, and they'd been adrift as a family ever since his loss. Danik must have been going through the same thing. But his situation was even worse. He'd lost his entire family. At least she still had Stacia.

"I believe you, Danik," Veru promised. "Look, I know I can be a little . . . off-putting. But you don't need to hide from me either. Even if your memory is gone, and you ask me the same question over and over and I lose patience and snarl at you, I'll still answer. I can't promise that I won't threaten to gut you at some point in irritation, but I can guarantee that I'm your friend too. And Verusha Stepanov defends her friends to the death."

"Now that, I believe," Danik said with a wink and a half grin. He held out his hands, offering to help her to her feet, and she was surprised with herself when she accepted and leaned against him, hobbling along, uncaring that she was not only depending on a man but showing weakness. It was a move she might have feigned once upon a time to get a man to spill state secrets.

Instead of despising herself for it, she let herself enjoy leaning on someone else for a change. Then, after a while, she began to like the way his muscular arm wrapped around her back, his hand clutching her waist. As they walked, she almost forgot the pain; instead, she focused on the warmth of his body pressed next to her own and the deep timbre of his voice as he hummed a tune in time with the rushing water nearby.

Veru was astonished to note how time passed as late morning became late afternoon, so wrapped up was she in the physical sensations of her body that she'd so long denied. She didn't even think of stopping until her stomach rumbled. Danik had only given her some berries that he'd found along the way, opting to walk as far as they could while she felt able, before resting to make camp. She was about to suggest they find a good spot for the night when they spotted a crooked little house on a craggy rock overlooking the river. A small column of gray smoke spiraled up from the stone chimney.

"Perhaps they'd welcome two traveling strangers," Danik suggested.

"Maybe," Veru said. "I suppose it couldn't hurt to ask."

"We'll say we're traveling musicians. People are often willing to put up groups such as that."

"But I'm not a musician," Veru said.

"That's fine. You can pose as my sister."

"A sister would be trained as a musician. What if they ask us to play?"

"That's true. Perhaps . . . a cousin, then."

"A cousin would need a chaperone."

Danik pursed his lips, obviously thinking hard.

Veru shook his arm. "I'll be your wife, Danik. No one can complain about that."

"But—but you'd have a ring."

"We'll say we've sold it. We're obviously very poor."

Danik rubbed his jaw and frowned. "I suppose it would explain why you don't have decent shoes. And why your dress is ripped." His expression suddenly brightened. "Wait a moment. *Are* we married, and I just forgot? You'd think I'd remember a thing like that."

"No. We aren't married. I'm the tsarevna, and you're taking me home. Remember?"

"Right. That sounds right." He nodded with certainty. "We're married and headed home."

"Close enough."

"But you can't sing?"

"Not a note." She took hold of his arm again. "Shall we, then?"

"I think we should."

There was a little path that led up to the cottage, but Veru's feet were really hurting by that point. She slipped on the gravel and nearly fell, but Danik scooped her in his arms and carried her up to the door, only setting her down once they were safely on the porch.

A lock of his thick, dirty-blond hair fell over one blue eye, hiding it from view as he leaned down. His hands were still spanning her waist, bearing most of her weight.

Veru found herself mesmerized by his full lips and the soft golden stubble of a new beard surrounding them. Reaching up, she pushed the hair away from his face and traced a long, dark eyebrow with her thumb.

The expression of concern and tenderness didn't change into something lustful, like she might've expected after a caress such as the one she'd just given him. But if she wasn't mistaken, there did seem to be a slight brightening of the blue in his eyes. Instead of causing Veru alarm, it made her breath quicken.

Danik smiled at her and said, "Your feet always seem to get you in trouble, don't they, little lapochka?"

Her mouth fell open, and she was just going to ask him if he was beginning to remember on his own, when the door behind them flew open.

Standing in the opening was a pale, thin woman with disheveled gray hair held back by a scarf. A thin blue film covered both her eyes, making Veru think she was blind, and yet her head moved back and forth between Veru and Danik as if she could see both of them clear as day.

The woman's nose and lips were pinched and thin, though her nostrils were quite large, especially when she took in great gusts of air, as she seemed to do often. Between her spindly legs wound a gray cat with eyes so green and bright they seemed to glow.

"Kto tam prishel, Maxsim, eh?" Reaching down, she stroked her cat's head with long, bony fingers. The cat dug its head into her hand and turned to look at Veru. Peering at her closely, it narrowed its eyes, then hissed and spat before darting back into the darkness of the cottage.

"Max!" the woman cried. "That's no way to treat our guests. Silly beast. No matter. Privet. You can call me Yuga. Did someone send you, or did you find my little hut of your own accord?"

"Greetings, Babushka," Danik said. "My wife and I came across your cottage on our own."

"Otlichno! Good! That is excellent. You two are most welcome. Newly married, are you?"

"We are," Veru replied.

"I knew it," the old woman said, reaching out to clasp Veru's hands. She missed, but Veru purposely touched her hands to the woman's fingertips and found them very cold—almost icy, in fact. When Yuga clasped them quickly, Veru was shocked to find her grip so strong. She was also confused to see the woman bring her hands close to her face and inhale deeply as if trying to catch her scent.

Veru watched the woman carefully, knowing there was much more to the old lady than there seemed to be on the surface.

Danik, however, appeared to already trust the woman completely. "If you have room, might my wife and I perhaps stay over for the night and share a meal? In exchange, I can offer a strong arm to chop wood or my skills as a hunter, or perhaps a bit of music to pass the long, dark hours. I'm a traveling musician by trade."

"Are you, then?" the woman said, never releasing Veru's hands or turning her rheumy gaze upon Danik. "My, my. You've made quite a catch, haven't you, my dear? A youth pretty of face who hunts, hauls, and sings to you by night. Hmm . . . yes. That would be quite lovely, young man. It's been a long time since I've enjoyed a song. Please, come inside and warm yourselves by my small fire."

When Veru hesitated at the threshold, Danik took her hand and said, "Are you coming in, my—my dear?"

Veru thought she saw the woman's eyes gleam in the darkness of the cottage. Her instinct told her something was wrong, but she couldn't figure out what it could be that was throwing her alarms. She'd always trusted her gut in the past, but everything in this dreamworld felt . . . upside down. For the first time in forever, she felt out of control. It was as if she hung on the side of a cliff, and there was no way for her to save herself.

Then she remembered the advice Kadam had given her before he disappeared. He'd said her strongest weapons would be her mind and her friends. Never in her life had she put her complete trust in a man before. Not even Nik. To do so now, when Danik could barely even recall his own name, seemed like the height of foolishness, but . . . she also knew that this dreamworld was a test. Perhaps this was a part of it.

Squeezing Danik's hand, she whispered, "Do you feel that this is safe?"

He stepped closer to her and cupped her shoulder. "You are wise to ask," he murmured softly.

Before she could stop him, Danik called out loudly, "Babushka? My dear wife is worried over our safety. You and your cat aren't planning anything nefarious regarding our persons while we are in residence, are you?"

The cackle that ensued lifted the fine hairs on the back of Veru's neck, arms, and legs. It was throaty, full of phlegm, and somehow contained a combination of delight and wickedness. All Veru wanted to do was turn her back to the place and never return. In fact, she shivered, took hold of Danik's hand, and tugged, intending to back out of the cottage slowly. But when she glanced behind her, the river was gone. In fact, the landscape was moving.

Veru wondered how she hadn't been aware of the movement. She was still standing on the porch, or at least halfway on the porch and halfway inside the cottage. But either the cottage was spinning, or the world was turning. Whichever one it was, it was a bad sign, a very bad sign. Just at that moment, the little house shifted, lurching suddenly to the right, and Veru stumbled into Danik. He caught her easily enough and braced himself against a table so they wouldn't fall.

There was a plaintive meow from Maxsim, the cat who'd been hiding beneath it, then the house tilted once again, this time to the left, and Veru and Danik found themselves jostling to the other side of the room.

The old woman called out to them, "The house will keep doing that until you make up your minds. Are you staying or going?"

Veru knew she definitely, surely, absolutely didn't want to stay, but before she could announce that decision to anyone, Danik proclaimed loudly, "Yuga, we're staying."

At that, the door behind them slammed with a definitive bang, while the house seemed to drop suddenly, as if it had fallen several lengths to the ground. Both Danik and Veru lost their footing and tumbled into a heap together as Maxsim the cat bound quickly over their fallen forms to settle himself in his seated mistress's lap.

"There," Yuga said, stroking her green-eyed feline. "Now that that's been decided, how about that song?"

CHAPTER 9

The One Who Crosses Wisely Will Master the Bridge

From deep within the bushes, a tiny voice pipped, "Please don't hurt me."

"Come out," Stacia cried, "and we won't do you any harm as long as you do no harm to us."

"Very well," said the voice. There was a great rustle, and then a beautiful little girl emerged from a perfect hiding spot.

Other than a smudge of dirt on her cheek and dress, Stacia thought she'd never seen such a pretty, well-kept child in her life. Crouching down in front of her, she asked, "What's your name, young one?"

"Zima."

"That's a pretty name. Where do you live, Zima?" Stacia couldn't help it. She fixed Zima's crown of blond hair, tucking in the loose strands of hair, and retied the blue bow of her embroidered pinafore, noticing it matched her eye color exactly. When she blinked, Zima's wide blue eyes reminded her of the forget-me-not flowers her mother had grown in her summer garden.

"I live in the town on the other side of the river across the bridge with my aunties." Zima lifted a plump white hand, plugged her thumb directly into her mouth, and began sucking.

"How did you get over here?" Stacia asked, mouthing to Zakhar to bring her some water.

"I got lost."

Stacia got her to drink a little bit of water, and then the little girl asked, "Can I pet your kitty? He's awfully big."

"You certainly can. He's very soft, and he adores children, especially those who tickle his ears. Maybe he'll even take you for a ride, if you're very good."

"Really?"

Her thumb came out, and she smiled widely, showing a rosebud mouth to match her little apple-pink cheeks.

"Do you think you can show us the way back to your home?" Zakhar asked.

At that, the little girl shook her head vehemently. "I know the way, but I can't cross the bridge. Trolls live underneath. They see through the planks and wait for you to drop through, then they catch you and cook you for supper. Then they use your bones to play music at night."

Zakhar asked, "How did you get to this side of the water if it's so dangerous to cross over?"

She shrugged. "They know how to get across safely. I was out hunting berries with my aunties. It must have been time to go, but I didn't hear them. I fell asleep, and when I woke up, they were gone."

Stacia and Zakhar glanced at each other. "How many days have you been out here by yourself?" Stacia asked.

"I don't know." Zima shrugged. Her thumb immediately went back into her mouth, and she began sucking it fiercely.

Smiling, Stacia said, "I'll bet you're hungry. Would you like something to eat?"

The little girl nodded, and Zakhar offered her a bit of bread with some meat tucked in the middle. She nibbled on it and edged closer to Iriko while she did.

"What's your kitty's name?" she asked as some crumbs fell from her lips and onto Iriko's coat.

"Iriko."

"That's a strange name."

"Yes. He says he likes scratches on his neck. Right here."

"You can talk to him?"

"I can. With magic."

"Oh. My aunties have magic too. That's how they made me."

"Made you?" Stacia asked. "What do you mean?"

"They said I'm their perfect little girl. They fashioned me from ice and snowflakes. I'm their little snow girl. That's why they call me Zima. It means frost." She laughed when the tiger chuffed. "I think he likes me."

"I think he does," Stacia said, looking at the little girl with new eyes and wondering what, exactly, Zima was and what the little girl might mean to them.

With Zima sitting on Iriko's back, the group made their way to the fork in the river, and then they passed over to the south side and continued on until dark. The next morning they walked for half a day, and every hour the river became wider and deeper. Soon they saw signs of other people. There was a trail that became a path and then a road. Signs pointed ahead to a village, and Zima confirmed that it was indeed her village that lay ahead. They were just wondering how they'd cross over and began looking for a good place, when they saw the bridge.

It was at this point that Zima became very agitated. "We can't cross there," she said. "I already told you about the trolls. They're going to grab us."

There was, in fact, a warning sign posted on the road nearby, with a wooden donation box beneath it. It read:

TRAVELRS CROSS AT YOUR OWN PARILE.

PAY THE TOLL.

MISERS RISK HIGHWAY ROBBERY.

OR WORSE.

Stacia stood there for a moment, reading the sign. Then she snorted and gave a cursory glance under the bridge. Seeing nothing, she scouted the trees and bushes nearby, then clicked open the blade of her walking stick and said, "Come, Zakhar. Stay just behind me. Iriko, stay behind him, if you will."

"But shouldn't we put something in the box?" Zakhar asked.

"Do we have any coins in our packs? I don't recall seeing any."

Zakhar shook his head. "No. Nothing like that. But perhaps they will take something else."

"We have nothing small enough to fit in the donation box. Besides, I don't see anything or anyone. I say we risk it."

"No. No. We can't," Zima said. "I told you—there are trolls."

"It's okay," Stacia said without looking back. "I'm a warrior. Don't worry. Iriko will keep you safe."

The little girl closed her eyes and trembled, burying her face in Iriko's fur and clinging to his neck tightly with her little arms.

"That's a good girl. You hold on to him. We'll get across just fine. You'll see."

Stacia started across the bridge, and everything went fine until they were just about halfway. Then they heard a hissing sound. The water below the bridge began bubbling, and the bridge rocked back and forth wildly. Iriko dug his claws into the wood as best he could, while Zakhar and Stacia grabbed on to the ropes, holding on lest they tumble over the side into the churning river.

Then it didn't matter. The boards they stood on, strung together by well-made ropes, jumped and bucked, though they could see no reason for them to move. Shifting, the wooden planks slid and rolled over, on top of and beneath one another, folding and bending in completely unnatural ways. Before the travelers could leap or prepare themselves, the planks beneath their feet were gone, and one by one, they tumbled into the river.

To their surprise, the water didn't carry them downstream, but it closed over their heads, and they sank down, down, down, until their feet touched the riverbed. Their hair and clothes floated around them, but there was a sensation that they were enclosed in an underwater room. What was even more astonishing was the fact that they could not only see, but they could somehow breathe and move, albeit slowly. They could see the river shifting around the pocket of space they'd fallen into, but as they pushed against the barrier, they found there was no way through. It was as if they were trapped inside a giant, stretchy bubble.

Zima began to cry, and as Stacia slogged slowly to her side, placing a hand on her back, she noticed the child's tears had turned into tiny diamonds in the thick, watery trap. She captured one and pinched it between her fingers. That's when she realized it wasn't a gemstone at all, but ice. She continued to rub the little girl's back in small circles, and eventually she sat quietly, sucking her thumb.

They didn't have to wait long for their captors to arrive. The liquid around them pulsed, and then a bubble pressed into the room, followed by a pop. Quickly, the room sealed itself behind the newcomer, repairing the hole made by him as perfectly as if nothing at all had happened.

The creature that stepped inside wore a long, tattered coat made of the skin of some type of amphibious animal and what appeared to be thick woolen pants, held up by a dark snakeskin belt fastened with a buckle made of shiny seashell or pearl. Where boots should have been, his legs were bare and covered with a hard, glossy armor that ended just at his extralong toes, which were connected by thick webbing.

His chest was bare, his belly blue-green and bulbous, and his long locks of hair looked much like floating seaweed. He raised a hand, beckoning them to come closer, and Stacia saw his long fingers ended in black talons, and the pads of his fingertips had suction cups. When none of them moved, he extended his arms, spreading those fingers, and she noticed the same webbing as his feet. With a powerful thrust of his arms, he was next to them immediately.

A heartbeat later, he ripped the weapon from her grip and seized her arm. Stacia knew immediately there would be no escaping the creature. He was unnaturally strong, and where she moved slowly in the water, he was incredibly fast and agile. Still, she looked him in the eye, bravely, like her parents had taught her, and accepted the consequences of her actions.

"I apologize if I've offended you, sir," she began, nodding her head deferentially. "We had no coin to offer you. Perhaps we can negotiate a trade instead, if you are amenable." Her voice sounded to her like bubbles, whistles, and pops, much as if she were trying to talk while submerged in her bathtub. Of course, if that had truly been the case, she would have drowned by now. She peered at Zakhar to see if he'd understood her, but he simply watched and shrugged as if he didn't know how to proceed either.

The creature blinked. Its eyelids closed from the bottom to the top and then from the sides to the middle. When it opened its eyes again, they gleamed with an eerie yellow light. The beam fell on each of them in turn, moving over them deliberately from head to toe as if searching each one for something unique.

When the light fell on Stacia, she could actually feel its warmth on her skin. It tickled and itched as it ran over her. It felt invasive, the creature's gaze, and she wanted to scratch her skin where it looked at her, but she dared not squirm as it finished its inspection. It paused for a long time as it considered Iriko, stopping at the tiger's eyes for a long while, and then it made a sort of popping noise with its mouth, puffing out its cheeks hugely as it did.

When it moved on to Zima, the little girl began to wail again. This time it was actually audible. Stacia was surprised she could hear her. Up until that moment, she had not been able to hear or communicate with anyone in the strange underwater realm except Iriko, and he didn't have much to say or any ideas on how to escape.

The light traveled over Zima again and again. There was rumbling and cheek-puffing from the creature, and he appeared to be quite excited about the little girl. Even his skin changed colors, showing off vivid hues of green, blue, and purple. The entire liquid room seemed to vibrate, and soon more bubbles erupted into the room, with other strange creatures joining the first one.

One looked decidedly more feminine, wearing what almost looked like a dress. Her coloring was more purple than green, and her face and limbs were longer. The next one wore a hat that shone with a fish-scale band, and he carried a pearl trident. Another had a belt adorned with little fish skulls. The last wore a crown of coral and had a deep scar across one cheek.

They erupted in conversation with clicks, guttural vibrations, color displays, and the puffing of various body parts. Finally, the first one who had entered approached Stacia and handed back her weapon, then said, "You want to trade for your life?"

"I do," Stacia said, nodding.

"Good. Give us ice child. We take. You go free."

On the word *free*, a hiss of bubbles rose from his lips and hovered right above his head, hitting the top of their little cage. Stacia looked up at them, and she could see the river above, flowing over their heads. If only they could reach it. As she watched, the tiny bubbles slowly rose higher, eventually penetrating whatever membrane was trapping them. Once they were fully outside, the current of the river caught the bubbles and carried them off downstream.

Stacia narrowed her eyes. "How do I know you'll keep your word?"

The creature bellowed. His whole body vibrated, and his cheeks turned bright purple. It took several moments for him to settle down. Finally, he said, "We are vodnik. Our deals are unbroken."

"Like your bridge?"

"You have warning. It is enough. Now, you make deal, or we keep all?"

"We make deal." Stacia felt a tiger head hit the back of her knee and Zakhar's hand on her shoulder at the same time. She held up a hand to calm her companions. "But I don't trust you. I'm not from here. We will exchange, but I want to set terms." She paused as if in thought. "You give me three of your bubbles to travel out of this place, and then we trade. Yes?"

The thick liquid around them pulsed as the creatures conferred with one another again. Then the big one turned back to Stacia. "We are agree. You have three pockets for travel, but no trickses. We watch you go first."

Stacia hadn't prepared for that. "I want my man going first," she said.

Zakhar shook his head hard, but she nodded and winked that it was okay and clapped him awkwardly on the shoulder in slow motion. After she moved away, the creature, his seaweed hair floating around his bulbous head, opened his mouth, forming a large circle with his lips, and then made a sort of gagging motion. Slowly, out came a bubble that grew larger and larger with each heave of his body.

Zakhar acted as if to move away from it, but one of the others grabbed his shoulders and held him still. The bubble touched one of Zakhar's hands first, and instead of popping, it grabbed hold of his hand and began crawling over his skin as if it were alive. Zakhar kicked hard then, writhing as if he were in pain, but soon the bubble was over his head, and then he calmed down and began breathing normally, his cheeks changing from red to a normal tone.

Stacia peered closely, and she could see there was no more liquid matter inside the bubble. It had completely encased him in the air. *Interesting*, she thought. Once it had re-formed and encompassed his body fully, the creature gave a snap of his mouth, and the bubble broke free. It began rising to the surface, taking Zakhar with it.

He knelt, his hands on the bottom of the bubble, shouting something that none of them were able to hear. Once it hit the membrane at the top of their liquid cage, it was slowly absorbed through, taking its human captive along for the ride. Zakhar kept his face pressed to the bottom for as long as possible; then, with a tiny pop, he and his bubble were gone, flying along the river current.

Turning with hands on hips, Stacia asked, "What happens at the surface? Will he be stuck in there?"

All the creatures started laughing with great puffs of their cheeks. "Don't be silly," the one with the crown said. "The minute he hits a rock . . ."

"Or a tree . . ."

"Or a root . . ."

"Or a fish . . ."

"Or even the air, it will pop," finished the big vodnik. "Them bubbles are fragile. Now, come closer, gal. It's your turn."

"But what if he doesn't know how to swim?"

"Not our problem," one creature said.

"Guess he'll learn then, won't he?" said another, laughing as he reached for Stacia.

"No. Not me," she insisted. "My cat next."

"No. No. We are the ones deciding. If you protest, we keep both."

He started blowing his bubble, and Stacia desperately cried out in her mind to Iriko: *What do we do? I don't know how to save her.*

Don't worry, Red. I've got this. Just go.

But without me, how will you see?

I can see from her eyes too.

What? How?

I'm not sure, exactly. But it started down here. When she began crying, I could see from her eyes too. I've been switching back and forth to make sure I wasn't imagining it.

But—

It's okay, Iriko said. *I have an idea. Let me take this one off your shoulders. Go.*

Iriko nudged Stacia's hand and she ran it over his head, squeezing his ear. *Just . . . take care of her.*

I will. I promise.

Stacia felt the bubble hit the back of her head, and soon it encompassed her just like it had Zakhar. The burning hit her lungs as the strange liquid evaporated instantly, causing her to cough and her muscles to spasm. Unlike the priest, she didn't kneel to watch Iriko and Zima as her bubble began to rise. Instead, she lifted her weapon and clicked the hidden switch, preparing to pop her escape device the moment she was clear of the vodnik's trap.

Impatient, she waited, watching as inch by inch the bubble rose out of the membrane, exposing her to the river above. Wide-eyed fish hurried past her, carried in the wake of the current along with flotsam and debris. Her vessel rocked, and then finally she was free and rushing along, tumbling head over heels. Within a moment, the bubble hit the sharp edge of her blade and popped with an ear-numbing blast that sent her down into the cold river.

It took her several moments to get her bearings, and she almost lost her precious walking stick in the process. Luckily, her bags were tightly tied to her back; otherwise, they, too, would have been lost. She could only hope that Zakhar had been as careful about his things. If he hadn't, they might have wasted many of their supplies. Stacia dragged herself out of the river, squeezing the water out of her tunic and hair and calling out for Zakhar while quickly heading back toward the bridge, which was now far upstream.

It was well past sunset, and as her eyes adjusted, she thought she spied a large rock ahead. But when she neared it, she found it wasn't a rock at all, but her fallen companion. She knelt and lightly slapped his cheek. "Zakhar. Wake up. Are you okay?" she asked.

He groaned and cracked open his eyes. "I'm alive, if that's what you're asking."

"Good. Come on. We've got to go back and help Iriko. He has a plan to save Zima."

"A plan to save Zima? What plan?" he asked as she helped him to his feet and adjusted his pack, picking up items that had slipped out of the bag and tucking them back in.

"But he did save me," a small voice behind them said. "See? I'm right here."

CHAPTER 10

A Wooden Bed Is Better than a Golden Coffin

Nik found the road easily enough and pressed on until he reached the small settlement. Not knowing what to do once he arrived and having no supplies or money to barter with, he located the nearest trading goods store and inquired about his friends inside. Unfortunately, no one had heard of or seen anyone fitting the description of the tsarevnas, Danik, Iriko, or Zakhar.

The owner asked Nik if he needed a room for the night and a meal, but as Nik had no money to offer in exchange, the man told him to try the local pub and ask if any of the farmers or herdsmen needed hands. He thanked the man and headed out.

Night was falling, and the streetlamps were being lit. Nik could feel the weather turning. It had been warm when he'd first arrived in this new land, but the air was now becoming cold. Very cold. He'd need a warm coat and supplies if he was going to head back out to look for Iriko, Zakhar, and Stacia. Perhaps if he worked for a week first, he'd earn enough to buy the supplies he needed. Then he could meet up with Pasha again, and the likho might help him find his friends.

He decided to focus on trying to be happy. If he could shrink the sorrow on his back, then maybe he'd not only help himself with his personal issues, but he'd fix the mistake he'd made in running away in the first place. The problem was, he couldn't think of a single reason he should be happy. Nothing that had happened to him since his beloved Veru had transformed into a tiger had gone his way. In fact, he had every reason to be unhappy.

Not only had he been the one to lead the Death Draughtsman to the palace, which is likely the reason the tsarevnas transformed into cats to begin with, but he hadn't even had a chance to explain himself yet. The sisters had lost their kingdom, their mother, and their very humanity, and it was all thanks to his clumsy attempt to help.

Then, on top of that, he had to relive the trauma of seeing the ghost of his past abuser, his own father, and had to kill him again—not once but twice. Instead of feeling jealous about the relationships between the tigers and the other men, he should be singing their praises for helping him save the twins' lives. It was like for every step he took forward, his past insecurities dragged him back, until he felt like giving up altogether.

Happiness felt like an impossibility to him. It was a dream as distant as the stars—a dance with his mother that turned into a nightmare—with her blood on his hands and her weight in his feeble arms every time he closed his eyes. Laughter and joy weren't something Nikolai Novikov deserved.

Passing a mother towing her two children, one on either side, Nik wished her well and forced a smile to his lips, saying, "Dobryy vecher." But the woman just sucked in a breath and hurried her children along as if he were a demon trying to steal them away from her sheltering, heavy skirts.

"So much for pleasantries," he murmured. The smile fell away from his face. It had felt forced and unnatural anyway.

Up ahead, he saw a few men heading into a log building. Warm light spilled out from the windows. When they opened the door, the sound of laughter and music echoed and was snuffed out when the door closed behind them. "Maybe I'll find some joy in there," Nik mumbled as he headed in that direction. "Or if not joy, at least a job."

Grabbing the pull handle, he tugged the door open and entered the pub. It was warm, perhaps a bit too hot, with a crackling pipe stove in the corner and several well-worn tables that looked to be hand hewn, each one with a set of matching log benches on either side. The exception was one large table set off to the side. It was well-worn and polished to a sheen. Instead of benches, twelve heavy, carved chairs were stationed around it.

As it was just approaching sunset, only a few men were in the pub. Nik guessed that they were the type who tended to stay all day, but there was also a handful of men in another corner playing a brisk melody together, stomping their feet to keep the beat. He watched them for a moment, thinking of Danik and knowing how much the young man would long to join them.

After they finished, he clapped along with everyone else, then approached the counter and asked if the brewer knew of anyone needing men for work, as he was new in town and needed to earn a place to stay for a few days. He hoped he didn't look as desperate as he felt.

The barkeep scratched his chin beneath his long, scraggly beard and considered. "Maybe. There might be a few men coming in tonight what would like some help. Here. Have a mug of sbiten on the house while you wait, and I'll point those who seem interested in your direction. Sound good to you, lad?"

"Appreciate it," Nik said, raising his mug of sbiten and taking it to an empty table in the corner of the room. He nursed it, keeping his eyes trained on the door. It wasn't long before the place was bustling and crowded, but none of the men came over to talk with him. The barkeep kept busy talking to every customer and even looked in his direction on occasion, which made Nik think that he was telling the men about his problem, but then they'd laugh and look him up and down and clap one another on the back or congratulate each other on one thing or another.

Nik sank lower and lower into his bench, certain they were laughing at him or found him lacking in some way. Sure, he was smaller than other men his age, and yes, he'd admit that he didn't look like much in the way of muscle or build, but he was smart and agile. He could work as well as the next man. Certainly someone, somewhere needed some help, even if it was just chopping wood or shoveling hay. If nothing else, he had plenty of experience mucking out stalls.

He closed his eyes, and he could almost hear his father's voice telling him over and over that he was worthless. That he'd never amount to anything. That he deserved every awful thing his father had ever done to him and more. Hunching over his drink, he took a long gulp and wiped his mouth with the back of his hand, willing the voice of his dead father to disappear.

His neck itched. Reaching up to scratch, he suddenly remembered the sorrow attached to his back and yanked his hand away. Placing his fingertips on the table, he stood, shoving the bench back with his thighs. There was no way he was going to let the sorrow win, not while he still had some fight left in him.

Forcing himself to smile, he reached into his secret pocket and pulled out the deck of cards given to him by the likho. Slowly, he strolled over to the large table and thumbed through the cards, examining them. It appeared to be a standard thirty-two-card deck. But in place of the king, there was a green-skinned demon of some kind wearing a crown. The queen was no tsarina, but instead was unmistakably the bolotnitsa.

Ignoring the rest of the cards, Nik cleared his throat, grinned at the men, and asked, "Anyone fancy a game of prefa?"

A large, ruddy-faced man stood, saying, "I'll play." He dragged his drinking buddy along with him.

Soon several others joined the group, and there were five or six interested players. Some were eager to play, others to watch and place bets. "How about we rotate players in?" Nik suggested, and the men nodded agreeably. "Now, what shall we wager on this first game?" he asked smoothly.

"What have you got, boy?" the man with red cheeks demanded.

"Not much," Nik admitted. "But I'm handy at mucking out stalls. Have any horses?"

"Yeah. Got me a couple."

"Good. Then I'll wager cleaning out your stalls all week long if you win. That goes for both of you. Either of you win, I'll do the work at both your places this week."

The men chuckled. "You're on, boy. Deal the cards."

"Hold on a minute," Nik said. "What are you two wagering?"

"I got a couple coins," the second man said.

"Nah. Put that away," his friend said. "Ya got no bargaining skills." He rubbed his plump cheek. "Tell ya what. You win, we buys you a drink."

"I've already got a drink. What else are you offering?"

"How about some dinner?"

"Done," Nik said, then thought and added, "I mean dinner and you pay for my lodgings for the evening."

Glancing at one another, the men finally nodded.

"Shake on it, then," Nik encouraged.

He smiled and shook hands with both men, then dealt the cards. He knew immediately he was going to win. Never in his life had luck been more on his side. Nik drew out the game a tiny bit, just to make the men feel good, and then played his hand. "Sorry, boys. I win."

"Hey now. You cheated."

"Not so. I won. Fair and square." Nik rubbed his hands together. "Now about that dinner. I'm mighty hungry."

"You dealt it wrong."

"Yeah," the second man said. "You must have slipped yourself the best cards."

Nik sighed and sat back in the chair. "Tell you what—we'll call that one a practice game. Let's keep the stakes the same. This time one of *you* can deal. Will that be acceptable?"

They glanced at each other and nodded. "Yeah. Hand 'em over."

The ruddy-cheeked man shuffled the cards awhile and then dealt a new hand. Again, Nik won easily. The other men cheered and clapped Nik on the back.

"Looks like you owe the boy a meal," the other men said.

"That's right. Let someone else have a go now," another man suggested.

The two men vacated the chairs and made arrangements with the barkeep to provide a very meager meal and lodgings for Nik, while he proceeded to make a new deal with the next two men. Soon Nik had a small pile of coins and other various little treasures growing in front of him. As his stash grew, the smile on his face grew proportionately. Hours passed, and Nik mused to himself, *I don't know what Pasha was talking about. Winning does make you happy.*

It was quite obvious that losing, however, was making the townspeople very unhappy. Oh, not in the beginning. At first they were amazed by Nik's success and rallied to his side, encouraging him and even cheering for his wins as if rooting for a favorite tournament champion. Nik had to admit—the victories went to his head, almost as if it were his skill being used to achieve the triumphs and not the magic of the cards doing the work. As the evening progressed, it seemed that one by one, he lost his supporters.

He didn't understand what he had done to make them turn against him. It was only a short time ago that he'd been their hero. Now they treated him like the worst of all villains. The men were almost united in their determination to see him lose, yet try as they might, they failed, time and time again.

Nik wanted to withdraw at that point, but they wouldn't have it. They insisted he give them a chance to earn back some of what they'd lost. He offered to just give them back some of their coins and baubles, but they had too much pride for that. They wanted to win. But they couldn't. Not using Nik's cards. He would have suggested using a different deck, but that would have made it obvious that his deck was a trick deck. If they figured that out, they might string him up from the nearest tree. His best bet was to just keep going.

Sweat broke out on his face. There was nothing he could do. He tried buying a round of drinks for everyone, but they poured them out on the floor while staring at him. Nik drank though. He downed glass after glass, hoping to fall into a stupor so he could stop playing.

The bets grew larger and more daring with each game, and Nik's smile grew watery, his vision blurry. The townspeople's expressions became dark and ugly. Some left the pub, while others spoke softly in dim corners, conspiring to destroy Nik one way or another. Man after man sat down trying to play and win against him, and all the while, Nik's pile of booty grew.

He shoved coins and gems into a bag as men eyeballed his stash, whetting their thumbs and running them over the edges of knives. Nik was certain the moment he left the pub he'd get a knife in the belly for his trouble. He considered donating all the money back to the town or loudly announcing it was all for the town orphanage, but he didn't think such a gesture would stop the men from pursuing him. They truly hated him now.

He knew there was no way he could trust the two who'd originally promised to pay for his lodgings. The owner claimed there were no beds, and they looked more likely to murder him than put him up for the night. How would he stop them all from coming to collect when he was asleep? He could clear out and head to the next town, but he'd seen no signs of any. He was more likely to get lost than to find somewhere safe, and it was too cold to camp out without supplies. Then an idea came to him. That niggling voice, the one that had protected him from his father in the past and had saved him from the kikimora, now gave him a thought.

"Well, boys," Nik said, stretching his arms over his head, "I'm sure tuckered out. You all have been so very generous and kind. Seeing as how I'm a stranger to your town, I'd like to repay the favor. I only need to keep enough of this to outfit me with traveling gear at the end of the week, but until then, I need a place to stay. I'm more than happy to work for my keep. If anyone will have me, and has room enough, I can leave the rest of these winnings with you as a fee for your kindness. You can keep it or redistribute it among your peers as you see fit."

Nik gave the group his winningest smile and hoped his generous offer would turn them back to his side.

The group was quiet for a long moment, each man looking at his peers, wondering who was going to take the deal along with the winnings. Whoever did would risk the danger of being robbed on his way home.

"Sorry, kid. No room at my place," one man said.

Another added, "My wife and kids are sick. Wouldn't want to spread it."

While another said, "Got no work for ya right now. All my crops are in."

Finally, the ruddy-cheeked man spoke up. "Here now. I got an idea. There's a place my family owns, just on the edge of town. It's a bit run-down. No one goes up there anymore. It's dusty and drafty. Likely full of mice. Probably find the kids have been using it for a playhouse." He laughed. "In fact, you might hear voices come midnight or such. You know how hard it is to keep those as wants to escape under control."

He glanced at his friends, who all shifted tensely but wouldn't make eye contact. "That right, Andrey?" he asked, elbowing his buddy.

"Uh, yeah. That's right," the man said, nodding furiously.

One by one, the other men quietly took their leave, slipping out the door and disappearing into the cold night.

"Anyhow," the man went on, "that money will sure come in handy to help us fix up that old place. Especially if you can keep an eye on it for us. Make sure it's secure and tight."

Nik rubbed the back of his neck. "Right. Yes. I can do that for you. Just tell me where to find it, and I'll stay there this week."

The man clapped his friend on the back. "We'll take you there ourselves, lad. Get you all set up. Sound good?"

An hour later, Nik stood in front of a dilapidated cottage tucked away at the edge of town. It looked to him like half the place had burned in a fire. Blackened boards and sooty windows marked one part of the building, while the other half looked like it was ready to fall over with wood rot and decay.

Grimacing, Nik said, "Are you sure you want to save it?"

"She was a beauty once," the man said proudly. "Owned by my own praded. He was the first town leader, Yuri Mer Minkin."

"I see. Well, we wouldn't want to tear it down then, would we?"

The man leaned down, putting his nose almost against Nik's. "No. We wouldn't." He took the lantern from his friend Andrey and handed it to Nik, along with a sack of food. "There's an old well behind the house with a bucket on the ground. You'll have to reattach it to the rope before dropping it down, else you won't get it back. The well's very deep."

"*Very* deep," Andrey echoed.

"The outhouse is out there as well. Careful of the door. It sticks. You'll find any tool you need in the shed. There's plenty of wood scraps out there for you to plug up the holes and to use as firewood. You might find some birds or other animals nesting in the chimney. Just poke at 'em with a stick, and they'll move along right quick enough."

"Right. Well, thanks, boys. I appreciate you giving me some work and a place to stay. Here's your money." He held out a bag to the ruddy-faced man, but he pushed the bag back toward Nik. "Why don't you hold on to it this week. At the end of the week, assuming everything goes well, you can pay me then. Like I said, if you fix up the place for me a bit, clean up the, er, undesirables." He turned to his friend and laughed hard. When the two of them were finished, he continued, "Then maybe I'll be so impressed with your work I'll be adding to your pot. What do you say?"

He held out his thick hand, and even though Nik knew there was a catch and the two of them weren't telling him everything, he slapped his hand into the bigger man's and shook it heartily, attempting to smile as if he were happy instead of trying to swallow a lump the size of his fearfully beating heart.

Every instinct he had told him something was very wrong as he watched the two men disappear, their little lantern growing smaller and smaller in the darkness until it vanished altogether. The house behind him felt like an evil presence watching him. As he pushed open the door and stepped inside, the wood creaked, groaning as if he were trying to pry open the top of an old coffin to expose the corpse inside.

Cobwebs and rats' nests filled every available corner of the front parlor, and the room was so dim, even with the light of his lantern, that he couldn't even make out what the furniture used to be, let alone if it was even still usable. Wandering through the front room, he entered what he thought might be a kitchen and found a sink and a potbelly stove. The wind whistled through the cracks and holes in the house, rattling the windows, causing the house to moan as if it were in pain.

After examining the other rooms, a small dining room, a library or sitting room, a nursery, and two other bedrooms, Nik decided that the cleanest and warmest of all the rooms was probably the nursery, as it was centrally located in the home. It was also the emptiest. The only pieces of furniture inside were an old rocking chair and what looked like the remains of a bassinet that was so covered in spiderwebs he wouldn't be at all surprised to find a nest of hoary spiders tucked beneath their silken blanket.

Shoving both to a far corner, he used his boot to swipe away the dust as best he could and dragged an old rug across the worn wooden floorboards to use as his mattress. He was so exhausted from his trek through woods and running from monsters that he figured he could probably sleep through pretty much anything. After turning on his side and nestling his head in the crook of his elbow, he closed his eyes and was out before he even remembered to douse the lantern.

It was the hoot of an owl that woke him, or so he thought at first. Nik was so deeply tired that he had no idea where he was at all. The lantern had almost died, and the sight of it helped him remember. He cursed himself for a fool. Nik needed that lantern and the little bit of oil until he could search out some more in the shed.

He was about to let his tired eyes shut once again, when he realized it wasn't an owl that woke him at all but the sound of a baby's cry. He sat up immediately, his eyes searching the pitch-black shadows. The nearby bassinet shifted, creaking—*squeak, squeak*—as it rocked. When it suddenly stopped, so did the baby's cry. Then the rocking chair moved, and he heard the hum of a mother hushing her baby and singing softly.

There was a bang as a door slammed in the other room, and the rocking chair froze in place. Slowly, Nik lifted the lantern and peered at the chair. It was empty. Ice crept through his veins, seizing his movement and making the fine hairs on the back of his neck and his arms stand on end. He heard breathing and footsteps as the floorboards creaked.

Someone, or something, was walking into the room behind him.

CHAPTER 11

All Who Possess a Knife Are Not Cooks

"What—what just happened?" Veru asked as she got to her feet and limped over to the table.

"Told you, didn't I?" the old woman replied. "The house settled when your minds did. It's funny that way. Now, what's wrong with your feet? You didn't say anything about an injury. I won't have you starting off injured. Makes any victory hollow, in my opinion."

"Victory?" Danik asked.

"Never you mind that just now. What you need to do is focus. Don't let that mind of yours wander. You'll get yourself lost if you do. And I won't be having none of that on my conscience. You hear that?" Yuga used a knobby cane to wrench her body up from her chair and hobbled over to her hearth. Then proceeded to knock the stump of her cane against the stone chimney. "If his mind wanders him off track, t'wont be my fault."

Danik frowned. As he wrapped Veru's arm through his, supporting her weight, he tried to see what or who the strange woman was talking to. Perhaps it was another cat or a mouse. For all he knew, it was a dust ball. Whatever it was, it didn't answer back, so she nodded and grunted, then turned her attention to the fire.

First, she poked the embers and added her last log, then picked up a ladle and stirred whatever was boiling in the large cauldron hanging on a hook over the hot coals. Then, when she was satisfied with that, she pulled several items from her shelf, opened various bags and small boxes, sniffing the contents, then discarded some and removed pinches and dashes of others, placing her concoction in a very large stone bowl.

After adding a shiny liquid, she began pounding her ingredients with a large stone club. She was so enthusiastic that it reminded Veru of the way Stacia beat her wooden dummies on the practice field. Veru didn't know if the woman was making medicine, tea, or preparing a sauce to baste the two of them in before roasting their flesh over the now crackling fire that seemed to be growing larger by the minute.

Veru found the knife she'd hidden in a skirt pocket and ran her finger over the catch to release the blade from its sheath. Her eyes roamed the little cottage, searching for other weapons or items she might possibly use as shields. She damned the flimsy material that served as her clothing but was surprised to be thankful for the corset. That at least felt a little like armor, and she knew the pinching metal would give her a bit of protection.

The dress hid her stance, which was nice. She bounced a bit on her toes in the soft shoes, wincing at the pain but biting her lip as she shifted her weight back and forth, back and forth, ready to spring like the cat she had been for the past several months. Meanwhile, Danik, who she'd disengaged her arm from so she'd be better able to defend him in a fight, stood nearby, his eyes transfixed on the process of pounding and mixing that seemed to be endlessly steady.

Suddenly, the banging stopped.

Yuga dipped a finger into her concoction, lifted it to her nose, and sniffed, then darted her tongue to it and grunted. "That should do it," she announced, not glancing in their direction at all.

Veru had managed to get a small end table between herself and the old woman. She figured she could pick it up and use it to trap her against a wall.

"Now, bring your young wife over to my chair, and I'll see to her feet," Yuga said.

"Yes, Babushka," Danik said, automatically reaching for Veru's arm and startling in surprise to find her several feet away from him.

When he stepped over and took hold of her elbow, an irritated Veru wrenched her arm away with a hiss. "I can walk on my own, Danik. Besides, I don't think I trust her. Do *you*?"

Danik looked at her, then at Yuga, who waited with thick eyebrows raised and a gleeful grin of expectancy on her mouth as she "watched" their exchange with her strange, too-seeing eyes. Veru noticed there was a large mole above her lip, with a curly black hair protruding from it. Her own lip quivered. Was she imagining it, or was the hut shrinking? She shouldn't be able to see such details in the dim light of the fire.

Shrugging, Danik replied, "I don't *not* trust her," he said. "She hasn't done anything but help us so far."

"Yeah. That's the thing," Veru replied quietly, though she was certain the old woman's ears were burning, and she could hear everything. "People don't help others out of the kindness of their hearts. There's always a purpose, and it's usually not a good one."

Considering, Danik took a moment, then said, "I think most people try to do the right thing. Even when they do wrong, they usually have a reason behind it if you look hard enough. You're smarter than I am. Look for her reasons."

Veru pursed her lips and finally blew out a breath, feeling herself relax. Danik was giving her permission to trust or not trust, to use her mind to figure things out on her own. Her experience in being dismissed as just a pretty face, while Stacia was hailed as the one with the mental ability to keep up with their father, made her touchy when it came to discussions of strategy. It was nice for a change to have someone else notice her brain, even if his own mental capacity was in question.

After taking a moment to think through her options, Veru clasped Danik's hand, hobbled over to the chair, and sat. "What is it?" she asked, before allowing Yuga to doctor her feet.

"There's nothing magic about it, if that's what's worrying you, dear," Yuga replied.

"You didn't answer the question," Veru stated. "If you want access to my feet, you'll give me a direct answer."

Yuga's eyes narrowed. "Who says I want access to your feet? I was doing you a good turn. It's no skin off my long nose if you're in pain or not. If you don't want the medicine, then don't use it." Yuga turned around on the little stool she'd pulled up in front of the chair and made as if to leave.

"Now, Babushka, she never said," Danik began, holding up his hands.

"Hold on," Veru interrupted, tapping him on the arm. "Babushka," she said, addressing the old woman directly. "Do you promise that this medicine will do me no harm whatsoever? That it will heal my feet, and that you don't mean to do any mischief to my husband or I during our stay?"

Yuga paused and turned back around. Her lips pursed as if she had just sucked on something sour, but there was a gleam in her eye as if she'd met an opponent she was very, very interested in playing a game against.

"I'll tell you what," she said, rubbing her lip and making the little hair that poked out of her mole stand straight up. "The medicine I made is a true medicine indeed. It will heal your feet, for certain. And I guarantee you, on the head of my beloved cat, Maxsim, that I plan absolutely no mischief between any married couple staying under my roof this evening. Will that do, young lady? Will you now let an old woman touch your precious *stupni*?"

Blinking, Veru shook her head, trying to ignore the woman's quivering lip and careful wording. "Da," Veru said with a sigh and a sheepish smile—she was likely reading too much into things. Her feet really did hurt, and they would only stay for a night or two. "And spasibo," she finished.

"Pozhaluysta."

Yuga began smearing the fragrant oil over Veru's blistered feet. It was warm at first, then it turned icy cold and painful. Finally, it soothed the ache and turned warm again. When the woman was done, she wrapped Veru's feet in lengths of cloth and then slipped large, knitted socks over them.

"There. Now leave those on overnight. They should be as good as new by morning."

Veru tried to pick up the stone bowl to sniff the contents herself but found she couldn't lift it. The old woman peered at her and huffed, then used her cane to rise from her stool and lifted the bowl easily, returning it to the wooden table.

"But how?" Veru said, standing quickly, but suddenly she felt lightheaded and sank back down.

"The mortar knows its master," Yuga replied. "Now, boy, the healing will sap her strength. Take the bucket by the door and head out to the well. Fetch us some water. She'll need it. Oh, and bring in more wood for the fire tonight. A blizzard's coming in."

"A blizzard? It seemed temperate to me earlier."

"Trust me. I've a nose for these things."

"Very well." Danik headed to the back door, picked up the bucket, and walked outside, surprised to see a very big change in the evening sky.

"Oh, and, young man," Yuga called after him.

"Yes?" Danik said, turning as he hefted the bucket.

"If the house presents its backside or topside or underside to you instead of a side that opens, you'll have to charm her."

"Uh . . . topside, Yuga? By that do you mean I'll be seeing the roof and chimney?"

The old woman waved a hand. "Yes, yes. Don't get caught up in the minutia. You did say you can sing, didn't you?"

"Yes."

"That'll help you a great deal. She likes music. She hasn't heard a lively tune in quite a long time. It's been ages since a body's danced on these old floorboards."

"Right," Danik said. "Um, who hasn't, Yuga?"

"The house, boy! Pay attention."

Muttering under her breath, Yuga thumped her cane twice against the floor, and Veru was certain one of the cupboards banged two times in response.

"Anyway, as I was saying," the old woman continued. "If the house shows you her backside when you return, charm her with a song. You can sing it any way you like, but make sure you use these exact words. 'Little house, little house, turn your back to the forest, turn your front to me. Little house, little house, lend your ear to my chorus, lend your guest the key.' Have you got it, boy?"

"Yes, I think I can remember that."

"Let's hope for your sake you do. I wouldn't want to be caught outside in a storm such as the one's brewin' right now. Best be on with you, then."

As the door shut behind Danik, Veru couldn't help but panic, wondering if she'd lost him to a magic spell, and if they'd made a terrible mistake. If she'd been physically able, she would have gone with him, but for the life of her, Veru seemed to be unable to lift her limbs. In fact, it took all her strength to remain conscious.

Yuga bundled a thick blanket over Veru and headed back to stir her pot of soup. It smelled delicious, and despite her efforts, Veru's eyes drifted closed. Something heavy dropped in her lap, but she was far too exhausted to move; besides, the something felt right somehow. It curled up in a ball and began to purr.

One hour passed and then another. The fire dwindled, and the little house grew cold. They could hear the wind tearing at the roof outside. Then there was a voice, a song. Through her stupor, Veru could just make out Danik's words. She was deeply relieved to know he was just outside and willed him with all the energy she could muster to return to her. The old woman appeared to echo her thoughts, and Veru's trust in their strange hostess grew a small fraction.

Yuga sat up straight in her chair. "Come on, boy," she mumbled. "Remember: If the house won't accept you, then no matter how strong your back, you're of no use to me."

Finally, the house shuddered and creaked, and the door flew open. Danik entered carrying a huge armful of wood and a bucket of icy water.

The door opened and shut twice, bringing with it the bite of winter air and bits of sleet and ice as he piled in more wood. Veru managed to crack open her eyes. Though his nose and fingers were red, and his clothing was soaked with sleet, his expression wasn't one of fear or concern. He was the same happy hunter she'd come to know, despite the fact he'd been caught outside in the cold for far too long due to his faulty memory. At least they'd all be warm enough, thanks to the wood he'd managed to bring in for the night. Veru closed her eyes and relaxed again, safe in the knowledge that her hunter had returned to her side.

"You were right about the storm," she heard Danik offer. "I'd say we're in for a blizzard all right. It's a good thing the house finally decided to let me in."

"I warned you. She needs a bit of charming."

"You'd think she'd like being warm too," he said as he added logs to the nearly dead fire.

"She doesn't think the way we do."

"Magical cottages wouldn't, I guess. The house kept walking away from me. I didn't see that it had legs before."

Shrugging, Yuga said, "Sometimes it does, and sometimes it doesn't. Depends on her mood."

"It almost seemed like she wanted me to chase her. She'd head off on those strange legs and hide in the forest, but never wandered so far that I couldn't see at least a bit of chimney smoke. Then she'd let me catch up, just in time to dart off again. It was like she was toying with me. After a while, the smoke gave out. Luckily, I'm a good tracker.

"Still, it got hard to see and even harder to carry the water and the wood. At one point, she knocked over my bucket, but then she must have felt sorry for me because she led me to a river. The better part of two days, I chased her. When I was about to give up, she stopped."

Veru shook her head, struggling to rouse herself. Had she heard right? It couldn't be. He'd be gone that long? That meant she'd been sleeping for . . .

"Only two days?" Yuga asked, rubbing her chin. "She must be soft on you. Still, she presented the wrong side, didn't she? Wouldn't make entering easy?"

"Showed me the underneath, I think. I sang the verse the way you said, but she only flipped to a different side. It was still wrong. It took several hours of singing and making up my own verses to finally win her over and get her to show the door."

"Is that right?" Yuga said. "Tell me, what words did you say that finally allowed you entry?"

"Instead of, 'Little house, little house,' I sang, 'Pretty house, pretty house, let me out of the forest, let me warm my bones. Pretty house, pretty house, attend to my calls, and I'll attend to your walls.'"

"Ah, I see. You bribed her. Flattered her."

"I'd say soothed her, more like. I calmed her is all. Much like I would a frightened animal in a trap."

"That's right. Before you slaughter them!"

Veru slit open her eyes again.

Danik blinked, unperturbed by the old woman's outburst. "That much is true," he replied evenly. "Calming them is about all I can do to ease their journey to the hereafter. I wouldn't take a life if I didn't need to though. And I keep my promises. You can rely on that much. I mean to work on the house, just like I said I would."

"I suppose that means you'll need to extend your stay," Yuga said, her filmy eyes aimed in his direction and her face screwed up in a calculating way. Veru wanted to warn him to be careful with his words, but she couldn't even lift a finger, let alone open her mouth.

"I'm afraid we can't pay you," Danik said. "We're poor folk. But we're happy to help you in any way we can."

The old woman clapped him on his arm. "I know you will, son. Don't you worry just now. Take your rest tonight. Soup's hot. I'm certain you're famished. Your girl will be resting tonight. She'll be as ravenous tomorrow as you, but tonight she'll sleep sound. Maxsim will make sure of that."

"Thank you for your kindness."

"I'll accept your thanks or not when you take your leave. Eat now and rest, boy. There's a bowl and spoon on the table."

As Danik began wolfing down his dinner, Veru heard the old woman mumble, "Congratulations on surviving your first challenge, boy. The rest of them won't be so easy."

The rest of them? Veru thought. The cat's purr intensified, and Veru sank into the depths of a sleep so deep she heard nothing else.

When Veru cracked open her eyes, the cottage was dark except for the banked fire. She could hear the shrieking wind whistling through the cracks in the logs, and the rhythmic snoring coming from the blankets on the floor nearby that indicated Danik was soundly asleep. The cat on her lap was still purring, but lighter this time, as if it were in comfortable kitty oblivion. In another chair, across from hers, she could just glimpse the small burning of a pipe and hear the inhalation and exhale of smoke.

"Yuga?" Veru said thickly, from deep within her blankets.

"Do you need something, child?" a disembodied voice replied in the darkness.

"Maybe some water?"

"There's a full cup on the table next to you."

Reaching her hand out from beneath her warm blanket, she gripped the handle of the mug and lifted the rim to her lips. Her hand shook as if the cup was the heaviest of swords. Still, she managed to drain the contents and then slipped her hand beneath her covers again. The air was so very cold that Veru couldn't imagine how it could have become so cold again so quickly.

"Are . . . are you warm enough, Yuga?"

"I'll be fine until the morning," she replied. "Go back to sleep now, young one. You've much to do tomorrow."

"Yes," Veru replied sleepily. "Much to do in the morning."

The old woman nudged Veru awake the next day when dawn lit the small, dirty window. "I've put some soup on the table. It's cold now, but that shouldn't bother you much, I should think."

Yawning, Veru stretched and replied, "No. That's—that's fine. I appreciate your hospitality."

Yuga harrumphed and bustled about the cottage collecting various items and placing them in her large stone bowl.

Sitting up, Veru asked, "Are you going somewhere?"

"Need some supplies. That man of yours is likely to sleep most of today and through the night. How are your feet feeling? Better now?"

Pushing aside the heavy blankets and the heavier cat, Veru stood up, feeling wobbly at first, but then, after taking a few steps and wriggling her toes, she pronounced that her feet felt incredible, better than they'd felt in ages.

"Good," Yuga said with a wide grin. "Good. That'll make your work go much more smoothly."

"My work?" Veru asked. "Of course I'm happy to help. What do you need me to do while you're gone?"

"Oh, not much, dear, not much. I'll just need you to clean the cottage while I'm gone. Wash the pots and pans, scrub the floor, clean the windows, that sort of thing."

Veru took a look around the dark little room and couldn't help but notice how chimney smoke covered most of the walls, and now that daylight had pushed its way into the house, it was quite easy to see the stains and crumbs that littered every surface. Veru guessed the woman's inability to see would make it very difficult to keep things tidy.

"Your man brought a bucket of water in last night, and there's some old lye soap and brushes in the cabinet below the sink by the window. And if you get to it, there's a bag of washing and mending by the door."

Closing her eyes for a moment, Veru steeled herself for the long day of domestic labor that lay ahead of her. It wasn't that she hated work. She'd certainly spent many a long hour training and sweating through tunic after tunic. And their mother was very keen on making sure they showed not only knowledge of but great appreciation for the work done by their servants.

Veru knew the difference between various linens and fabrics, what types of soaps removed stains the best, how to hire the best cooks, what foods should and shouldn't taste like, the proper ways beds should be made up for guests, and much, much more. She'd even personally overseen the staff and training from time to time to make certain she was well-versed in how to run the palace.

But that didn't mean she enjoyed that type of work. Truthfully, if she had to choose, she'd much rather work in the stables or build homes. She wasn't afraid of manual labor, but there was something about the types of work considered traditionally "women's" that made Veru feel very uncomfortable.

Perhaps it had something to do with the way men viewed the maidservants. They were ogled often, and that was even despite their mother's frequent attempts to pass laws protecting them and the changes made to their uniforms. It was as if men just couldn't help themselves. It was often unattached women who worked in those positions, and men somehow saw them as fair game.

Veru always wanted to distance herself as much as possible from such tasks so as not to give men even more opportunities than they already took with her person. Not that many did. They wouldn't dare. But still, she could always feel their eyes on her, and that was almost as bad.

Smiling distractedly, Veru nodded and said, "I'll do my best. Have a nice day."

"Oh, it will be more than a day," the old woman said gleefully. "Which is good for you. You'll need a while to get all I expect of you done."

"All you expect?" Veru frowned.

"That's right. If the house is properly cleaned, I'll bring back a present. It'll be something the two of you could really use. I'll have you know I'm highly picky when it comes to cleaning though. I don't give gifts lightly. You'll have to make it worth my time."

"I see. And if I *don't* meet your expectations?"

The old woman grinned, and it frightened Veru, which wasn't something that happened often.

"Well now, if you don't finish . . . then I suppose you'll owe me something. That sounds fair, doesn't it? I am letting the two of you stay here free, after all."

She began whistling and added a few more items to the pot. When she was done, she opened the door and said, "Oh, and I left a few bones for Maxsim by the fire."

"Bones?"

"That's right. Keeps him hungry for mice. Dos vedanya."

With that, Yuga stepped outside, and the door shut behind her. Veru ran quickly to the door and twisted the knob, but try as she might, she couldn't get it to open. Giving up, she turned around with hands on her hips and stared at Maxsim, who sat on the floor, his tail twitching as he looked at her expectantly.

"Well, Max," she said, picking up the platter of clattering mouse skeletons. "I'm not sure if you're a spy or a friend, but either way, there's no way I'm letting a fellow feline subsist on a pile of mere bones."

CHAPTER 12

A Child with Seven Nannies Has No Guardian

Kneeling and taking the child by the shoulders, Stacia peered into the face of the little snow girl. "Zima," she said, trying to be patient. "Tell me what happened under the bridge after I left."

Her thumb was back in her mouth, and she was soaking wet and cold. In fact, the little girl was so frozen her lips had turned blue, and her breath was turning to fog. Perhaps it was a trick of the light, or a lack of it, but Stacia thought Zima's pretty blond hair was turning white.

"Zakhar?" Stacia said. "Can you start a fire, please? Quickly? She's freezing."

Even Stacia herself could barely suppress a shiver. A brisk wind blew across the river and prickles of sleet came with it, pelting their already wet skin. They'd need to find shelter and fast. Saving Iriko would have to wait. They needed to get the girl warm, then they'd head back to the bridge.

"Wait," she said as Zakhar turned to begin looking for firewood. "Zima? How far is it to your aunties' house from here?"

"Not far. Why?"

"It's getting cold. I'm going to take you home, and then Zakhar and I will head back to save Iriko." To Zakhar, she added, "Maybe in town we can trade something for coin. We'll find out what the vodnik are likely to exchange for one of their victims. We'll have to hurry, though, before they decide to have him for supper."

"Oh, they're not going to eat him. Not yet, at least. I heard them arguing about who was going to get to keep him for a pet."

"My, you have big ears," Stacia said, smiling and standing. "But that's a good thing. Don't you worry a bit about Iriko. He can handle being a pet for a while."

"But they use their pets for fighting," the little girl added.

"What's that?" Zakhar said.

Zima pulled her thumb out of her mouth. "Fighting. They have all sorts of pets. Giant fish with huge teeth. Monsters that live at the bottom of rivers. Huge snakes or swamp creatures. He might have to fight some of them. Then if he dies, they'll probably eat him or feed him to one of their pets. That would be very sad."

Zakhar and Stacia glanced at each other. Grabbing hold of Zima's icy hand, Stacia said, "Yes. It would be very sad. Let's walk a bit faster then, shall we? It's sure getting cold out here."

"I'm not too cold yet," Zima said, "but my aunties get cold, too, sometimes."

"Do they?"

"Oh yes. They complain about it all the time."

They hurried along, listening to Zima tell stories about her aunties and how they only seemed to be happy when it was warm. Then Zima started crying about Iriko, and the sleet fell in thick sheets, soaking their clothing and hair. She kept saying she was sorry as the icy teardrops fell like diamonds from her eyes and pebbled her pinafore, creating two tiny icicles.

It wasn't long before the warm lights of the little town came into sight. The sleet and Zima's tears finally stopped, thanks to Zakhar's tale of tigers pulling sleds, but by the time they reached the outer walls, the wind had grown so fierce their clothes were stiff and crunchy with frost. Zakhar believed the temperature had dropped at least thirty degrees since they'd crossed the bridge. It didn't make sense to them. In fact, it seemed the more emotional the little girl seemed to be, the more frigid the weather. And it appeared that the young lady was indeed very concerned about Stacia's beautiful cat that had been left behind—not that Stacia blamed her; she, too, was worried about Iriko, but first she had to take care of their tearful ward.

Zima's skin had become so pale and cold that Stacia feared for her life, and yet the little girl insisted she was fine. Stacia peered at her tiny hand in the moonlight and noticed her fingernails had become blue in addition to her lips. If she couldn't get her seated by a fire soon, she feared the young thing might lose her fingers and toes. Every so often, Stacia would rub Zima's hands between her own and blow on them to keep them warm.

The gas lamps at the town gate were lit, but there were no guards stationed, so they passed through the entrance easily enough. Most people appeared to be tucked inside their homes, which made sense considering the current weather. They could see little cottages lining the main road, along with some small businesses. All the windows were dark. The homes had puffs of smoke coming from chimneys and flickering candlelight behind their curtains.

Zima's face brightened as she began to recognize the streets of her home. Her pace increased, and she tugged on Stacia's hand, hurrying through the dimly lit streets, ignoring the barking of dogs and the clucking of chickens while ducking between different buildings until she found a path lightly dusted with snow. "That's the way," she said. "I live in a cottage on the edge of the forest on the other side of the town."

She began to skip, and snowflakes fell heavy and thick around them as they walked up the path. The flakes clung to her lashes, skirt, and hair, but she didn't dash them away and still didn't appear to be affected by the cold. Stacia shivered violently and wished for her tiger body. Her fur coat had kept her warm in the deepest of cold weather.

The snow was up to their ankles now. Zakhar slugged along next to her, saying nothing. She hadn't told him how grateful she was that he'd been willing to come on this journey with them. He was a good soul. *Maybe they could use a priest at the palace*, she thought. An adviser such as him would be a welcome addition.

Finally, a house came into view, tucked into a copse of trees, just as Zima had described. It was a large cottage. Definitely big enough to house several adults. What was better, it had two chimneys, and both of them were spewing a good amount of smoke. Stacia didn't think she'd ever seen a more welcome sight. She couldn't wait to warm her hands and backside by a crackling fire and get a dry change of clothing. A hot meal to warm their bellies wouldn't be a bad thing either.

Zima had skipped far ahead of them. They could hear the echoes of her laugh carried on the wind. The dark clouds hung over them, ominous but silent, as if waiting to see what would happen next. It was a reprieve they needed. Stacia and Zakhar were grateful not to have to shield their eyes, even for a little bit, from the snowfall and the sleet.

Before they reached the door, it opened widely, and she could just make out the outlines of several figures. Stacia could tell they were conversing with Zima, who had stopped dead in her tracks just in front of them, but she couldn't make out what they were saying to her until they got closer. When she did, what she heard was shocking.

"Why did you return?" one woman asked.

"Look what you have done, child," the other accused.

"You know it isn't time."

"What will the others say?"

"You know they will blame us."

"They'll say we can't control ourselves."

"How did you get across, anyway?"

"We made a deal."

"They shouldn't have reneged."

"I told you we should have left well enough alone. But you wanted to be a mother."

"You know I wasn't the only one."

"It isn't her fault. Let the girl come in. She's probably hungry."

"They're always hungry. Children eat and poop all the time. That's what they do."

"Stop being so moody. You're getting old."

"We're all old."

"Some of us more than others," a voice said who wasn't standing at the door. "Stop being rude and invite the strangers inside. Can't you see they're cold?"

The three old women, framed in the door, looked up then and noticed Stacia and Zakhar for the first time. "Who are you?" an older lady with gray braids and a moon-shaped face asked.

"Dobry vecher," Zakhar said, bowing stiffly. "I am Zakhar Balakin, a humble traveling priest accompanying my tsarina, Her Royal Highness, the Empress Stacia Stepanov. We discovered this lost malyshka on the other side of the river and took it upon ourselves to escort her home. She told us of seven lovely aunties who care for her. Are you perhaps the ladies she mentioned, or can you point us in the direction of their home so that we might find respite for the poor child?"

Stacia peered at Zakhar with a side-eye, a raised eyebrow, and just the tiniest lift of her lip, showing she was impressed. *Well done, Priest,* she thought. If she didn't know better, she'd think Zakhar went to her father's diplomatic charm school. He was far too good to be a simple priest. He had some *skills.* She'd correct him on the tsarina title later. Technically, neither she nor her sister had accepted the role as of yet. They were still tsarevnas. But she supposed it didn't matter to these women in either case.

She could actually see the bitter melting off the old lady as she batted her nonexistent eyelashes at Zakhar. "Why, yes, we are Zima's aunties. Thank you so much for escorting her home. We are in your debt, good sir. Please," she said, nodding more to him than to Stacia, "won't you two come in and warm yourselves by our fire for a bit before you return to town?"

"What a kind offer," Zakhar replied, smiling warmly at the woman. He then quite obviously blew on his hands and managed to blush, deftly apologizing. "I'd offer my hand as a token and a blessing on your home, good lady, but I'm afraid they're quite cold, and I wouldn't want to offend anyone with skin so delicate."

All three of the women nearly simpered at that one. Stacia could barely contain a giggle. Instead, she disguised it with a delicate cough, a trick her mother had taught her. Instantly, Zakhar turned to her with an expression of concern. "My dear tsarevna, are you becoming ill? What a dolt I am to be escorting you about in weather such as this. Your parents will give me a tongue-lashing, that's for certain."

"Do come in and we'll put both of you by the fire."

"Yes," another auntie said. "Come in. Come in. Zima, take off their boots. We must get those wet stockings off."

"You are too kind, Aunties, truly," Zakhar said. "But I can tend to the tsarina while you must be anxious to care for your niece."

"We won't hear of it. Let us take care of her."

Two more aunties entered the room and tugged Stacia to a corner away from Zakhar. In a matter of moments, her wet things were stripped away behind a changing screen, and she was dressed in a woolen nightdress far too large, with heavy, itchy socks hitched up her feet; then a warm blanket was wrapped around her, and she was tucked into an oversize chair by the fire. Zima was quickly whisked away to bed.

Meanwhile, Zakhar could barely keep their hands away from him. He was able to insist on changing his own clothing, though, and soon disappeared behind the screen alone. Stacia sipped a hot cup of tea and warmed her toes, waiting for his return, along with the seven other women, who stared at the screen with anxious eyes. Stacia smiled, enjoying the sweet brew, content to let Zakhar take the lead on this one.

She'd learned long ago that women, especially older women, tended to respond better to young men. In fact, her parents employed a bevy of attractive diplomats of both sexes of various ages and engaged them as useful tools whenever necessary. Plying state secrets from others using honeyed sweets rather than pointed threats was often far easier. When her parents were younger and single, their looks had been used to charm others, but after they committed to each other, they vowed never to do so again.

But that did not mean using charm was off the table completely. They simply employed beautiful people to do the job for them. And, like it or not, Veru was one of them. Oh, they never made Veru go too far. She simply had to dance, flirt, and make promises she didn't intend to keep. They never wanted Veru to compromise herself in a way that made her feel uncomfortable. They did, however, want her to understand the benefits and hardships that came with beauty.

As for Stacia, she considered herself fortunate she was blessed with something other than traditional beauty. Stacia was statuesque, imposing. Most men weren't nearly as tall as she was, and that made them uncomfortable. Sure, Stacia could hunch to make them feel more manly, but she didn't want to. She liked her height. If they couldn't measure up to her, then too bad for them.

It had been a long time since Stacia had felt attracted to a man, or could even look up to one. Not since her father, anyway. Even when a man did happen to best her in a physical capacity, she often found his mind was pale by comparison. Truth be told, she hadn't found anyone interesting at all, not until a certain surly, bare-chested someone made an appearance and decided to help them. If they couldn't rescue Iriko . . . Stacia didn't like to think about what was going to happen to him if they couldn't. They just needed to . . . that's all.

Her thoughts were interrupted by Zakhar's return. Once he was seated next to her, sipping a hot mug of tea, the sisters brought out a loaf of brown bread, freshly churned goat butter, and lamb stew. Stacia's mouth watered, and she dug into the food immediately, grunting her appreciation, if not voicing it outright, but Zakhar took the time to fawn over every bite. He made appreciative little noises as he ate, praising the cooks and calling the butter "ambrosia made with angels' hands" and the bread "manna." When he got to the stew, he told the aunties they were guaranteed a seat in heaven.

Stacia thought he was laying it on a bit thick, but when she glanced over at her traveling companion, he did seem to be genuinely relishing his meal. One would think the man had never eaten before. He closed his eyes with every bite and chewed slowly. If she didn't know better, she'd say Zakhar was in love. Stacia had only met her mother's father once, but he was a man like that.

Tomas Dalle had no great loves in his life, other than dogs, hunting, and horses. He wasn't overly fond of his granddaughters either. Stacia remembered that too. Her mother had been very vocal about how Veru and Stacia should act around her father. He was a man who believed women were less valuable than men. There were a lot of men like that in the world. But their mother still took care of him and even loved him in her own way. She played a role with her father, one that made him happy, and Mila Dalle didn't seem to feel that it diminished her in any way to do so.

Stacia had watched her mother serve her father food. She'd ladled extra gravy on his beef, just in a certain way, half on and half off his slices, and even cut his meat for him, just the way he liked. He'd pat her on the head and smile at her like she was one of his horses or his dogs, and then turn and talk to his men or some visitor who was much duller than her brilliant mother, while her mother would simply smile and nod and occasionally dab her father's lips with a napkin as he slobbered gravy on his expensive tunic.

"Why do you do it?" Stacia had asked her mother when they'd left. "Why serve the man when he treats you that way?"

"Because he expects it."

"But you are better than that. He keeps you under his boot. You're worth ten times what those men are. You're an empress! What are they? Tiny barons or local law keepers. They're nothing."

"Our title doesn't make us important. Nor does serving others make us unimportant."

"But he listens to them because they are men."

"That's his choice."

"But he ignores you because you're a woman!"

"That's his loss."

"Doesn't it make you mad?"

Mila turned to Stacia and took her chin, holding it gently in her hand. "Listen to me, dear one. You are strong. You always have been. You're much like me. But you are also like your father. You want to mend what's wrong in the world. There are many things you will be able to fix because you have been given the power to do so. But"—her mother smiled—"you will find that you cannot force someone to alter their thinking. All you can do in those cases is to try to show them a better way by example. Anger, my love, never fixes anything."

Weaving her arm through her daughter's, Mila continued, "And here's a bit of advice for you to tuck into your pocket for safekeeping: The way to your grandfather's heart—and to most men's hearts, for that matter—is to add a bit of gravy to his plate."

Stacia smirked. "I'll keep that in mind."

Thinking about that long-ago day with her mother, Stacia watched Zakhar sop up all the gravy from the stew with the remaining piece of brown bread and stuff it into his mouth and thought, *Truer words were never spoken, Mama.*

"More?" one of the aunties asked, taking Zakhar's plate.

He looked as if he was considering saying yes but instead managed to say, "Perhaps later."

The aunties looked disappointed but nodded and removed the plates, then returned to straighten Zakhar's blanket and ask if he needed a refill on his tea. Finally, they asked if their guests would like to stay for the remainder of the evening, and Zakhar found his opening to mention their missing friend.

"There is nothing more we'd like to do than accept your generous offer of hospitality," he said. "Unfortunately, though we managed to escape the trap at the bridge set by the vodnik, we left a friend behind. We must return to save him. Perhaps you know of these creatures and can help us negotiate a trade of some kind? They seem to want coin, but we have none to offer."

At the mention of the vodnik, the aunties tensed and gave each other long, guilty glances. One asked Zakhar, "What, um, did they want from you?"

Stacia answered, "They wanted Zima. We wouldn't give her over. How could we leave a little girl in their clutches? They'd gobble her up for certain."

One auntie said, "Oh, we don't know about 'for certain,' though, do we?"

"It's more likely they'd just keep her for a spell."

"Yes. Probably just to listen to her stories. They do like a good yarn, those vodnik."

"Ladies, I'm afraid I don't understand," Zakhar began.

"I think I do," Stacia said, standing and tossing off her toasty blanket, regretting it immediately. "You left her on the other side of the river on purpose, didn't you?"

"It were only for the summer," one auntie began, crying.

"The townspeople been beggin' us," another chimed.

"What are we to do? She's a powerful child. We've tried to help her control it, but she's too small."

Stacia put her hands on her hips. "Who are you? I think it's time you told us."

"Yes," Zakhar added. "And then you'll help us rescue Iriko."

One of the aunties rubbed her hands. "If we agree to help you with your friend, then we'll need a favor in return."

"What favor?" Stacia asked, her eyes narrowed in suspicion.

The auntie with gray braids held up her hands. "We'll help you. Give you things to aid your journey."

"Yes. We just need you to take Zima with you. Only for a bit."

"Long enough so the townspeople have a summer."

"What has Zima got to do with summer?" Stacia asked.

The aunties all blinked and looked at each other, then back at Stacia and Zakhar. "She's the snow child," they said as one.

When they stared at the aunties blankly, one of the younger aunties looked at the eldest and said, "You'd better explain who we are."

The eldest sighed and said, "Very well. Please," she added, holding up a hand. "Sit down, and I will tell you how we made Zima."

Once they were seated, she said, "My name is Daz. My magic is in gift-giving, motherhood, sunshine, the renewal of life, and weddings. These are my sisters. Stribog—her gifts include manipulation of the wind, the ability to travel on lightning, and the ability to jump high and far. Moksha has power over death, fertility, fields, and herds. Veles can manipulate the waters and the earth. Sima controls all things in the sky, including birds and storms, while her identical twin, Yaryl, manages all the living things on and beneath the earth, including plants and animals. Last is Peruna, who controls fire and weapons."

Both Stacia and Zakhar had heard these names before. They were the names of old gods and goddesses their ancestors had worshipped for millennia. Neither of them knew what to say. Never had they expected to meet these . . . goddesses and see them act like real people. People who served them lamb stew. What was this place?

Zakhar, in particular, didn't know what to say. He didn't believe in the old stories. They weren't real. Were they? Then again, he didn't used to believe in magic either. He cleared his throat. "Perhaps you'd better tell us how you created Zima and why you want us to take her."

The aunties looked at each other. Daz continued speaking. "We were traveling when we first came upon Zima's lost soul. She didn't know who she was then, or how she'd become lost."

"She no longer possessed a body," Moksha explained.

"So we made a new one for her," Yaryl added.

Peruna added, "All of us helped. Each of us added a bit."

"For the magic to work, we had to search the world until we found her original body. It had been lost in the ice," said Stribog.

Veles explained, "We took a bit of hair, then fashioned her new form. We didn't expect the ice to stay with it."

"We just wanted to know what it felt like to be mothers ourselves," Sima said softly. "We help so many mortals but never get to experience it."

"She's our little snow child, you see?" finished Daz. "But the snow stays when she does."

"Yes. The townspeople want summer. They need summer for their crops," said Moksha.

"So we made a deal with the vodnik and warned her about crossing the bridge."

"They weren't going to hurt her," one auntie added.

"No. Only keep her for five or six months if she tried to cross."

"Just to make the townspeople happy."

"But . . . could you not relocate your home, at least in the summers? Perhaps to a snow-topped mountain or some such?"

Sima replied, "We are bound to this home so long as we reside in mortal form."

"And we must remain in mortal form so long as the child lives," Velas added. "At least until the price has been paid and she is freed."

"Freed?" asked Stacia, but her query was ignored.

"But we also have a responsibility to the people. They need to eat," Daz said.

"And Zima needs friends," Sima finished.

Zakhar thought but didn't say that friends wouldn't have agreed to cast a poor child out into the woods for several months alone.

"I see," Stacia said, managing to hold back her personal opinions on their mothering abilities. "But whatever the case, now the vodnik have Iriko."

"They'll trade. We have things they want," promised Daz. "If you take Zima with you, we'll give you plenty of things you can offer in exchange. Is it a bargain?"

Zakhar held up a hand. "We only need to keep her for the next five or six months? Then you'll want her back?"

"Oh yes," Moksha said. "We love her. We will take her back in the winter months."

"But it will hail, sleet, and snow when we're with her?" Stacia asked.

"Yes, unfortunately. But we can give you warm clothing and gifts, like we said. We have many things to help you," Sima said.

"And are the vodnik likely to kill Iriko before morning?"

The aunties looked at one another and conversed quietly, then shook their heads. "No. We don't believe they will. At least not until we speak with them. They will wait to find out if we are angry at them for letting Zima go free."

Stacia gave them a long look, then nodded and yawned. "Very well. You have a deal. Give us a few hours to sleep, and then you can give us what we'll need to make the trade."

The relief on their faces was palpable.

"Wonderful! Zima will be thrilled," Yaryl said.

"Yes. It's great. Looking forward to eternal winter myself," Stacia said. "Now, spokoynoy nochi, ladies. See you in a few hours."

The aunties nodded and, one by one, left the room.

"What do you think they meant by Zima needing to be free?" Zakhar asked.

"I don't know," Stacia answered. "But I have a feeling she'll be better off with us."

"Agreed." He shuffled around and flung out his quilt. "I hope we made the right decision," Zakhar said before leaning back in the chair and shutting his eyes.

"So do I, Zakhar," Stacia said, doing the same. "So do I."

CHAPTER 13

Don't Go Praising the Chimney When the House Is Cold

Nik's heart nearly burst out of his chest. He'd faced some terrifying creatures, but for some reason the idea of a ghost frightened him more than monsters. Demons and monsters, he could kill, but a ghost? Being haunted by a specter, either visible or unseen, chilled his blood until his limbs turned to water.

Hand trembling, he lifted the lantern and turned it toward the shadowy hallway beyond the door. "Who's there?" he asked, ashamed when his voice sounded as weak and frail as a young boy's. He could hear breathing and the slight squeak of the floorboards, indicating someone stood just in the doorframe, unseen.

Then there was a voice. It was dark and deep. It said, "Come away now, Katya."

The rocking chair began moving again. "Not just yet, Yuri. The kroshka needs me."

"She's fine. Put her down and obey me now."

"But she just started to nurse."

"Do I need to tell you again?"

"No, Yuri. It's just that—"

Heavy steps hit the floor right next to the spot where Nik was lying. His entire frame vibrated with each stride. He winced hearing the strike and knew it was a backhand to the cheek and that it had also disrupted the baby's feeding. The newborn began screaming plaintively, and if there were more children in the home, they'd be cowering in corners or beneath their beds.

Though the entire scene was played out by invisible apparitions, Nik could almost see it clearly in his mind's eye—that was how familiar he was with the characters. The mother immediately began shushing the babe, comforting her as best she could, and rose instantly, tucking her newborn in the bassinet before following her stomping husband out of the room. Nik could barely detect her footfalls on the floor.

He lay there listening to the pitiful cries of the ghostly babe as it soothed itself and eventually fell asleep. Then the entire house went silent. Nik, too, though terrified by what he'd heard, was also somehow soothed, just as the baby had been, by the mother's obedience and the calm that came upon the home afterward, and he fell into a fitful sort of sleep.

Never in the many years since he'd lived on his own had he ever sank into the blissful, dream-filled sleep of the innocent. It wasn't just that he knew he deserved the nightmare-plagued torpor he called slumber that filled his evening hours. It was that he'd long since trained his body to doze in small bursts, with eyes slit just a little open, like a cat. That way he could always remain alert, always be wary of predators. Though fatigue was a demon that constantly chased him, he'd rather be chased by exhaustion than some of his other monsters, and the habit had saved his life on more than one occasion. It was a problem both he and his tsarevna shared, and he relished the long talks they'd had when neither of them could find respite on the trail.

It did mean, however, that he took rest when he could. It wasn't quite dawn when he was startled awake again by a scream, but this voice was different, younger. This time it came from outside. Nik heard the stomping of many feet headed down the hall, small as well as large. There was the telltale sound of a bed creaking in the far room and boots sliding onto stockinged feet.

"What's going on out there?" the man he'd come to know as Yuri shouted as he stomped out the hall and toward the front door.

Nik peeked out into the front parlor. There was just enough morning light to see no one was in the room, but the front door of the home creaked open and remained that way as if waiting for Nik to come and see what had transpired.

Though he knew better, he was pulled toward the yawning opening. His stockinged feet left prints on the dusty floorboards. The early-morning air was frigid. He could see his own rapid breaths coming fast as he approached the door. Quickly, he scanned the courtyard, looking for anyone trying to play a trick, but his stomach and nerves told him this was no trick.

The fine hairs on his arms stood on end, and he felt a surge pass through him. It made him want to throw up. That's when he saw the unmistakable imprint of boots appear on the dew-covered steps. The prints were large. Even larger than his father's had been.

Swallowing, trying to muster his courage, Nik followed the invisible specter's boot prints outside. In the predawn light, he spotted many other footprints, some made with shoes, some with bare feet. Most of them were obviously young children. They stopped at the trunk of a large tree, gathering in a cluster. He heard a soft sound that grew in volume and realized it was the keening of crying children.

A little voice said, "Why, Papa? Why did Mama do it?"

"Because she's a coward. That's why," the ghost named Yuri answered brusquely.

He began mumbling to himself, and Nik saw the boot prints move as the ghost paced by the tree. Suddenly, they stopped. "We'll burn her," the man said. "Say she was sick, and we didn't want to risk it spreading. Then we'll bury her ashes in the church cemetery. The townsfolk'll accept it. I'll get a nursemaid up here to help for a while. Have to find another wife real quick. Give it a few months for mourning. That should do the trick."

The boots stomped over to the group. "Not a word of her slit wrists to anyone. You older boys understand me? If I hear even a whisper about it, mark my words, ther'll be hell ta pay."

"Yes, Papa."

Nik heard the cowed acceptance from at least a half dozen children, one of them holding a crying baby, perhaps the same one who'd cried itself to sleep the night before. The ghost father, Yuri, stomped toward him, and Nik froze, unable to move. He could almost feel the malice and hatred emanating from the specter. It passed through Nik again and disappeared into the house. The door slammed shut, and the little footprints by the tree, along with the children's sobs, disappeared just as the sun broke through the forest.

This time Nik couldn't stop it. His stomach heaved. Bending over, Nik vomited all over the steps and then began to cry.

Collapsing onto the steps next to his sticky puddle of rvoty, ribbons of phlegm streaming from the bottom of his lip and his nose, and tears raining down his cheeks, he felt and smelled like a wet bag of puke. He couldn't even look at the tree, fearing he might see the mother there, her wrists red with her blood, the knife still in her hands, with her children looking on. He thought at least he'd spared his siblings the sight of their mother and the bloody knife that killed her.

He was sick with the thought that it could have been him standing there, holding the newborn babe, looking at his mother, knowing she was released from the grip of their father, but his life would go on, the terror would continue, and he would now bear the brunt of it alone. Yet was what he had done any better? He'd always told himself it was. That he'd released all of them. Only he was alive to suffer. To remember.

When his face was dry, with no more tears to shed, he pushed himself up and went behind the house, searching for the well. He found the old bucket easily enough, but the rope had long since rotted away. Picking up a rock, he tossed it into the well, and true to their word, it took a long time until Nik heard the plink of the stone into water.

Dropping the bucket, he went in search of the shed and had another ghostly encounter with the father who was punishing several children in a brutal manner. It was nothing Nik hadn't experienced himself. This time he chose to ignore the ghosts, closing his ears to the screams of the children and the lash of the belt or horsewhip.

Finding a long cord and knowing it was probably used to tie up more than livestock, Nik headed back to the bucket and attached it to the handle, then dropped it in, hoping the cord was long enough to reach the water. It wasn't. He had to go back to the shed three times to find more lengths of rope or cord to finally reach the bottom.

When he drew up the first bucket, the water was clean, which he supposed was good news. Nik couldn't say the same thing about the bucket. It took three bucketfuls of water to clean both himself and the bucket before he was willing to drink from it. Finding a yoke in the shed as well as another bucket and a scrub brush, he went to work on the nursery first, cleaning the windows and floors until they sparkled.

Taking the rug out, he beat it for more than an hour until he couldn't see any dust at all. He was surprised to see it wasn't gray at all but a beautiful soft blue with small pink flowers. There were some small sections he had to spot clean and one corner that had been nibbled on by rodents, but there was nothing he could do about that.

The rocking chair and bassinet he took outside. After several buckets of water, he uncovered two hand-carved pieces that must have been loved at one time. The quilt inside the bassinet had to be thrown out, and he had to do some repair work on the chair so it rocked without tilting, but he felt rather proud of his work when he was finished. As he had no paint, and the wallpaper would have to be stripped, he ignored the walls and repaired any holes he could find leading to the outside.

Thirsty, he headed back to the well and found a small pile of just-ripening gooseberries on top of the stone. Nik looked around and called out, "Hello?" But there was no answer. He tasted a berry and found it delicious. After he ate his snack and drank his fill, he went back to work, starting in the kitchen. He'd barely began cleaning when the sun sank again. Out loud, he said, "I'll need to hunt tomorrow or head into town for supplies, I suppose. If I can get this kitchen tidied up, I can cook a meal in here tomorrow."

He was more than happy to bed down in a clean room that night and was doubly thrilled to have found enough oil to fill his lantern for many more evenings. Laying down on the newly cleaned rug, he made himself comfortable, and just as he started to close his eyes, he heard the soft creaking of the bassinet and the movement of the rocking chair.

This time, the mother's hum seemed content, sleepy even. She spoke to her little baby, telling her, "Aren't you the prettiest little thing? You know your mama loves you, don't you, little one?" Then she sang a lullaby, one Nik remembered his own mother singing to him when he was young, and it was like the ghost mother was speaking directly to him as she sang.

> Sleep, my beautiful good baby,
> Bayushki bayu.
> Quietly the moon is looking
> into your cradle.
> I will tell you fairy tales
> and sing you little songs,
> but you must slumber, with your little eyes closed,
> Bayushki bayu.

She skipped the verses he knew well and went ahead to the last verse, changing the words slightly.

> On the morrow, I'll give you
> a cherished family tin,
> and with the help of God, you'll
> place it right in front of you,
> while playing the most dangerous game.
> Please remember your mother.
> Sleep, good boy, my beautiful,
> Bayushki bayu.

Nik's heart beat wildly in his chest, and he sat up abruptly. "Mama?" he cried in the darkness, but the rocking chair had gone still, as had the bassinet. Though the ghostly voice had sounded like the woman from the night before, her voice had changed with the second verse. Perhaps it was a trick, but Nik was certain that voice sounded like his own mama.

As he lay back down and attempted to still his racing pulse, he tried to remember the words. There was something about a dangerous game and a cherished family tin. His mother had little treasure boxes passed down to her by her parents. They were all locked with tiny keys. He hadn't thought to take any with him when he left. All of them were long gone by now. Nik thought of the music box she'd shown him. He'd loved it at one time. He'd always known it was meant to be his someday. Now someday would never come.

Maybe the ghost meant he was to find something similar. Something she'd left behind. But why would he need to place it in front of him during a dangerous game? It didn't make sense. He fell asleep thinking about it.

The cruel specter named Yuri didn't appear that evening, and Nik slept soundly until sunlight touched his eyelids through the newly cleaned nursery window. Stretching, he headed to the kitchen and was surprised to find freshly baked apple cakes left for him on a little plate. They were covered with a clean towel and still warm.

Lifting one to his nose, he inhaled and took a bite, then lifted the cake to the empty house. "Thank you," he mumbled, tucking a few moist crumbs back into his mouth. Not questioning the magic of the house, Nik finished his repast, drank deeply from the cold well water, and began working on the kitchen. He wore out several brushes on the floor but uncovered the loveliest purple tiles and spent time polishing each one and cleaning the grout until the gray grime filling the space between the tiles turned a creamy white.

Though the cabinets were empty, he wiped them down and found wood rubbing oil. Once he began oiling the surfaces, he noticed the kitchen woodwork was extremely intricate and detailed. In fact, the more he worked, the lovelier it became. Tiny carved details appeared richer and more striking every time he turned to dip his cloth.

Shelving that had once seemed cracked, split, or gauged appeared to heal upon a swipe of his cloth. Boards with insect damage or sun rot looked brand new after Nik spent a few minutes working on them. When he went outside to refill his bucket of water and returned a short time later, gold filigree had surfaced along all the cabinet edges in complex swirls and patterns underlaid with fine purple lines that matched the floor tiles.

Nik wondered if the water was magic or if it was the house itself. He also considered it might be the kindly mother ghost helping him restore the home. Whatever the case, Nik was grateful for it. At the end of the workday, when the sun sank, Nik found a hot tub of water in the nursery along with a bowl of stew, a freshly made loaf of bread, and a heavy bar of sweet-smelling soap.

The chair in the corner moved, creaking softly. Nik began unbuttoning his shirt, happy to be able to sink into his bath, but then went into the next room and took the old dressing screen and dragged it into the nursery, placing it between the tub and chair.

"Spasibo, Mama," he said, taking a big bite of the black bread before sinking into the hot tub.

He heard a soft humming and the suckling of a baby as a reply and alternated between scrubbing himself clean and shoveling spoonfuls of the delicious solyanka into his mouth, sopping up the last of it with the remaining bread. When he was done with his meal and his bath, he lay back with his eyes closed and relaxed until the water cooled, surprised that he'd fallen asleep for just a few minutes.

Jerking awake, he looked around, and the stew bowl on the little table near the tub was gone. Instead, he saw a fresh towel and his clothing, which had not only been washed but also dried and neatly folded. Nik toweled himself off and picked up his shirt, finding beneath it a small box.

"What's this, Mama?" he asked. "Did you leave me a present?"

Not hearing a reply, he set it down and finished dressing. By the time he'd put back the dressing screen, the tub had disappeared. He sat down on the blue carpet with the pink flowers, trimmed his lamp for the evening, and examined the little box. It did indeed open with a key, but as far as he could tell, there was no key to be found.

"Maybe you'll help me find the key tomorrow, Mama?" Nik suggested. "In the meantime, if there's a certain room you'd like me to work on, let me know, will you?"

The next morning, Nik found a book next to his lamp.

"Ah, the library. Very well. I'll start on that room next."

Just like the kitchen, the library practically cleaned itself. As Nik dusted each book, cleaned the floor, and polished the furniture and shelves, the room came to life, restoring itself to pristine condition. Even the fireplace began crackling all on its own accord. Once again, a nice breakfast and luncheon were provided for him on the beautiful old mahogany table. He tried searching the desk drawers for a key but found none.

As he'd finished the library before dusk, he returned to the nursery and wiped down the walls. He watched in awe as lovely pink- and blue-flowered wallpaper, which had been ripped and yellowing, was suddenly stripped of dust, dirt, and insect debris. Pieces that had been torn and sagging reattached themselves once Nik gently pressed them into place. Faded colors brightened and seams tightened until they could no longer be seen.

When he began working on the floor, he uncovered beautiful, nearly white oak floorboards. Nik realized then that the rocking chair and the bassinet were made of the same base materials along with a softer-woven wood in between, perhaps made with rattan. Now that he looked closer at the rocking chair and bassinet, he could see that they had changed just like the cabinets in the kitchen. Along the outside, Nik noticed ornamental fretwork carvings, and the same pattern was echoed on the back of the rocking chair. He traced a fingertip over it.

"Beautiful," he said. "I wonder who made this. I doubt it was Yuri. Maybe it was passed down in your family, Mama?" Nik mused. Standing up, he lifted his arms, stretching them over his head, and cracked his neck. "Well, spokoynoy nochi, Mama," Nik said. "I'm worn out.

See you in the morning." He lay down on his familiar rug and trimmed his lamp. "Or I guess I won't see you. Sleep well."

After two more days of cleaning rooms, Nik headed out the front door one morning with his cleaning bucket, thinking he'd tackle the windows and clean up the walkway. Setting down his supplies at the bottom of the steps, he turned around to count windows and see if he was going to need a ladder or if he should scare up some clippers to tackle the hedge first.

To his shock, he discovered that the dilapidated old cottage that he'd wanted to burn down when he'd first seen it had transformed into a glittering mansion complete with curved balconies, arched stained-glass windows, and bright-colored tiles adorning the roof and lintels. There was even a mosaic trim around the door and windows depicting flowers, birds, and, upon closer inspection, wolves and other fairy-tale monsters.

He got to work trimming bushes and trees and sweeping the stairs, and almost instantly, the landscape around him began to shift and take shape. Though it was winter, and the air was cold and crisp, flowers erupted from the ground. Ivy, once dead, came to life and wound around forms that straightened of their own accord.

As he clipped hedges at the side of the house, he uncovered a hidden door. Tugging on the handle, he discovered a secret passageway that led beneath the house. Deciding to explore that area last, he continued his work, pressing on until the house was completed and there wasn't a room left that he hadn't scrubbed and renovated with the special magic. He wondered what the owners would think when they saw what he had done. Would they be grateful and let him keep all the money he'd won?

As he sat in the hot bath that night, he frowned. *If there is one thing I know about people, it's that, more often than not, their mistrust of magic runs deep. It's most likely they'll string me up from the nearest tree, take all the money and the house, and forget I ever existed. Maybe that's how all the ghosts wound up here in the first place.*

After he finished his pelmeni and drank the rest of the delicious broth directly from the bowl, Nik spoke to his quiet specter. "Mama?

I still haven't found the key. Aren't you going to tell me what you want me to do with your little box before I leave?"

He heard the sound of doors slamming in various places around the house and the rocking of the chair accelerated.

"Now, now. I know you're lonely. You miss your family. But now that the house is fixed up, maybe a family will move back in, and you won't be so lonely anymore."

The rocking ceased.

Nik sighed. "You can be upset if you wish, but the men are returning tomorrow. I don't really have a choice. There's only one more thing I have to do before I leave, and then, if all goes well, you'll get a new start. Spokoynoy nochi, Mama."

When Nik drifted off that night, he could have sworn he heard a woman weeping.

The next morning, he decided to try his luck with his boots, just in case something went wrong and he needed a fast exit. Lacing them up, he stretched, bouncing up and down, and then launched into a quick jog, but only made it down the lane to the gate at a normal speed. The little gate wouldn't even open, so he hopped over it and ran down the road, then turned and ran back. It seemed Pasha was right. The boots were still recharging. At least his tunic should work if he needed such a thing.

Turning back to the house, he politely thanked the invisible helper that now willingly opened the gate to admit him, walked back to the front door with a whistle, and took up his cleaning supplies and lamp once more, this time heading to the side of the house to see if there was anything he needed to do with the newly discovered underground passage. When he tugged on the handle of the door, it wouldn't budge. He braced his feet against the frame and pulled with all his might. It jiggled a bit, and he got the sense that he was being prevented from opening it.

"Now, House, or, Mama, or whoever is trying to stop me. I aim to finish what I start. This isn't going to keep me from leaving, so you might as well let me complete the job." When he said that, the door sprung open, almost by itself.

Lifting his lamp, he picked up his basket of supplies, stepped inside, and began descending the stairs into the blackness. He'd only just cleared the doorframe when the heavy wooden doors lifted on their own accord and slammed shut over his head. Nik heard the snick of a key in a lock and a familiar voice say, "What have you done?" before he was struck on the back of the head and collapsed down the dark stairs into an even darker hole. Thankfully, he was unconscious before he landed.

CHAPTER 14

Cast No Dirt into the Well That Provides You Water

In answer to Veru's question, Maxsim the cat meowed plaintively, obviously wanting breakfast. This was followed by a rather nasal snore from Danik, who slept on the floor next to her chair and under a pile of dusty blankets, one of them stuffed beneath his head. Shivering, Veru headed over to the fireplace and noticed most of the wood Danik had brought in hadn't been used. She stirred the coals to life and placed two more logs on the fire, then sat on the hearth with her cold bowl of soup.

She'd only eaten two bites when Max began rubbing his large body back and forth against her leg.

"Here you go," she said, placing his small dish of discarded bones on the floor.

The cat batted at them a bit, kicking a few out of the bowl and then made another plaintive mewling sound and began kneading her stockinged foot with his paws.

"I know. It's not much for a cat's belly, I'll grant you. But who knows when your master will return? I may end up needing to roast *you* over the fire, you know."

The cat hissed in response.

"Believe me—it wouldn't be my first choice either."

Veru took another bite, and another.

The gray cat sat and stared at her with his big green eyes, and Veru decided she wasn't as hungry as she thought. "Fine, you greedy beggar," she said. "You're lucky I have a very soft spot when it comes to felines."

Placing her bowl on the floor, she removed the spoon and headed over to what served as a kitchen sink in the little cottage. After finding an old scrub brush, a bucket, and a cake of soap, she ladled enough water for herself and Danik to drink into the stoppered bottles provided by Kadam, and then poured the rest into the large cauldron hanging on a hook and swung it over the fire to warm.

She knew the meager amount of water left in the cauldron would only be enough to clean the kitchen, and they'd run out of drinking water if the woman was gone for more than a day, but Veru figured they'd worry about that later. It took her three bucketfuls of water and the entire contents of the cauldron, just as she'd suspected, to clean the sink, the inside of the little window, and the table and counter.

She wrung out the small cloth she'd found in the filthy water and wiped her brow on her sleeve. The cottage was warm. A bit too warm now for her. Even Danik had thrown off his blankets in his sleep. Fortunately, the little sink had a pipe that led outside, so at least she'd been able to discard the dirty water. She only wished she had reserved some water to wash her face and hands.

Heading back to the cabin door, she twisted and turned with all her might, but it still wouldn't budge. She even tried quietly singing to the house like Danik had said he'd done. Veru's voice wasn't as beautiful as her mother's had been, but it wasn't bad. Still, the "pretty house" didn't seem to like what it heard. Sinking into her chair, she wondered what she'd give Danik to eat when he woke. She wanted to put her head into her hands but wouldn't, knowing how filthy they were.

As she shook out the blanket she'd used and saw the dust and crumbs of meals gone by rain down to the dirty floor, she imagined all kinds of vermin and bugs crawling across her body while she'd slept the night before. Though she'd lived outdoors as a tiger for many months and had even *eaten* vermin, there was something about being back in her human skin that made her feel vulnerable.

As a tiger, there was nothing she could do about insects other than jumping into a body of water, but a tiger's coat was built to slough off most irritants. Human skin wasn't. Her whole body itched, and she wanted nothing more than to sink into a hot tub like she had when she'd once lived at the palace.

Maxsim hopped up onto the table and nudged the bowl she'd cleaned with his paw. He meowed hopefully.

"You can't be hungry again already," Veru said. "You ate my entire breakfast. I'm afraid both of us are going to starve now, unless you want to scare up some mice I can roast over the fire."

Meow? the cat replied, sitting beside the bowl and cleaning his paw. Veru frowned and thought her eyes must be playing tricks. Steam rose from the cauldron, which shouldn't be possible. It was empty. She'd even pulled it away from the fire so it wouldn't scald. If she wasn't mistaken, she smelled something too . . . something good. She rose and looked inside.

The cauldron was filled to the brim with thick solyanka. Closing her eyes, she inhaled the delicious scents of garlic and dill, sour cream and tomato. Her mouth watered. Picking up a ladle, she stirred the stew and saw it was filled with thick chunks of potato, carrot, mushroom, beef, sausage, and even bacon.

"It looks like both of us are eating a hearty lunch today, kotenok."

The ladle froze. "Kotenok?" Veru whispered. "Why did you call me that?"

"What?" Danik asked. "I didn't." He rubbed his chest, and his shirt moved, revealing a very strong, muscled abdomen. "At least I don't think I did."

Veru quickly looked away, trying to hide the flush that crept up from her neck and colored her cheeks and shoulders.

He dipped a finger in the stew, brushing his lanky form against her body, and she dropped the ladle and moved away. *What was wrong with her?*

"I was talking to the cat," he said, sticking his finger into his mouth and sucking off the juice from the stew.

Veru couldn't help it. She watched his mouth and tongue enjoying the taste of the meal, and something nearly feral came over her. It was almost like her tiger had returned. The overwhelming impulse to attack or leap filled her frame. It was all she could do to suppress the desire. It wasn't appropriate. Especially for a tsarevna. Instead, she said something banal, like, "That's as I thought." She flicked her hand as if dismissing him.

Danik just gave her a confused look, then shrugged and filled a dish of stew for himself.

Picking up the dish with the bones, she tossed them in her refuse pile and selected the nice meaty bits a cat would appreciate for Max, then blew on it to cool it off before setting his plate down. Maxsim slunk over to the dish and licked delicately at the glistening bits of beef before devouring whole chunks like the small, ferocious feline he was. Veru watched him for a moment with a wistful half smile, then waited while Danik ate two helpings and was contemplating a third when he asked, "Don't you want any?"

"Of course," Veru replied. "Unfortunately, there's only one bowl and spoon and no clean water to wash them with."

"Ah," he said. "If you don't mind sharing, then?"

She swallowed and held out her hands for the offered bowl, but he shook his head and rose, bidding her to sit. "Allow me."

He filled the bowl to the brim and cleaned the spoon as best he could on one of his own shirts that he pulled from his hunting bag, then passed both to her the with a tiny bow and a flourish.

"Priyatnogo appetita, my lady," Danik added with a grin that widened in appreciation when she offered a smile in return.

"Spasibo"

"Pozhaluysta." He turned away to stir the stew and picked out a large piece of meat, placed it in his mouth, closed his eyes, and chewed with a sigh. "I had no idea you possessed such talents."

"I don't," Veru replied, sitting back in her chair, shoving spoonfuls into her mouth. "I think the cat made it."

Raising his eyebrow, Danik mumbled, "The kotenok? How?"

"Dunno. Maybe he's made of magic, like his mistress."

"I suppose it's possible. If the house is magic, why not those who live inside it too?"

"Why not?" Veru twirled her finger over the knob on the chair. "Danik?"

"Hmm?" he murmured while going through his bag.

"The lady of the house left for a bit and asked me to clean up and do laundry. The thing is . . . I'm out of water. Do you think you might be able to sing the door open and get more? I can't seem to turn the knob."

"I see," he said, setting down his bag. "Thing is . . . even if we did manage it, the well's afar off. Don't think we'd be able to find it at this point. I suspect Yuga wanted me to lose my way back. The only reason I didn't was because the house didn't want me to go."

"The house?"

"Yes. In fact, I wonder if the reason the door is locked now is the house is trying to keep you, or perhaps us, in on purpose."

"Do you think?"

"She likes me. Or both of us, maybe."

Veru thought about it and considered if maybe Danik was right. "The stew did appear out of nowhere. Well, someone likes us. I wouldn't count on it being the old woman. That leaves Max or the house. Either way, it couldn't hurt to ask for help, I suppose."

Danik tilted his face up and said to the dark ceiling, "Well, pretty house, I promised I'd fix you up today, didn't I? It might be very hard to do such a thing if we can't get you clean first, so I can see what needs to be done, wouldn't you agree? We'll be needing more water, soap, brushes, and cleaning cloths. Also, a bit more light might be nice."

At that, they heard the creak of hinges, and a hidden closet popped open. Inside, they found buckets, shelves full of fresh cleaning cloths, a mop, cleaning brushes, a broom, and several lanterns with oil and wicks. There was also a key hanging on a hook. Danik took the key and found it opened not the locked door to the outside but a hidden door inside the closet.

When Danik glanced at Veru with eyebrows raised, she shrugged, indicating his guess was as good as hers. Twisting the key in the secret door, he turned the knob, and it opened easily. They were greeted with a warm breeze and sunshine streaming into the little closet. Marveling, they peeked outside at the new landscape. Max darted out first, and the two young people followed, stepping onto a wide porch overlooking a lush wheat farm ripe with grain ready to harvest—a stark contrast to the wintry blizzard outside the kitchen window.

Danik noted a heavy-duty water pump attached to the porch and began filling bucket after bucket with sweet, fresh water. He drank his fill while enjoying the fragrant summer air and then headed back into the small closet and stepped into the dark little cottage, carrying the first of many water buckets.

As much as they preferred the summer breeze and pleasant day, they knew they owed the little house a debt, so Veru and Danik worked together scrubbing and cleaning the cottage well into the evening, and by the time they decided to stop, they had cleaned and polished all the furniture in the front room, and Veru had washed and hung out to dry the first batch of blankets and sheets. They flapped on a line Danik had strung on the summer porch.

Maxsim, having found his way to the warm floorboards of the magic porch, sunned himself there all afternoon long, lazily flicking his tail back and forth, back and forth as he dozed. As Veru worked, she would often glance at him, feeling slightly jealous, remembering the time when she, too, would take long catnaps in such a way.

In the evening, the cat reluctantly returned with them into the house and hopped up onto the table expectantly. Veru was happy to fill his bowl with another helping of the cooling stew, and she and Danik took turns finishing off heaping bowlfuls, as they were famished with the amount of work they had done. They only left a little in the bottom of the cauldron for their breakfast in the morning and fell into a deep sleep as only those who are hardworking are able.

The next morning was crisp and frigidly cold once more despite the fact that they'd thrown half of their remaining logs on the fire, and they rose with muscles aching in places they weren't accustomed to having hurt. Veru groaned, unused to sleeping in a chair and unwilling to sleep on the old woman's rickety bed. She pulled a thin sheet over her head and shivered, hoping the blankets outside were dry.

A furry paw sneaked its way beneath the sheet and batted her nose, willing her to get up and fix a meal. "I know, I know, you're hungry again, aren't you?" she said as she pulled herself out of the chair. "Let's see if there are any good bits left for you."

Heading to the dark fireplace, she picked up the poker to stir the ashes when her arm brushed against the cauldron. It was hot! This time the lid was in place. Grabbing a towel, she carefully lifted the lid and peeked inside.

"I don't know if this was you, Maxsim, or your house, but thank you! Danik? Wake up. It's kasha!"

Picking up the bowl, she spooned a generous portion of buckwheat porridge, caramelized onion, crispy bacon, forest mushrooms, and soft-boiled eggs, their yellow yolks oozing and mixing into the fresh cream and dill dolloped on top, then handed it to a still sleepy Danik. Next, she prepared a bowl for Max, spreading out the tasty bits so they cooled quickly, and placed it on the table, choosing to nibble pieces for herself right out of the cauldron.

"So good," she said between bites.

"Tastes like my tetya's," Danik said. "She always used fresh goose egg when they were in season. These are goose eggs. I'm sure of it."

"Delicious," Veru agreed. "If you ate this well at your auntie's house, I'm surprised your fingers aren't too fat to play your instruments."

Danik laughed heartily. "I'm not sure that can happen. I've met some musicians who were very round and portly, and I think it made their tone that much more interesting."

"I'm sure it was more interesting. More interesting to watch, maybe." Veru imitated what she thought a large musician might look like trying to play for a crowd. She liked the way Danik's eyes laughed the same way his face did. He hid nothing.

"That's nothing like it would look," he said. "It would be more like this."

He stood and began tromping around the room, dancing and tooting on an imaginary horn as if he were a giant animal, but somehow still managed to sound melodic. At some point he reached down and grabbed hold of Veru's hands, despite her protests, and danced around the chair and table, twirling her this way and that, bouncing her off his "enormous" belly or his "bulbous" backside.

When he got to the chorus of his song, he spun her around and around until she became so dizzy she nearly fell and grabbed on to his arms for balance. He stopped quickly and held her steady. They both panted. His hair had fallen over one eye in that appealing way she liked. His large hunter's hands held her loosely at her waist. She knew if she pulled away he'd let her go, but for the first time in her life, Veru wasn't sure she wanted to move back.

Lifting a hand, she pushed the hair from his brow and slid her palm down his cheek, then she took a step closer, knowing that was all she'd need to do. Men were easy. Give them a wink or a smile, and she'd have them right where she wanted them. But with Danik, she didn't want to play games. Veru wasn't sure exactly what she wanted from him, not yet, but she did know she was ready for more of something.

Their bodies were close. So close. Not quite touching, but almost. Just a whisper of cloth between them. She waited, her hand trembling on his face, and watched his expression change from joy and slight concern to confusion, to something raw and hungry, and then to something . . . sad?

He stepped back, his hands still supporting her, making certain she was steady before letting her go; then he smiled, and for the first time, she saw he seemed to be hiding something from her.

"Shall we get to work, then?" he asked.

"Danik?" Veru said. "What is it? What's wrong?"

"Nothing. I'm fine. Are you fine? Is something wrong with you?"

"I'm good," she said, confused.

"Are you certain? I can work on my own today if you're in pain."

"No. I can work. It's just . . . did you . . . are you remembering . . . something?"

Danik began whistling and opened the little door to the summer porch. "Not that I recall," he said, turning back to offer her an easy smile.

She stopped him with a hand on his arm. "Please, tell me."

He let out a sigh. "It's like—it's like the pictures in my head are a bit jumbled. I'm not resetting like before. My mind is staying with you now. Long as I focus on you, I can remember who I am and where we are and what we're doing. I just don't remember the before, except the parts you fill in. You tell me I'm a hunter, and I believe you. I can track the mice even without seeing them. In fact, without thinking, I fashioned a little knot with a string and set it in just the right place. This morning I found a rat caught in my makeshift trap. For some reason, I thought about giving it to you, but before I could, the kotenok grabbed it and finished it off."

"You're remembering when I was a tiger. You fed me mice in a barn."

"Did I?"

"Yes. We took care of each other. I saved your life, and you saved mine. I rescued you from wolves. Remember?"

He shook his head. "No. But it sounds like I got the better deal."

"Perhaps," Veru said, and turned away, disappointed that Danik still couldn't remember her from before.

"Hey," Danik said. "For what it's worth, I'm glad to have the chance to get to know you as a person. I can't imagine traveling with a tiger. It must have been . . . difficult."

"In some ways, I suppose. But I think you liked me more as a cat."

"Really?" Danik smiled. "Must have been because you never talked back."

Veru punched him on the shoulder.

When they stepped outside, there was a long line of strange creatures, all of whom had buckets, bowls, barrels, bottles, pots, kettles, jugs, or cups. "It's Flower of the Well Day," a short, bald man with a shovel and bare feet chirped the moment they opened the door. "As I'm the first one here, I should get to draw the water."

"Says you!" shouted a very tall, very thin woman standing about ten paces back. Her nose was as long as her arms. "You know best as anyone—they get to decide. Have to judge, they do."

"Well, stop your yappin' and let 'em get on with it, then. Some of us don't got all day, do we?"

"If you don't want to take the time, 'ur welcome ta leave," said a very bulbous gentleman with a nose like a pig and hooves for feet."

Veru held up her hands. "Can someone please explain what's going on?"

"Certainly, 'ur Graciousness," the pig-man said, bowing regally.

"Stop flirt'n with the garl. T'won't get you anything," the thin woman groused.

"Ya never know, do ya?" he replied, wiggling his eyebrows suggestively.

Danik picked up a stick and rapped it against the porch. "Here now. You'll treat my lady with the proper respect as befits her station. If you want to address her, you'll have to go through me first. You there," he said, pointing to the first man in line, "what's this about the water?"

"Once a year a pure white flower grows in the witch's well. When that happens, she grants a wish to them as is deserving. Of course, one must be worthy, and that depends on her whims, don't it? She's just as likely to curse ya as to help ya. But to some of us, it's worth the risk. Since it's her beautiful daughter as is keepin' house this time instead of Her Fearsomeness, more of us are steppin' out of the woodwork, as it were, hoping for something good ta happen."

"Kak stranno. But, my good, er, man, perhaps you will understand my confusion. You see, this is not a well, but a pump. And I see no flowers here, white or otherwise."

At that, the ranks of creatures parted, and where there had been nothing in front of the summer porch before, suddenly there was a pretty little stone well. It was covered with the most beautiful green ivy, and twined through the ivy was not one but hundreds of the most delicate white blossoms Veru had ever seen. The wind carried their delicate scent to Veru's nose, and even without her tiger senses, she could smell their fragrance. It reminded her of her mother's favorite blossoms, the flowers they'd planted by her grave. Her heart lurched, and her eyes stung for a moment. She blinked quickly to clear her vision.

"Very well," Danik said. "What do you need us to do?"

"Decide!" the thin woman cried, raising her bucket in the air.

"Decide!" another echoed.

"You must hear our reason for wanting a wish and choose who gets it."

"But what if someone lies?" Veru asked.

"A witch's daughter will punish all liars," a man's voice called out from the side of the house. They heard a neigh, and a knight wearing silver armor and a white cape and riding a white horse came into view. When the horse neighed again, it shot the palest yellow and white flames from between its teeth. Everyone backed away, clearly frightened.

Veru started to say, "But I'm not a—"

Shaking his head in alarm, the man held up a hand to Veru, then removed his helmet and drew his sword, pressing it to his forehead in a dramatic fashion. Veru couldn't help but notice his gleaming smile and sunshine hair. "My lady," he said very loudly. "I am Zarya, the Knight of the Sunrise. I offer my services and protection." Quietly, he added. "Just play along with the people. If they suspect you are anything other than the witch's daughter, they will report your activities to Yuga. You wouldn't want that. You help them and you might get something in return. Yuga never needs to know."

"Th-thank you, Knight," Veru said. "I, um, we welcome your help."

Danik didn't appear to be upset or jealous over the knight's appearance, only concerned about the newcomer and, even more, the newcomer's sword. The hunter angled himself slightly differently, just in case the knight decided to try anything, but Veru noted his stance still appeared to be relaxed. She was impressed with his calmness in a potentially volatile situation.

"We were just about to hear the locals make their cases," Veru said. "Danik, would you be so good as to fetch me a chair? This might take a while. And while you're at it, would you also ask our friends, Maxsim and our *cook*, if we have enough food to share with everyone? Perhaps they have some ideas that might be of aid as well?"

As Danik passed, he squeezed her arm and said, "Why don't you make it easy on yourself and just tell everyone to take a flower? There seem to be more than enough for everyone here."

Veru smiled regally at the crowd that was becoming more agitated by the moment and replied, "We don't yet understand what it is they want. For all you know, they want to invoke a famine on the land or curse their neighbor's horse. My parents taught me long ago, when it comes to ruling an empire, the easiest way is always the wrong way."

Raising his eyebrows, he shrugged and said, "Very well. I shall bring you that chair." When Danik returned, she summoned the first person forward.

Each one passed by the knight, who guarded her carefully with his sword. He allowed the person to present their proposal, then they were sent over to Danik to receive a parting gift and be escorted from the porch. Veru thought the whole process wasn't unlike receiving dignitaries at the palace. In actuality, it was a bit more interesting than her normal line of work.

Politics bored her, but the problems real people had were much more fascinating. A farmer wanted his cows to give more milk, or a young woman wanted to find the man she should marry. A father wanted his baby daughter to survive an illness, or the leader of a village wanted his people to prosper and be safe.

None of the wishes were for riches or glory or fame. In fact, if she could have granted every one of them, she would have. As strange as all the forest creatures were, they were essentially like Danik. Just good people at heart who wanted a simple life. Veru didn't get the impression any of them were lying to her. She shuddered to think what Yuga would do to them though. Would she have granted them their wishes or played an awful trick on them for visiting her home?

Then she met two men who argued bitterly over a property line. Apparently, a very old tree had grown right on the line, and one of them wanted the tree felled since the roots were making it impossible for him to farm that piece of land. The other loved the tree and wouldn't see it fall. Around and around they went. Both men were right in their argument and selfish in not hearing the opinion of the other.

No matter what she did, Veru couldn't get either of them to budge. Then, an idea came. "How old is the tree?" she asked.

"Near eighty," replied the tree-loving man.

"How many more years do you think it will live?" she continued.

"Could be past my lifetime!" the other man complained loudly.

"Then here's my proposal. The tree stays." She held up a hand before the loud man could cry out again. "But this one compensates you for loss of your land until such time as the tree dies."

"Now hang on. I can't afford ta—"

She held up a hand again. "If such payment cannot be made, when the tree does die of natural causes, then the owner wills the tree and any proceeds from it to his neighbor or his neighbor's descendants."

Both men were quiet for several moments, working their jaws, trying to come up with something different but unable to speak. Then, at last, they nodded, shook hands, and parted ways.

It was many, many hours later when Veru had finally heard the last person and told them she would retire to her chamber and muse on their wishes for a time before announcing her final decision. After each one had presented their case, they were allowed to fill their container with water from the pump, which she assured them also held magical properties, perhaps not wish fulfilling but nevertheless still special. Then they were also given a bundle of bread, cheese, meat, fruit, and vegetables provided by the house, and finally, a white flower was plucked and handed to each person.

Most were so happy with the arrangement they no longer wished to wait for the announcement and left completely satisfied with what they had already received. Still, about a third of the contenders remained, sitting on the grass in the sunshine, picnicking on their gift of food while they waited for the witch's daughter to make up her mind regarding their fate.

"And what of you, good knight? You have served me well today. Do you not have a wish for yourself?"

"It is not my place to seek boons from those I serve, mistress. However, I am humbled that you would take notice of one such as myself."

"Tell me, is there indeed magic in this well? Is it in the water, the flower, the drawing up?"

The man said simply, "There is magic in all those things when you consider it, isn't there?"

"Must I truly just select one to draw water from the well?"

"It is tradition. But you may alter tradition as you wish."

"I'll consider that." Veru peered at the man. "Have you always served Yu—my mother?"

He shook his head. "She captured me and my brothers. We are bound to her with chains much stronger than our armor. I am afraid we must serve her to the end of her days. Or the end of ours. Whichever length of time is the shortest."

"But is there nothing that could break those chains?"

Sheathing his sword, he climbed onto his prancing stallion. "What can break steel?" he asked. Stretching out his hand, he reached for hers and kissed it. "I must go now, my lady. My time is far gone."

"Of course."

After she and Danik had "retired" into the house, Veru sank into the chair. "What do we do?" she asked him, pressing her head into her hands. "Which one do we let draw the water? So we keep with tradition, or do we alter it? I don't want to set a precedent when we don't intend to stay here."

"That's true. But sometimes traditions need to be changed."

Veru sighed. "They all made good cases. I wish Stacia was here. She's the smart one. She'd know which one to pick. What to do."

Danik knelt in front of her and pulled her hands away from her face. "You think your sister is smarter than yourself? Granted, I don't remember much about her. Have I met her?"

"Yes. But only as a tiger."

He grunted. "Doesn't matter. You're one of the smartest people I've ever met. You'll know what to do. But just in case . . . I sneaked over to the well and drew some water." He held up a small vial. "If you want to keep the wish for yourself, I wouldn't blame you. You could wish yourself out of here or you and your sister back home. It's my fault we're here in the first place."

"Oh, Danik," Veru said, standing and cupping her hand around his containing the vial. "That . . . that was sweet of you, but it's not your fault. Even so, I'd never leave you here alone, and I'm not one to take the easy path. We're here to learn, right? I don't think wishing our way out, as nice as that sounds, is the right thing to do."

Biting her lip and keeping her hand in his, she headed back outside. When they stepped on the porch, everyone came to attention and stood.

"Thank you all for your patience," Veru said. "It's time for us to make a decision."

CHAPTER 15

God Prefers a Trinity or Maybe a Troika

Stacia and Zakhar were jostled awake by the strange sisters. "Come quickly. You must arise. If you mean to rescue your man, you'll have to hurry, else you'll be too late."

"What?" Stacia said, rubbing her bleary eyes. She felt like she'd just fallen asleep. "I thought you said we had time."

"We thought so as well, but it seems the vodnik like your man so much"—they glanced at one another—"at least in his current form, that they no longer wish to trade. They want to use him in their games, and they've already left for the snowcapped mountains of Bogatyr."

"Once he's entered, he must fight for his life, for only those who are crowned at the end and drink from the gold and silver horns of the aurochs will live to tell the tale."

"We are sorry, but we didn't know he had gifts of his own. If we had, we would have warned you."

"Perhaps we should give them our gifts now, Sister. For they have a long journey ahead of them."

"You are right. We must hurry."

"But you don't understand," Stacia said. "Iriko is blind. Yes. He's strong. He's in his tiger form, but he cannot see. He relies on my eyes."

"We do understand," said the sister called Stribog. "You are bonded, here." She touched the place on her own chest covering her heart. "Is this not so?" she asked.

"I-I suppose so. In a way," Stacia replied with a confused shrug, looking at Zakhar for help.

He explained, "Iriko, Stacia, and her sister, Veru, make up what we call the Transcendent Troika. Do you know what this is?"

"Ah!" All the sisters nodded knowingly.

The one called Daz said, "This is the Holy Trinity."

Zakhar squeaked and chuckled, slightly uncomfortable. "Oh no. I'm afraid you ladies misunderstood me, or mayhaps I misspoke. The Trinity and the Troika are two different things. One is a godhead, as in the Father, the Son, and the Holy Ghost."

"Perhaps I am indeed confused," Daz said. "I thought you were speaking of power."

"Oh, but I am," Zakhar said, nodding sincerely.

"Ah, then there is no misunderstanding after all, for we are as well."

"But . . . but how?" Zakhar asked. "What I am speaking of belongs to the heavens above and to the church."

The women laughed. "Now I think it is *you* who are confused, good priest," Daz said. "For the power you and I speak of, indeed the very power from which we draw our own strength, cannot belong to something so mundane as a building constructed by men."

"Indeed," echoed another sister. "Even as something as expansive and as beautiful as the heavens above couldn't possibly contain the Source of all things."

"I'm sorry, ladies," Zakhar said. "The, um . . . the Source?"

"That is right. Have you ever wondered why there are always three?" Moksha asked.

"Do you mean three tigers?" Stacia asked.

"Yes," said Stribog.

"And, no," said her sister Daz.

"If it is the Trinity you speak of, then I know from my studies that they serve as a witness of one another. Particularly the Holy Ghost,"

Zakhar suggested. "When it comes to law, there must always be at least two to witness a truth."

"That is right," the youngest sister, Veles, interjected. "Witnesses serve as supporters of truth. As we also exist to support one another."

"As in ancient days, we unite for a purpose greater than ourselves," Yaryl said. "The Troika is the same."

"A triangle is strong. Three is always stronger than two. You can build a great city on the back of three," said Stribog.

"Or seven," said Daz. "Seven is also good."

"Or twelve," mused Zakhar.

"Yes. But three are always required."

"But why three?" asked Stacia.

Daz picked up a stool and showed her the legs. "It cannot stand without three. Nothing in this world or any other can. Each leg symbolizes our purpose."

Veles touched the first, saying, "We have a duty to take care of our world and all the life and resources available upon it. Seeing all of them as gifts given by the Source to be used responsibly and carefully. Life is a precious thing. No life should be ended without much consideration."

"The second leg is about community, home, family, relationships, nurture, growth, and many more such things that are somewhat difficult to define," said Stribog. "Choice, opportunity, and certain freedoms must be enacted for civilizations to develop and for people to thrive and be happy."

"And this one?" Zakhar said, pointing to the last leg.

"This last one is about work," said Moksha. "Without industry and effort, civilizations collapse."

"The balance seems tricky," Stacia said.

"Oh, it is," replied Stribog. "Too much of one, and another weakens. All must be given an equal amount of attention. Just as all legs of a stool must be measured and cut the same, else the stool will be off-balance."

"But the point here," said Daz, "is to remember that *we* are not the

Source. We serve it. We draw upon its power, yes. But all of us lend our strength to the same cause in the end."

"But . . . but I still don't understand. What *is* the cause?" asked Zakhar.

"You of all people must know the answer to that question, don't you?" said Stribog.

"I . . ." Zakhar stood there open-mouthed. How could he tell these goddesses of old he was coming to doubt his purpose in life for the very first time. That he was concerned that he'd joined the priesthood for the wrong reasons. That he feared coming on this journey might mean the loss not only of his core beliefs but of his place in the hereafter. The path he stood on now was not only uncertain, it was dark. He felt blinder than Iriko, and unlike the tiger, he'd been left without a guide.

"Perhaps he will find the answer on his journey," Sima added kindly.

"Yes, perhaps," Moksha said. "Come, let us present our gifts and send them on their way. They must hurry if they wish to save their friend from the Games."

Veles was the first. She pressed a coin into Stacia's hand. "As I am the goddess over the waters, toss this coin into any cup of water you drink from or bathe in, and the waters will heal you from injury."

Peruna gave them a metal cup and moved her hand across the top. Blue flames erupted from within, glowing hotter than anything Stacia had ever felt. When she passed her hand over it again, the flames disappeared. "This is a burning cresset. You can use it to start fires or warm yourselves. If you pour out the flames, they will flow like hot pitch, encompassing whatever they touch. You must always remember to turn it off before stowing the cup."

Next was Yaryl, who gave them her pet ermine and a bag filled with very rare red gold. Zakhar took to the ermine immediately. The furry white animal climbed into his coat and curled up in one of his large pockets and went to sleep.

Moksha gave them a bag of barley and another of rye, both of which would always remain full, no matter how much of it they used.

Then the last three sisters combined their abilities into one great gift. "Come and see," said Daz.

Stacia and Zakhar followed the sisters outside, where they found a great swollen dirizhabl' of some kind with a small wooden vessel attached to it with a series of ropes and pulleys.

"What is it?" asked Stacia.

"Your mode of transportation," said Stribog. "I call it a Rackapelterly Aeroflation. Climb inside the structure. I'll teach you how to control it with my ability to manipulate the wind, jump far distances, and travel on lightning."

"Don't forget harnessing the storms and using my birds," said Sima, just as a large network rose before the balloon. The air in front was now filled with hundreds of winged creatures all screeching and cawing and tweeting. Each one was leashed to the structure via a harness so small it could barely be seen, but it was somehow effective enough that none of them twisted around one another or became trapped or stuck.

"How? How are you doing that?" Stacia asked, darting around to the front to see the miraculous setup.

"Simple," said Sima. "I asked them. They have control over the harnesses. If it gets twisted or uncomfortable, they simply unlink it with their minds. When they're ready to pull again, they link back in, and it reattaches. It's constantly in flux, but because there are so many, someone's always pulling."

"That's amazing!"

"It is, isn't it?" Sima grinned. "Now, you take good care of my babies, and they'll take you where you want to go. Bogatyr Mountain, my sweet things. You're headed to the Novgorod Games. Make sure to stay warm in that freezing weather."

Sima bumped into Stribog, and while they argued over who could board the transport first, Daz shook her head and smiled.

"And where are you in this thing?" Stacia asked.

"Isn't it obvious?" Daz asked.

When Stacia just frowned and shook her head, Daz laughed and ballooned her cheeks, then made a shape with her hands over a rounded belly. "I'm the goddess of motherhood. Remember?"

"Oh, you're responsible for the . . ." Stacia pointed out the great rounded shape above them floating in the air. "Does that mean we should expect something else in a few months' time?"

Daz shrugged. "Not necessarily. But you never know. Do you?" She leaned closer. "I've also smuggled aboard a bagful of sunshine. When you need a break from the storms and lightning, just toss one overboard. You won't get anywhere for a few hours, but at least you'll have a nice sunny day. With Zima around, it will still be cold. But the sun helps."

"I understand. Spasibo," Stacia said.

"Pozhaluysta. Speaking of which, I'd better fetch her so you all can get going. And here." She pressed another bag into her hands.

"What's this?" asked Stacia. "You've already given us too much."

"It's nothing. Just three extra biscuits. I have a feeling you'll need them. Remember: Once the Games begin, your friend must see them through to the conclusion."

"I've got it. Now, teach me how to drive this thing."

Stacia hooked arms with Daz, and they followed the other sisters and Zakhar into the very strange transport.

Zima and Zakhar were much more enthusiastic about the new means of travel than Stacia, who much preferred having her claws dug into the dirt or in the bark of the nearest tree trunk. It was strange to her that she missed her tiger. She felt . . . off-balance without it. Like she was always teetering on the edge of a cliff, almost on the verge of falling over.

When the birds rose in the sky, taking them along for the ride, Stacia's stomach lurched. She even feared she'd lose the contents of her belly over the side of the ship and sank down to the bottom of the vessel, putting her head between her knees and taking several deep breaths to steady herself.

Meanwhile, Zima and Zakhar were studying all the instruments, pressing every knob, and flipping every switch, then taking careful notes as to what resulted from each button push. Zima seemed to make a very good scribe-in-training. The only problem was that the inkpot kept freezing. They solved the problem by switching over to chalks and charcoal pencils.

Zima told them the ermine's name was Belizna. The furry white creature stuck its nose out of Zakhar's pocket and slid out onto the floor, then hopped on its short legs over to Stacia. With twitching whiskers, it sniffed around her and quickly found the bag containing the biscuits Daz had given her.

"Oh, no you don't, little lady," Stacia said, taking the bag away and stowing it in her own coat. "Here, you can have some rye or barley instead. This stuff won't run out. If you want it cooked, you're going to have to wait."

The animal sniffed the grain and hissed at her, baring its teeth.

"Don't like that, eh?" she said.

"She doesn't eat things like that," Zima said as she scratched on her paper.

"Well, what does she eat?" asked Stacia.

"She mostly hunts for herself. She eats birds, mice, lizards, that sort of thing."

"Ah, you're more like me, then, aren't you, little girl?"

Zima looked up from her drawing. "Did you say she's like you?"

"Yes. Like me and Iriko."

The little girl frowned. "You're not like Iriko."

"I used to be," Stacia said softly as she began petting Belizna. "How are we going to feed you, I wonder?" she said as she scratched the white ermine's soft ears. "I'm fresh out of mice, and I don't think Sima would take too kindly to you eating one of her birds."

"Perhaps she can hunt when we put down for the night," Zakhar said.

"Do we need to? Set down, I mean. Wouldn't it be better to keep going? Get there as fast as possible?" Stacia asked.

"I think our bird friends need a break, and we could use a fire to keep warm, I should think."

"Not to mention cook our dinner," Zima said.

"Yes. That makes sense," Stacia agreed. "Let's find a good place, then."

She stood up and discovered Zakhar had been making aerial maps as they journeyed. They were crude, he insisted, but to her, they were astonishingly detailed considering how quickly they'd been moving.

"I'd suggest we set down in a clearing," he said. "It would give us more room for maneuvering."

She nodded and said, "See to it, Navigator."

They touched down with only a slight bump or two, and Zakhar told her to hop out and take the lead rope and tie it off on a sturdy tree. Once that was done, they tied off two more ropes, and the birds disconnected themselves and headed off in search of food and water.

As for them, they made camp and used the gift of the burning cresset to start a fire, remembering to pass their hand over it to turn it off before stowing it in their bag. Finished, they filled water bags at a little stream and boiled up a potful of barley for their supper. They agreed that they would share one biscuit together every night after Zakhar told them he estimated their journey would take three days, based on the distance he'd discussed with one of the sisters.

They'd just pulled one biscuit from the bag and were preparing to divide it when an old man hobbled into their camp and asked if he could warm his hands by their fire.

Zakhar rose immediately. "Please, sir, sit in my spot."

Just as Zakhar sat again, farther from the flames, Belizna returned to his feet with a dead mouse in her jaws. She stretched out by the fire and began eating. Soft snowflakes fell around them. Stacia shivered and drew her coat around her shoulders, with her fur-lined hood drawn down. Zakhar, too, drew in his knees and stuffed his hands back into his gloves, then pulled his hat down, only then noticing the man at their fire wore just a long-sleeved shirt and well-worn boots. His balding head was bare, as were his hands, which he continually rubbed and held to the fire. He was thin, his face drawn.

"Are you hungry, sir?" Zakhar asked. "We've finished our dinner, but we're happy to boil up some more to eat."

"I don't want to be a bother," the man said. "You should save your grain for your girl. She looks cold."

"I'm not," said Zima. "I'm quite warm enough. You aren't though."

"You're right, Zima," Stacia said. "He isn't. I insist," she said. "Take this biscuit, at least, and some water. We've a few blankets too—if you'll stay the night by the fire, we'll keep it hot."

She held out the biscuit and a cup of water, and the old man reluctantly took them. As he ate, the crumbs fell on his thin chest. "Spasibo," he mumbled, his watery blue eyes twinkling in the firelight. "You've been very kind. I'll remember this kindness."

"Don't worry about it," Zakhar said. "Rest now, Dyedushka. Sleep well."

Zakhar gave him his own blankets, then made sure Zima was comfortable before laying down with his own back to the fire. Stacia could see him shivering every so often. With Zima near them, the cold was back with a vengeance. It seemed like every minute the temperature grew icier.

The next morning, Stacia had to work to get her eyes open. Her lashes were frozen together. How she missed her thick coat of fur. Even if Iriko were with them, she knew she could have curled up next to him and been very warm. The fire had gone out. In fact, the flames had frozen in place!

Stacia worried that the man might not have lived through the night. She hurried to beat some life into her frozen limbs so she could check on him, but she was surprised to find that the old man who had visited them the night before was gone. The blankets he'd borrowed were carefully folded up and placed next to the fire, and a note had been pinned on top of them with a rock.

With a gloved hand, she picked it up and read it: "Your hospitality saved an old man's life. I don't have much to leave you in exchange, but please accept this nose bag as a token of my appreciation."

Stacia mumbled to herself, "Nose bag?" She looked around, picking up the blankets and glancing around the dead fire and saw nothing. Then she shook a shivering Zakhar awake.

"Zakhar. Zakhar! Wake up!"

"What? What is it?" he mumbled, frozen air lifting from his lips. "It's so c-c-cold!"

"I know. Here. Here's your blanket."

She tucked it around him, and he buried his head inside and sighed in relief.

"Did you see the old man leave?" she asked.

"No." Stacia heard his faint reply from inside his blanket.

"I did." The answer came from Zima, who she hadn't noticed was awake. Zima sat up and let her little blanket fall away, and in her hands, she clutched an old knapsack.

"Zima?" Stacia said. "Is that the bag the man left on his blanket?"

"Yes," answered the little girl. "And I think it's got magic," she added.

"Why do you say that?" asked Stacia.

"Because I wished for something, and it hopped right into the bag."

"What did you wish for?" Stacia said, crouching down next to the little girl. "Will you let me see?"

Zakhar lowered his blanket to see as well but still wasn't warm enough to do much more than that.

"I . . . I thought Belizna might be lonely out here with us."

At that moment, something hissed and bucked inside the bag. Stacia thought it was probably the white ermine, but just then a sleepy Belizna crept out from Zakhar's blanket and stared at the bag, whiskers twitching. Stacia got a bad feeling.

"Honey? Why don't you hand that over to me?" The little girl was barely able to hold on to it. Whatever was inside it wanted out. "So you were saying you thought she was lonely . . ."

"Yes. So I wished for a boyfriend for her."

"A boyfriend," Stacia said. She glanced at Zakhar, who immediately sat up. "And you say he jumped right into the bag?"

"Yes. The minute I wished it, he came and scooted right inside. He was very angry about it too."

"I imagine he was."

Zakhar was standing next to her now, and he took hold of the other side of the bag. They walked several steps away from the camp, and then she mouthed, "Odin, dva, *tri*!" They pulled open the bag at the same time, leaving the top wide, but the creature inside remained as though there were an invisible window keeping him tucked down into it.

Like Belizna, he was a snow-white ermine but with a black-tipped tail. He was beautiful and huge and very, very mad. He hissed, kicking and bucking against the bag, but made no attempt to escape the top even though they'd opened it for him. Stacia dared not insert her hand or fingers lest he bite them.

"You can leave," she said to him, but he remained inside. "Zima? I think you're going to have to be the one to tell him he can go," she said. "It's a nice thought, but he's a wild ermine. I don't think a wild and a tame ermine would get along too well."

"Yes. I think you're right," the little girl said. "Okay, boy, you can go."

It was like the animal had been released from a trap. He screamed and leaped a foot in the air, twisting his body as he did so; then he plopped down in a snowdrift, did a little ermine dance, and was off as fast as he could go. Soon the only thing left to show he'd been there at all were his tiny footprints in the snow.

Zakhar took hold of the pannier. "Now that's interesting. Do you think it will work with other animals?" he asked.

Before she could stop him, Zakhar said, "How about a nice big rabbit?"

Not a moment later, a fat, fluffy rabbit barreled out of a nearby hole they hadn't even seen. It screeched madly as it did and leaped high just as he opened the bag, then fell right inside it. Once it was in, it seemed to rethink its decision and began bucking just as the other animal did.

"Well now, that's a fine thing, isn't it?" Zakhar said. "I fancy some rabbit for breakfast."

With a quick twist of the neck, the rabbit was dead, and he was quickly able to get the fire going, skin the creature, and skewer it. It wasn't long before she could smell the roasting meat.

Reaching down, Stacia picked up the pannier, folded it, and placed it in her bag. "We're going to have to be very careful with this," she said.

"Indeed," replied Zakhar as he pulled off a piece of crisping leg meat and blew on his fingers before nibbling. "We will indeed," he said.

When they'd eaten their fill, they broke camp, climbed back into their large balloon, and stowed all their gear. Zakhar and Zima plotted their course and summoned all the birds who'd just linked up when a winter storm hit. The sisters had warned them about storms and had even taught them how to use storms to travel, but never in her life had Stacia seen a squall move so quickly. The sky, already dim for morning, turned black as night.

They lost all sense of direction. That's when the birds abandoned them, and the funnel descended. They began to spin.

CHAPTER 16

If You Want to Sweep the Steps Clean, Start at the Top

Nik cracked open his eyes, but he couldn't see much of anything. His lamp had broken, and the light had gone out. The space where he'd landed was damp; the earth beneath him soft. At least that had prevented him from breaking any bones. He cautiously moved his limbs and found them in working order, but the lump on the back of his head told him he hadn't imagined the beating he'd taken. Someone had hit him. And it wasn't a ghost. At least he didn't think so.

He lay still, listening, but heard nothing. Nik was good at remaining still, even in the most uncomfortable and appalling places. After waiting a length of time he deemed appropriate, he shifted to a standing position, then stretched out his hands to feel around him. At first he attempted to climb the stairs and exit the tunnel, but the door was locked from the outside.

Unable to get his lamp lit again, he decided to look for another exit or at least try to find some supplies to shed a little light on his surroundings. Reaching the bottom of the steps, he stretched out his arms and came upon the stone wall on either side of him very quickly. Keeping one hand on the right wall, he followed it all the way to one end, estimating it stretched the length of the house, then turned and began tracing its length back on the other side, hoping there was more to the place than just a long tunnel.

That's when he found the little alcove. It's also when he stumbled, stirring something that made a strange sound that sent chills through his body, though he couldn't place the noise. *Chink, chink.* The sound was loud at first, and then soft, and then went still.

Nik guessed the room he'd found had once served as a root cellar or dugout. Many old houses had such spaces used to store items. His father had wanted one, but their land had proved far too rocky.

Wind chimes, he thought. *That's what it sounds like. But no, that doesn't make sense. Who would put wind chimes in a place like this?*

His foot brushed something, and he heard it again. *Chink, chink.*

He felt a cool kiss of air on the back of his neck and realized he was sweating profusely. Swiping his forehead and upper lip, he called out quietly, "Is anyone here?"

There was no answer but the sound of his hot breath as it peppered the viscous dark. "Of course no one's here," he said, forcing a meager chuckle that deflated too quickly. Groping for a shelf or a barrel, Nik came up with nothing. He slid his foot forward again, but something definitely blocked his path, likely the same thing that had caused him to stumble. *Chink, chink, chink.*

"What is that?" he said. "Glass bottles, perhaps? Maybe this was where they stored wine."

Crouching down in the pitch black, he gingerly felt for the obstruction. His hand found the clanking chains first. A part of him was relieved to know the source of the sound, but then, when his fingers slipped through the ring, and he ran his fingertips up the chain to the place where it was embedded in the wall, a cold dread filled him. Nik knew what he'd find next. He didn't want to be right, but he was well-versed enough in the depravity of men to trust his gut.

If he could have run, he would have. The last thing he wanted to do was confirm his suspicions. But he needed to know if there was a way out somewhere beyond this room. Steeling himself, he swallowed, the blackness feeling as thick to him as the borscht his mother had sometimes made.

He'd always despised that soup. His father never let her use meat or potatoes. He always demanded it be made the way his own mother had done it back in the old country. It was as sour as his disposition—full of vinegar and as red as his cheeks and neck when he was drunk and angry.

Nik's hands brushed cloth, then a thin arm. He pulled back. The sound of weeping filled his ears. Closing his eyes, Nikolai licked his dry lips and stretched out his hand again. He took hold of the arm, wrapping his hand around it, feeling with his fingers. It was nothing but bone. Nikolai heard a snap, and a spark of light filled the tunnel behind him. It came from his forsaken and now broken lantern that lay near the bottom of the stairs.

Carefully, he made his way back, following the tiny, flickering flame. Picking up the lamp, he again tried to leave the way he'd entered but found it locked as before. His shoulders slumped. "Now that I know, you want me to see. Is that right, Mama?" he asked. "Very well. Show me what you will."

Returning to the room, he lifted his little lantern high and gasped. In a small room, maybe twelve feet wide and twelve feet long, he saw more than a dozen skeletons all seated next to one another with arms stretched up over their heads. It looked as if the skulls shrunk in size from the right side of the room to the left.

"The man killed his own children," Nik said. Sinking to his knees next to the smallest skeleton, he picked up a hand-carved horse on wheels. His eyes were hot. Burning with hate and rage, but there was nothing he could do about it. It was too late. These children were gone.

He heard the crying again. It was Mama.

"I'm so sorry, Mama," Nik said as he sat in the hall of horrors. "I see what happened to all your deti. Was there no one to protect them from the monster?"

Suddenly, Nik couldn't breathe. It was as if his own mother was crying, and she was asking Nik why he didn't stay and protect her deti. Instead, he ran. He became the monster that killed them.

"Forgive me, Mama," he begged. "I loved them too." Nik clutched the toy horse to his chest and sobbed. "Please, Mama. Take me with you. I don't want to be alone anymore. It's too hard. Don't make me see. Take them away."

Just then he heard a voice from above, and it wasn't his own mother or even the ghost mama. "Weren't supposed ta see this," a deep male voice said.

Nik froze, feeling the prick of a sword at his back.

"Technically, he wasn't supposed to survive either," another man said.

"Right, but he did. Can't let him now, for sure. He'd spread word, wouldn't he?"

"Not like you were plannin' on it anyway."

"Right. Was hoping the fall woulda killed ya and done the job for me, but seeing as how you're still alive, I suppose we're gonna have to take care of ya all proper like."

The other man said, "House is lookin' real nice though. Ya did good work, boy."

"Shut up, Andrey!" the other man said. "Ya garrulous lout."

"I'm just sayin' since we're keepin' the house, the rubles, and killin' 'im and whatnot, least we could do is honor 'is effort. Otherwise, we can't expect ta mundify ourselves, can we? How we gonna hold our heads up in front of the townsfolk or at church? If we gonna do it, best do it proper like. Now do ya wanna prick him here, string him up, or chain him with these poor lost souls?"

Nik raised his hands in a show of surrender. "If you're worried about your souls or holding your heads up among the townsfolk, then have no fear, for I am more worthy of death than most. As far as the coins or the money, I care nothing for it. You can have it. But if you are truly related to these poor children in any way, I beg you to lay them to rest in a proper fashion. Their mother mourns grievously for them. I'll help you, if you wish, just . . . just restore this poor family. Redeem them. Please! Do what you will with me when it's done."

After a few seconds of silence, he heard the second man, Andrey, speak. "He's right. These deti were the brothers and sisters of your dyedushka. We need to do right by them. Besides, I believe him. Look at the house. The old dom is beautiful! Clearly your prababushka ghost likes him. That must mean something. Da?"

"Maybe you're right. But what about Yuri? You know what he's capable of."

"I'm not scared of Yuri," Nik said, though, if he told the absolute truth, he was terrified of the ghost. Yuri was pure evil. Much like his own father. Only there was no destroying *him*. How could one kill a person who was already dead? But Nik had stood up to evil before, and he could do it again. At least, he thought he could.

"What do you propose we do?" the big man said, then sheathed his sword. "We're not killing you, at least, not yet, so put your hands down and turn around."

Obeying, Nik stood and rubbed the back of his neck. "I think we should bury them. But I also believe there's something Mama—I mean, your prababushka's ghost—wants us to find or wants us to see. She gave me a box, but I need a key to open it."

"You stay here," the big man warned.

The two men headed down the tunnel to talk over their plans. Nik found it interesting that though he knew they were talking about when or if they were going to kill him, he had no fear of death whatsoever. In fact, the idea that his impending demise might be looming felt somewhat freeing in a way. He supposed that it should bother him, but it didn't. *What does that make me?* he wondered.

"Okay," the large man finally announced, "you can come up with us. Show me the box, and I'll see if I can find a key. But understand: If there's anyone what's going to deal with Yuri, it's you, my friend. Also, we want the money now. It's our insurance policy, just in case he kills you."

"Or frightens you to death," Andrey added. "It's been known to happen."

"Very well." Nik picked up his broken lamp and made his way up the stairs, with the two men marching up right behind him. Trailing his hand against the house as he walked, he felt the warmth of Mama protecting him. "If you two will stay outside here," Nik said, "I'll head in and get the box as well as the money."

"Fine," the first man answered, backing away from the windows and the light they cast, hiding instead in the shadow of the large tree in the front yard, the very same tree where Mama had taken her own life. If they knew the scene that had played out there, it would have been one of the last places where they'd feel safe.

He heard the second one say, "How do we know he won't just lock himself in there?"

"If he does, I have a key, bolvan."

"Right." Then there was a pause. "But just so's you know, I'm not goin' in after him."

"Don't matter. He's got to come out sometime."

Nik just shook his head and went inside the house, their words trailing off as he left them behind. When he entered the nursery, he found a mug of water and some powdered pain medicine to soothe the growing lump on his head.

"Spasibo, Mama," he said, mixing the powder into the water and gulping it down. Then he turned and uncovered the little box and the bag of winnings from their hiding place in the corner of the room and began heading out the door, when he noticed that in place of the mug of water, there was a shiny gun.

He stopped. "No, Mama. I understand you want to protect me. But this man is your potomstvo, your offspring. I don't want to hurt him. Perhaps he can help."

The rocking chair began squeaking, and Nik smiled at it and nodded, then left the room, heading outside. He found the men there, pacing.

"What took you so long? This place makes me polzet. What's the word?" he asked his friend. "Oh, popeyed."

"That's not right. It gives you the fish in the belly, not fisheyes."

"Yes, that's it."

"Calm down, you two," said Nik. "Here. This is the box Mama gave me. Do you recognize it?"

The men studied it for a moment and then shook their heads. "Sorry. No."

"Hold on. Didn't your dyedushka tell you when he crawled out of the well he dropped something?"

"He did what?" asked Nik.

Ignoring Nik, the large man answered, "Yeah. That's right. I forgot. What was it my mama told me . . . It was something about a tin and a game."

"A dangerous game?" Nik asked.

Both men stared at him. "You know it?"

"I think so. Mama sang me a song my first night here." Nik hummed for a minute and then sang.

> On the morrow, I'll give you
> a cherished family tin,
> and with the help of God, you'll
> place it right in front of you,
> while playing the most dangerous game.
> Please remember your mother.
> Sleep, good boy, my beautiful,
> bayushki bayu.

"I didn't understand it when she sang it," Nik confessed.

While he stared at the box, the big man said, "My mother told us that until the day he died, my grandfather insisted that when his brothers and sisters started disappearing, a beautiful angel, his own mama, came to him, wrapped him up in a blanket, and lowered him into the well. She told him it was a game. That he had to stay very, very quiet until she came to fetch him, and that when he came out, she'd leave him the key to a tin containing the family secrets or family treasure or some such thing.

"Turns out, she never did come to get the lad. When he finally crawled out after he was nearly dead himself from hunger, he discovered his entire family was gone, including his father. The key, which was left at the top of the well, was forgotten. When he did return to retrieve it, the key slipped back into the well and was never recovered."

"How old was he when it happened?"

"I don't remember. Five or six, I think. I was named after him. He was called Eldar."

"Was Eldar the last baby your prababushka had before she died?"

"Yes. Why?"

Nik nodded. "No reason. It's just . . . I think she wants us to recover that key." Nik put one hand on Eldar's shoulder and his other one on Andrey's. "I have a fairly strong rope, but I'll need the two of you to pull me back up."

Nikolai soon found himself dangling painfully from a very thin rope wrapped over his shoulders and between his legs, supporting him like a harness. Strapped to his chest was a too-hot lantern that dribbled oil on his pants and threatened to send him up in flames. It wasn't the best of his ideas, but it was all he could think of in that moment.

It didn't take him long to search the rocks at the top, which was where he'd hoped the key would be found, but there was nothing there. Once he got past the rocks, he knew there was no place for the key to go but all the way to the bottom. Nik also knew the likelihood of finding it was slim to none.

Pressing on, the two men lowered him down, down, down, until the tiny circle of light at the top became so small Nik felt like he'd descended into the depths of hell itself. The only way he could cope with the tiny space that closed in on him, stealing the breath from his lungs, was to shut his eyes and focus instead on the pain caused by the rubbing of the ropes on his skin.

When his boots finally splashed into water, he breathed a sigh of relief that he could at last focus on the task at hand. Oh, how he wished he could use them for their magic, but the best they could do at the moment was give a weak flutter of shoelaces. They were barely more useful to him than a regular pair. In fact, they were even letting foul water into the top, soaking his feet and turning them numb with cold—something he hadn't experienced since he'd owned them.

"Zamechatel 'no," he mumbled to himself before calling out, "I'm down!" But there was no answer from above. It was likely they couldn't hear him, which was soon proven true when he was lowered further, not that it mattered much. The water was only thigh-deep anyway. It was frigid though. He knew he wouldn't be able to work very long before he lost feeling in his hands as well as his legs.

"This is ridiculous," he said, standing there, lantern raised over the black water, shivering with cold. Letting out a sigh, he hooked the lantern on a root that protruded out into the well and, seeing no other options, sucked in a breath and dove underwater, using his hands to feel for a key.

When diving in a well, one finds a myriad of strange and awful things, especially when probing with bare fingers. The men had given him a bag with which to collect items, so anything Nik brushed against that felt hard and smallish went into the bag. He was fairly certain some of them were pebbles, but he couldn't tell.

He didn't consider himself a squeamish fellow, but the amount of mucus-filled globules and pulsating, tentacled things he found shocked him. When he exited the well, he was sure he'd spend the next few hours focused on the sanitation of his person. The only problem was that the well was the place from which he drew his bathwater.

When Nik was absolutely sure he had to leave or else lose his extremities, he yanked on the rope and then began the slow ascent. He couldn't remove his fingers from the rope by the time they pulled him out.

"Gaw! Boy's near froze off his yaytsa! Better put him near the fire."

"Ya know I don't like goin' into the house."

"I'm not much for it either, but we got no choice if we want to save the lad. Ghost won't let us have the treasure if we don't. She'll hide it from us again. You know what she's like. She's taken to this one."

"You're sure there's a treasure?"

"Durak. I told you my family was wealthy. Look at this place. There has to be an inheritance. Why do you think I've been coming out here facing these ghosts all these years?"

"Fine. In we go, then build him a fire, and back out. Agreed?"

"Agreed."

The door opened as they carried him into the house, and a blazing fire sprang to life in the hearth. Nik tried to mumble a, "Spasibo, Mama," but his lips just knocked together along with his teeth.

Andrey ran from the nursery with a change of clothing for him, which was, of course, provided by Mama, and the two men helped him into them. As Nik thawed by the fire, sipping a warm mug of sbiten that had appeared at the hearth, the greedy men grabbed the bag he'd scrounged from the well and headed to the front door, which slammed and locked of its own accord.

"Rotten luck, that," said Andrey.

"Don't think it's the bad one though," replied Eldar. "Calm yourself, Prababushka," he said loudly. "We'll help the boy."

"Yeah. We'll keep an eye out."

They sat down and started sifting through what Nik had found at the bottom of the well, discarding most of it as rubbish. The two men jumped nervously every time they heard a noise.

When Nik was sufficiently warm, he slid closer to the table, examining the pile of items they were keeping, which included a few coins, an earring, and some metal pieces they might be able to reuse. None of the things they'd collected looked like a key. Then one of them set aside a matryoshka nesting doll.

"What's that?" Nik asked.

"A child's toy," Eldar said.

"May I see it?"

Eldar pushed the muck-covered doll over to Nik and continued pawing through his pile.

Picking up a cloth and dipping it in hot water, Nikolai cleaned the doll's face and uncovered a sweet-faced grandmother wearing a dress bright with the same purple-and-cream tones that he'd uncovered in the kitchen. Her bow mouth and cheeks were pink, and her bright eyes were rimmed with lashes. "Hello, Mama," Nik said softly.

Carefully, he opened the nesting doll and found another woman. This one had white hair, not gray like Mama's. Her dress was blue. The next one was a redhead who looked a lot like Stacia. Then a blond who reminded him of Veru. The last was a child.

Nik twisted the tiny doll, trying to open it.

"It's likely the last one. Most of them have five."

"Some have more," Andrey said. "My mama had one with ten."

Ignoring them, Nik kept at it. Finally, it gave. Inside wasn't a doll but a tiny silver key.

"Hey, fellas?" Nik said, holding up the key. "I think I found it."

"Now look," said Eldar. "Before you go getting any ideas. Anything in this house, including that there tin box, belongs to me. It's my rightful inheritance, see?"

"That's right," Andrey said. "Belongs to him."

Nik raised his hand with the key between his fingers. "That's fine with me. If you two want it all, you can have it. I won't fight you for it. You'd clearly win. I mean, it's two against one. Now, if you were to go up against me in cards, that's a different story. No one can beat me at that. Cards are my game. I *always* win."

"That so?" Eldar said.

"Yep," replied Nik. "It's just a gift. I was born with it, I think."

"Okay. Tell you what—let's play to see who gets to open the tin. Now, it's just to open it, mind. Don't mean you win the contents."

"Sounds fair to me. Though I might want to raise the stakes a bit. Say, if I win, I get to live."

Andrey looked at Eldar and shrugged. "Seems fair enough. Boy almost did die to bring us the key."

"Yeah, all right. But we get to deal."

"Only if I get to cut the cards."

Eldar grinned and lifted his hand to take the cards from Nik, but then the deck lifted away from both of them, and a chair was yanked away from the table. The cards landed in front of the empty chair, and they heard a voice say, "I think tonight it's my turn to cut, don't you agree?"

A gleaming knife with a sharp blade sank into the wooden table, and the invisible specter laughed. The cards flew around the table as if controlled by unseen forces, whirling incredibly fast. The two men screamed and tried to run, but something pushed them back down in their seats. The laughter suddenly cut off.

"I said we're going to play, and tonight I think I'll be in charge of the stakes."

Sweat and tears began rolling down the faces of the other men, but Nik remained still and calm, at least on the surface. "Hello, Yuri," he said, plucking his hand of hovering cards from the air. "I've been waiting for you to make an appearance."

Chapter 17

A Silk Dress Does Not Mean Clean Undergarments

"All of you good people have come seeking aid. I'm here to tell you today that I've heard your wishes and judged your hearts and found all of you worthy. That is why I've chosen to break with tradition. My decision is not to help one of you today, but all of you."

There were gasps of amazement from the crowd, along with claps, shouts of joy, and even scoffs coming from those filled with skepticism. Veru had expected that and prepared for it. Holding up her hands, she waited for them to quiet. "I'll admit, I am not Yu—my mother. My magic is weak compared to hers. But I will offer you what I can. In my hand, I hold a vial of the first draw from the well. My companion, Danik, will mix it with our own water from the pump and give all of you an equal share to drink or use as you see fit.

"Perhaps the magic will be diluted this way. Perhaps not. We have already distributed food and the flowers that sprung from the well. I see this as a sign. My hope is that all of you will benefit from it and have a blessing from the Flower of the Well come your way. But know this: If what you seek does not come to pass, return here, and I promise to do my best to render what aid I can."

As Danik mixed the water and those who remained formed a line to accept their offering, Veru placed her hand on his shoulder and said,

"Can you summon them and provide them with water in the following groups? First, I'd like to see the man who wanted his cattle to prosper and the one who needed his grain to grow hale and hardy. After that, I'd like to see the young woman looking for a husband and the three lonely widows whose sons are wandering."

Rubbing the stubble on his face, Danik grinned and nodded, listening closely as Veru introduced the first people called and spoke of how they might help one another. The man with cattle might offer fertilizer to the man with the grain, who in turn might provide feed and hay to the cattle. They walked off talking of a new partnership, both toasting the future possibilities with their jugs of water. Danik marveled that Veru never forced them together in any way. She just spoke to them of how she'd seen things successfully done in other villages, cleverly making it seem as if it their new partnership was their idea all along.

Then, with the next group, she somehow got the three widows to all offer up their homes to the beautiful girl, hoping she might entice their wayward sons to return home to settle down. The young lady was quite enthusiastic about the prospect of three eligible bachelors, especially with mothers-in-law all vying for her attention.

The man with a sick daughter was introduced to a medical student who needed a place to begin a practice. There were no guarantees that he could save her, but he was bright and energetic, and he wouldn't give up hope. His youthful enthusiasm would be infectious, and he'd lend that optimism to the parents and give them a reason to keep trying. In turn, they would give him a place to stay.

Again and again, Veru skillfully arranged partnerships among those who needed help, usually without them recognizing her efforts. The only one she couldn't seem to find a solution for was her silver-armored white knight, who had mysteriously disappeared for the duration of the day. No matter how she considered his problem—or her own, for that matter—there didn't appear to be a way to free him or her and Danik from the old woman's clutches.

When everyone was satisfied and gone, Danik and Veru toasted their success by downing a mug of the water themselves.

"What do you wish for?" Danik asked her.

"Do you mean other than a good night's sleep that isn't in a hard wooden chair?"

He chuckled. "You're welcome to bunk on the floor with me."

She gave him a quick, piercing look but saw no hidden agenda behind his words. It almost made her feel melancholy, especially as she remembered his rejection of her before. It was puzzling. No man had ever been uninterested in her. To be fair, it had been some time since she'd bathed or brushed her hair. In fact, she probably looked a mess.

"What do *you* wish for?" she asked, avoiding answering his question.

"Hmm, would it be wrong to say I'd really like a bath?" he asked, echoing her thoughts.

Veru laughed. "I was going to say the same thing."

"Then wish granted." Danik stood up suddenly and looked around. "It will be much warmer out here than inside the house. Not to mention there'll be privacy. Let me see what I can scare up."

"Privacy?" she scoffed as he disappeared inside the little house. "Did you forget all the people who were just here? I'd say this porch is anything but private."

"You just leave it to me, Tsarevna," he called out.

Veru began unknotting her braided hair, wincing at the tangles and the sticks and weeds she found twisted in them, and sincerely hoped she wasn't going to find any bugs. As she worked, she heard the movement of large pieces of furniture inside the house.

"What are you doing in there?" she called out.

"Don't worry about it," he said.

There was a hiss and a meow, and Max ran outside and sat at her feet, licking a paw furiously, obviously irritated.

"Did he step on you?" she asked, stroking the cat's head. "Poor kotenok."

Danik appeared just then, carrying what looked like a huge copper bowl. It was even larger than the stone dish the old woman had taken with her. The thing barely fit through the closet door.

"Think it'll do?" he asked. "The house thought it might."

"I'll make it work," Veru said, eyeing the large pot. "What on earth do you think she used this for?"

"No idea. It's heavy though. Had its own stirring spoon, but I left it in the secret cupboard. Apparently, the house is full of them. Didn't think you'd need the stirring rod since you're not making soup of yourself. Here. Brought you some salts and soaps. Choose what you like while I bring out the water."

Danik brought out pails full of steaming water from the cauldron inside and tried arranging the dried blankets still hanging on the porch to give her a semblance of privacy. She shooed him away and fixed them herself, almost creating a private room on the porch. The last thing he did before adding just one bucket of cold water to offset the hot was to set a clean blanket on the little stool next to the tub so she could dry off.

Stripping off her now worn and torn blue gossamer dress, Veru gingerly stepped into the steaming bath and sank down as low as she could. It wasn't nearly as roomy as her old tub back home, but it was large enough to at least get her limbs wet, so she commenced scrubbing herself clean. She set to work right away, lathering the large cake of soap into her hair, wincing at the astringent smell, hoping it would at least stave off vermin and insects. It certainly wasn't the pleasant floral scent she was used to, but it would do to get her clean.

When she was finished, she dunked under the water, getting as much soap out of her hair as possible. With bubbles still dripping down her shoulders, she found herself missing her maid and wondering if she should consign herself to staying soapy, when she noticed that Danik had left her a bucket of warm, fresh water to rinse with. Grateful for his thoughtfulness, she stood in the tub and carefully poured it over her head, getting all the soap out of her hair and off her body before stepping out and wrapping the blanket around herself, using it to squeeze the excess water from her hair.

"Danik?" she called out. "I'm finished. If you want a go, it's all yours," she said. "I'll bring you a fresh bucket to rinse with to return the favor."

"That would be wonderful!" he said.

"Thanks for letting me go first," she said, her body cocooned by the blanket. "Next time you get the first turn."

"I don't mind," he said, removing his shirt and ducking around her, not even paying attention to the woman in the blanket. "I just hope the water is still warm."

"It should be," Veru replied.

She heard a splash and exited with her back to the tub so as not to catch a glimpse of his naked form. Her face colored as she picked up her clothes and hurried into the house. Veru's breath froze when she entered the cottage, and she realized for the first time all day just how cold it still was inside the little home. She'd nearly forgotten. Quickly, she threw the last of their logs onto the fire and danced on the floor, hurrying to put on the knitted stockings Yuga had given her.

After she adjusted her blanket, she headed back to the summer porch and cleared her throat outside the makeshift bathing chamber.

"Um, Danik? Can you pass me the bucket so I can bring you some rinse water?"

"Here you go."

His very wet, naked arm appeared, holding the bucket, and Veru couldn't help herself. Her eyes trailed up the arm to his handsome face. His blond hair was dark and slicked back from his forehead. With his eyes closed, she felt braver and let her eyes drop down from his stubbly bearded cheeks and chin to his chest.

Veru had worked and sparred with many soldiers and thus had seen many chiseled male forms in various stages of dress. She'd schooled herself well to take no notice of it, and in most cases, she never did. To her, seeing a well-built male was much like seeing a well-built stallion. She appreciated such a creature and could even admire it and recognize its value, but never did it inspire feelings of lust.

With Danik, there was something different. It wasn't that his body was particularly muscular, though he was certainly much larger in the chest than she'd anticipated. Veru had always considered him to be on the thin and lanky side, but perhaps that was more due to her having seen him through the eyes of a tiger. Any man would look small when compared to a tiger.

Where the copper tub had been sufficient to hold her legs and allow her to clean her body, it barely contained him. His long legs hung over the sides, giving her a good view of his heavy thighs. Her gaze traveled back up those legs to the dark water hiding the bits of him she couldn't see but was somehow very curious to, and her lips parted. Veru jumped when the bucket moved against her hand, and her eyes locked with a set of stormy ocean-blue ones. She was suddenly very aware she was as naked as Danik.

As she tried to leave, he refused to let go of the pail. Once again, she felt as if she were caught in a trap, but this time she had stepped into it willingly. She could let go and hop out of the pit anytime, but there was something about this hunter; it was his voice or perhaps the way he looked at her. She kept circling him, getting closer and closer. Instinct told her it would be the death of one or both of them. Veru could almost feel the snarl of the cat tickle her throat and the claws curl her fingers. She narrowed her eyes, preparing to pounce.

Quietly, not in his musical or soothing tones, but in a voice of warning, he said, "I am not a piece of string for you to play with, little kotenok." He let go of the bucket, and she faltered back a few steps. The blanket fell into place, shielding him from view. She stood there, silent, thinking about what he'd said. Then she heard him speak again. It was almost a whisper. She could hear the sorrow in his tone. It reminded her of when he had to kill an animal. "When a string breaks, the instrument can no longer be played."

Veru didn't understand. Danik thought . . . he thought she meant to injure him? *Does he fear me?* If so, why? He had called her kotenok. Perhaps he was remembering her time as a tiger. Veru had frightened off many a man in the past, that much was true. She was formidable, even deadly, when brandishing her knives, but Danik had never seen that. Or maybe she had it wrong. Maybe he thought he was going to hurt her, like he did the animals he hunted.

Whichever one it was, it was clear he wanted Veru to keep away from him. Whether it was to protect himself or her, she didn't know. It was even possible that Danik didn't know the reason, or didn't remember it, but Veru didn't think that was the case. He seemed pretty certain about his feelings. If only Veru felt as sure of her own.

Turning, she said, "I-I'll bring you some more water."

She hurried to ladle hot water into the bucket, adding only a bit of cold, and slid it next to his tub without another word, then sat in her chair finger-combing her wet hair, wishing for a hairbrush as hot tears slid down her face. She had meant it when she'd called him her companion. He was more of a true companion to her than Nik or even her sister had been in a long time. Danik's quiet ways were soothing. He was kind and gentle. But perhaps her perspective had been tainted by a cat's perspective.

Maxsim climbed in her lap and began to purr, making her wonder what his feline view of her might look like. What did he see when he glanced in her direction? A weepy, bedraggled woman? A tsarevna trying to do her best to keep herself and her hunter alive? Did he see the missing cat she'd lost? Could he know where her tiger was? How Veru could find her again?

Veru didn't speak to Danik again that night, choosing instead to curl up in her blanket in her chair while petting Max and trying to sleep. She kept her back turned to her traveling companion. But even when his peaceful snores filled the little home, rest still eluded her.

The next morning it was Danik who woke her. Veru had a beast of a headache. Her eyes felt sticky, and it was painfully obvious to her that she wasn't wearing anything beneath her blanket. Her traveling companion, however, appeared to be in the best of spirits. He was dressed in the same clothing he'd worn the day before and somehow looked refreshed despite the fact.

"Here," he said. "Eat up. You've got visitors."

"What?" Veru said, rubbing her eyes and adjusting her blanket as she took the bowl of leftover porridge. "Who?"

"Your admirers are here, and they're bearing gifts. I took the liberty of bringing in this bundle now. I thought you could use it. Your other dress is washed and hanging on the line outside. I'll leave you here to change in peace."

Danik headed toward the secret cupboard door that led to the summer porch but turned before shutting it behind him. "There's a fresh bucket of hot water by your chair with some soap and a clean cloth. See you outside."

Veru nodded her thanks from the depths of her blanket but doubted he could see the slight movement. The door closed behind him with a snick, and she hurried to inspect the bundle of fabric he'd left her. It was a new skirt and blouse, leggings, a knitted sweater, and the finest pair of stockings and boots she'd ever seen. When she lifted the skirt, the most delicate undergarments fell onto the chair as well. They looked to be made of butterfly wings and were embroidered with pink flowers.

Usually, Veru rejected such feminine wares, preferring the standard undergarments worn by soldiers. They were durable and warm. These would hardly serve a purpose, as scanty as they were, and yet knowing they were a gift from the grateful townspeople, she took the time to run her fingertips across the embroidery and admired the craft and the effort it took to create something so lovely.

Dropping the heavy blanket, she washed quickly and donned the slips of fabric and found she quite liked the way they molded to her body. The stockings were warm but smooth and silky and attached to the undergarments with tiny buttons. It was quite cleverly done. The skirt and blouse were heavy but well-made and fit her perfectly, and the sweater was as soft as a newborn lamb. The ribbons that tied it around her shoulders could be easily untied so when she was overwarm she could hang it nearby.

Since she couldn't brush her wild hair, she let it hang loose, then ate a few bites of breakfast, leaving the rest to Maxsim, and headed outside, excited to see what the new day would bring. Veru opened the door to find Danik with his arms full of wood. It was stacked so high that it covered his face.

"Do you need some help?" Veru asked cheerfully.

"No. There's quite a line waiting to see you. Go meet with them, and I'll get to work on the house like I promised. It feels good to remember what I wanted to do today—seems I'm able to remember the things that are happening here, just nothing from the past. Maybe it's the magic of the house that's helping."

"Oh. Yes. Maybe." Veru stood there fidgeting for a moment with her hands. "Okay. But don't you think I should be in there helping you? Yuga did ask me to clean, you know."

"And you have. This is different. I'm not cleaning, really. I'm . . . restoring. That's different. You need to be doing the work with the people. You're good at it. I'll just be in the way. Now this load of wood is heavy. I'm heading in. Do skoroy vstrechi."

"Yes. Well . . . have a good day, then. With the house, I mean. Do skoroy vstrechi."

"You as well."

"Let me hold the door for you."

"Spasibo."

When he disappeared inside, Veru shut the door behind him and felt disappointed that he didn't want to spend the day with her. She tried to justify his desertion by telling herself that he was simply keeping his promise and not angry with her. Then she shook her head, wondering why she was acting like such a fool. She was a tsarevna, a spy, a soldier, and, until recently, a tiger.

Verusha Irena Vasilia Stepanov didn't moon after men. Or weep when they didn't shower her with flowers, chocolates, and affection. If Danik Andronovich desired a relationship of any kind with her, then he should be so lucky. And if he didn't . . . then so be it. She would seek friendship and perhaps other things . . . elsewhere.

Just then she heard a neigh, and the white-clad knight, Zarya, appeared. She gave a shout and raised a hand in greeting. He returned it and galloped up to the porch, then removed his helmet.

"Privet, my lady."

"Dobroye utro, Zarya. How do you fare today?" Veru asked, ducking just in time as his horse lifted his head to blast a golden-white pillar of flame in the air.

"I am well this morning. I wish to give my thanks."

"Thanks? For what?"

"For helping my people. You gave them guidance when I could not."

"It was nothing."

"It was not nothing. You showed you cared about them. You listened to them. You thought about their problems and made them your own. You prioritized them, worrying about them more than yourself. It's what a leader does. I wish to give you a token as a sign of my appreciation and gratitude."

"Really, it's not necessary."

"But it is." The knight lifted his leg from his horse and slid down, then reached into his cloak pocket and pulled out a wooden-handled tool. After he set it into her hands, she touched a fingertip to the sharp barbs on the comb end. At first glance she thought he'd given her a brush, which she could've sorely used, but she quickly realized this wasn't a hairbrush.

"What is it?" she asked. "It looks like something the weavers use, but I've never seen one quite like this before."

"You're right—it is used for weaving. It's called a spinning hatchel."

"Is it for wool or flax?"

"Yes."

"I don't understand."

"It's for wool, flax, reeds, vines, hair, moss, leaves, or just about anything you can think of."

"What?"

"It's a magic hatchel. It spins whatever you place into it. If you can conjure it, the hatchel can spin it. But I'll warn you—it is only to be used to create things of beauty. If you try to use it to make something deadly or dark, it will disappear. This gift is a gift of light."

"It's like you and your horse," Veru said.

The knight smiled. "That's right."

"I wish I had a gift of equal measure to bestow upon you." Her face brightened then. "Can I use it to spin a way to free you?"

Zarya shook his head sadly. "There is no spun magic strong enough to counter Yuga's chains, little one. But take heart—there is still hope for you and your man."

Veru gave the knight a smile. "Perhaps. Shall we go and see to your people, then?"

He nodded, and he and Veru spent the day greeting the people who came to see her. Many returned who'd left early before, hoping to hear some of her wisdom and perhaps get a little food and a bit of the water the others had managed to receive. Veru willingly shared what she could and matched up many people who needed help.

Other visitors came bearing gifts. Veru was surprised to realize that many weeks had passed in their time, though it had only been a day for her and Danik. The young girl looking for a husband had indeed found one, and she was more than a month pregnant with a doting mother-in-law. The family with the sick child was holding out hope thanks to a promising new treatment the new doctor was trying.

In addition to the new clothing, Veru was gifted with a newborn calf, baskets of fruits and vegetables, bundles of wool, bales of hay, and even a basketful of combs, hairbrushes, and hand-carved hair accessories. Each gift was received with great praise for the work and even hugs for the women. Two of the women even came forward shyly, clucking at Veru's hair, and began swiftly combing and braiding it for her as she sat talking with visitors. Never had she enjoyed diplomatic meetings as much as she did with those simple people.

When the day was nearly over, and everyone set out for home, Veru said farewell to her white knight and asked if she would see him again the next day. He surprised her when he said no; it would be his brother coming to visit her next, if she was indeed allowed to return at all to their summer haven. When he bowed and took her hand, placing a kiss on her knuckles, Veru felt emotional. She put her hand on his head and said, "Bless you, good knight. If there is a way to save you, I vow I will do my utmost."

"Spasibo, my dear, dear lady," he said. With that, he clicked his heels, mounted his horse, spun, and rode off into the sunset.

Veru dashed the tears from her cheeks and turned toward the door on the summer porch, but standing in it, framed in its light, was Danik, who stared at her with the strangest expression. If she wasn't mistaken, he was grinding his teeth. Her normally easygoing, sweet-natured friend was livid.

CHAPTER 18

You Can Get Used to Anything—Even Hell

"Can't you do anything to stop this?" Stacia yelled above the squall as their dirizhabl'—or Rackapelterly Aeroflation, as Stribog called it—twirled dangerously like a child's toy held under a giant's thumb. Each one of its passengers clung tightly to the ropes as the dark and threatening sky pressed heavily against them.

Zima cried as she held on to Stacia's leg. "It's not me!" The poor girl wept frozen tears that rained like sleet down her pink cheeks. Soon her lips and eyelids turned blue, then purple, and the clouds puffed up darker and rained slush on them to match her mood. As her voice choked out a sob, they heard the crack of thunder, and lightning streaked across the sky.

Stacia's dark red hair was plastered to her neck and cheeks. Her own lips and fingers felt as icy cold as little Zima's. She wrapped her heavy coat around both of them, but it didn't serve to warm them at all. They were quickly drenched. "Zakhar!" she yelled, trying to reach him through the storm. "Zakhar!" she tried again.

The priest turned to her, squinting in their direction, and took a few steps closer, trying to hear them through the storm. "I fear we're going to be lost!" he cried.

"What?" Stacia shouted.

"Lost!" he screamed. "We're being dragged off course!"

"But didn't they say we could use the storm? Ride the lightning somehow?"

When he didn't understand her, she tried to gesture to him by moving her hand like a snake and then twisting her other fingers to hop on top of it and zoom away. But she had to grab for the rope again as the balloon lurched suddenly. When she righted herself and steadied Zima, she thought she saw the spark of understanding catch in his eyes. He quickly turned about and began adjusting levers and buttons.

"Brace yourselves!" he cried loudly.

Crouching down next to the girl, Stacia wrapped her arms around her and said, "Hold on to me tightly, little one. We're going for a ride."

"But we're already on a ride," Zima said before plugging her thumb back into her mouth and closing her eyes.

Stacia nodded to Zakhar, who turned to the sky, watching carefully.

Zakhar had no idea if such a thing would work. Truthfully, the very notion that one could "ride a bolt of lightning" was something out of an old wives' tale. Such fantastical stories and superstitious practices that were still observed among townspeople, especially those born in the smaller communities, were very difficult to eradicate.

Zakhar and his brethren always found themselves at odds with old traditions and belief systems, and they struggled to implement the new Christian ways of doing things. What would his brothers think to see him operating a contraption such as the one he was in now? He'd be lucky if he wasn't immediately excommunicated. After saying a quick prayer and asking his Lord for forgiveness, ending with the sign of the cross, Zakhar spotted a streak of lightning and pressed the button, turning the lever indicated at the same time.

The little switchboard hummed to life, and he shrieked as the lightning bolt switched direction midair, turning toward them instead. The buttons he'd been pushing lit up, and the hair on his arms, legs, and head stood on end. He'd only a fraction of a second to think, *What have I done?* At the same time, he was mouthing the word, "Amen."

He never got to finish his prayer, though, because the air around him crackled and sparked, as did his fingertips. Never in his entire life had he felt such energy. It practically filled his frame. He was acutely aware of his own heartbeat, and there was an itching sensation all over his skin. It was as if time somehow slowed. Zakhar heard a hum in the air; then there was a pop, and he heard nothing at all for several seconds.

A scent tickled his nose. It reminded him of the cleaning solution he used to wipe down the church pews. Then there was a taste in his mouth, as if he'd been sucking on the coins left in the collection box. He wondered if he'd killed them all. Perhaps they were dead, and this was what the resurrection felt like. Or maybe he was being changed into spirit, like the Holy Ghost. That wouldn't be so bad. To be a thing filled with the power of God.

But what if he hadn't been good enough? He had been questioning much as of late. If anything, the quest he'd been sent on had certainly tested his beliefs, his faith. What if the energy he felt was not the glories of heaven but the fires of hell? Was having doubt enough to send him *there*? Zakhar didn't think he'd done anything worthy of hellfire and damnation, but he knew there were those who believed the merest deviation, the simplest infraction, or even defying your superiors would qualify.

Zakhar didn't consider himself authorized to decide who was and wasn't going to heaven. He figured it was up to God. Even men smarter than himself still argued over minuscule points of scripture, so who was he to tell them who was right and who was wrong? Still, at that moment, he feared he hadn't done enough. How could he ascend to God's throne, look Him in the eye, and say, "I did my best," and "I deserve a seat at your table?" The very thought filled him with shame and made him want to "hide under a rock," as the Scriptures noted.

It wasn't that Zakhar was a bad man; he just wasn't godly enough. Not for a priest, anyway. He hadn't even joined the clergy for the right reasons. All he'd wanted was three meals a day. What kind of man did that make him? He closed his eyes and consigned himself to his fate. At least he knew God was merciful. Perhaps He would allow Zakhar to do penance. *Maybe a forty-day fast?* Zakhar didn't think he'd survive that either. His stomach rumbled immediately.

"I can't do it, Lord!" he shouted.

Then the lightning hit.

Everything turned white. The ship stopped turning and began moving forward, faster than he believed possible. They bounced slightly, like a rock or a pebble skimming the surface of a still pond. Quickly, they passed beyond the storm and were deposited down on the outside of it. The lightning bolt fizzled away. They fell a short distance and were then caught by the air as they stabilized. In the distance, they could see the storm raging—all purples, grays, and blues. They had moved away from it, but the weather was still unbearably cold, and clouds still covered the horizon as far as they could see.

Stacia stood, removing her sodden coat, and waved her hand over the burning cresset, igniting the blue flames. They stood around it, trying to warm their hands and faces. It would take forever to get warm. Picking up the bag of sunshine, she opened it and inspected the contents, not sure how to use it. Seeing nothing of interest inside, she shook it out over the edge. When that didn't work, Zima said, "You have to throw the whole bag overboard."

She climbed up on a box, held out her little hands, and when Stacia handed her the bag, she closed the top and twisted it shut. Though Stacia had seen nothing in it before, this time there was clearly a bouncing ball moving around inside. With a heave, Zima tossed the bag as far as she could. The minute she did, the wriggling ball broke free and burst outward in all directions, pushing away the clouds, dissipating them until they could no longer be seen. Warm sunlight filled the blue sky, and steam began rising from the ship.

"Thank you," Stacia said to Zima, giving the girl a wink. "And thank you, Zakhar. It's a good thing you were paying attention. You really saved us back there."

"Yes," Zakhar said. "Paying attention." He spun and picked up a sodden paper map, barely clinging to the side of the vessel. Tracing his finger across the blurred lines, and studying their position, he said, "But we're further from the mountains than before. It'll take longer to get back. Especially if we have to skirt the storm."

"The snail will come, but who knows when it will arrive?"

"What's that?" Zakhar asked.

"It's just something my mother used to say. It was her way of telling us to act. Not just wait around for things to happen."

"Right." Zakhar gave Stacia a lopsided grin, then turned back to the controls. "Tsarevna," he said, "speaking of not waiting for things to happen, we, umm, aren't moving."

"What?"

"Yeah. It seems without the birds or the wind, we don't go anywhere. At least not anywhere we want to. The wind blows us around a little, but not in any particular direction. There's no way to control it. We just end up where we end up."

"So what do we do?"

Zakhar shrugged. "I don't know. Wait for them to find us?"

"Use the bag," Zima suggested.

"What?" Stacia said.

"The nose bag. The one you trapped the rabbit with."

"But those birds are a good distance away."

Zima shrugged. "Couldn't hurt to try."

Stacia nodded, and Zakhar opened his soggy pack and found the nose bag.

Loosening the tie that secured the opening, he said, "Collect some birds."

Within the span of a few seconds, birds of all types began darting toward the balloon, careening to the open bag and diving inside. Once in, they screeched and banged themselves against the sides. At first it was only small birds, then larger birds appeared, including falcons, hawks, and owls. As they, too, joined the group, the bag grew larger and larger. Slowly, it filled the space where they stood until they began to be crowded out.

"Make it stop," warned Stacia as she threw a leg over the side.

"You can stop now, bag," said Zakhar, but the bag kept on collecting. Bird after bird soared into the bag, filling it to bursting.

Zima began crying as the creatures bucked and screamed inside. She was certain some of the big ones were killing the smaller ones. Stacia suspected she was right. The tsarevna grabbed the little girl just before she was crushed against the side of the vessel and pulled her into her arms.

"That's enough!" shouted Zakhar, climbing on top of the bag. He attempted to pull the opening tight and close it, but it wouldn't stop.

Then he tried a different tack. "Now set the birds free."

Hundreds of birds poured out of the bag. Zakhar yelped as he fell halfway inside it. Many of the birds had cuts and torn wings. Some flopped brokenly on the deck of the ship. Others never made it out at all. Their lifeless little bodies remained inside the bag, and Zakhar removed them one by one, tossing some overboard. Others he kept, intending to roast them for supper.

Zima turned her head, unwilling to look at the little birds and cried herself to sleep in Stacia's arms. When the job was finished, they saw the nose bag had returned to its normal size. Stacia quietly counseled Zakhar. "Perhaps the trick is to be specific and only request a small number at a time."

The priest nodded and tried again, opening the bag. "Bring me ten of Sima's birds, making certain to give them enough room so that they are not harmed."

It took some time, but eventually ten little birds arrived and flew into a stretched-out bag. They circled inside, coming to no harm until Zakhar told the bag to release them. He experimented with larger and larger numbers until he found he could hold up to two hundred small birds without endangering them. Once they had what they felt was approximately enough winged creatures to pull them, they set off on their journey once again.

"We've wasted a lot of time," Zakhar said, "but at least we're headed in the right direction."

That night for supper they roasted birds to eat along with their barley and rye pottage. Zakhar even pulled the meat from the bones and made something of a stew out of it. But poor little Zima took one look at the dinner and refused to eat any animal meat. In fact, she warned them the nose bag should never be used to summon animals in such a way again. "It just wasn't right," she said.

Stacia and Zakhar agreed as the sky darkened overhead. They feared another storm would hit if the little girl's despair was not mollified.

They mutually agreed to let her have an entire biscuit to herself while they ate the stew. Unfortunately, when they turned around to search for the biscuits, the snow-white ermine, Belizna, in her desperation to get at some bird meat, knocked over the entire pot and began eating. With their dinner in the dirt, Zakhar and Stacia contented themselves to fast until they could make another pot of porridge for breakfast. Zakhar seemed determined to spend the evening in prayer, saying things like, "The Lord is indeed merciful," and, "One meal is not too much to ask for a spot at the table."

Zakhar handed the biscuit, which was now becoming hard, to Zima and sat back, pulling his knees to his chest. "My brothers and I used to make trips to feed the hungry children," he said. "We kept only the simplest of fare for ourselves. What I wouldn't give for some good black bread, cheese, and sbiten," he said. "A hard biscuit isn't much for a little girl."

"Stop," Stacia said. "Now you're making me hungry."

"What would you like? Right now? I mean, if you could have anything?"

"I don't know. Ginseng tea sounds nice."

"Huh. I've never had that."

"It's imported. Very rare. Oh, speaking of rare. Beluga caviar. Toasted bread with a bit of fresh butter, a very thin slice of salmon and caviar on top. Then you take a bite and just let it melt in your mouth."

When Stacia opened her eyes, she found Zakhar staring at her mouth. She frowned and grew slightly uncomfortable. His cheeks colored all the way down to his neck.

"F-forgive me," he said. "I've just never had such a dish. It sounds . . . intriguing."

"Well, if we ever make it back to the palace, you're welcome to come try some. My sister doesn't like it. She's got a sweet tooth. I was never much for sweets. My preferences tend to skew toward the savory."

"S-sweets?" Zakhar's voice squeaked. "Such as what? I'm afraid we give up most delicacies in the brotherhood and keep to simple fare."

Stacia frowned. "But your stores held plenty . . ."

"Oh yes. That is true enough. We have more than enough to eat. But like I said, it's not elaborate in any way. Just your basic everyday items. But you were saying your sister enjoyed the palace sweets?" he prompted. "Such as?"

"Oh, you know. She had her favorites. Trubochka, ponchiki, bliny, pastila—she loved most everything. Nikolai knew it, and he would often ply her with sweets when he wanted something, which was all the time." Stacia laughed. "I swear, he knew every merchant in the empire, especially those who specialized in chocolate or candy making."

"What's chocolate?" asked Zima.

"Shokolad," explained Stacia. "And why haven't you eaten your biscuit yet?"

"The two of you aren't eating," the little girl said. "If you can't eat, I don't want to eat either."

"But we're older, milaya devushka. We can do without a meal or two. But you? You still have some growing to do. Don't you want to get big and strong?"

"Oh, I'm never going to get any bigger. That's what my aunties say."

"What do you mean?" asked Stacia.

"I'm the snow child," she said simply, putting her thumb in her mouth.

Just then a wagon seemed to appear just outside their camp. It was drawn by two large horses. When they came to a stop, a very pregnant woman, her husband, and their two young children approached.

"May we share your fire this evening?" asked the husband. "My wife is nearing the blessed day of our next child, and it would be nice to save a bit of time and spend it with her instead of hunting firewood."

"Of course you may," Stacia replied.

"Spasibo. My name's Fyodor. My wife's Dinara, and our two young ones are Klara and Kiril."

"Rad vstreche," Zakhar said.

"To you as well," Dinara replied, groaning as she sat down, leaning back against the wheel of their wagon. Her husband hurried and placed some blankets behind her back and tucked them around her, then sat the children next to her and put thin blankets around them as well, before tending to the horses.

They all warmed their hands. "It's so chilly tonight, isn't it?" Dinara said. "But your fire is toasty. We're lucky, aren't we, kroshkas?"

"Yes, Mama," the two children replied.

They buried their little faces in the blanket, and soon the father passed them a small cup and a piece of bread. "It's all we can spare," he said, whispering to his wife.

The mother smiled brightly at her children anyway. "Look what your handsome papa has brought us!" she said. "A cup of milk and the softest bread in the world! He must love us more than anything, da?"

"Yes, Mama," the two children said as they looked up at their pretty mama with hope-filled eyes.

She broke off the largest pieces for them, saving only a tiny bit for herself, then took a sip from the cup and made sure each child drank down a good share.

Before Stacia could intervene, Zima got up with her saved biscuit and walked over to the group. "I have an extra biscuit," she said quietly. "Would you like some?"

The mother-to-be smiled her softest smile. "Well, aren't you just a ray of blessed sunshine on a bitter cold night? Thank you, sweetheart," Dinara said.

Stacia could see the sparkle of tears in her eyes. When Zima turned as if to leave, the mother shifted, opening her blanket. "Come, child.

Would you like to sit with us? We'll dunk your biscuit in the milk to soften, then we'll all have a bite, da?"

Sucking her thumb, Zima smiled, nodding vigorously. The woman didn't complain about Zima's cold skin but tucked her in close against her own body, along with her children. When the father returned, conveniently just after the food was finished, he pulled the little boy onto his lap and scolded all of them about keeping the warm blankets to themselves. He put his arm around his wife, and the children asked for a story.

Stacia said, "Before you begin, we have grain. We can boil some up for you or put on a pot for the morning, if you like."

"We're well enough off tonight," the father said. "Perhaps in the morning we'll take you up on your kind offer. Now, then," he said. "Shall I tell you the story of 'The Duck That Laid Golden Eggs'?"

"Oh yes! That's one of my favorites!" said Klara.

"I don't know that story," said Zima.

"Well then," replied the father, "you're in for a treat. Especially if you're fond of birds."

Zima began to cry. "I love little birds. But so many of them died!"

"Oh no, my dear one," the mama said, pulling Zima close. "You must remember that little birds are special. They never stay dead for long. It's why they have wings, you know. God turns them to angels right away. He doesn't even need to judge them. They're already perfect."

"They are?"

"Absolutely. They're His best little souls."

"Which is why, in my version of the tale, the duck wins. Every duck has his day, you know. Didn't deserve to get eaten, in my opinion. Are you ready for the story?"

Zima nodded, her eyes wide, and the father began. "A long, long time ago, there lived a very poor family. The papa named Abrosim, a mama named Fetinia, and a young man named Ivan. When their last crust of bread was stolen by a sorrowing spirit living behind their stove, they begged her to return it. She refused, but instead promised to send them a very special bird . . ."

Stacia could feel her eyes drifting shut as she listened to the story. She didn't know when she fell asleep, but it was dawn when she woke. The fire had burned down to just embers, and she realized it was her trembling body that had woken her. Zakhar was still sleeping nearby, snoring lightly, so she glanced over at the place where the wagon and the family had been the night before, only to find them gone.

Throwing off her thin blanket, she stood, wobbling as she rubbed the sleep from her eyes. The only sign that the wagon had been there at all was a blanket left in the snow, covered by a thin layer of white powder on top. Stacia dashed over to it and saw neither footprints, horse prints, nor even a trail of wagon marks. It was as if the family had never existed at all.

Crouching down, she dusted the snow from the blanket and felt a form underneath it. Gasping, tears filling her eyes and panic making her choke, she hurried to lift the edge of the blanket, thinking she'd find Zima's lifeless body. Then, when she saw the little girl suck on her thumb and take a breath, the steam coming out from around her thumb, the relief was so palpable that her hands began to shake and the tears spilled out, blurring her vision completely.

Stacia cupped her arms beneath the child and lifted her up, carrying her back to the fire, and got it going hot again, then began cooking their breakfast. The smell of hot food, even if it was barley and rye, roused Zakhar. It took him a moment to realize the wagon was missing. Stacia put a finger to her lips to shush him, pointing to a still-sleeping Zima.

He spoke in low tones. "Only a snool would leave in such a way."

"A snool?" Stacia couldn't help but grin. "The old man left in the same fashion, and you didn't suspect him."

"That's right. I normally welcome strangers. But twice in a row is becoming suspicious. What did they steal? I fear we are being taken for fools. We are carrying magical tokens. We must be more careful."

Stacia didn't like to admit she hadn't even thought about what they might have stolen. She'd only cared that Zima was safe. "I don't know," she admitted. "You're right though. We need to be more wary of strangers."

Just then a sleepy Zima rolled to a sitting position. "They didn't steal anything. They were nice to me," she insisted.

"I know you liked them, sweeting. We just want to understand why or how they disappeared."

"They didn't need to be here anymore."

"What do you mean?"

"The test was finished. They gave me my gift."

"Gift?" Stacia said. "What gift?"

"This."

Zima held out what looked like an hourglass, but it was more intricate and elaborate than anything Stacia had ever seen. Whorls of silver, gold, and brass flowers adorned each side, and on the top was a sort of clock or compass, but the handles were spinning of their own accord. The very strange thing was, there was sand on both ends—white on one side and dark as ebony on the other—and neither one flowed into the other. It looked like they were trapped on either side of the glass and couldn't mix, and yet both of them flowed.

"What is it?" asked Stacia, handing it back to Zima. The little girl shrugged. "Mama said I had to be careful with it. She called it the Glass of Death."

CHAPTER 19

A Clear Conscience Makes a Soft Pillow

"Though I suppose saying 'appearance' is giving you a bit too much credit," Nik said to the invisible specter.

The other two men at the table gave Nikolai a horrified look, and Eldar mouthed, "What are you doing?" While Andrey whimpered and said softly, "Please don't make him mad."

But Yuri, the ghost, didn't seem to be mad. In fact, he laughed again. "Oh, I plan on appearing a great deal more after this, young man, especially now that you've discovered the key. I suppose I should thank you for that."

"Oh?" Nik said, sorting his cards. "And why does that have anything to do with your ability to"—he screwed up his face as if searching for the right word—"transmew?"

"Because, as my pravnuk here likely knows, that little tin box doesn't hold the title to this dilapidated old house or the directions to any hidden treasure. No. He already owns the land, and if there were any money to be found, he would have already discovered it. My great-grandson, you see, is after something more. Something bigger."

"Is that right?" Nik said, turning over a card. "Trump is diamonds. I attack first. Your move, Pravnuk."

Eldar stuck out a trembling hand and swallowed, a visible lump in his throat bobbing up and down. He gathered his cards and played one to defend the attack. Nik attacked again. Soon it was Andrey's turn to attack. The poor man was sweating profusely. He put down a card, and the ghost to his left defended. He put down a second, and no card was played.

Nik took that opportunity to ask, "I know the stakes *we* were playing for. I'm assuming you'd also like to play for the right to open the tin box?"

"Not at all," replied the ghost. "I cannot open it. I rely on human hands to do that bit for me. All I care for are the contents."

"Why can't you open the box? Obviously, you're able to manipulate corporeal elements. You're playing cards with us as we speak."

Nik felt a breath of cold air wash over his face. It was fetid and reeked of all things rotted and decayed. Lifting his collar to his nose, he coughed once, trying not to gag, and then took a few steadying breaths before lifting his mug of sbiten and sipping.

"The tin is protected. It was locked and sealed by my lady wife. To open it, one must have earned her favor. And I, unfortunately, have never earned that. Not in my mortal lifetime. Nor will I earn it in the hereafter."

"But what does it contain?" Eldar pressed.

"Is it a map to treasure?" asked Andrey.

"He already said there's no money," Eldar said.

"But money and treasure can be two different things," Andrey replied.

"That much is true," replied the ghost. "But what is inside the tin is much, much better than anything you can possibly imagine."

"Better?" said Andrey. "What's better than treasure?" His face brightened. "Oh, I know. Gold!"

Eldar cuffed him on the back of the head. "Same thing, durak."

"Life," Nik guessed.

"Life?" echoed Andrey. "What do I need that for? Already got it."

"Perhaps not for long," the ghost said, chuckling as he played a card. "Aren't *you* playing for your life, Nikolai?" he asked.

"Indeed I am," Nik replied, defending the attack.

Eldar then took a huge number of cards. The play continued in silence until the draw pile was exhausted. Finally, it was down to two players: Andrey and the ghost. Back and forth they went, until Yuri put down a card, and if Andrey could have played, it would have been a draw. Unfortunately, he couldn't.

The ghost said, "It appears as if *you* are the durak, my sad little friend."

"Yeah . . ." His face fell, but then it brightened. "Yeah! Means I win, don't it?"

"No. I'm afraid you lose." The knife rose in the air and then whipped back and forth in two quick slashes. Blood gushed from Andrey's throat, and he clutched at it, then slipped from his chair to the floor.

Nik gathered the cards and began shuffling. "Was that fair?" he asked. "You didn't negotiate the stakes before gameplay commenced."

"Nothing in life or death is fair, is it? Didn't a great man once say, 'Not being able to pravit the world, I pravit myself'?"

"Is that what you did to your children?" Nik accused. "You governed them to *death*?"

The table holding the cards began to shake.

Eldar pleaded, "Nikolai, stop antagonizing him!" Turning to the ghost's chair, he said, "He didn't mean anything by that, Praded. He was only . . ." The knife rose in the air again, and the tip pierced Eldar's neck. A drop of blood trickled down his throat.

"Keep quiet, boy, if you want to live," Yuri warned. "Remember: I have no problem killing my own flesh and blood."

"Why?" Nik asked.

"Why, what?" asked the ghost, picking up his cards.

"Why did you do it? Kill your children."

"You think I wanted to?"

"Are you saying you didn't?"

"Of course I didn't. Why do you think I'm here, haunting the place? It's because *she* won't let me leave. Won't let me forget."

Nik paused in the middle of the deal. "You're saying *Mama* keeps you here?"

"That's right. She forces me to relive all the horrible things I've done, over and over in some sort of countervenge."

"Then why do you want her box?"

"Ah!" the ghost replied. "Because that's the ticket out. You see, my wife was something of a witchy woman. A long time ago, she told me that the tin holds a spell—her greatest one, in fact. I once overheard her tell our children that the one who inherited it would be a lucky soul indeed, for whoever did would obtain their true heart's desire. And my heart's desire, my boy, is to live again. Why? So I can leave this place once and for all. I want to start over and forget my old life, these children, my wife, this town, everything. The only way to do that is to open that box."

Nik nodded thoughtfully and picked up his hand.

Eldar turned over the first card in the stack. Queen of Hearts. "I attack first," he said.

When half the round was played, Nik said, "I still don't understand why you had to kill your children. I know you abused your wife, and she killed herself. Then you wanted to cover it up and remarry. Did you do it because you couldn't find another wife?"

"I did find another wife, and a third after that. The problem was, each wife went crazy. Driven that way by my first wife's ghostly visits. The second lasted just two years and the third only eight months. The townspeople started suspecting things after that. My first wife cursed me.

"After my third wife's death, I lost the respect of the town and my position, especially after seeing the bruises on her wrists when she was buried. I told them I had no choice but to tie her up, to protect her from herself. They saw how she caused her own death by throwing herself out the upstairs window. I was even telling the truth that time, but I could see they didn't believe me. I knew it was just a matter of time before they came for me."

"I might believe the window, but I don't believe the wrists. I've seen the show, Yuri. I know you abuse women." Nik defended two attacks, then played his own. "How did the kids end up chained under the house?"

"The crying wouldn't stop. It started off with me just trying to scare them silent. Then it got so quiet I forgot about them. Two of them died from no water. After that, I knew it was over for me. The town would never let me go free after that. I chained them up and waited for them all to go. My oldest was the last. Couldn't bear to do the deed myself. Would have been kinder. Least they all had each other in the end. Then I hanged myself from the same tree where I found my first wife dead. Only one of the children survived. I never could remember how many I had. Apparently, he hid."

Nik continued to play, thinking about the dead man's story. It wasn't that much different from his own. He, too, had feared being discovered. True, he hadn't been the person doing the abusing, but he had committed murder, accidental or not. Just like this man, he had killed innocents. He was no better than this ghost. Weight pressed down on him, and he remembered how the little man he'd met, Pasha, had told him he carried a sorrow on his back. He imagined it was fairly huge at present.

After a few more attacks, Nik said, "Well, at least we know the stakes. It seems we're playing for our lives, Eldar. He needs one of us to open the box. Best of luck."

The big man nodded. As he played, he alternated holding his cards in one hand and wiping his sticky palm on his pant leg with the other.

Soon the ghost played his last card. "I'm out, boys. Let's see which one of you gets to live."

Nik set down his cards. "I forfeit. It should be your kin," he said. "If you really want a fresh start, then try doing a kindness to your kinfolk. And while I got a say, I'd like to raise the stakes."

"You would, would you?" the ghost said.

"Yes. No matter what you do, or who wins, let us bury those poor kids first. Mama wants it done. It won't hurt you none."

"If you're thinking that once you're out in the yard I'll have no power over you, you're wrong. I can kill the two of you faster than the time it would take for you to reach the tree. You'd be dead before your body even hit the ground. I owned this town and this land. My roots run deep."

Eldar whimpered and began sweating profusely.

"I wasn't thinking of escape," Nik said smoothly. "Were you, Eldar?"

The other man shook his head and squirmed. He looked like he was about to faint.

"Good," the ghost replied. "Is that all, then? Is there anything else you want to add?"

"No. That's it," Nik answered.

"Very well. I'll agree to your terms."

"Otlichno." Nik relaxed in his chair and continued playing. Out of the corner of his eye, he thought he saw the fire burn just a little brighter for a few seconds and imagined his gesture had made Mama happy.

"But I want you to finish the game first. No forfeits allowed."

"Fine. Just so long as you know that Eldar wins in the end."

"Didn't I just say no forfeits?"

Nik scowled.

"That's fine with me," Eldar said. "I don't fancy ending up the sluga for my praded."

"You will if you want to live, boy."

"He'll do as you ask," Nik said, warning Eldar with raised eyebrows.

Eldar set down a card. "Let's just see how it plays out, shall we? I'm sure I can beat him."

Nikolai knew it didn't matter. He'd win no matter what. He was using the magic cards given to him by Pasha. He didn't think he could lose if he tried. In fact, when he attempted losing, it backfired. Eldar played even worse cards than he did before.

"You've got to be kidding me, Eldar," Nik said when he won attack after attack. "What kind of chepukha hand were you dealt? Or are you just that bad of a player?"

"Hey, you're the one with the gift. The one who never loses. Remember?"

Eldar and Nik played furiously until, finally, they neared the end.

Both of them only had a few remaining cards. Nik attacked, then Eldar. Then it was down to one card apiece. It was Eldar's turn. Whatever card he held would decide both of their fates. He smiled widely. He had a high trump card left—the Queen of Clubs. There were only two cards that could beat it. He leaned forward, his hands clutching the table so hard his fingertips turned white. Nik sucked in a breath and played one of the two—the King of Clubs. It was a draw. It was the best Nik could do without stomping him.

"What—what happens now?" Eldar asked in a shaky voice. "Do we play another round?" he suggested hopefully.

The knife that had dropped away from his throat lifted again, first pointing at him, then turning to point at Nik.

"Well," the ghost said. "Since we've decided to bury the children, I suppose it will go much faster with two. I've waited this long. I suppose I can bide my time for just a tad bit longer. Come along. Let's get this over with."

They all rose from the table, careful to step around Andrey's chilling body, and headed outside. Nik obtained shovels from the shed, and they began digging underneath the old tree. Once they had moved enough earth to hold all the little bodies, and Andrey's, they began moving everyone to their new resting place.

The job took most of the night.

By the time they were finished, Nik was dead on his feet and nearly ready to crawl into the hole right next to Andrey's body. Instead, Nik picked up his shovel and scooped dirt on top of him. He was about to turn and ask Eldar if he thought they might be able to catch a few hours of rest when he was hit over the back of the head. The world spun. One minute he was looking down at Andrey's dead body, half covered with dirt, the next, he was lying on top of it, looking up at the leaves of the tree. Then he closed his eyes and could see no more.

Nik's dreams were mercifully dull. He slept deeply and long and only woke when he was jostled smartly on the arm.

"Wake up. Wake up! Surely I didn't cuff you that hard!"

To his horror, Nik found he was slow of speech, drooling, had blurry vision, and was indeed sleeping next to the very dead, very cold, and now putrid-smelling Andrey. Flailing his arms and legs in a vain attempt to extricate himself from the shallow grave, Nik managed to flop over like a dead fish, which only served to put his drooling lips on top of the dead Andrey's, causing him to finally gag and vomit a bit into the dead man's mouth, which upon seeing it, made him vomit even more.

At least it served to rouse him fully from his stupor, and he stumbled from the dirt at last and thrashed his way to a standing position. "What? What did you do to me?" he managed to ask as he tried to straighten his clothing, brush dirt from it, and wipe vomit away from his person all at the same time.

"I figured if I knocked you senseless, the ghost would let both of us live. Turns out, I was wrong."

"Wrong? What do you mean?"

Eldar sank down to his knees. "You should run. Run while you can."

He fell, turning to his side, and that's when Nik saw the knife plunged into his back and the other stab wounds that leaked blood down his shirt. Reaching down, Nikolai pulled out the knife and rolled Eldar over, only to see his eyes had already turned glassy. He was gone.

"Why did you do that?" Nik asked. "Why did you kill your only kin?"

"I told you. I don't want to remember. Keeping him alive is just a reminder of the past." The leaves on the tree began to quiver. "Now, do as I say. Bring me the tin and the key. Stand here under the tree and open it. Then read me the contents of the spell. Be quick about it, boy!"

His leg still slightly twisted, Nik limped back into the house and found the box and the key he'd put back inside the nesting dolls. Taking them outside, he paused at the door and said, "If there's anything I can do to stop him, Mama, then make it known to me."

Clouds had gathered, and cold sleet began falling, leaving icy rivulets trailing down the sides of the house and the trunk of the tree. He stood beneath a heavy branch and lifted the box to the sky. "It's here!" he shouted. "I'm opening it now!"

"Help me, Mama," he murmured.

Inserting the small key in the tiny lock, he turned it, and the top of the box popped open. Inside the box, he found a rolled scroll of paper wrapped around a stick. Again he felt a shock of cold, fetid breath on the back of his neck. "Read it to me," Yuri mumbled in the storm. "Read what gift shall be mine."

Careful to keep the paper away from the rain and sleet, Nik unrolled it and began to read.

Dear One,

Herein is contained that which you desire above all else.

It is more precious than diamonds, gold, glory, fame, or even love.

I hope you can use it to start anew and find happiness.

Know that I will always
watch over you,
Mama

The gift is . . .

Nick turned the paper over to see what was written on the back.

Forgiveness

Flipping it over again and again, Nikolai read and reread the letter until his vision blurred with tears. It was as if it had come from his very own mama. Could it be that this mama had somehow given Nik the thing he wanted most in the world instead of Yuri? He collapsed to his knees, sobbing. "Oh, Mama," he cried. "Mama," he said, over and over again. "I'm so sorry. I love you."

"What is this?" the ghost said. "Why are you crying? You want Mama's forgiveness? You think this is a gift?" Yuri shouted. "I don't care if you forgive me or not, old woman! I don't forgive you! You have trapped me here for decades. You think you have suffered? I have suffered twelve times over! I had to see our dead children, not you. I had to stay behind and care for them when you left. You should be asking me for forgiveness, eh?"

While Yuri kept yelling, Nik got up, found a bag with all his things packed at the bottom of the house steps, stuffed the tin and the nesting dolls with the key inside, and said dosvidanya to Mama.

He'd only just exited the town and entered the woods when he heard a familiar voice.

"Hey, kid."

"Pasha?"

"That's right."

"Whew! I thought you were going to try to shrink that thing. You haven't been gone for more than a week or so. I know I'm a little late, but I thought the time without your power would do you some good. What could you possibly have found in there to make a sorrow grow like that?" Pasha climbed up on a stump and began probing Nik's back and shoulders.

He tried to push the one-eyed man off. "So you're responsible for this? It figures. I thought you were coming for me! What happened?"

"I got caught up in a gig. Couldn't help it. Anyway, you're a big boy, aren't you? Don't need a nanny."

"No, I don't. So clear out, would you? Just leave me alone," he demanded.

"I'd like to, but first off, it's hard to look away from that thing on your back. That sorrow looks like a tick that's been dining on a blood blister. It's like a giant slug waiting to explode." When the little man slid down, Nikolai noticed a strange look on his face.

Trying to ignore him, Nik started walking, and the man followed, saying, "Reminds me of this one time I found a pustule growing on me backside. Raw and red, it was. Festered something fierce. Very difficult to excrete. Couldn't quite reach it, you see?"

Spinning, Nik said, "That's quite enough explanation. Thank you, though, for the very vivid imagery."

"You're welcome. Now, seeing as how you failed your task, I believe you owe me a debt as well as my cards back. I'll be taking those now, thank you very much."

"Er, your cards?"

"Don't tell me you lost them. Not my lucky deck."

"Uh, no. Let me just check my bag."

Rummaging through the bag, Nik began to panic when he didn't find them. Then he had a thought, opened the nesting dolls, and took out the key. When he inserted it in the little tin box, he found the same paper with the note as before as well as the lucky deck. "Whew! Here they are," he said, handing them over.

"They'd better all be here," Pasha said, riffling through them. Picking up a card and sniffing it, he winced. "Killed a few people with these, I see."

"Not my fault," Nik said. "The ghost did it. And only one was during the card game."

"Haven't you learned yet, boy? Everything in life is a game. I told you, didn't I? Walking away with your dignity intact, shaking hands with everyone at the table, that's how you play. Don't matter if you win or lose. Don't matter what hand you're dealt."

"Yeah? Well, nobody ever said anything about playing with ghosts!"

"Ghosts? What are you doing playing with ghosts? Can't trust the likes of them."

"It's not like I set out to do it."

"Yeah, well, didn't learn much, did you? Same lesson still applies." He sniffed again and grunted.

"Shows what you know. I won forgiveness in a deadly game. That's not bad."

"Yeah. You're right. Not bad. Not bad." Pasha kicked Nik in the shin.

"Ow! What did you do that for?"

"Because! You're letting a precious gift like forgiveness go to waste. Here you are letting your sorrow suck the life out of you while you carry around a trump card like forgiveness in your pocket and never play it. I suppose it serves me right for letting you go off on your own. The young people of today are idiots. What a waste. If I had your wiry frame, your hair, and your, ehm . . . let's just call it vim and vigor, not to mention your two eyes, coupled with my vastly superior mind and experience, why, there's no telling what I could accomplish."

"Hold on. Letting me go off on my own? Pushed me, is more like it."

"Are you still dwelling on that when I'm talking about vim and vigor, boy? You really need to pay attention to the important stuff. Besides, you say apples, and I say apples. Now then, as to the terms of our agreement. I believe we said something to the effect of you shrinking that sorrow and I'd reunite you with your friends. I was generous too. Gave you much longer than a week."

"You did. Yes. *Very* generous."

"And that if you didn't, you'd do something for me."

Nik sighed. "Right. Yeah. Well, what did you have in mind?"

"Oh, not much. Not much," Pasha said, rolling back and forth on his large feet.

He scratched his head. "It's just that, well, my gal has made up with me, and she says I never take her anywhere. I told her to name the place and time, and she did. She wants me to take her to the Games."

"The Games?"

"Yeah, the Games. There's betting. Food. Lots of action. It's a real good time. The thing is, she's got this sister."

"Wait. What?" Nik started backing away. He put his hands up and shook his head. "No way. No! Absolutely not!"

"I'll cover all the costs. I'll rent us some nice transportation. You'll have a lovely time. I promise!"

"You're kidding me, right? Tell me you're joking."

"Sorry, kid." He held up two fingers. "You should know that Pasha

Pogodin never jokes about two things—women and gambling." He paused and put up a third finger. "Also, food. Can't forget food. Not necessarily in that order. Come on, boy. We've got dates waiting."

"Pasha! I said nyet!"

"Come along, mal'chik who doesn't deserve to be young! Let's see some bounce in your step. Vim and vigor, lad. Vim and vigor!"

CHAPTER 20

Keep Your Ears Wide and Your Mouth Narrow

"Danik?" Veru said. "Are you quite fine? You seem . . . you seem off. Are you perhaps overworked? What's vexing you?"

He let out his breath and stepped aside. "It's nothing, Tsarevna. I simply hit my thumb with the hammer."

"Did you? Let me see."

"Nyet. It's fine. Ne volnuysya. Don't fret. Go inside. I need to cool off out here for a bit."

"Cool off? But it's cooler in the house."

"Just go. I'll be in soon."

Veru shrugged and moved past him to enter the house. To say she was shocked at the transformation was an understatement. He certainly had been busy. The stone fireplace had been cleaned to the point that it looked almost new. The grate and tools gleamed as if they had just been polished. The stones were no longer black but a light gray, and the heavy mantel was stained and glistened in the light of a new fire.

The tables, chairs, and floors had been cleaned, repaired, sanded, and oiled. Where there had once been water damage and rot, she saw new boards and a white coat of chinking sealant. She didn't understand how he could have accomplished so much while she had been outside. Such a great deal of work should have taken him weeks.

Veru went to the little door and opened it. "Danik?" she called out, searching for him in the dimming light.

"I'm here," he replied.

"How did you do so much in one day?"

He shrugged. "I don't know. It was like the house wanted to be clean. It helped me. At least, I think it did. Anyway, nothing new for supper tonight. I scraped up the rest of the porridge and already ate my share. Left the rest in the bowl for you."

"That's okay. I brought in a few baskets of things the villagers gave me. The cow is tied up outside. I gave her the hay. The chickens and ducks are grazing on the lawn. There might be eggs in the morning."

"That's fine. Let's put the rest in our bags. The house wouldn't let me bring in more than one log today. I think it's trying to tell me something."

Veru agreed, and they stuffed their bags full, each eating a few pieces of fruit and feeding Maxsim some dried jerky. They had just laid down to sleep when the locked door blew open with a bang, and Yuga entered carrying her large stone pot and stomping on the newly cleaned floor with her muddy boots. The winter wind outside blew in wet snow that melted in puddles around her feet.

Lifting her long nose in the air, she inhaled deeply and clicked her tongue with great dissatisfaction. "The two of you are still alive? How is that possible? What's more"—she ran a finger down the length of her table and rubbed her thumb over it, sniffing carefully—"how were you two able to clean this place?"

Yuga thrust her heavy bowl onto the table, scratching its surface and making Danik wince at seeing his newly repaired work abused. "Max!" she bellowed. "What have you done? You traitorous feline! I'll teach you to offer aid in my absence. You know better than that. Cheating is what it is."

"You want to talk about cheating?" Veru stood and accused. "You left us without food and water. You locked us in the house where we couldn't even get outside to retrieve firewood. You're lucky we aren't dead."

"No. *You're* lucky you aren't dead. Speaking of that, where exactly *did* the two of you get the firewood to warm yourselves? Did you break all my furniture and burn it? Others have done that before you. There's a price to pay for that, I'll have you know."

"We didn't break your furniture, Babushka," Danik said. "You'll find it all here. And I'll thank you to be taking better care of it. Spent all my time restoring it for you, and I'd like it to stay in nice condition, if you don't mind."

The old woman narrowed her eyes and stalked over to every table, chair, and cabinet, running her hands over each one and mumbling to herself as she did. There was a meow, and Maxsim leaped up onto the table next to her. She grabbed him then and felt his stomach. "He's fat! You've been feeding him more than bones, haven't you?" she accused.

"You did say he feeds himself by hunting rodents. Didn't you?" Veru asked innocently.

"Hmph," Yuga replied as she pushed the cat away from her. Max walked over to Veru and jumped up on her lap, kneaded her with his paws, and turned in a circle, then lay down and began purring.

"Come now, Babushka," Danik said in a soothing tone. "You've had a long trip. Why don't I play some music while you settle in and we'll all sleep. Then, when you wake in the morning, you'll feel much better. I promise."

"Very well, boy," Yuga said. "Play me a song, and tomorrow we'll discuss the payment for your stay."

Danik and Veru gave each other a meaningful look—one that said they both knew they'd been lucky, and they'd better keep quiet about how the house had helped them—then Danik pulled out his domra and began to finger the strings. He played random tunes for a time but didn't add his voice until Yuga climbed into bed. When he began to sing, Veru was surprised, since it was a song she hadn't heard before.

Fading Embers

In the shadows of my memory,
I can feel your soul so clearly.

But the warmth has now gone cold,
like a story left untold.

Every touch and word we share,
echoes of a love declared.
If I spark, ignite this flame.
Will it prove a vicious game?

Fading embers I once knew,
in a world that feels so new.
Just two strangers turning pages,
trying to break out of our cages.

But maybe all this is a dream.
Perhaps we'll wake beside a stream.
Recall the place where once we fell
as we sought a tale to tell.

Fading embers I once knew,
in a world that feels so new.
Just two strangers turning pages,
trying to break out of our cages.

Fading embers in the night,
fill me, heal me with her light.
Fading embers set me free.
In her arms, I want to be.
But everything's . . . fading . . .

"Oh, Danik," Veru whispered. Her words were so soft she was certain the only one who heard her was Max.

"It's a pretty song, boy," said Yuga. "We'll see if you still feel that way tomorrow. Sleep well."

With that, the old woman rolled back and forth, making her old, rickety bed creak and groan loudly in protest, and then grabbed her stirring wand that protruded from her stone pot, which she'd placed on the floor next to her bed and wrapped her arm around it, cradling it to her cheek like a young girl would a doll, and then began to snore loudly. Veru settled back into her chair, managed to close her eyes, and even slept when Maxsim purred loudly, vibrating his body on her lap.

The next morning, Veru was determined to confront the old woman once and for all.

"We thank you for your hospitality," Veru said bluntly, "but we really need to be moving on. As for payment, we've more than sufficiently paid you for our stay. You asked us to clean your home, and we did as you asked."

Babushka Yuga seemed very pleased with herself. She even hummed as she stirred whatever concoction she was making over the fire. "Oh yes. I agree with you, dear. You certainly kept your end of the bargain. My home has never been this clean. As promised, you are free to leave. You'll find the door unlocked."

"Thank you," Veru said.

Before the old woman could change her mind, Veru picked up her bag and headed to the door. She sucked in a breath and twisted the knob, then let it out when she found out it opened. Turning back to offer a winning grin to Danik, her expression of happiness faded into one of confusion when she saw him still standing in place with his bag over his shoulder. She gave him a meaningful look, but he simply shook his head.

Yuga paused. "Oh, didn't I mention? The agreement was for you only. Your man must stay until he accomplishes a task of his own."

"You're kidding me. Another task?"

"Of course, you're more than welcome to aid him. I imagine he helped you a great deal in finishing your work."

The old woman giggled, dipped a finger into the pot, and tasted her stew. "Not quite finished yet. Needs a few more ingredients, I think."

Veru threw down her bag. "Okay, let's put all our cards on the table, shall we? I don't like games."

"And I don't like cheaters."

"The definition of *cheating* depends on the rules. If you don't define the rules well, it's not my fault. I can see you're one who likes to change the rules mid-game, according to your whims, to affect the outcome. You're going to have to be"—Veru leaned forward—"very explicit; otherwise, we are allowed to win your so-called game any way we must. Our lives depend on it, after all."

"Oh, please. Don't be so dramatic. You haven't been hurt, have you? Both of you look hale and hearty to me."

"Nevertheless. If we're going to negotiate, let's negotiate properly. I want a contract."

"Bah! I never put anything in writing."

"You will this time."

"And why would I do that?"

"Because I'm going to offer something you want in exchange for something I want."

"You don't know what I want."

"I certainly do."

"And what's that, young woman?"

"A lifetime of servitude."

The old woman paused and sniffed. "You'd willingly offer up yourself and your young man to me for the rest of your lives?"

"Only"—Veru held up a finger to illustrate her point—"only if we lose."

Yuga narrowed her eyes. "And if I lose? I assume the two of you go free?"

"Oh no. Not just that," Veru said. "I think you'd better sit down."

Veru had been trained by a master negotiator. Never ever do you go into a negotiation asking only for what you want. No. You go in asking for the moon and the stars and the sun and the planets and then when items are removed, you act as if each thing is terribly painful. In the end, the other person should believe they are getting a bargain when, in fact, you are giving only a fraction of what you were willing to part with, while they are giving away much, much more than they were ever wanting to give in the first place.

Also, never show your hand before they show theirs. They lay down their cards first. Never commit to anything until you're sure you've seen everything. This one was wily. Veru would have to work at her best to beat her at her own game. If only Yuga was a man, Veru could use her other considerable "talents" to distract her. If she were doing this at home, it wouldn't be Veru who was sent into this negotiation, but her mother, or Stacia. They always did much better when it came to women. But there wasn't a choice. Veru would simply have to succeed. There wasn't another option for them.

She closed her eyes for a moment, trying to steady herself and remember all the rules of engagement her parents had drilled her in. She could almost hear her father's voice. "Just remember: If they are not willing to pay the price you desire, then you simply stop the transaction. At the end of the day, you should always be seen as the one having the most valuable commodities. Thus, more traders will want to strike bargains with you in the future."

Unfortunately, Veru didn't think this particular situation was one she could simply get up and walk away from. If she could, she would have. She didn't trust Yuga and would normally have tried to follow her instincts, but she didn't see another way out of their situation. Taking a breath, Veru, having found a pot of ink, a quill, and some paper, began cataloging a long, long list of what she wanted from Yuga, including everything she could think of, citing all the items she'd come across while staying, as well as things she hadn't seen. Obviously, she put down freedom for herself and Danik, but she also added changes of clothing for each of them, two weeks' worth of food and supplies, money, transportation, information, a map, and even added the house, the stone pot Yuga seemed to love, and her cat, Maxsim.

It was when she thought to tack on the freedom of the knight, Zarya, and his brothers that she got into trouble.

"Aha!" the old woman said. "I knew you had help. That mischievous rascal Zarya must've been passing you victuals and wood through the window. I knew I should've bolted it down. Ah, well. Lessons learned."

"You're a miserable wretch. Has anyone ever told you as much?" Veru said bluntly.

Yuga laughed, and it was a dreadful sound. "Usually not when they want something as much as you do. In most cases, I deal with flattery."

"I prefer honesty."

"As do I. Though you aren't terribly familiar with it, are you, my dear?"

Veru stiffened. "I'm not sure what you mean."

The old woman snorted. "Come now. No need to pretend with me, Princess. I wrote the book on deceit. I may be practically blind and old, but I can see clear as day, and you, my beauty, are about the shiftiest little thing to ever have sat in that particular chair. In fact, the only way I can pin you down is to have Maxsim hold you in place, and that takes a powerful charm, believe you me."

Narrowing her eyes, Veru bit her bottom lip. It was one of her tells, and she typically had to force herself to avoid doing it, but she allowed it now since she knew the old woman couldn't see her anyway. Glancing down at the cat in her lap, she stopped petting him and purposely picked him up and set him down on the floor. He meowed and rolled to his side and began licking his paw as if he didn't care.

"How interesting," Veru said demurely. "Do go on. I find what you said fascinating."

It was one of her catchall lines that she'd memorized long ago when she didn't know what else to say. She was sure it wouldn't work with the old woman, but she figured it would at least buy her some time to come up with something else. Luckily for Veru, the woman chose to further explain.

"The boy was easy. Wasn't much left there to find. Just a nudge here and a push there, and I was able to get all I needed from him. But you? You're a much harder read. Shifty. Like I said."

"Am I to assume by all this that you are implying you can read our minds?" Danik asked.

"There's no implying about it, boy," Yuga said. "Let's call it one of my gifts."

Danik pressed, "And what exactly are you seeking?"

"Not the secrets of the universe, if that's what you're worried about." Yuga snickered in a condescending tone, and Veru frowned. She didn't like how the woman was treating Danik. It was as if he was too simple-minded for her to take notice of him. From what Veru knew about the young man, he was anything but simple. He was a man of deep feeling. Danik was sensitive. He noticed things. Things that others didn't.

Veru's parents had taught her that intelligence shouldn't be measured by certificates, degrees, power, money, or anything else most people put stock into, but that it should be weighed more by how a person observed and evaluated the items that impacted their worldview. This meant that wisdom could be found just as much while seated at the feet of a humble sheep farmer as it could listening to a clergyman. That answers might be sought at the table of a baker making rolls or at a table of diplomats.

She knew that there was a difference between intelligence and knowledge. Natural gifts and talents could be something one was born with, but if a gift wasn't developed, it could decline or never develop its potential. On the other hand, a person with a mediocre ability could work hard and practice until they became a master craftsman.

Knowledge could be taught, but it didn't come only from teachers and mentors. She'd seen some develop great gifts on their own, simply by reading. Others would take to the mountaintops, meditate, or commune with the skies until they achieved wisdom or enlightenment. This, also, was knowledge that descended from above, dropping like dew from the heavens, to bestow truths upon the minds of those who diligently sought answers.

"If a person wanted to discover the secrets of the universe," Veru said, "I would think someone capable of and willing to unlock the mind of a hunter who loves animals might just be worthy of such a treasure."

Yuga pursed her lips, wrinkling them as she considered first Veru and then Danik. Then she shook her head and smiled craftily. "Ya get nothin' for free, young miss. Told you flattery won't work on me, pretty though the words may be."

Veru folded her arms. "That wasn't flattery. That was truth."

"Bah. Let's get on with it. Now I've heard your exhausting list. And in exchange, here's mine."

She started listing things on her knobby fingers, but Veru stopped her immediately by grabbing her hands. "Before you continue, you should know that the eternal servitude is the only thing we're putting on the table. You demand anything else, and we're done."

"Is that so?"

"It is."

"What if I were to offer up something else? A prize you didn't consider?" she tempted.

"Such as?" Veru asked.

The woman drummed her fingers on the table, considering. "Tell you what—I'll agree to your terms. In fact, I'll give you everything you've asked for, including the aforementioned prize, if the two of you agree to complete not one but three more tasks before I return with the ingredients I need to finish this potion I'm making."

"Tell us the tasks, and we'll decide if we agree."

"Very well. Since you've been helped by my knights—and losing them would prove a huge loss to me—the tasks will be associated with them. If they are meant to be freed, then perhaps the tasks will not be so hard for you, eh?" Yuga began cackling, and it made the hairs stand up on Veru's arms.

"The first task is to take this cup and dip it into the water where the white knight's emblem rises each day. Then fill my barrel here with the water. The second is to shear all the sheep guarded by the red knight, then weave it into a bolt of cloth. The third is to take this jar of white sesame seeds and this jar of black sesame seeds and give them to the black knight. While he holds them, you will be allowed to gather the wheat he watches over.

"When this is complete, he will allow you to come collect the sesame seeds once more, which *you* will then return to me, along with the wheat. Once I have all these items in my possession—the water, the wheat and sesame seeds, and the cloth—your tasks are complete and you will have won your freedom, along with the prizes you have stipulated and the gift I have promised you."

"And you'll put all of this in writing?" Veru asked.

"I will."

Veru turned the paper to the woman. But when she said she couldn't write, as she couldn't see well, she proceeded to dictate her words and had Veru copy them down for her, trusting that the tsarevna would complete it, as she put it forth after she ensured such by murmuring a truth incantation. When Veru tested it by deliberately trying to write the wrong word, the ink kept drying up. The cackle from Yuga every time that happened told her all she needed to know. There would be no tricking the woman.

When all the items were listed, and the tasks were marked down in order, Veru pored over it, searching for traps.

"And we can accomplish these tasks in any way we see fit?" Veru asked.

"You may. If you enlist the help of my knights, then so be it." The woman smiled as she said the words, and a shiver went down Veru's spine.

"So that's it, then? We schlep water, shear sheep, and harvest grain."

The woman held up a finger. "And return the sesame seeds. Don't forget. I'll need those for my recipe."

"Right. Return the seeds, both white and black." Veru turned to Danik. "What do you think?"

"I've sheared sheep a few times. Grain is pretty easy. How long will it take you to gather your remaining ingredients, Yuga?" he asked.

Veru was ashamed she hadn't thought to ask that question herself.

"Oh, I'd imagine about the same length of time as the last. Maybe a bit longer. Will that do?"

"Depends on the size of the herd and the size of the field. Not to mention the amount of water we're talking about."

Yugas rheumy eyes twinkled. "Clever boy. Clever. Very well. The size of the herd—you can mark this down, girl—will be no more than two hundred animals. The barrel, you can see here, and the cup"—she picked up a wooden mug and slammed it down—"is right here. As for the water source, it's larger than a typical stream, smaller than an ocean. Now, for the size of the field . . . I'd say a team of oxen or horses could plow it in two days. Is that sufficient enough information for you?"

Danik nodded, then gestured to Veru. "Write it all down."

She did. When she was finished, the old woman said, "Now don't forget to add on what the two of you are giving up should you lose."

Veru thought about lying, about changing the wording, but she knew Yuga's spell would not permit it, so she wrote down the awful words:

> *If Verusha Irena Vasilia Stepanov and Danik Andronovich should fail to accomplish the three tasks set forth in this contract, then they agree to forfeit their freedom and remain servants to Babushka Yuga for the remainder of their natural lives or until such time as they are released, whichever comes first.*

Then at the bottom of the document, Veru signed it with a flourish and slid it over to Danik, who also signed. They spun it around to Babushka Yuga, who pretended to read it for a moment but then groped for the quill and sank it into the pot of ink before stabbing the paper with it and signing as well.

> *Verusha Irena Vasilia Stepanov*
> *Danik Rodion Andronovich*
> *Bony Shanks*

"Very good," she said, when she was finished. "I suppose all that remains now is for me to leave so the two of you can get started. As I said, your cup is here." Reaching into her bag, she took out two containers and shook them. "Here's one container of black and another of white sesame seeds, as promised. When you're visited by the knights, they can direct you to the field and so forth."

Picking up her huge stone bowl, she shuffled it through the door-frame. To their surprise, she climbed into it, picked up the large spoon and her bag, gave a command, and the bowl rose into the air with her inside. "I'd say good luck," she shouted back at them, "but it won't matter much. Keep 'em alive, Max. I'll have things for them to do when I get back."

With that, the door slammed shut behind her, and Danik and Veru were left alone again in the little hut.

"Danik?" Veru said.

"Yeah?"

"What have we done?"

CHAPTER 21

A Clean Fast Is Better Than a Dirty Breakfast

"No. Oh no. Did you say it was a Glass of Death? May I see it?" Zakhar asked.

Zima shrugged and handed it to him. Once he had his hands on it, Stacia could see he handled it gingerly, turning it over and over, carefully examining the device.

"I thought so," he said, after tracing his fingers over the clockwork piece at the top and mumbling to himself as he translated the inscription found beneath the levers. "It isn't a Glass *of* Death; it's a Glass to *Summon* Death."

"Summon Death?" Stacia said. "I've never heard of such a thing."

Zakhar set it down and wiped his palms on his pant legs. He seemed to be very, very nervous. "I wouldn't exactly call this a gift," he said softly, attempting to address Stacia and purposely exclude Zima. "It's more like a curse," he hissed in a whisper.

He angled slightly away from the little girl, trying to distract her with some breakfast first, then continued, "There are certain of us among our brethren who study, shall we say, forbidden relics. Items that would be deemed useful to those wishing to practice in secret orders. These clandestine groups that our brethren aid and even participate in can range from the mundane, such as those who might share an affinity for—for felines, for example, to those who worship things so dark and twisted that they would frighten even the bravest of heroes.

"I've even heard that one of the churches has an antiquarium of sorts in the basement. It's filled with all manner of antiquities and artifacts ranging from pagan gods and goddess idols to tokens representing physiolatry and paleolatry. Items said to be possessed of gramaryes. Then there are grimoires, books that explain alfridaria, others describing cults of the nullifidian order, that sort of thing."

"And is this particular relic something that falls into the dark and twisted category?" Stacia asked.

"Truthfully, I don't know if this would be an item considered good *or* evil. Perhaps it entirely depends on the wielder or upon how it is used. There are many such items."

"What . . . um, what does this one do, I wonder?"

"Mama told me it summons death. Like Zakhar said," Zima explained as she spooned up another bite of porridge.

"My you have big ears," Stacia chided.

"Can't help it when you're talking about me," Zima replied. "But if you want to know what it does, that's easy enough. I'll just use it."

Before they could stop her, she grabbed the timepiece and pulled it back to herself. Next, she adjusted the clockwork on top, angling the dials toward herself. Then, just as both Stacia and Zakhar shouted, "No!" she flipped it upside down.

They stared at it in wide-eyed horror as the white sand began mingling with the black, then the particles passed through one another. The black began filling the top and the white filled the bottom. Stacia covered her mouth with her hand while Zakhar said, ominously, "You shouldn't have done that."

Zima, who had simply begun eating again, replied, "There's no sense in worrying about something if you don't know the truth of things. It's better to find out. That's what I think, anyway."

Stacia felt like she couldn't breathe. Couldn't talk. Her whole body shivered, and she wished there was somewhere she could hide. She could almost feel death breathing down the back of her neck. She kept looking over her shoulder to see if someone was there, but nobody ever was. It was unsettling, to say the least.

Meanwhile, Zakhar had managed to scrounge up a pencil and tore off a section of map he could use to jot down notes. He was furiously scribbling even now. Stacia could find value in the fact that he could act when she was frozen in place, and yet how he chose to act bothered her. She knew the saying—"The sword lacks the power of the pen"—and she understood and even believed it, and yet there were many, many times when a pen was useless, a detriment even, as was the man who wielded it.

Didn't the Scripture say, "For everything there is a season, and a time for every matter under heaven"? Surely that meant there was a time to take up a sword and a time to set it down. The salt-and-pepper stream thinned, broke, and then stopped completely. Zima set down her spoon. Stacia felt her fingertips tingle. It always happened just before she entered a battle. But this time she was without a sword, without armor.

"Dobroye utro," a smooth male voice said. "How may I serve you today?"

Stacia spun, staggering slightly, and then managed to get to her feet. Standing there, between Zima and herself, was one of the most handsome men Stacia had ever set eyes on. His hair was dark, as were his eyes, which settled on her only briefly.

"Who are you?" Stacia demanded.

The man's eyes now looked her up and down, and she got the impression he found her lacking. "I don't answer questions to which the answer is obvious," the man replied. "Besides, I didn't come for you. I was summoned by someone else." He inclined his head to Zima. "Do you wish to know the past or the future?"

Zima blinked. "I don't know."

"I can only tell you one. Most people only get one. You get two. You're lucky. I'm going to be visiting you twice."

"Oh! I am lucky, then." She smiled, showing a dimple in her cheek, and the man smiled back.

Stacia sucked in a breath and thought if such a man waited to greet her upon her death, perhaps it wouldn't be such a bad thing after all.

Zima screwed up her face. "Past then, I guess. I suppose since I'm so young and all, my death is probably far off, if it will ever happen. My aunties say I'm never going to grow up."

"Do they now?" The good-looking man bit his bottom lip and rocked in his boots, then bent over and touched his fingertip to Zima's pert nose. "Well, who am I to contradict aunties?"

Giggling, Zima rubbed her nose.

"Okay," he said. "So you want to know about your past death. I'm not allowed to give you all the details, mind. Only clues, so to speak. That means you must pay very close attention. Understand?"

Zima nodded, her little face very serious.

"Good. Now take my hands. Hold on to them tightly."

He studied her face and then said, "I see . . . love, a family, sacrifice, a brave girl, toes pointing to the sun, a little boy, and a proud mother."

"Was I a mama?" Zima asked soberly.

"I can't tell you that, little one. What I can tell you is that you were loved and still are. You did not waste away or die in war. It was an accidental passing. You were younger than most. The most frequent question I get next is, when? As in, when will it happen? In your case, it doesn't much matter, does it? It's already done. I try to encourage most people not to ask it anyway. I find that when they know, they just dwell on the time they have left, and they stop living. What's the point of that? Life is meant to be kept; the purpose of it is to gain experiences, and to feel joy. Why grieve the end of mortality before it happens?"

"But . . . but there is an afterlife, isn't there?" Zakhar asked.

"If you want to ask me questions, you'll have to use the device yourself," the man said softly, not bothering to look at Zakhar. "But I'm not certain a conversation with Death is what you really want, is it, Priest?"

Zakhar swallowed, and Stacia could almost see him shrinking back.

Death squeezed Zima's hands. "Do you have any other questions for me, little one?" he asked.

"Yes. What am I supposed to do with your gift?"

Grinning, he said, "Not many would consider it a gift. I'm happy you do. I don't like to think of myself as a monster. You might be surprised to know that there are many who pray for me to come."

He turned at that moment, and his eyes connected with Stacia's.

She gasped as he gave her a small nod. *He knows!* she thought. Somehow he was aware of the dark thoughts she'd had just after the death of her mother. And when her sister was lost as a tiger, she'd prayed again for Death to take her. Stacia hadn't even told her sister. She hadn't been able to. Honestly, even if she had been, Stacia doubted if she could share such feelings. Veru was so sure of herself, so full of life. She didn't think her sister would understand the dark places Stacia went in her thoughts when she was alone.

Thoughts such as—how could she lead the empire her parents left behind? Stacia knew no one wanted her to lead. They wanted her beautiful sister, not a woman who fought like a man with hair redder than the flag. And besides, who would marry a girl who could outride and outfight them? Not to mention a woman who was a handspan taller than most men. Her mother had always said that it didn't matter what a woman looked like, so long as she acted like what a man expected, they'd get along just fine.

That was the problem. Stacia didn't want a man she had to change for. She wanted a man who respected her and one whom she could respect as well. Was it too much to ask for a man worthy enough to be able to look in the eye and not be disappointed? If not mentally, then at least physically? Stacia shook her head. Who was she kidding? She wanted it all. Someone smart, interesting, attractive, and tall. Such a man didn't exist.

And now, with her parents gone, there was no more time for her to look. A choice would have to be made and soon. Of course, that was assuming there was even an empire in existence, should they be able to return and reclaim it. They had mucked up everything. Royally, it seemed. But what else could be expected of twins who couldn't even decide which one had been born first?

Death began speaking again and caught her attention, his eyes narrowed as if he were reading her mind, studying her. "Though most think of life as a blessing," he said, "it is not always a kind or pleasant, easy journey. Yet all mortals must . . . what is the saying? 'Suffer the slings and arrows of outrageous fortune and take arms against a sea of troubles'?"

Stacia broke eye contact. No wonder she'd been courting Death. Apparently, she found him very attractive. He was just tall enough too. Suddenly, she felt all the sorrow accompanying her father's death come back, making her heart feel heavy. Was he doing that to her? Playing with her emotions? Reminding her of . . .

I'm so sorry, Mama . . . Stacia could hear her own voice whispering the words and see the ground far below as she stood on the parapet atop the highest balcony of the palace, ready to jump. She hadn't leaped into Death's arms that long ago day. Life had a way of intervening, as it often did, but she frequently remembered that dark time. In fact, she still had to fight to keep that darkness from consuming her.

The personification of Death laughed in that moment, and the vision disappeared. It seemed Zima didn't understand his words. "Never mind, dear one," he said. "What you do is simply what you just did. You use the device to summon me to someone's bedside. Leave the rest of it up to me. I'll take it from there."

He straightened and stood. "Now, as for the two of you. I'll tell you this once as a courtesy, lest you get any ideas. This gift was given to Zima for a reason. Knowing the details of one's own demise can be a comfort to those who are truly at death's door. But for those who are not, it can be . . . well, let's call it a millstone.

"The weight of that knowledge will burden a person for the entirety of their lives and can sink them into a dark place, where no one can ever find them again. There is a difference between knowing who you are and where you're going, between faith and purpose, and just driving toward a dead end. Think about that the next time you want to touch the hourglass."

Stacia wet her lips, which she found had gone suddenly dry. "We—we will," she said.

"See to it." Death stood up, dusted his hands, and winked at Zima. "Farewell, young lady. Use that gift wisely."

"I will. Spasibo."

"Thank *you*." He seemed about to leave, but then hesitated. "Oh, and just so the two of you know, there can be a great deal of healing found if one takes advantage of the—what is it called—oh yes, the Seal of the Confessional. In my experience, the roles of priest and parishioner do not need to be strictly adhered to for counseling to remain effective."

With that, Death disappeared.

"What, um, what do you think he meant by that?" Zakhar asked.

"I have no idea," Stacia replied. "Unless there's something you'd like to talk about?"

"No. Nothing on my end. What about you?"

"No. Not at all. Ya v poryadke. I'm in apple-pie order."

"Good."

"Khorosho."

"Otlichno."

"Let's go then, shall we?"

The little group was quiet and rather sober as they struck camp and climbed back into the balloon. Zakhar navigated, and they proceeded to move ahead quite rapidly, making up a good deal of distance. By the time they set up camp that night, he announced they should arrive at the mountains sometime the next day.

They camped near a rushing river, and Zakhar stood next to it and used the nose bag to catch a large salmon that leaped right out of the water. Belizna, the white ermine, was happy to eat any pieces of the fish that came her way. When they were finished, they all lounged by the fire, enjoying the warmth and their full bellies.

After they tucked Zima into her makeshift bed near the fire, with Belizna curled up in her arms, Zakhar offered to stay awake for a while to keep an eye out for strangers. Stacia and he had decided not to eat the last biscuit. They were full of fish and didn't need to, but they'd also agreed that if a stranger appeared again, they wouldn't simply offer it to them either, at least not without consulting with each other first. Stacia and Zakhar weren't sure the gift given to Zima was a good thing, though they both thought that the nose bag had come in handy.

After Stacia had slept a few hours, Zakhar nudged her awake, and then he rolled into his blankets and fell asleep quickly. To keep herself busy, Stacia decided to sharpen her only weapon: the staff given to her by the old man. Truthfully, she hadn't given it much thought at all. She never used a walking stick, and with Iriko at her side, she had preferred using his claws as weapons rather than the stick, but she had practiced stick fighting a bit when she was younger.

Pressing the hidden button that released the spearhead, she examined it carefully in the firelight. The carved bear with its open, roaring mouth had a hinge so delicate and detailed she couldn't see it or even hear it. And when she peered into the mouth when the blade was hidden, there was absolutely no sign at all that it was inside. The craftsmanship was excellent.

She'd found a stone adequate enough to sharpen the blade, but once it was exposed, she didn't have the heart to touch such a rough, everyday object to something so exceptional. The blade was almost jewellike. Stacia wondered if there was a whetstone built into the staff, because when she pressed her thumb to the surface, it bled instantly.

"Okay," she said softly, pressing the knob to shield the blade. "You don't need sharpening. Guess I'll practice instead."

Stepping away from the fire so as not to wake the two sleeping campers, she found an area clear enough and began working on some old staff techniques. Her heavy outerwear soon proved cumbersome, so she removed her coat, tossing it over a nearby boulder, just working in her close-cut trousers, her snow boots, and a long-sleeve blouse.

As she moved, her boots pressing down into the packed snow, twirling the staff from arm to arm, across her back, and thrusting it at invisible adversaries, her breath formed pillowy clouds in the frosty air. Picking up speed, Stacia twirled and dipped, using the staff as a launch device. It helped her push off tree trunks and kick higher, harder, faster, farther.

Then she began twisting it in her palm, quickly unsheathing the blade, then using the back of her foot to kick the staff the other way so the blade could be thrust directly into the heart of an enemy. Stacia practiced this maneuver over and over again until she felt confident she could use it if they were attacked.

Stopping for a moment, she twisted her arms and neck, shaking out her limbs, preparing to go again. She felt good. Warm, despite the chill in the air. A sheen of sweat had risen on her arms, and there was moisture in the little cleft at the bow of her upper lip. She licked them and rolled the staff over her forearm a few times.

Then she slipped on a patch of wet snow. Stacia quickly corrected herself and recovered her footing, but not before she nicked her other arm with the exposed blade. She hissed, feeling the sting, but it was nothing compared to the cuts and injuries she'd had before. In fact, the pain disappeared very quickly. She was about to start working again when her vision went blurry.

Stacia staggered, and the staff fell from her hand and landed in the powder at her feet. Then it was like a heavy coat dropped from her shoulders, and she felt lighter than she'd ever felt before. Her perspective shifted. It was almost like she'd boarded the balloon ship again and had risen a few feet in the air. Confused, Stacia looked at the campfire, a good distance away, and then down at the staff again.

Someone had fallen next to the staff. No! On top of it. And what was worse—the staff that was so very, very important to the shaman that it was only on loan was now broken in two! One piece lay on each side of the body. Speaking of which, why was there a body? *Did I kill a person accidentally?* Stacia hadn't heard anyone nearby. The light had changed. Everything was brighter. Different. Colors that had been muted suddenly weren't, and things normally bright were dull. Stacia focused on the fallen person. She couldn't see the face, but there was something about the hair and the boots. The hair was braided and . . . and red! It was her!

But . . . how? Stacia looked down and could still see her hands and her legs, but she was somehow floating in the air. *Wait!* Hadn't the White Shaman said something about the blade severing her from her body if it cut her? Oh no! What had she done? She should have been more careful. How was she going to fix this?

Help! Oh, help! White Shaman? Can you hear me? Death? she tried. But there was no answer.

Stacia had no idea how long she had floated there next to her body. It could have been minutes or hours. She watched as the limbs on her body grew blue, starting at the fingers. It was soon up to her wrists, while the tips of her fingers turned white. She knew what frostbite looked like and that there would be no recovery. Lowering her head, she despaired. How would she save her sister or Zima or Iriko now?

Was it not even a day ago she'd conversed with Death? Now it seemed he'd come for her, and Stacia was surprised to find she no longer wanted it. What had changed? She wasn't sure, but one thing was certain: Before she greeted the handsome Death again, there were a few items of unfinished business she had to take care of first.

"I'm not ready!" she called out to the bitter-cold sky.

Just then she saw a funnel of ice and snow appear at the edge of the woods. The trees nearby crackled as icicles grew on every limb and snow swirled about each one. Smaller branches broke and fell to the ground below. Out of the funnel galloped a huge white bear, and harnessed to him was a silver sleigh carrying a wizened old man.

"On, Lednik!" she heard the man cry as he flicked the reins. The bear roared and lifted his powerful paws, stretching his legs and sinking his claws into the ice as the sleigh slid along quickly behind him. Then the man pulled up and they came to a crashing stop, casting silvery snow that dusted Stacia's unmoving body with a fresh coat.

While the bear shook out his fur and panted from his run, the man climbed down from the sleigh and inspected her body. Then, to Stacia's surprise, he looked up straight at her hovering form.

"Well," he said. "You're caught in the valley between two glaciers, aren't you, my dear? The question is, which wall of ice are you going to climb, I wonder?"

"Who are you?" Stacia cried.

"Who am I? Who am *I*?" The man began laughing. "She's asking who I am. Can you believe it, Lednik? It's like her parents never read her any bedtime stories. Or perhaps they just weren't that important to her. Is that it?"

"Of course they were important to me. What has that got to do with anything?"

"It has everything to do with why you're here. And everything to do with who I am and who you are, for that matter."

"What? You've got to be kidding me! This uzhasnyy dreamworld of yours is nelepyy. I don't give furry rat's zadnitsa who you are or even who I am at this point. I just want to go home, okay? I want everything to go back to the way it was. I want my sister, my mom, and . . . my dad. I want my dad back."

The big man sighed and leaned on his cane. "Young woman. *Tsarevna*," he said more sharply, trying to get her attention.

To Stacia's shock, the world around her had blurred again. The deep heaviness was back. It was pulling her down, down, down to the dark place where she didn't want to go. While she'd been floating above her fallen form, she hadn't felt anything—not cold, not pain, not emotions. Now she could. The pain was flooding in, and if she couldn't find a way to hold it back, to numb herself from the waves, she feared she'd drown.

She heard the man say, "Look at me. What do you see? Focus."

Something about his voice helped her rise from the turmoil happening inside herself. She managed to see him the way her mother would, taking in all the details, from his clothing to the way his boots were polished. Stacia focused on his hat, taking the time to look at the jewels and the shape of the dome, the star in the middle, and the ice-blue color and how it matched his robe and belt.

She was able to figure out the value of his gloves, see they were made of the softest kid leather, and notice how his cane was taller than he was, that it was meticulously carved and that only one section was covered with ice. Next, Stacia studied his boots, his thick, heavy coat lined with white fur, and she saw how his thick white brows were neatly brushed, as was his mustache, which was as long as his hair and beard, which ended just below the belt.

Though she suspected who he was immediately, it gave her a great deal of satisfaction to catalog all the details, storing them away in her mind. It made her think of her father and her mother. She could almost hear their voices speaking to her as her thoughts worked through each piece of his clothing. That he didn't mind her scrutiny helped.

"You're Morozko," Stacia said at last. "Father Frost."

"That's right, young lady," he said, gifting her with a smile that softened the lines of his face. "And I have a question for you."

"Go on, then," Stacia replied, expecting the typical question that came in the next part of the fairy tale. He was right. She knew it well. A kind widower with a daughter had remarried, and the new wife hated the daughter, so she forced him to leave his girl out in the cold forest. With no other choice but to make his new wife happy, he did as she asked. When Father Frost came and saw the shivering girl, he asked if she was cold.

She replied, "No, I am warm enough." That night he left her a beautiful coat. This happened again. Each night he left her with gifts, jewels, and he eventually drove her home in his own sledge. The jealous stepmother then put her own daughter out in the cold, hoping for the same treatment, but her daughter complained instead and insulted Father Frost, calling him an "old man" and basically treating him badly enough he froze her.

When Stacia first heard the story, she asked her father why the father didn't put the stepmother outside instead. Her mother had laughed at that. Then Veru had asked why Father Frost liked a girl who lied and said she wasn't cold when she was. Why was that a desirable quality? She thought they were supposed to tell the truth. Stacia agreed with her sister. Their father hemmed and hawed a bit, saying something about humility and other such rubbish, but both girls agreed that the father should have been frozen for casting out his daughter.

Now here Stacia was, years later, wondering what her answer was supposed to be. When Father Frost asked, "Are you cold, child?" she could say something truthful like, "Hell yes," or "What the bloody hell do you think?" She could play the diplomat and answer, "Niggling, Father Frost. Worry yourself not a bit." Then again, she could say, "You do have eyes, don't you?" or simply answer, "Obviously."

Stacia didn't think she had it in her to say, "No, I am warm enough." She might as well shout to the sky, "No! I don't need a family. No! I don't care if I ever see my sister again. No! The empire my parents built means nothing to me. No! I don't ever want to see the real world again!"

As she hovered there, almost trembling with a deep-seated anger at the injustice of the world and at the uncertainty of her place in it, she waited for his question.

Finally, it came.

Father Frost asked, "Do you have anything for me to eat?"

CHAPTER 22

Don't Offer Advice to Those with More Experience

Pasha opened a passageway through the nearest large tree, grabbed Nik's arm, and yanked him through the portal. Nik found himself caught in a strange twilight dimension, where passageways and doorways of every kind surrounded them. If it weren't for Pasha, he would have no idea where to go or how to move. He relied completely on his strange guide.

After checking a few doors, Pasha selected one, twisted the handle backward and forward a few times and then opened it outward, peeking first to make certain it was the place he wanted to go. When he was satisfied, he tugged Nik along with him, and the two of them popped out of the in-between place and back into a forest, albeit a very different woodland than the one they had just been in before.

"Coach'll be here momentarily," Pasha said. "Gotta get you cleaned up before it arrives with the ladies. Hold still a minute." The man gathered some water from a nearby leaf, rubbed it between his hands, and began painting the air. Nik could feel his hair moving as if invisible brushes were working at it. Then his arms lifted on their own, and he suddenly had the sensation of his entire body being scrubbed by something that felt unmistakably leaflike.

"Hey!" Nik complained as the invisible force exfoliated his body, shuffling even his underneath clothes while his body still occupied them. "Cut that out!"

Then it abruptly ceased, and he was just about to relax, when a sharp, stinging sensation pulled at his cheeks. He realized his beard had been shaved away brusquely. "Ow!" he screamed, rubbing at his jawline in a futile attempt to protect it. "Stop it. I wanted to keep that! It was just starting to come in nice."

"Ha!" Pasha laughed. "Better nothing than that abandoned bird's nest you're tryin' ta pass off as a beard. Trust me. Keep shaving for a bit longer, and it'll start coming in thicker." The shaving finally stopped, but Pasha still wasn't done. Before Nik could guess what was next, his clothing was whisked entirely off his body, shaken in the air above his head, twisted, turned inside out, penetrated with water particles, steamed, and then shoved back on and laced or tied back up.

Nik was panting, red-faced and very angry, when his ablutions were complete. He pointed a finger at Pasha's nose as the man began working in a similar fashion to clean himself. "Never, ever do that again," Nikolai warned.

"What can I say, kid? You needed a bath. You smelled like death."

Blinking, Nik realized the man was probably right, but said, "Nevertheless. I never want to experience that . . . that personal torture again. Understand?"

"Sorry if I offended your sensibilities, Princess," the man said, his back turned to Nik. "I didn't have time for your usual rose petals." He snickered, then his clothes whipped off just as Nik's had a moment before. Completely unembarrassed, Pasha turned around and stood there as naked and proud as the day he was born, with his fists on his scrawny hips as if daring Nik to say something.

"Uh, can you hurry this up?" Nik asked.

"What?" Pasha said. "Am I making you uncomfortable?" He twirled a finger, directing his clothes to be cleaned above him in the air. "Why do you think I gave you your bath with your clothing on? Delicate. That's what I call you. Now me, on the other hand, I'm all man. That's right. Behold my glory. I expect others to stare. I know. I'm impressive. Even my mother said I'm huge for a man my size."

"Your mother sees you naked?"

"Doesn't yours?"

"No! She's dead. And even if she weren't—no!"

"What's wrong with you, boy? Someone's gotta check you over for leeches and the like. If you don't got a gal, then who?"

"I don't get leeches. Even if I did, I suppose I could check myself."

Pasha squished his face in pity. "Ah, I see. Got a wee one, do ya?"

"No, I don't got a . . ." Nik grunted. "Just mind your own business!"

They heard a snap in the trees nearby, and all Pasha's nearly finished clothes suddenly fell to the forest floor. "It's the carriage coming. They're almost here! Quick, take these flowers."

Two bouquets of strange-looking flowers appeared on top of a stump, and the still-naked man thrust them into Nik's arms.

"Look, I don't want to go on a date with you and one of those swamp creatures that tried to eat us," Nik said. "Forget it."

"Swamp creature?" Pasha said, wriggling into his pants. "That wasn't my gal. That was who my gal was feeding me to. Very different thing."

"Ah, that's right. Well, in that case . . . *no*!"

"Need I remind you, boy: You *owe* me."

"*I don't care.*"

"You will! I can make that wee package of yours smaller, ya know!"

Nik's mouth fell open. After gasping, fish-mouthed for a few seconds, he yelled, "*Still. Not. Doing. It.*"

"Stubborn. Muleheaded. Stump-kicker!" Pasha hissed. "Woulda thought I had you with that one."

Just then a huge carriage pulled by six of the largest plumed birds Nik had ever seen pulled up next to them. Their talons and bills were sharp, and he had no doubt they could sever his arm if they wanted to. And yet they were well controlled by the driver, who handled the reins expertly. One of them cried out, and Nik had to cover his ears.

"What are those?" he asked Pasha. "Why use those instead of horses?"

"Because the Games are on top of a mountain, boy. We have to fly there," the likho said.

The carriage door opened, and a lady stepped out. She was graceful in her own way and looked a bit like Pasha. She was the same height, but instead of one eye, she had two. He caught her hand and helped her down, then kissed it a sickening number of times, saying, "My lovely darling, my honey muffin, my kukolka."

"Nikolai," he said, turning around. "I want to introduce my malyshka, Polina."

"Kak dela, Polina," Nik said, bowing.

"Khorosho, a u vas?" she replied.

"I'm well too, all things considered," Nik said.

"Wonderful. I'm so happy you agreed to take us, my luchik, my sweetums," she said to Pasha. "I've so been looking forward to the Games, as you well know."

"I do know, rodnoy. I was just telling the boy here all about it."

"Oh good. How fortunate you found a traveling companion for my dear sister. I just know you'll love her as I do. Pushka! You can come out now."

"I'll come out when his lips are off you. Is he finished yet?"

"Never," Pasha said loudly.

Polina giggled, and Nik rolled his eyes and said under his breath, "At least we have something in common."

"There, you see, boy? You're bound to have a great time. Hop in. Let's be off. Come, my dear," he said to Polina, helping her back into the carriage. After his girlfriend was settled, he turned to Nik, who stood there stubbornly with his arms folded across his chest and said, "Look, if you come with me, I'll teach you a bit of magic. Deal?" Pasha could see the spark in Nik's eyes and knew he had him.

"Fine," Nik said, finally agreeing. "Just don't leave me alone with the sister. I don't want her getting any ideas."

"Okay, whatever. Just don't blow this for me."

"Get into the carriage, lover boy."

Pasha climbed in, and Nikolai hopped in behind him and settled on the only open seat, wincing when he saw he had an up-close-and-personal view of Pasha and his girl, Polina, giggling and necking on the opposite bench. Trying to steel himself for a very long and uncomfortable weekend, he turned away from the lovebirds, hoping to start up a conversation with his date, only to find her veil lowered over her face. It was probably a way for her to shield her sister and her lover from view.

Pasha came up for breath long enough to introduce Polina's sister. "Nikolai, this is Pushka. Pushka"—he nodded—"meet Nik."

"Charmed," she said drolly from behind her veil.

"Likewise," mumbled Nik. He laid his head back against the cushion and wished he had such a device. It would come in handy at the moment.

Rolling his eyes, Pasha went back to kissing the very long arm of his much taller girlfriend, leaving Nik to muse on the physical mechanics of such relationships. Then he remembered the strange pairing of the kikimora and the leshi and thought that might have been an even more difficult pairing.

As for himself, his sights were set on merely the impossible—a tsarevna who may or may not be at that very moment a tiger. *Where are you, Veru?* he thought. *Are you safe?* Since the day he'd met her, they'd never spent time apart. At least not until he'd rode out to meet Grigor, the powerful man in the woods who'd destroyed everything. It was his fault. He'd done this. Nik suddenly realized that it wasn't forgiveness he needed—it was power. Power to destroy the man who'd come to destroy his dreams. If he could somehow go back and undo the things that had been done, maybe then he could stop the tigers from coming into their lives in the first place. But that was impossible. Wasn't it?

The ride was bumpy and uncomfortable not only due to the lack of conversation and the couple making out in the carriage but because there wasn't an actual road for them to travel upon. That would seem an obvious necessity to Nik but apparently not to Pasha. Not only that, but the bird creatures pulling the carriage didn't have the smoothest gait. In fact, they didn't seem coordinated in any way at all. Soon it didn't matter, though, because the driver shouted back, "Clearing ahead. Prepare for takeoff."

Nikolai didn't know what to expect, but apparently everyone else did. The osculation session stopped, and they all gripped a bar overhead. Not thinking to do the same, Nik fell awkwardly into the lap of his seat partner when the carriage suddenly lurched sideways, and then they took to the air. He apologized and sat up, but the girl didn't even respond. Out the small window, he could see the driver clearing the tops of the trees and then the man lifted a knout, cracking the whip in the air above the heads of the strange birds, who had spread out and were flying in two long lines, pulling the carriage behind them.

He looked out the window and saw they'd climbed high and far. A wide, ice-clogged river ran snakelike through the forest and up toward some glacial peaks. Far out on the blue water, he could just make out a narrow, wooden fishing boat, struggling to haul in a catch. Sometimes he felt like that fisherman—caught between summer and winter, toiling in an in-between place, waiting for one season or the other to take hold just so he could move on with life.

Imagining he was that fisherman, Nik thought about just how easy it would be to simply kick one leg and then the other over the side of the boat and slip into those icy waters. There were days when it seemed to him that the effort was just too hard. Were fish even worth that much work? Did anyone care if he came back with a catch at all? Who was he doing all this for, anyway?

The carriage lurched again, and Nik caught himself staring directly into Pasha's eyes. The man shook his head with a too-knowing expression and pointed to his own back, mouthing, "The sorrow." Nik ignored him and turned back to the window. If there was a giant sorrow weighing him down, it certainly *would* sink him down in that river quickly enough. He wondered again if Veru would even miss him, assuming she was still alive, and if she was, she probably blamed him for all that had happened. He certainly blamed himself. Nik hadn't been smart trying to run after her. If he had stayed where he was, at least he'd be with the others. Fat lot of good his special gifts had done for him. If Veru *was* dead, that was on him too. It would serve him right to lose the only person left the world who meant anything to him. The seat groaned as he sank in it further. He did feel it that time. His boots might work now. Maybe he could run. Go looking for her again.

Someone tapped him on the shoulder. "I've got one too, by the way."

"Wh-what?" Nik asked, distracted from his thoughts.

"A sorrow. Pasha says mine's small, but it's still there. Yours is big enough even I can see it. *Sorry*."

"Oh. I can't. See yours or mine, I mean."

"Yeah. They say when they get that big, they cloud your vision. Make you blind to reality. Makes sense now."

"I guess. So you're . . . Pushka, right?"

"Da. Fun name, isn't it? My sestra teases me about being pushy. I'm not though."

"I wouldn't have assumed you were," Nik said. "Or that you had a sorrow. Is there a way to get rid of them?"

"It's hard to do. There's something about finding your inner peace or making peace with who you are. I don't know. Theories abound on the subject."

"Pasha said I have to experience ultimate joy."

"Yeah. He told me the same thing. Then he also said most people carry around a little sorrow. It's like the common cold. Everyone gets it at some point. The trick is not letting it defeat you. Or building up an immunity to it or something."

"I guess. The thing is, I don't think I ever have."

"Ever have what?"

"Experienced ultimate joy. I mean, I don't know what it would feel like."

"You mean you've never been happy?"

"Well, I've had moments, I suppose. But true bliss? No. You?"

"I'm not sure, I guess."

"Of course you haven't," Pasha declared, interrupting. "You two are babies still sucking at the teats of the world. Does a baby feel bliss? No. A baby is content, or a baby is upset. Bliss can only be achieved by those who are enlightened enough to understand the hardships of the world. How can you know the difference between joy and pain, between sadness and happiness, if you don't have enough life experience to compare the two? What you need to do is to stop wallowing in your tiny little life puddles and go for a swim in the big people's pool. There's an entire ocean of experiences waiting out there for you. Put a few decades beneath your boots, and then I'll listen to you talk about sorrow. Right now, at your age, there's too much life ahead of both of you to give in to that beast."

"But you don't know what I've—"

"Been through? Son, don't forget who I am." Pasha leaned forward. "I'm the Bringer of Misery, remember? I've cursed them young and old, and I've seen it all. The thing is, a curse can be broken, and even a one-eyed demon of disaster can find love. I've seen it. Do you know there are some people in this world who are so determined to be happy that they can find it no matter how difficult their life circumstances? They are special souls indeed. I call them the 'cream of the crop, for they rise to the top.'"

"I've heard of people like that," Nik said. "They 'paint the world in roses,' or so the expression goes. That means they're ignorant of reality. Simpleminded."

"No, boy. Not simpleminded. Not ignorant. They simply have a gift for finding the good. They let the bad fall away from them and hold on to the good no matter how small it may be and learn to find joy in that little thing. That's why they're the cream. Cream rises to the top of the milk jug. It's all the fat. All that's good in the world. You just need to learn to find the joy, boy. Float on it. Float to the top. Let the rest sink away like dregs."

"Find the joy, you say? Float to the top?"

"That's right." Pasha leaned back. "And there's no better place to float than the Novgorod Games. And don't think of running either. I see it in your expression. A deal's a deal. Trust me. You don't want to get on my bad side."

Nik frowned. "Fine. I'll stay through the end of the Games."

"That's all I ask."

A faint cheer rose in the air, and Polina clapped her hands. "We're almost there! Can we place some bets?"

"Of course, my dumpling," Pasha said. Turning, he called through the window, "Take us straight to the gambling section."

"Yes, sir!" the driver replied.

Nik glanced out the window and was shocked to see not only huge mountains but many such vehicles in the sky circling the largest of them. There were even what appeared to be dragons flying in the air.

"Incredible!" he mumbled as he leaned out further to take in the sights.

Banners of multiple colors flew from every direction, and as they passed over many arenas, he saw a myriad of creatures gearing up for battle games as well as spectators of all types waving flags, queuing at vendors, buying souvenirs, or heading to tents or coaches or chariots that hovered or were parked at various places all over the mountain. Smoke rose from multiple cookfires, bringing with it the smells of succulent roasting meats and vegetables or baked goods and sweets. Suddenly, he found he was anxious to get out and see everything.

"Glad you came, boy?" Pasha said with a too-smug grin on his face.

"I am. Though I'm still holding you to your promise to teach me a bit of magic."

The man held up his hands. "A bargain's a bargain."

They pulled up alongside the main thoroughfare and the door opened. Pasha got out and helped Polina. Once Nik and Pushka were on the cobblestone path, the birds screeched, and the carriage took to the sky. Pasha tucked Polina's arm in his, then tossed Nik a small bag. "Here. This is for you and Pushka. Show her around a bit. Place a few bets. Get something to eat. We'll meet you back here in a few hours."

Nik hissed. "We're supposed to stick together, remember?"

"It's only for a while, boy. You don't want to watch us do *everything*, do you?" Pasha said, his eyes wide.

Wincing, Nik said, "I suppose not. Fine. Two hours. No more."

"Six hours. See you around, boy. Have fun. Find something *joyous* to do."

"Right. Joyous." Nik and Pushka watched them leave, and then Nik offered her an arm and said, "Well, shall we find something joyous and floaty?"

Pushka laughed, and it didn't make him nervous like when he was with Veru. She was a bit taller than her sister but still on the short side, which made Nik feel rather tall. She took hold of her purple veil and tossed it over her head. She had two eyes like her sister. They were blue. Not a deep blue, like Veru's, but they were still nice. Her jaw was very square, but she had a nice smile.

"Would you like to place some bets or get something to eat?" he asked politely.

"Eat, definitely. But I'm also happy to follow your lead."

Nik had always served the tsarevnas. He'd never had someone ask him what he'd prefer before. He rather liked it. "Why don't we look around at the different vendors first and see which looks most interesting, and then we'll try a few things?"

"Sounds perfect."

They spent the next couple of hours sampling a variety of foods, some of which they really enjoyed, others they found they had differing opinions on, while others they both loathed entirely. It was a rather fun game. Soon they were both stuffed and declared they couldn't take another bite. They sat and watched one of the events, and Pushka seemed happy to listen to Nik describe the various skills in the different contenders. She suggested that since he seemed to know so much about fighting, he should observe the warriors and then keep a tally so they could place bets using his knowledge and therefore improve their odds of winning.

Pushka volunteered to take notes while he made observations since she couldn't abide bloodshed. They purchased a little book with a few pens and had made several entries by the time they met up with Pasha and Polina again. Nik was actually a bit sad to see his time with Pushka end. He'd found her a rather interesting companion and easy to talk with.

"Well," Pasha said. "I see the two of you have been getting on."

"Yes," Pushka said. "We were just getting ready to place some bets. Would you like to come with us?"

"What's this?" Polina asked her sister, taking the book from her gloved hands. She thumbed through the book, and Nik could see how doing so irritated her sister.

Offering his arm again, he said, "Pushka, bring your notes and we'll place our bets before the evening events begin; then we should get some dinner, don't you think?"

"Perhaps that little Strike It Rich Cantina we wanted to try?"

"The one where we have to pan for our supper? Sounds interesting."

"And you never know. You might find a gold nugget along with your side salad," Pushka said with a laugh as she took Nikolai's arm.

"You two are welcome to join us, if you like," Nik said smoothly as he lifted Pushka's notebook from Polina's grasp and then turned his date toward the betting booths.

Polina sulked at the treatment, but Pasha grinned. "Look at that, why don't you?" he said under his breath.

"What?" Polina said, fluffing her hair.

"Boy's sorrow shrunk at least an inch. Told you your sister would be good for him."

"As good as I am for you?"

"Now, darlin'," Pasha said, turning to his date, "nobody is as good as you. And don't you know it!"

Polina brightened and rubbed noses with Pasha, then wound her arm through his. As they strolled behind the others, she said, "Every man needs a good woman. Those who don't have one end up being truculent to everyone else around them and a plague to themselves."

"Don't I know it," he agreed.

They approached the betting station where Pushka was checking the notes in her book and Nik was scanning the upcoming events. Suddenly, he turned, his face white.

"Pasha!" he said, taking hold of the shorter man's coat. "My friends are here! At least one of them. Maybe more!"

"What do you mean?"

"See that?" Nik said, pointing to the headline event happening later in the week.

"Which one?"

"The one that says 'tigers.'"

"You're friends with the tiger trainers?" Pushka asked, confused.

"Not the trainers. With the tigers."

"I don't think I understand what he's saying, Pushka," Polina said.

Frustrated, Nik ran a hand through his hair. "It says right there on the program—a black, a red, a gold, and an ivory tiger. Those are my friends. They can change into tigers. Those are their tigers' colors. Well, not the ivory one. I have no idea who that is. But the others. That's Veru, Stacia, and Iriko!"

"You're saying those tigers are people?" Pushka asked.

"Yes!" Nik nodded excitedly.

"Is this possible?" Polina asked.

"Stranger things have happened," Pasha said. "Why don't you stay here, lad, and let me see if I can find out more."

The three had been waiting for what seemed like an eternity when Pasha finally pushed his way back through the crowd to their sides. "Okay. Here's what I learned about them. A group of underwater creatures called the vodnik brought the black tiger here. He was recently sold to a high bidder who has arranged the big match between him and the other three cats for a high-stakes game. It seems he owns all of them. There's no word on any of them changing to a human form. Sorry, lad."

"Can you get me in to see them?" Nik leaned in. "Just tell me where to go. You know I could get in on my own with the tunic and boots."

Pasha rubbed the back of his neck. "The contenders are very heavily guarded, son. By magic. Magic that could very well *see through* other magic, if you take my meaning. It's dangerous. Not even I would risk trying to pull off something like that."

"You've got to, Pasha. Please! They . . . they're my family."

"Oh, won't you help him?" Pushka asked.

"He does seem rather sincere, pumpkin."

Pasha looked at the three hopeful faces and said, "Very well. I'll see what I can do."

CHAPTER 23

One Cannot Shear a Naked Sheep

Not wanting to waste a single moment, Danik and Veru set about the first task immediately. Taking the wooden cup, the list of instructions, and their bags, they headed out to the summer porch in search of the white knight. They didn't have to look long before they came upon him.

"Let me see this list," he said. "Ah, it's as I feared. She's given you tasks impossible to accomplish."

"But are they truly?" Veru asked. "Just show us where the water is found, and we'll take it from there."

"That's the problem. My emblem is the dawn. The water she's referring to is the place where the sun crests upon the water at daybreak. That could be any place around the world at any time, for the sun casts its light upon the water for but an instant. I fear by the time you traveled to any one location, it would have moved on to the next one, and so forth. It would take you eons to fill the barrel, if you even could."

Zarya took the cup and dipped it into the well, then lifted it to his mouth to drink. Tiny, unseen holes at the bottom of the wooden mug dribbled water over his hands and breastplate quickly enough that by the time he pressed the edge to his lips there was nothing left inside but a few drops.

"See here? The cup is riddled with tiny slits. She's made certain you will fail."

He handed the container back to Danik, who tried his luck. Just as with the knight, water streamed out the bottom in thin rivulets. "Deceitful old woman," he said, watching as the contents quickly drained before his eyes.

"Yes," Veru said. "She's a crafty one." Pacing, Veru clasped her hands behind her back and bit her lip.

"You have an idea," Danik said.

"Maybe." She turned to Zarya. "There isn't a certain place where your emblem rises, then? Nothing in particular she's referring to?"

"I wouldn't think so. It could be a stream, an ocean, a lake, anything really."

"Right. So long as it's water." Veru stopped. "Her instructions specifically say to take the cup and dip it into the water, *then* fill the barrel. It doesn't say we have to use the cup to fill the barrel. It also doesn't stipulate that the barrel cannot be moved. So, here's what I'm thinking: We bring the barrel with us, find a stream or a lake that the rising sun will touch, dip the cup, then fill the barrel using whatever means we can, and bring it back. Will that work?"

The knight pulled off his helmet and rubbed his jaw. "The fastest way to find the dawn would be to use my mirror. It's how I make my way home when I must replenish my energy."

"Your mirror?"

"Yes. It's how I traverse realms quickly to serve the needs of my mistress. When I cast my mirror down, it becomes a body of water near a distant shore where she wishes me to go. Most every town and city are built near water. I simply state my destination, then I wait for dawn's light to create a passage between.

"You see, my horse travels along daybreak's band of light. But without my armor, I fear the fiery rays would burn your fair skin and leave you blind. I dare not expose you to that danger. Only the magic binding us to this servitude protects us from harm."

"I'm not giving up," Veru said. "If we can accomplish her tasks, then you and your brothers are to be freed as well."

"Though I am grateful for your kindness in thinking of us, it is likely your generosity that has caused her to create tasks that are so very difficult. I fear the two of you are doomed along with us to continue on in this half-life until you pass from this mortal realm."

"Not if there's a breath left in my body," Veru vowed.

"What about your cloak?" Danik asked, interrupting.

"My cloak?"

"Yes. I'd assume your clothing helps protect you. Do you need your cloak?"

"I've never tried moving between places without it."

"What if we used it to shield something? Have you ever brought items with you across the divide?"

"Yes. Now that you mention it, I have fetched ingredients for her various potions from distant places. They haven't burned up. But she always lent me her stone dish to carry them in."

"You mean the big one?" Veru asked. "The one she rides in?"

"No. A smaller vessel. It has a handle I can lash to my saddle."

Danik disappeared into the house and returned with a smaller version of the stone pot. "Is this what you're talking about?"

"Yes. That's the one."

Examining the vessel, Danik said, "It's been fired. Something made of wood might burn. What we need is a wheeled cart made of stone, something small and not so heavy that your horse can't pull it, but large enough to fit me and the barrel."

"I believe I understand what you intend," the knight said. "Remain here. I know of a place where such things are made."

Climbing on his horse, he rode around the house and disappeared. Within the span of just a few moments, they heard a heavy thump. There was a neigh accompanied by the crack of thunder and lightning. The white horse turned the corner, rolling its eyes and shooting golden flames from its mouth.

Attached behind him was a heavy chariot that looked as if it had been carved from the most exquisite, flawless white marble. Every part of it—from the spokes to the axle to the shaft—was made of stone.

Danik ran his hand over it. "It's beautiful!" he said. "Are you certain she can pull it?"

"Over land it would be difficult, but on the dawn highway, she will draw energy from the sky. We become weightless. You will see."

"But won't we still burn in the back?" Veru asked.

Shaking his head, Danik said, "I'm thinking you ride inside the barrel for protection, and we'll use the cloak as a cover to shield our heads. Do you think it will work?"

The knight considered and replied, "As long as the two of you keep your eyes tightly closed when we are traveling along the dawn road. Make certain your limbs are well hidden so you won't be burned. I feel I must warn you though: I have never brought back a living thing without a lid covering the stone basin. I fear for your lives."

Veru and Danik looked at one another and then nodded. Veru said, "We would rather risk our lives trying than end up in servitude."

The knight let out a small sigh, then moved to help Danik lift the barrel into the back of the chariot. When it was tightly secured, bound with strong ropes tied to inner hooks of marble, Veru climbed inside, and the lid was placed on top. After the cloak was tied down as well, they were told to make ready, and it seemed like only a moment before Veru felt her entire body lift into the air. She heard the hiss of something sizzling, and there was an intense heat.

The knight warned them to close their eyes, and even through her closed lids, there was a brightness like nothing she'd ever seen before. Then a jolt that made her bite down on her tongue and bang her head against the inside of the dank barrel. The bright light dimmed and then vanished.

"You can open your eyes now!" shouted the knight. "Dawn approaches quickly."

The top of the barrel was removed, and Danik lifted her out, then they rolled the barrel out of the chariot. They crouched down beside a quiet lake, the trees around it white with snow. Veru paused above the water with the mug, ready to dip, watching the knight for his signal.

He lifted his gloved hand. "Wait," he said. "Wait for it. It's coming. Almost . . ." Then he pointed his finger. "Now!"

She dipped her cup just as the dawn broke over the water, the rosy golden light kissing the lapping waves as they filled the cup. Veru placed her hand over the bottom to contain as much of the liquid as she could and then unceremoniously dumped the contents into the barrel. It was a pathetic start, and she knew at that rate it would take weeks, if not months, to fill the entire thing. It didn't matter, though, because then the knight and Danik lifted the barrel and dunked it into the lake, filling it completely before capping it.

When they rolled it out, they waited a moment to make certain the barrel was watertight before positioning it onto the chariot, then they secured it again, preparing for the return. The problem they hadn't considered was how tight the trip home was going to be now that the barrel was filled with water.

"We could make two trips," Danik suggested. "You go first, Veru, and then he can come back and pick me up later."

"That would work," the knight said, "but dawn is fleeting. The time draws to a close even now. If we don't leave within a few moments, I fear we will be stuck in this place for another day."

Veru held out a hand. "Come on, Danik. We'll make do. I'm not leaving you here that long. I'll just sit on your lap."

Danik's expression became unreadable, but he stalked forward and climbed into the chariot, scooting as far into the back as he could, then pulled his knees to his chest, wrapping his arms around them.

Veru rolled her eyes. "That's not going to work. Relax your knees, open your arms. You're going to have to hold on to me."

She climbed into the chariot, positioning herself on his lap, elbowing him when he sat so stiffly she was uncomfortable. "Relax! Would you? I'm not going to bite you. Neveroyatno. Put your arms around my waist. Tighter. I'm going to fall out if you don't hold on to me. That's better."

"Are you settled, then, my lady?" the knight asked.

"We are," Veru answered. "Please take us home."

He secured the cloak, and they were plunged into the dark. The chariot began moving, and Danik's fingers tightened over hers, weaving between them. Veru leaned back against his chest, and she felt him finally relax. They were warned to close their eyes, and when she did, Danik pressed his cheek against hers. She felt the rough stubble of his jaw and loved the sensation so much she turned her head just a bit so her nose and lips came into contact with his skin.

She inhaled deeply and found she loved the scent of him. It was different from when she was a tiger. There was the lingering fragrance of the soap he'd recently used and the tang of woodsmoke and snowy pine that always clung to him, but there was also something . . . primal. It was very difficult to describe.

As a tiger, she'd hunted things with velvet skins, fur coats, and leather jackets. Beneath the outer layer, she'd find pulsing life that could sustain her. She wasn't particularly hungry, but if she didn't know better, she'd think she wanted to rip into Danik's jugular like one of the wolves who'd once stalked him. The impulse was almost to the point where she had to bite back the growl developing at the back of her throat. Veru could almost taste his pounding pulse at the base of his neck. Her breath quickened.

Their bodies rose in the air as the white horse galloped along the dawn highway, and Veru let out a soft gasp and whispered Danik's name. He grabbed on to her head and hip, trying to shield her from hurting herself when they fell. Veru shifted in his arms, angling toward him even more. Her mouth moved to the corner of his, and she couldn't help it. Her tongue flicked out for a taste. He froze, his fingers flexing on her hip as if he were uncertain about what to do.

Then his hand slipped into her hair and around her waist, wrenching her to him fiercely as his mouth found hers. He kissed her deeply, drunkenly, passionately, and then they crashed down, hard, and broke apart suddenly.

"We're back!" came the shout from the knight, and Veru could have wished a pox upon the man in that moment despite how much she liked him. "You can open your eyes again," he said.

Veru didn't want to, but she did. Danik was still near. It wasn't like he could escape her in the confines of the small chariot, but she could still sense the growing distance between them. He regretted what had just happened. She knew it. The arms that had held her a moment before with such passion and intensity were now iron bars keeping her locked away.

Ah, she thought, still drunk from the moist heat of his kiss. This tiger has had a tantalizing taste of flesh and wouldn't be forgetting it anytime soon. She pondered this and sat quietly, waiting for the white knight to remove the cloak. When he did, she took his offered hand and stepped out of the chariot, watching as he and Danik positioned the barrel on the summer porch.

"Spasibo," she said to the knight when the task was complete. "We couldn't have done it without you."

"It is I who must thank you," he said in return with a courtly bow. Then he took her hand and placed a warm kiss upon it before turning it over and gifting her with his little mirror.

Veru gasped. "Surely you don't mean to give us your means of transport. This is how you and your horse sustain yourselves."

She tried to give the token back, but he refused. "Please. Keep it. Like you, we will fight or perish. The time has come to make a stand. Perhaps all I needed was a reminder of what a valiant heart looks like." Zarya squeezed her arm, and Veru saw the telltale signs, the beginnings of dreamy-eyed affection she saw in the expressions of so many, but she thought perhaps in this man, she might not mind it so much.

Glancing over at Danik to see if he noticed, she saw he'd left and frowned. Her tiny bubbles of joy popped, but she still managed to smile. "What's next?" she asked Zarya.

"I will depart and send my brother. He will come at noon. Watch for him. Eat heartily. You will need the energy. I'll take my leave, fair one."

After the knight left, Veru made her way to the porch and found Max curled up on a chair next to a steaming bowl of stew and a hot loaf of brown bread. "Keeping us fed, kotenok?"

She sank into the chair and had finished most of the meal before

Danik decided to make an appearance. He leaned against a post as she used the last bit of bread to soak up the rest of her stew. Veru had a lot of practice with patience and waiting for others to speak first, but Danik had a knack for being calm and cool under any circumstance. While she sat, playing over what he should be saying again and again in her mind, he thumbed a tune on his thigh as if he hadn't a care in the world, and as if their shared kiss had never happened at all. It was driving her crazy.

Determined to make him suffer more than she was, she said nothing at all herself and left him alone until she heard a neigh that indicated the arrival of a new knight.

"Privet?" she heard the shout and headed outside to the greet the brother of the white knight.

The minute he saw her, he reined in his prancing sorrel stallion who rose on his hind legs and opened his mouth. Red-and-orange flames erupted as the horse shook his bright red mane and danced on his hind legs before the knight hopped down. The man's armor and cape were as red as his beautiful horse. When he bowed deeply and then removed his helmet, Veru laughed when he shook out a head of hair as bright, thick, and shining as his horse's tail, and every bit as red to boot.

"Why, I'd say my sister would be a bit jealous if she saw your hair. That color is quite beautiful. Is that appropriate to say to a man?" Veru smiled as she teased him.

He answered with a twinkle in his eye. "When a lady as lovely as yourself calls me beautiful, I would daresay it's appropriate under any conditions. Now, how may I be of service? And please say you need an escort of some kind," he added while tossing his lustrous hair over his shoulder.

Veru laughed. "I'm afraid it's nothing that fun."

Danik was beside her instantly. She had no idea where he'd come from. "We've a task to complete," he said brusquely. "Here are the instructions." He handed the knight the paper and stood there waiting with his arms folded.

The knight eyed the two of them and unfolded the paper. After reading, he winced. "I can take you to them, but there's a problem."

"What is it?" Danik asked. "Do they have fangs? Is their wool poisonous?"

"No. Nothing like that. They are, er . . . well, they're naked."

"Naked?" Veru said.

"Yes. So you see, there isn't anything for you to shear."

"I've never heard of such a thing."

"It's very rare. Supposedly, they come into their wool under just the right conditions, but it hasn't happened yet."

"Do you know the conditions?"

"No one does. Not even my mistress. I was tasked with guarding them and given every tool at my disposal to, shall we say, encourage the growth. But so far, nothing's worked."

"I see," said Veru. "Well, this is quite the embranglement, isn't it?" She sighed. "Is the way far?"

"It is. The sheep reside in a hidden forest, but my brother said he gave you his mirror . . ."

"He did. I would just like to consult one of our local sheep farmers before setting out, if that's agreeable to you."

"Very well. When you are ready to attempt your task, simply tell the mirror you wish to find the hidden forest guarded by the Polden Knight."

"Polden. Is that your name?" Veru asked.

"For now, it suffices."

"Then we'll seek you out soon."

The knight departed, and Veru and Danik set out to find the sheep farmer Veru had met before. He indeed proved a fount of wisdom and appeared to know much about the very sheep she mentioned.

"Special ones, them are," he said. "Need ta be fed on the hair of virgins."

"What?" Veru replied, gasping.

"That's right. Supplemented with flowers if you want the wool to grow out colored special. Otherwise, it grows the same color as the girl's hair—black, white, gray, blond, you get the idea. Mind, they're voracious eaters. They prefer it fresh. Fall asleep next to one and ya might find they've eaten off your very scalp!" He visibly shivered. Then he whispered to Danik, "I once heard a one young lad as had a lambkin. Loved it like his own babe. Fed it from a bottle. Then, one night, it came inta its teeth and began nudgin' the boy at his ankles. He was a hairy one, the lad. Took after 'is da. Wouldn't ya know, the lamb licked the fine hairs clean offen his legs, even up to 'is nethers. Some say it even nicked 'is wee kolbasa."

Danik straightened and his entire face turned red, while Veru tried her best to smother a snort. The short farmer turned to her. "Poor boy's legs were ever after as smooth as a babe's popka. But I says he was fortunate. Even a virgin girl with hair down to her feet ain't enough ta satisfy one of them adult bugger bears."

Veru cleared her throat. "Okay, so flowers and hair. Is there anything else we need to know?"

Danik managed to find his voice and asked, "Anything special about the shearing?"

"Naw, nothing special. Oh! Except once they eat, their wool grows immediate like. Ya have ta shear them before the full moon appears; otherwise, it all falls out and you need ta start over again."

"But if they need hair to grow wool, what do they eat in the meantime?" Veru asked. "How do they stay alive?"

"Same as every other flock of sheep. They eat grass, clover, hay, that sort of thing. They just can't produce wool."

"It's strange," Veru said. "I don't understand why anyone would want to go to so much trouble."

"I'll tell ya why. If ya can manage ta weave the wool—and mind, it's near as an impossible a task as gettin' the beasties ta grow it in the first place—the fabric is the finest, strongest, and most beautiful you've ever seen."

"Better than the silks of the Orient?" she asked.

"Better than dragon silk. Better even than phoenix leather."

Danik raised his eyebrows and gave Veru a look. "How, um . . . how is it different?" he asked.

"Not only is it more beautiful, but once it's sewn into clothing, it withstands flame like phoenix leather and also has the magical properties of dragon silk; then it also lends the wearer something else."

"What is that?"

"It depends on the virgin and the flower. They combine to create something unique. It could be a scent so overwhelming that anyone seeing the person wearing the gown would fall at their feet, or it could be astonishing beauty, or the gift of great discernment. Like I said, it depends on the blend."

"I see. And, umm, a final question. If I may."

"Of course, lass," the farmer replied.

"How do the sheep, er . . . tell?"

"How do they tell what? They don't talk, if that's what you mean."

"No, good sir," Danik said, interrupting. "I think she's asking, how do the sheep know a virgin from a nonvirgin?"

"Ah!" The farmer touched his finger to his nose. "Excellent question. They leaves them as nonvirgins alone, to be certain. It's believed they can sniff them out, a bit like a hound dog. I don't know how it works. Not really. It must be within a certain age as well. Turns off after a woman is past birthing age. And they don't bother children either. But there's no camouflagin' it. Olfactory is what it is. Show them hair from the same person cut as a child and ya get nothing, but once they reach marryin' age, the poor girl is downright discerpible."

"I see. Thank you so much for your help," Veru said.

They left the farmer's home and headed up the road. "No wonder Yuga wants the wool so badly. Where are we going to get that much hair?" Danik asked.

"Let's not worry about that just yet," Veru said. "Let's find the knight first and let him know what we discovered. Maybe we'll think of something."

Danik nodded and Veru pulled the small mirror from her bag and checked her braid first, tugging on it to see how long it was and wondered how much of it she could cut off to feed to a sheep and if it would be enough to produce even one bag of wool. Then she placed the mirror on the ground and said, "Take us to the hidden forest guarded by the Polden Knight."

The mirror shimmered and boiled and grew, spreading out and lengthening until it became a bubbling river. Trees erupted all around it, and the countryside surrounding them changed, turning and twisting. The little farm disappeared, and in its place was a hidden pasture with a river surrounded by trees. On a distant hill, the red knight sat upon his horse as he watched over hundreds of naked pink sheep, all of them crying *baa* as they jostled for position, trying to stay as close to the warm knight as possible.

Calling out, Danik waved, and the knight kicked the sides of his horse, galloping over to them. Veru bent, picking up the small mirror that had shrunk to normal size once again. She tucked it into her bag and offered the knight a smile.

"Hello!" he said. "That was fast."

"I'm afraid what we learned isn't going to help much," Danik said.

"Tell me," the knight replied, getting down from his horse. The sheep made their way over to the knight, basking in the warmth that naturally exuded from the man. They drank deeply from the stream and grazed while the people talked.

"The answer is hair," Veru said. "Virgin hair and flowers. In great quantities, apparently."

"Really? How fascinating." He removed his helmet and ran his hand through his own lustrous red locks as he thought. "So they are to ingest it?"

"Apparently," Danik said. "And then they'll grow wool right away. We'll need to shear it before the full moon; otherwise, it will all fall out."

"That gives us"—the knight closed his eyes—"approximately one week." He blew out his breath. "I suppose we'd better get busy, then."

"Get busy?" Danik frowned. "I doubt we could shear all these animals in a week, let alone find that much hair and convince the virgins to give it up. Also, there's a catch. Once she has the wool and turns it into fabric, she'll use it to make clothing, powerful clothing that I'm certain she'll use to trap others."

"Yes. That is a conundrum. But first let's see if this will work, then we'll cross that bridge if we must."

"Very well," replied Veru. "Let's go round up some virgins."

"Oh, that won't be necessary," the knight said, opening a hidden pocket in his cloak and pulling out a jeweled comb. Then he gestured at the two of them and winced. "I'm assuming, though, the two of you haven't, umm . . . That is, you're still . . . ?"

Veru frowned and folded her arms. "If you are asking if we . . . the answer there is no!"

The knight half smiled and nodded sheepishly.

"Then . . . perhaps . . ." The knight stepped forward, glancing at the two of them, then paused at seeing their confusion. He cleared his throat. "You see, it is often assumed that when the hair of a virgin is mentioned, it is meant that a woman's hair would be required, but in actuality . . ."

Danik blinked and then caught Veru's arm. "Then you should take mine. Hers is so beautiful. Please, leave it be."

He approached the knight and turned around. Just as the knight lifted his arms, Veru spoke.

"Wait a minute! Danik, how do you know you're a virgin? You can't remember what happened before you arrived in this place."

"Well, you didn't volunteer, so I assumed—"

"You don't get to assume anything. It's none of your business"—Veru noticed the knight's raised eyebrows and interested expression as he peeked over Danik's shoulder—"or yours either," she added angrily. "But, yes, I'm a virgin!"

"Good. Excellent," the knight said. "Then this"—he held up his comb—"should work fine on both of you."

"What will work?" Danik asked, glancing back.

"My comb. It's how I keep my hair as nice as it is."

"And how is your fancy-man hair supposed to help us?" Danik asked, tucking his own longish hair behind an ear, causing Veru to smirk.

"Just wait." He turned back to Danik's hair and began combing. Soon Danik's blond hair began to grow. When it was at his waist, the knight lopped it off with a sword, dropping it on the ground. The sheep approached it, nibbled at it half-heartedly, and then soon it was gone.

"Umm, if I may, my dear?" He raised his hands, the one containing the comb, indicating he wanted to use it. Though she was a bit uncomfortable with the idea of him touching her, she shrugged and turned around. The knight loosened her braid and ran his fingers through her hair, stretching it out along her back so it fell in long waves, then he began to comb it, tugging gently through the knots until they untangled.

She bit her lip, then her thumbnail, wondering what was happening, and watched Danik's expression change from one of irritated annoyance to one of awe.

"What?" she asked, demanding he explain what he was seeing. "What's happening?"

"Your hair!" Danik exclaimed. "It's growing. And quickly!"

"Of course it is," the knight said. "My mistress gifted me the comb hoping it would aid me in cultivating the wool. Sadly, it doesn't seem to work on the sheep."

Within a few seconds, Veru's hair was down to her knees, and the sheep were jostling one another, becoming extremely interested. Some were even drooling. They bumped against her knees and baaed with open mouths. Danik shoved several aside, but it was becoming more and more difficult to hold them back. One of them managed to get a mouthful and yanked hard. Veru screamed and fell and was trampled within the span of a few seconds.

Danik picked up animal after animal and tossed them aside, then grabbed Veru, and when he couldn't free her from the biting, chewing beasts, he pulled out his trusty hunting knife. With a quick slice, the long length of hair fell to the ground, where the entire herd trampled one another to get at it.

"How fascinating," Danik said. "It's a very different reaction than they had to my hair."

Veru snickered. "Maybe you aren't a virgin."

"If he wasn't, they wouldn't have eaten it," the knight said.

"Maybe they just like your soap," he said, his warm breath a whisper that kissed the bare skin where her shorn hair tickled the back of her neck.

"I used the same soap you did. They probably just didn't like the taste of a hunter," Veru replied, but her comment didn't have the bite it usually had. In fact, she very much wanted a taste of the hunter who held her close in his arms. All she could think about in that moment was pressing her lips to the warm pulse beating in his neck and tracing a path from there to his jawline, feeling the scrape of his rough beard against her soft cheek until she made her way to his mouth.

Instead, she shivered, clinging to Danik, her arms wrapped around his neck. She could still feel the demanding mouths gnawing at the back of her neck—the hunger, the tugging, the ripping. She wanted to sink into him. To lose herself. But Danik set her down a distance away and lightly touched her trembling shoulders, swiping away the fat tears on her cheeks. Never had he seen the tsarevna look so vulnerable.

"Hold still," he said. "Let me check the damage."

He winced at the cut he'd made to her beautiful hair, but that wasn't what pained him the most. Large chunks of hair had been pulled right out of her scalp, and there were multiple bite marks on her back and neck. When the knight approached, he glared at the man. "Can you get me hot water, a clean towel, and some salve?"

Nodding, the knight departed, and Danik smiled and spoke calmly to the trembling woman. "There now, little lapochka. Try to be calm. It's not so bad. Perhaps you can tell me a story while I tend to your wounds, eh? Maybe something to help me remember from before?"

Soon he began humming quietly, and she felt the stinging sensation of a warm cloth pressed against her neck. "I-I don't heal like before, when the tiger was with me."

"You healed as a tiger?"

"Yes. You took care of me then as well."

He listened as she told him of meeting him for the first time when she'd been caught in a trap, and by the time she finished her story about her saving him from the wolves, Danik was finished cleaning her wounds.

Taking her still-trembling hands, he pressed a soft kiss on her palm and instructed, "I'd like you to rest away from the flock for a while." Glancing around at the meadow and then staring up at the large trees, he said to the knight, "Bring your comb."

Danik took Veru's hand and guided her to the tree line. The flock followed them, hoping for another delicious serving of virgin hair. Once he found a tree he was satisfied with, Danik began to climb, then held out a hand for Veru. He settled her in the crook of a tree and then asked Polden to hand him the comb.

"Good," Danik said. "Now, Polden, I'm going to need you to gather every dark and evil flower you can find as quickly as you can. I'll loan you the mirror if you need it."

"No need. I can travel in much the same way as my brother, but by using the noonday paths. What do you intend to do with the flowers?"

"I'm hoping to give Yuga a surprise she didn't count on."

"But your young lady . . . she's in pain."

"I know. I'm not planning to use her hair. I'll use my own. Hurry back. Some of them are already sprouting wool."

The red knight looked at Danik thoughtfully. "I see. You know I'd stay and offer up my own hair, but . . . well, I don't think they'd be interested in mine."

"It's fine," Danik said. "You find the flowers. I'll take care of this."

"Very well. Good luck to you, hunter."

"And to you."

The knight lifted his helmet to his head, and with a crack of red-and-orange lightning, he disappeared.

Veru's head throbbed. Danik had instructed her to keep the cloth pressed to her scalp, but she couldn't find a place to lean against the tree without it hurting awfully. Finally, she turned her head enough to watch him work, and that at least distracted her. He began combing his hair, and it grew longer and longer. The sheep below began leaping into the air in an attempt to catch it in their mouths.

When it was sufficiently long, well below his feet, yet still above their reach, he'd use his knife to cut it off, hacking it off in great chunks and tossing his dirty-blond hair to the waiting beasts below, who leaped upon it like they were starving in winter and it was lifesaving hay. Over and over, he'd comb and cut, comb and cut. An hour passed, then two, and three.

He paused to check on her, and his hair was long, past his shoulders and covering his face. She brushed it behind his ear. "There. Now I can see your eyes."

"How do you feel?" he asked.

"Sore. Painful."

Danik helped her lean forward and tried to gently check her wounds, but the cloth was now stuck to her scalp. Instead, he took a bottle out of their bag. "Here, drink. Eat something and rest. What you need is medicine." He froze. "Wait. We have the mirror. Why didn't we think of this before? Why don't we simply use it to travel home? Find your sister? Get all of us out of this place? Escape Yuga?"

"Do you think it could be that simple?" Veru asked.

"It couldn't hurt to try." Danik took the mirror from the bag and placed it on the tree limb. "Go ahead."

Veru wet her lips. "Take me to the palace," she said.

The mirror glimmered, then went black. After a moment, it cleared as if nothing had happened.

She tried again. "Take me to my sister," Veru commanded.

Once again, it was the same result.

"That won't work," the red knight said as he approached the tree. "Until you are free of Yuga's enchantment, you won't be allowed to go anywhere she wouldn't wish. Believe me—my brothers and I have tried."

"Is there a way to get her medicine?"

"Yes, that much is possible. Take her to that young doctor friend of yours. He can help her, and you can return to help me shear the wool. Even now it grows." He tossed a large bag at the base of the tree. Awful-smelling and ugly flowers of every type spilled out. "I brought the flowers you wanted: pitcher plant, cobra lily, ghost fungus, bleeding tooth, spider orchids, mask flowers, death root, fang ferns, Dracula vampiras, hooded skull dragons, Venus flytraps, witch hazel, octopus stinkhorn, corpse flowers, doll's eyes, bat flowers, bladderwort, carrion flowers, spider mums, strangle tare, and devil's walking stick."

"That's . . . that's great," Danik said, eyeballing the strange flowers, most of which he'd never heard of or seen before.

"You take her to the doctor, and I'll feed them the flowers." He put his hand on Danik's shoulder. "But I also gathered a special batch, just for the two of you. I'm going to section off a small group of them and give them these."

He opened a small bag filled with the most beautiful flowers Veru had ever seen. Her mother would have wept at such a sight. Veru recognized lilies, tulips, peonies, and roses, but never had she seen such colors or smelled such fragrance. Reaching into the bag, she stroked the delicate petals. "They're amazing!" she said to the knight.

"As I said, they are for you. When we shear these, we will bag the wool separately. Now take her. There is much work to be done."

Danik told the mirror where he wanted to go, and in an instant they were at a small creek next to a little cottage. He knocked on the door, and they were welcomed by the young family with the sickly daughter and their live-in physician. Veru was settled in, fed, and while she was tended to, Danik disappeared.

It turned out that she needed stitches in the back of her head, but she was no stranger to pain. The young mother even volunteered to try and style her badly shorn hair and gave her scarves to wear. After a few days of rest, she began helping with the chores and wishing Danik would return. Finally, after the removal of her stitches, she heard a neigh and the sound of thunder and lightning outside.

She got up to find the red knight and Danik, his hair still a bit too long, cut at his shoulders, but with a large, satisfied smile on his face.

"Is it done?" she asked expectantly.

"More importantly, how are you feeling?" he asked, reaching for her hand.

"I'm well. I've been taken very good care of," she said loudly. "This family has done us a great service. We would do well to return the favor."

"And we shall," Danik said.

The father replied, "You've helped us more than enough in the time you've been here. You owe us nothing."

"We're just happy to see you well again, my lady," the physician said.

"And back with your man," added the mother.

"Yes," Veru replied, surprised to feel the sting of a blush color her cheeks. "Well, thank you all."

As they headed down the road, she asked, "Where's the wool?"

"Back at the house," Danik replied. "We used the spinning hatchel on it."

"Really?"

"Yes. Nothing else worked," the red knight replied. "That hatchel of yours did the trick. We've a lovely bolt of the blackest, magic fabric Yuga's dark little heart could desire."

"But we also have another bolt, a second one," Danik said. "And the house wanted us to hide it. The minute we finished it, another secret closet opened. When I placed it inside, a key fell out of the lock." He reached into his pocket and showed it to her. "I think we're meant to take it with us when we leave."

CHAPTER 24

The Tiger May Leap
But the Tamer Collects the Money

"You want . . . you want something to eat?" Stacia asked.

"If it wouldn't be too much trouble," replied Father Frost.

Folding her arms, Stacia considered him for a moment. He didn't look particularly hungry. She was sure that big bear of his could eat. Probably her lifeless body that grew bluer by the moment if his master allowed it. She sighed, knowing it was some kind of test, but no longer caring. She just wanted it over and done with so he would leave, and she could figure out how to reconnect her split soul to her freezing body and try to repair the broken staff before the White Shaman returned to reclaim it.

"Fine. There's a biscuit in the left pocket of my coat. You'll have to find it yourself, as I don't seem to be able to get myself back down there. If that's not to your liking, head over to the fire down that way and wake up the sleeping man. He'll prepare you and your bear some porridge. Just don't hurt the little girl. Now, if you don't mind, I need to figure out how to remedy my current mistake so I'll be able to continue working on my last one. Appreciate your visit. I'm sure you have many things to tend to, as do I. Have a nice day."

Father Frost didn't move. He just stood there considering her. He reached up and stroked his perfectly smooth white beard and mustache as if he had all the time in the world. His very blue eyes twinkled as he studied her. Stacia found it disconcerting. She'd dismissed him, and he had the gall to ignore it. But what could she do about it? Nothing, exactly.

"You've a bit of sour grapes about you, my dear, wouldn't you say?"

"Sour grapes? Am I to assume you're referring to my mood? That's right. Men always believe when a woman is irritated, annoyed, or upset, it's related to mood, or the weather, or the cycles of the moon, or some other such nonsense. Of course, when a man is angry, he has every right to stomp and fuss and go to war. In most cases, he's celebrated for such things. But women aren't allowed to have such emotions. It's unbecoming. Is that it?"

Father Frost removed his hat and set it down on the nearby sledge. "I think you misunderstand my meaning. I am not referring to your mood or temper. Do you know the story of 'The Fox and the Grapes'?"

Stacia shook her head.

"Then, if you'll permit me." He waited a beat, and when she didn't protest, he began. "One day a clever fox with fur as red as your delightful hair went out hunting for his breakfast. He passed a grapevine simply bursting with the ripest purple grapes he'd ever seen and thought, 'Why, I believe those would make a perfect meal.' Circling below the vine, he leaped, his jaws snapping at just the right time, but the vine was wrapped around a tree, and the bunch of grapes was simply too high.

"Undeterred, he took a running start and leaped upon the trunk. He came closer this time, but still, he missed the mark. A clever fox, he tried again, using every trick he could think of, until his body was exhausted and his paw was injured. When he sat down in disgust to lick his wounds, he decided to find breakfast elsewhere, telling himself, 'I must have been mistaken thinking those grapes were desirable. Certainly, they must be the most sour, awful-tasting grapes in the land.' From that day, the fox vowed never to visit that vine or tree again, no matter how hungry he or his kits might be."

"I see. So am I to assume by your tale that I am the too-clever-for-his-own-good fox, a creature cursed due to its own stubbornness, or the too-high-and-lofty-therefore-they-must-be-sour grapes?" Stacia asked.

"You are neither," Father Frost replied. "You are simply a clever young woman sitting down at the base of a tree, licking her wounds. You have not yet decided to give up and declare the grapes unworthy of your attention. Nor are you the tempting fruit dangling just out of reach."

"So, what's the answer?"

"What do you mean?"

"Am I supposed to give up? Or am I supposed to keep trying?"

"I guess that depends on how badly you want breakfast."

"I hate metaphors. Can't you just speak plainly? Telling stories like that reminds me of my father. He always wanted me to think and analyze instead of just telling me the answer. He'd never give me the satisfaction of saying I was right or wrong either. Are you referring to my current predicament or to something else?"

"Yes."

Stacia grunted in frustration.

Father Frost, eyes twinkling again, leaned down and fished the biscuit from the pocket of her inert form. He tried to take a bite, but the biscuit was too hard from the cold. "Nearly broke my tooth," he said. "I suppose that'll teach me to be careful where *I* look for breakfast." He winked at Stacia and tucked the biscuit into his pocket, then patted it. "I'll just save it for later."

He turned and made as if he were going to leave, but then stopped. "Oh yes. I almost forgot." Unbuckling his jeweled belt, he removed his heavy, fur-lined cloak and draped it over her body, still lying in the snow. "That should heat you up in a bit," he said. "Polar bear fur is quite warm. Keeps me cozy in all kinds of weather."

"I shouldn't think your bear would like to hear that."

"Oh, you're referring to Lednik? Hmm. Yes. Well, not everything that appears bleak and terrible at first glance always is. He knows the warmth of my coat from personal experience. That fur belonged to his mama. Both of us loved that old girl. She gifted me her magic when she died. Old souls like that keep watch over those they care about. Just like your parents do for you, child. After all, who is it do you think that sent me, little Tassie?"

Stasia let out a soft gasp. No one had called her Tassie except her parents and her sister when she was young. Tears filled her eyes, and she clutched at her heart. She could feel it beating, hard. Warmth spread from her heart through her chest. It rose and fell, rose and fell, as she breathed in thirsty sobs. Above her, she could see the cold, dark sky with bright pinpoints of starlight, and then soft purple-and-blue glimmers shone down.

She began to sink.

"They're still there," Father Frost said. "They aren't beyond your reach, and you don't need to leap to find them. They're always near you. They watch over you, just like those stars. And they'd want you to know—want you to remember, lass—if there's something you want, something good, and you can't grasp it, just circle back. It may be that you just have some growing to do. Perhaps you'll find that the next time you come 'round those grapes will be easy to reach after all."

Stacia covered her face with her hands and began sobbing anew. She drew up her knees like she used to do in her bed when she was a child and frightened of some monster hiding underneath it, calling out for her father to come to her room and save her.

But instead of her papa, the voice of Father Frost soothed her. "All will be well, child. Sleep and let my pelisse work its magic. You've more work to do before joining your ancestors. Hush now. Sleep. Sleep."

That was the last thing she heard.

Stacia woke with the sun shining brightly in her eyes. She blinked and groaned. Her body felt stiff, but she was warmer than she'd been in a long time and didn't want to move. Fur tickled her nose. Becoming alert at once, she sat up and the heavy cloak fell from her shoulders, taking several inches of snow with it.

"I'm back in my body," she mumbled, pulling her fingers out to examine them. They were pink and healthy. She checked her feet, wiggling her toes, and they were also warm and unaffected by frostbite. Unfortunately, the staff was still broken. Careful to shield the blade, she picked up the two pieces and, finding a large pocket inside the cloak, placed them inside, then wrapped it around her body and headed back to camp.

Zakhar was calling her name as she approached.

"I'm here," she cried as she rounded some trees.

He sighed in relief. "We were worried. We thought a bear had made off with you," he said, his words trailing off as he saw the cloak. "What's this?"

"I had something of an adventure last night," Stacia confessed. "I wanted to practice using the staff, and I didn't want to wake you, but then I accidentally cut myself and had what you might call an out-of-body experience."

"Are you quite well?" Zakhar asked.

"I am. I . . . ran into Father Frost out there."

"Father Frost?" exclaimed Zima. "Did he bring you any presents?"

"In fact, he did," replied Stacia. "He gave me his coat. But I'm sorry to say, I broke the . . ."

Stacia reached into the cloak pocket to pull out the pieces of the staff, but when she did, she only found one piece. Panicking, she dug around for the other part. "Oh no! We have to find it!"

"Find what?" asked Zakhar.

"The staff. I lost the other half. I was here, but . . ."

She pulled out the half that was still there, but found it was no longer a half. She kept pulling and pulling until the entire staff emerged from the pocket. "I don't understand," she said. "It was broken."

"May I take a look?" asked Zakhar.

Handing it over, Stacia crouched down and stirred the porridge, coaxing Zima to eat.

"I found the break," Zakhar said. "See here? It's a very thin line where it was reattached. To me, it looks like clear glue or . . ."

"It's ice," Stacia said.

"Ice? But wouldn't that crack easily?"

"I don't know. Let's check."

Before he could stop her, Stacia took the staff and bent it over her knee, trying her best to snap it in two. If anything, it was harder than before. "Whatever it is," she said, "it's not ice."

Zakhar touched the fur on the cloak, then the jewels on the sleeve. "This belonged to Father Frost?" he asked.

"Yes."

"And he just . . . gave it to you?"

"Yes. No. He asked for food. I told him he could have a biscuit."

"Then this is your gift," said Zima. "It's magic. It fixes things."

"I-I suppose it does," Stacia said.

"I should like to draw it," Zakhar said. "Perhaps if we have time."

"Maybe later. Right now we need to get to that mountain."

"Yes. You're right. Such things can wait until later."

They quickly ate and broke camp, then they called for the birds and were underway. By the late afternoon, they could tell they were headed to the right place. The air was filled with the cries of cheers and the clash of battle. Even from a distance they could see several trails up the mountainside, each filled with travelers. As they approached, the sky also appeared to be peppered with flocks of various huge birds or winged contraptions.

One such *bird* broke away from its pattern of circling the mountaintops and headed toward them. As it got closer, they realized it wasn't a bird at all but a dragon! Zakhar didn't know what to do. He asked if they should turn around or run, but Stacia said to hold their course. Soon they saw the dragon had a rider.

"It's a bogatyr!" cried Stacia.

"But don't they usually fight and slay dragons?" asked Zakhar.

"Perhaps not in the dreamworld."

The bogatyr pulled up alongside them and introduced himself.

"Privet!" he called out. "I am Dobrynya Gorynych. Are you here to compete or to observe?" he asked.

"Observe," Zakhar said. "Definitely observe."

"Otlichno. Then if you will kindly show me your invitations."

Zakhar began patting his pockets as if that would produce anything.

Meanwhile, Stacia could see the bogatyr's smug expression, his grip on his spear tightening, and the fresh columns of steam coming from the nostrils of the dragon as it angled its head in their direction. She knew the man meant to destroy them.

"What my master means to say," Stacia intervened, "is that *I* am competing, and *he* is observing."

Zima began pulling on Stacia's cloak, shaking her little head in fear. Stacia shushed her and held her hand tightly.

"Ah, I see," said the dragon rider, buckling his spear at his side. "If that is the case, then you must follow me, and we'll get you registered and assigned barracks. After that, your *master* and his . . . daughter"—he nodded toward Zima—"will be free to wander the stands as he sees fit."

They followed the dragon-riding bogatyr, and the trio were soon immersed in a cacophony of noise and splendor the likes of which none of them had ever experienced before. In the hollow of the mountains, a great coliseum with multiple arenas had been created, some of which overlapped. One of the battle areas was a series of small islands or tree structures surrounded by water.

Stacia spied another dragon fighting in one arena against a flying lion. Cheers erupted when fire blazed from the mouth of the lion, and something like molten metal poured out of the dragon.

"Tsarevna," Zakhar said. "I don't think—"

"You can't go!" Zima protested. "You'll get hurt!"

"We have to help Iriko," Stacia said quietly, not wanting to cause Zima to panic. "Remember: He's fighting beasts like that. If we can find him, maybe we can free him before he gets himself killed." She bent down to Zima. "We have to save the tiger, Zima. Please understand."

"But remember what the sisters said: After he's entered, he has to fight until the end. The only ones who live are the winners."

"I guess we'll have to make sure Iriko and I are the winners, then."

Zakhar shook his head. "I refuse to allow you to enter. How could I call myself a man of God and send someone to their death?"

The bogatyr flew to their side again. "This is where you part. Say your farewells."

Stacia quickly hugged Zakhar, who only awkwardly returned the embrace, telling himself it was simply a friendly farewell, and possibly one to a brave woman he would never again set eyes upon. He quickly spoke last rites, just in case, offering an official blessing over her bent head while she said her goodbyes to Zima, who cried huge tears causing clouds to gather overhead.

They had drawn up to a large barracks at the top of the coliseum. A huge man strode up to them along the thin plank that jutted out over the side of a cliff. One step to the left or right meant a fall that would bring certain death. Peering over the edge, Stacia could see there were many so-called warriors who had seemingly decided to take that route rather than enter into the Novgorod Games. She breathed a sigh of relief not seeing a broken tiger body among the rocks.

He waved away the bogatyr, who rode off with a flick of his dragon's tail. Then the huge man thrust a form into Zakhar's hands.

"What's this?" he asked.

"Waiver of rights to your warrior. When she dies, depending on how well she fights, you'll be compensated for her death. If she goes over the plank, you get nothing. Collect your earnings at the end of the Games. Go to the owners' booth. Claim number is at the bottom."

Zakhar read through the rules quickly. "It says here she can bring her own weapons?"

"That's right. We won't issue any. Least not until the end."

"And she can keep her clothing?"

The man grinned and looked Stacia up and down. "Unless you want her to fight naked. She probably won't last as long, but we might go easier on her for entertainment's sake. Put her in the warmer arenas."

"No. No. She'll wear her clothing."

The man looked disappointed.

"And you'll feed her?"

"Yeah, yeah. She'll dine like a princess. Now, is she coming or what?"

Zakhar signed the form with a flourish and handed it back, along with a small piece of red gold. "See to it she is fed well and housed well and more of this will come to you later," Zakhar said.

The man's eyes lit at the sight of the rare gold. "Whatever you say, moy gospodin." He gave a slight bow, then said, "Come on, girl."

Stacia knew Zakhar had made a mistake. That man was not one who would take a bribe. Oh, he'd take your money for certain, but he'd also take your life. He was just as likely to throw her into a dungeon to make a point. But there was nothing she could do about it now.

"You must be careful," she said. "Watch your back. You're all Zima has."

"I'll watch out for him," Zima said.

Stacia couldn't help but laugh. "Good. Take care of each other. Watch out for pickpockets."

"You just worry about finding Iriko and winning."

Stacia nodded.

Zakhar helped her put on Father Frost's cloak, handed her the repaired staff, then slipped the burning cresset into one of the pockets and the coin that could heal in the other one. Then he gave her the bag of rye. "In case they don't feed you," he said.

Just as she threw one leg out onto the plank, Belizna, the white ermine, hopped off Zakhar's neck, ran up her leg, and climbed into the pocket of her coat. She glanced at Zakhar, who nodded earnestly. With that, Stacia quickly followed the large man toward the barracks, and when she glanced back, she saw the balloon that had brought them to the mountain flying to the opposite side of the coliseum.

"Where will they be staying?" she asked her warden.

"Where all the paridels stay," he replied. "In the gambling section."

They entered the barracks, and Stacia saw not rooms but cages. The few women she noticed were hard and filthy. One huge bear of a man lunged for her, stretching out his hands to grasp her coat. When he couldn't reach her, his fingernails grew, and he bucked and scrabbled, trying to scratch her as they wove around him.

"Get back, you great lumping beast!" her guide said. He lifted a small rod attached to his belt and flicked it sharply. It expanded before her eyes, and though the man retracted his nails and whimpered, trying to back away, the guide still touched the caged man on the chest with his device, giving him a powerful enough shock to blow him back against the wall and knock him out completely.

"I appreciate your stepping in," Stacia said diplomatically, "though it did seem he was cowed enough by your presence to back off even without your needing to take action."

"That's right," the man said. "I like everyone to know I mean business, lest they get any ideas."

"Yes. It's quite obvious you have a nose for business."

"What's that supposed to mean?"

"I mean it cannot be just anyone who could be trusted to supervise the greatest champions of the realm. The one who put you in charge must have known you are much more than just a strong arm. A person running games like this has to be wily, clever, smarter than everyone else who crosses his path. Take my master, for example. He tried to bribe you, and I could see it on your face—you're not the sort of man who dallies in whipsawing. You'd know that accepting bribes from various parties, whether dangerous-looking or not, is just as likely to cut the floor from under you as it is to benefit you in any way."

"What are you getting at, girl?"

"I'm simply saying I can tell you're a smart man, and a smart man might be interested in something more than money."

He laughed outright. "Yeah. That's right. If it's yourself you're offering, the other gals have already tried that. You are cleaner than most,

I'll give you that, but there's no sense in offering what I could easily take, is there?"

"True enough, my friend, true enough. But it's not myself I'm offering."

The man frowned, then rolled his eyes like he'd heard every offer under the sun. He placed a meaty paw on Stacia's chest and shoved her aside, then opened an empty cell. "Here's your palace, Princess. Dinner will be served to Her Majesty in an hour."

"Don't you want to hear my offer?"

"Lady," he said as he slammed her cell door shut and locked it, "I've heard it all. Nothing you could say would surprise me."

"This one will."

He sighed. "Fine. Seeing as how I got a nice piece of rare gold in my pocket, and knowing how you're going to die tomorrow anyway, I'll indulge you. Who is it you're offering up for me to have a nice *long* visit with? Is it your mother? Your sister? Your best friend? A cousin maybe? Believe me—I've heard it all."

Stacia placed her hands on the bars and smiled. "No, it's nothing like that. I'm offering you a visit with a very charming fellow. One who might answer a question you've dreaded the answer to for quite a long time."

Her jailer snorted. "I hate to tell you, but I don't go in for that sort of thing. I'm disappointed. You weren't even original."

As he turned away, she called out, "I think you misunderstand. I'm not speaking of a man, exactly. I'm talking about Death himself."

He stopped. "Death?"

"That's right. I . . . well, we, have the power to summon him. If we do call him to visit a certain person, he will tell you the means and date of your own demise."

Turning back to Stacia, he folded his arms across his chest. "Really?" After staring at her for several seconds, a grin lit his face. "You know, you did surprise me after all. I can truthfully tell you I've never heard that one before. Death? So what will he do? Summon a boat and usher me down the River Styx? Give me a vision of the future?"

"Something like that."

He rubbed his lip. "You know, it would almost be worth my exhalation to try to smuggle you out of here just to see what kind of game you're playing."

Stacia backed up. "Oh no. I don't want to be smuggled out."

"You don't?"

"No."

"Ne veshay mne lapshu na ushi, woman. You fill my ears with pasta."

"Nyet! I'm not lying. I want to stay. I'm looking for someone."

"Ah ha ha. Now I understand. You seek your springat stripling. Your attractive young man. Your beans are in flower. It makes you stupid and sick with love."

"What? No! No beans are flowering here. You don't understand. You—"

He waggled his finger. "Poor little zaychik. Little bunny chasing her wolf. What a stupid little bunny you are."

Stacia hit the bars with her palm. "I'm not looking for a wolf, and I'm not stupid or lovesick. I came because—because he needs me. He can't see without me. He's blind."

Turning around, Stacia slid down the bars to the cold concrete floor.

The man didn't leave. In fact, he crouched down next to her. "Look, I'm sorry if your man was brought in. It happens. But there's nothing I can do once a contract is signed. I can try to find him, make sure his death is quick. Yours too. There's nothing else I can do for you. Just tell me what to look for; give me a description. There are more than three hundred combatants."

A teardrop plopped onto Stacia's cheek. She swiped it away.

"What color is his hair? Is he tall? Short? Medium build? Just try and give me something."

"He's a tiger," Stacia said softly.

"He's what? I couldn't hear you. Say it again."

"I said," Stacia repeated, speaking louder this time, "he's a tiger."

"A tiger? Huh. Well. You *are* full of surprises."

He stood and rubbed his jaw with his palm. Stacia remained sitting on the cold floor, feeling defeated. She listened to the scraping sound of his whiskers against his hand.

"At least that narrows it down a bit," he said. "We've only got four of them. One of those is bound to be him. Not that it will matter much. They're all meant to be pitted against each other in the morning. Fierce beasts, those. Beaten all who've come their way."

Stacia quickly got to her feet, determination on her face. She reached through the bars and grabbed the man's tunic, refusing to let go even as he stumbled and grabbed the weapon at his waist.

Just as he commanded her to let go before she got the shock of her life, Stacia said, "You've got to get me into that match."

Chapter 25

The One with the Most Toys Still Dies

Pasha had arranged sumptuous accommodation for his party to stay in all week long, hoping that he'd convince Nik to remain once he saw the sights and tasted the food. It was his good luck that the boy had stumbled upon the very people, er, tigers, he was looking for within the first few hours of arrival. The being known as the Ghoulish Gnome of Grotesquery hadn't been at all certain the "family" Nik had been looking for would be found at the Novgorod Games at all.

In fact, as a betting man, he would have put down money that they were long since dead, knowing all the dangers and lethal creatures that inhabited the world in which he resided. Without some sort of magic or weapons, they were very likely to either be food fit for a beast, stolen away as chattel, or worse—that is, if they survived at all. As he well knew, there were things in this world much more terrible than death.

Still, he had hoped to convince the lad that staying the week would be good for both of them. The chances *were* better that Nik's friends would be at the Games. At least, finding them at the Games or hearing word of their whereabouts would be easier than just searching blindly. That much *was* true. Often strays and stragglers were rounded up and tossed into the Games by unscrupulous rustlers, looking for entrants that might make them a coin or two.

The boy was hopeful right now. Pasha didn't have the heart to tell the poor lad that the arena being constructed for the tigers and the game they were designing for them meant that only one was supposed to emerge a victor. One of his contacts had set up a meeting with the new owner of the black tiger for him that evening. He was hoping he could purchase ownership in exchange for a few favors. If there was a contract on the man's head, Pasha had the power to cancel such things if the man was open to negotiation.

Then there were also rumors of a young man of the religious persuasion with a small girl. The two of them appeared to be asking a lot of questions about the tigers, and what was worse, the man was flashing around red gold, a surefire signal that he wanted to be hauled off to the nearest gambling den so someone could see what else the good priest had tucked beneath his robes.

Unfortunately, there were a lot of unsavory elements circling the pair already. He'd have to try and locate the two of them as soon as possible before someone made them disappear permanently. Pasha would have to work quickly indeed. But tonight was about keeping up appearances. He didn't need the boy following him. He'd wait until they were all asleep, then sneak out to meet his contact.

"Come, my sweeting," he said to Polina. "I'll escort you to our suite of rooms, then fetch the finest of tidbits to tide you over until morning." Leaning over to Nik, he whispered, "I'll find out what I can, boy. Long as you promise to watch over my girl and her sister. There're ruffians about. Deal?"

Nikolai gave a brisk nod in return, and Pasha straightened with a charming smile, blinking his one large eye. "We'll be headed up to my personal luxury suites. You'll love it, Nik," Pasha said. "Panoramic views of the Games, personal chefs, a full-service bar, even a special system that lets you tune in to announcers covering each arena so you never miss an event. It's large enough I could host a party of up to one hundred guests, but since we can style it however we like, I turned the space into guest suites where we could spend the evening as well. Maids will come make it up for us in the morning or come clean it at the ring of a bell."

"Sounds expensive," Nik said.

"Oh, it is," Pasha replied. "Not that I pay a dime. The Gamemakers consider it 'curse insurance.'"

"Must be nice."

"My Pasha is such an important man, isn't he?" Polina said.

"I'd rather have a good one," Pushka said.

"But he is good!" Polina said. "He's good to me!"

"I suppose that's all that matters, then," her sister replied drolly.

As the two girls began arguing, Nik winced and Pasha ran a hand down his face, rubbing his one eye.

"Sorry if I started something," Nik said.

"Don't worry about it, kid," Pasha answered. "The two of them squabble all the time. Serves me right for bragging. I just like enjoying this part of my job, you know? The rest of it is—"

"Yeah. I get it."

"Okay. I'm heading out now. Sorry to leave you with that. Order them up something sweet. The staff are gone for the night, but someone's always on call. Just ring the bell and tell them what you'd like. If you can't think of something, say, 'Bring the usual,' and tell them how many people."

"Got it."

"See you in a few hours, kid."

"Pasha?"

"Yeah?" He turned, holding the door.

"Be careful."

"Always."

Pasha left, quietly closing the door behind him. Then Nik rang the bell and ordered "the usual" for four. After that, he sat down and waited for the girls' argument to lose steam. They were just winding down when he heard a quiet knock on the door. He opened it without checking first, thinking it was room service.

On the other side was a huge man, or at least a huge half man and half something else.

"Can I help you?" Nik asked.

"I'm here to escort you to your meeting with the owner of the tiger," the man said.

The two women hissed at one another to be quiet.

Hesitating only a moment, Nikolai answered, "Yes, that's right. Lead on, man." He turned to the women. "You two wait here for Pasha. Tell him where I've gone and that he shouldn't worry."

"I don't like this," Polina said.

"Nik knows what he's doing," assured Pushka. "We'll tell him," she promised.

He nodded his thanks and followed the big man out through the maze of streets, which was still crowded with partygoers. Though the Games were over for the evening, the vendors remained open, and bright lanterns danced from stalls and tree limbs in the cold wind. Feather-like snow fell, covering the paths, but rotating heaters bathed the attendants in warmth and melted the dusting as quickly as it fell. Nik longed to examine the strange machines, wondering if they were man-made or magical, but he dared not stop.

The man led Nik down the hill, farther and farther. The lights and noise of the parties faded until all he saw around him were darkened tents, torches, and campfires. Finally, the man stopped at a large gate built right into the side of the mountain. Pulling a key from inside his shirt, he inserted it into a heavy lock and swung open the gate. Nodding at another man, he said, "This is where I leave you. Follow Sergey the rest of the way."

"And you're certain this man is the one who owns the tiger?"

"He owns everything," was the only reply. "You're lucky to be granted an audience. He must think you have something of value to trade," he said. "Most people who ask something from him end up being killed."

Nodding too quickly, Nik swallowed and offered a sheepish grin. "Right. Right. I've got something valuable. Absolutely. Wouldn't be here otherwise. Right?" He laughed awkwardly, but it sounded too loud and hollow in the dark, huge space, so he stopped and cleared his throat. "Shall we go on, then?"

"This way, Bringer of Misery," Sergey said.

The gate closed and locked behind him as Nik realized what had happened. These were the men Pasha was supposed to meet. Obviously, there had been a misunderstanding. Either that, or Pasha had been delayed, or worse. What should he do? Should he play it as if he were Pasha? Would they know? Had they met before? As they walked in the dark, Nik quietly removed his shirt and pulled the tunic out of his secret pocket, then slipped it on over his head backward. He wouldn't have the luck that came with a goat kicking him or the butt of a horse, but it would have to do. Pasha had said these men could see through magic. Nik sincerely hoped he'd been wrong. Putting his own shirt on over the top of the tunic, he followed behind his guide and hoped he wouldn't need to make a quick escape.

Sergey stopped at a wide door and threw a lever. A series of lights came on, and he realized he was standing next to a large iron cage of some kind.

"What's this?" Nik asked.

"Get in."

"Are you putting me in prison?"

"No. See? I'm getting in as well. It's a levitator."

"A what?"

"A levitator. It takes you up inside the mountain. Runs on pulleys and gears. Waterfall does the work so's we don't have to haul things to the top or climb stairs. Get it?"

Glancing up the dark shaft lit only every so often by tiny gleaming lights, he said, "Brilliant. Is it made by magic? Did you install those snow heaters outside as well?"

"Don't rightly know. Boss is a bright one. Wouldn't never cross him. Look at him wrong, you're dead. You'd do well to remember that."

"I will," Nik said.

The man shut the cage, pulled a lever, and they began to slowly rise, ascending level after level. Nik was certain he heard the roar of a tiger at one point.

"Are the tigers kept down there?" he asked.

"Some are," the man replied.

"How many does he own?"

"You ask a lot of questions. I don't make it a habit to answer. Answering gets me killed. Understand? I'm only courteous to you being on account of who you are and all."

"I see. Thank you for explaining. You don't need to answer. I won't ask any more."

"Appreciate it."

The levitator finally came to a stop in a luxurious and well-lit entry. "These are the boss's personal quarters. Keep your visit brief and to the point, and you might live. Good luck."

"Thank you." Nik stepped out, and the man immediately left, descending back down to where he'd come from. Without knowing what to do next, Nik decided the best thing would be to simply knock on the man's door. So he did, and when it opened, he was greeted by a rather tall but fairly young man. "Come in, come in, make yourself welcome. Excuse me while I finish my shave."

"Not a . . . not a problem," Nik said, entering the sumptuous room, following the well-dressed man with a steaming towel pressed to his face.

"Have a seat," the man said, "and I'll be back in just a moment."

Nikolai had mingled with royals on many occasions and had seen what great amounts of money and power could purchase. He was always curious about the items put on display. They never failed to tell him a great deal about the owner.

Those who arranged comfortable furniture for guests tended to be the best diplomats and were centered on such things as human rights policies and treaties. Others who displayed fine art or statues were typically focused on trade, export, and economic prosperity. Some would showcase items from far-off places, indicating ties to nature, wildlife, the Arctic, or the oceans. While those who exhibited flags, weapons, or heroes of the past were more dedicated to patriotism and protection for their country.

It didn't matter whether the home was an extravagant palace or a hovel in the smallest town. People always showed their colors. Family portraits meant the person, or couple, took great pride or comfort in their legacy. A bare space indicated that whoever lived in that home had not put down roots or meant to leave at any moment.

As the man cleaned his face, Nik looked around for signs to gauge what type of person he was dealing with. The chairs were luxurious, something he'd expect in such a space, but the cushions were clean and simple—an indication the man did not want to stay or put down roots. However, there were subtle signs that showed he prized something . . . rare. Something not often seen.

Politics didn't interest this man. He didn't care for people either. He had no photos of family or friends. The art on the wall was expensively framed but meaningless. Generic. As were the carpets.

The few books he saw were also common—simple classics most would include in a library. But there were a few standouts. Those were what interested him, in addition to a few simple items that sat on one of the shelves. His fingers itched to examine the books as well as the relics. Nik immediately knew them to be magic—he recognized a rune carved into what looked to be a wand.

Hearing footsteps, he reluctantly sat down, noticing only at the last moment the bowl of stones on the table beside him. He ran his hand over them lightly and felt power, but it wasn't coming from the stones inside the bowl. *Ah*, he thought, *a ruse*. Sliding it aside, his eyes widened as he realized the entire table was a section of carved Sledovik cup stones that had been lifted from a glacier and polished to a high sheen. Running his fingers over the three indented cups, he could feel the hum of power coming from there.

"So," Nik mumbled quietly, "you collect magic."

Quickly, he moved the bowl back where it had been before and affixed a smile on his face, preparing himself to greet the man as he entered the room, knowing he'd have to do his best to play the part of someone else. Nik was good at acting. Hiding his true feelings and fears was something he was well accustomed to, especially when dealing with powerful men.

Still, when the man entered, the unexpected shock sent even a man as practiced as Nik aback. His smile faltered and his heart raced. It took him too many seconds to recover, but he managed and rose to shake the man's hand, saying, "I certainly appreciate you seeing me on such short notice."

"Not at all," the gentleman replied. "Please sit. To what do I owe the pleasure of a visit from one such as yourself this evening?"

Nik studied the man he'd come to know. He was young. Much younger than when he'd met him, but there was something in his eyes. Yes. It was the same. He was still deadly. And clever. Oh-so-very clever.

Leaning forward, Nikolai rubbed his hands together, slowly, and glanced up at the man, seeing just a hint of impatience. Deciding to scrap his plan and go a completely different route, Nik began. "I'm not who you think I am," he said.

"Is that right?"

"That's right. But then again, you aren't who people think you are either, are you? What are you called here? Do they refer to you as the Death Draughtsman yet? Or is that a name that comes to you in the future? Do you pose as a monk? I see you've been collecting magic. Have you discovered all the relics you seek yet? Perhaps you use your other name here. Grigor Sobol Petrovsky?"

The man was upon him in an instant, his dark eyes flashing daggers. He grabbed Nik by the collar and pulled him to his feet. "Where did you hear that name?" he asked softly. "Tell me quickly, before I slay you where you stand."

Nik was surprised the man didn't try to probe his mind or send clouds of magic or fog or summon his undead minions. He realized in that moment that the man hadn't yet come into his full power. That meant they had a chance to kill him—a much better chance here in the dreamworld than they did on the outside. Nik smiled.

"I heard that name from your own lips, Grigor. How many years have you been trapped here?"

Shock registered on the man's face. He thrust Nikolai back and he tripped, falling onto the settee.

The man began pacing. "You've met me, you said? In the future?"

"That's right. You're quite the magician."

"And I've been collecting relics?"

"Yes," Nik replied. "In fact, you're the one who sent me."

"I sent you?"

"That's right."

"I'm supposed to help you get out of here. But to do that, you're going to have to help yourself."

"What do you mean?"

"I mean, you're going to have to show me exactly what magic items you've collected so far. One or more of them might be tying you to this place. Also, you've got to let the tigers go. You can't get home until they do."

The Death Draughtsman appeared to be considering Nik's words but then dashed to the shelf and grabbed the wand.

Quick as a flash, Nikolai whipped off his shirt and disappeared. By the time his adversary mumbled an incantation and spun to aim it at Nik, he was nowhere to be found. Both men waited silently, listening for the tiniest sound, for an exhale or a shift of a boot on soft carpet. Finally, the man pocketed his wand and said, "I know you're still here and that you do not possess the power to curse me. If or when you return, I will kill you on sight. I know a thief and a robber when I see one. You are a fraud, nothing more. If you want me to believe you, bring me proof. Show me evidence of a relic and I will listen. Otherwise, your life is forfeit."

Lifting a bell, he rung it and a dozen men appeared immediately. "Sweep the room from top to bottom. When I leave, bar the doors. There is a thief inside. He is invisible. When you find him, kill him, and bring me his bleeding body. If he escapes, all of you will be killed in his place."

The men immediately fanned out and locked the doors. Nik knew he had no choice but to follow the Death Draughtsman. Staying as close to the man as possible without touching him, he closed the gap between them, narrowly avoiding being sliced open by multiple swords as they methodically began sweeping the room from top to bottom, side to side. He barely made it through the heavy door as it was locked behind them, and he heard the cries of the men as they searched.

Quietly, he followed the man as he returned to his quarters and sat at his desk. He stood in the room as he gave orders, signed papers, examined artifacts, and even personally murdered an assistant. When the body was removed, Nik followed it out, hoping they were going to take it outside to be buried. Instead, he barely avoided spewing the contents of his belly when they hacked it to pieces and fed it to not one but seven large tigers.

He recognized three of the cats. One was Iriko. The other two were Veru and Stacia. But how had they ended up caged there? Four of the seven cats refused the macabre dinner, but three of them ate with gusto.

Nik approached cautiously. He'd have to find a way to rescue them, but there was no way to do it alone. He'd need Pasha's help. He stopped at Veru's cage first. She roared.

"Hush," he mumbled. "I know you're probably mad."

Her paw came out and swiped at him.

"Stop that," Nik said. "I'm going to rescue you. I promise. I'm just glad to see you're all alive. I'll bring help. You're scheduled for the Games, but I'll try to get you out before that. You're owned by the Death Draughtsman. He's not at full power yet. We can beat him now if we put our heads together. Stay safe. I'll be back."

Just then two men turned the corner. "Did you hear something?" one guard said.

"Nah. Don't know why you're always thinking someone's down here. Just us and the cats and the man who's staying over for dinner." He started chuckling.

"I don't think it's funny. Bound to be us one of these days."

The other man shrugged. "We're all zoophagans, ain't we?"

"What's that? Zookeepers?"

"Nah. Carnivores. They eat meat. We eat meat. Only fitting we end up meat for something."

"Not me. I'm top of the food chain."

"No, you ain't. Lots of things what can eat you."

"Like what?"

"Like them, for one."

"Yeah? What else?"

"Snakes."

"Snakes? I don't think so."

"Yeah, they can. Great big ones."

The two men wandered off and turned a corner, still arguing.

"Glad you have men smart as carrots taking care of you," Nik mumbled. "I'll hurry," he promised, and followed behind them.

It took another hour for him to find his way out of the compound, and then two more hours to make his way back to the main game area and then to the section that looked familiar enough to him that he could find the rooms where Pasha and his girls were staying. He discovered the right floor, turned the corner, smoothed back his hair, and prepared to knock—when he noticed the room had been abandoned, and everything inside it had been destroyed.

Chapter 26

You Can't Live All Your Life in One Set of Feathers

"We've got her bolt of fabric, then," Veru said. "I suppose we'd better try to complete the third task before she returns."

"This one will take the longest time, I fear," the red knight said. "I wish you luck. I'll send my brother to you. He'll be coming this evening." He picked up Veru's hand and bent over it, placing a kiss on the back and then turned it over and gave her his magic comb, folding her fingers over it as he did.

"Oh, Polden, no," Veru said. "I couldn't."

"But you must. Don't you see?" he said. "She will ask how it was done. I dare not keep this with me. She will gather virgins and use them. I won't have it."

"But won't she do that anyway?" Danik asked.

He shook his head. "It's unlikely. It would take far too many and too much hair to grow the wool for even one sheep before a full moon. Without the comb, she won't be able to get more of the precious wool. She has enough to keep her happy for the time being. I'm hoping by the time she realizes what has happened, you'll be long gone with the comb."

"But can't she simply conjure another comb?" Veru asked.

"The comb was not made of her magic. She acquired it as she does most of her magic—by stealing it from others. What she doesn't understand is that the most powerful magic never works well when stolen, only when gifted. This is why I am gifting it to you."

"Very well. I'll keep it for now. But I plan to return the gift someday, my friend."

The knight nodded his head. "As you wish, my lady. Good luck to the two of you. Fare thee well, my friends. Dos vedanya."

"Dos vedanya, Polden."

He took his leave and Max leaped onto Veru's lap as Danik dished out a heaping bowl of hot porridge for both of them. They ate and considered the two jars of sesame seeds.

While Danik cleaned the bowls, Veru reread the contract and asked, "Why do you think the black knight needs to hold the jars while we're harvesting the wheat?"

"I don't know," he said over his shoulder. "Maybe it's a toll thing? We can only harvest while he's holding on to something in exchange?"

"Maybe."

Veru shook the jars, listening to the seeds roll around inside. Max stared at her with his big cat eyes. Opening her bag, she dug around inside until she found the flask Kadam had left for her. Uncorking it, she emptied the water into a mug and then dumped all the black seeds into it, then did the same with the white sesame seeds and Danik's water flask. He came over as she was finishing up.

"What are you doing?" he asked.

"Hedging our bets. Now, I need something small. It would have to sound like the sesame seeds."

Max jumped off her lap and headed over to a bin in the corner. He meowed and tapped it with his foot. When Veru opened it, she found rice.

"Interesting. I can't recall rice being here before. But it's perfect, Max. Thank you."

She filled both containers with approximately the same amount of rice and closed them up again.

"I've been meaning to ask how your scalp is healing," Danik said.

"It's better," Veru replied. "Still a little tender in the back, but the doctor said the sutures he put on my scalp would absorb on their own and promote quick recovery. Apparently, it's not made of catgut or silk like in our world but spun from some rare tree-dwelling spider creature found in this place. I tried not to ask too many questions. And honestly, I prefer not thinking about it too much. When I do, it makes me want to scratch."

"Interesting. May I take a look?"

Veru nodded, forcing herself to keep her hands at her sides, and Danik stepped behind her chair and gently parted her shorn hair. "There's a scar, but it looks very good. Mostly healed, I'd say. There's still blood on your hair though."

"He wanted me to wait another week until I got it wet again," she explained. "I figured most of the hair was so new anyway it probably didn't matter that much."

"It's been that long. I can help, if you like."

Veru sputtered. "Help? Help me . . . bathe?"

"No. Not that, of course. I meant wash your hair. It's so short now that it wouldn't take long, I should think—that is, unless you'd rather bathe. I'm not sure we have the time, but if you want to . . ."

He trailed off, and Veru could see his neck turning red.

"No, I think it's a good idea. My hair, I mean. Not a bath."

"Okay. You just sit there. I'll get what we need."

Danik bustled around the cottage, opening the closet to find clean towels, a basin, and soap. He poured hot water into the bowl and mixed in some cold water from the pump outside, then had Veru turn in the chair, plumping a pillow behind her shoulders so her head hung over the side. He draped a towel around her shoulders and gave her another for her face.

"Are you sure about this?" she asked.

He shrugged. "My mom had sores on her feet on occasion and I bathed them, tending to the wounds to keep the infections at bay from the time I was young," he explained.

"Do you know why?" she asked as he carefully poured water over her head and began to lather in soap.

"The doctors didn't know. Something to do with her blood and the circulation. She always complained that she had ghost pains in her toes and ankles. Then she stopped feeling anything at all below the knee."

"I'm sorry. Is that how you know so much about herbal medicines and poultices?"

He paused. "Did I tell all this about myself before?"

"Not about your mother, no. When my paw was in a trap, you gave me something to make me sleep. I healed too quickly for you to treat me, but I saw what you'd made and dropped as you ran out. You put a lot of work into it."

Danik grunted. "She always called me her miracle boy. Didn't have me until she was older than most. When they got sick, I tended to them, hoping I *was* a miracle. That I was sent to them to save them. I never got sick. Not even a cough." Danik began rinsing her hair and then paused. "Mama died first. I was holding her hand so tight. Her body just . . . just stopped fighting. It relaxed. She looked at me and smiled and said, 'My angel.' A tear leaked from the corner of her eye, and she was gone."

He took the towel and began squeezing the excess water from her shorn hair. Then he stood, leaving the towel wrapped around her head, and tossed out the water, putting away the bucket and the soap.

"What about your papa?" Veru asked. "Do you remember?"

Sighing, Danik nodded and looked through the bag, removing the comb. Then he took the towel from her head, and she sat up. As he began working through the short hair, he said, "Papa was delirious. He didn't even know Mama was gone. I buried her with my uncle's help, then sat with him for two more days, trying to feed him broth and soaked bread, anything my aunt left at the door. But he wouldn't eat, wouldn't drink. He was gone before the third day."

"How old were you?"

"Not yet twenty. After my father was buried, I stayed away from my cousins long enough to ensure I didn't carry what my parents had, then I left with my older cousins on a hunting trip to help. Soon after I was assigned my own route."

His hands stopped moving over her hair. "There. I think it's long enough now."

Veru's fingers darted up to her wet scalp. "I didn't realize you were using *that* comb."

"I thought you might like your hair to be your usual length. Not that I don't like it short."

Standing, Veru removed the towel from her shoulders. "Thank you for helping me."

"You're welcome."

"So, can I ask . . . when we first arrived, and you were searching for your home . . ."

"I was lost."

"Which makes perfect sense. This is a strange place, after all," Veru said, taking a step around the chair.

"It is," he said, setting the comb down on top of the chair and narrowing his eyes at her, wondering what she was up to.

"And then I was a perfect stranger as well. You having only known me as a very large cat." Veru walked her fingers along the arm of the chair and slid her foot closer, closing the gap between them.

"That's right," Danik replied, not moving away but not bending toward her either, which was frustrating to Veru. Never in her life had she had to woo a man, and she found the exercise both taxing and, to her surprise, also exhilarating.

When she was right next to him, her arm brushing against his, she wondered how she should approach him. Veru knew he cared about her. The kiss they'd shared before proved he wasn't immune to her charms. So, what was it? Why did he hold back? What was it that he'd said to her before? Something about him being string or an instrument that might be broken?

She thought about the words of his song. He'd been concerned about being a pawn in a vicious game. It was possible he'd been talking about their situation, but there was a niggling part of her that wondered if he wasn't speaking of her. Did she even deserve someone as good as

Danik? His mama's miracle child, her angel boy? Surely if she was looking down on them from heaven right now, she'd choose someone else for her only son.

While it was true that Veru was a tsarevna, a royal, born of noble blood, she'd always felt like an impostor. What would it be like to be loved not for your face, your body, or even your blood, but simply for who you were? Loved enough that someone would kneel at your damaged feet to ease your pain. Seen for your humor, your mind, and appreciated or not, depending on your actions and not on your appearance.

Perhaps a more direct approach might work, she thought.

"Danik?" she began.

"Yes?"

"Do you think there's a possibility that a hunter—"

"A musician who hunts," he clarified.

"Right." Veru picked up his hand, turned it over, and began lightly tracing the calluses on his fingers, trying to figure out which ones were made from playing instruments and which ones were made from wielding a bow or setting traps. She started over. "Do you think it's possible for a musician who hunts to find happiness with the very thing he's been hunting for?"

Danik frowned. "That tickles. What are you saying?"

"Do I have to spell it out for you? You came here searching for something. A home, right? Well, how about it?"

"How about what?"

Veru shoved his arm. "*Me*, you durak."

"You," he said bluntly. "You want to take me home, with you. To the palace? As what? Your butler, your dvoretskiy? If you want to hear me play, to serve as a visiting kompozitor of songs, I'm more than happy to do so, my lady. But if you want to install me as one of your lyubovnikov, then my answer is unequivocally nyet!"

Becoming angry, Veru retorted, "I think you misunderstood. That's not at all what I—"

"It's always taking, isn't it?" he accused. "It's not enough that I had to give up my family home and most of the instruments. Do you know how much in taxes my uncle has to pay each year? That it's based on the number of children? How is it their fault how many they have?"

"What?" Veru said. "What are you talking about? Number of children? What does that have to do with anything?"

Danik snorted. "There's a tax for everything. Even dying. Did you know that? Wasn't it bad enough that I lost my parents, but then I had to lose the instruments they played as well? And for what? To fund diplomatic balls? More dresses? Wars in far-off locations? Or perhaps pay for your mother's pet programs to help people who aren't even citizens of our country?"

Veru's face turned red, and her neck felt hot. "That's not fair. I lost my parents too, you know."

"Yeah? And did you lose your home as well? Have to change jobs? Move in with a relative to help support them simply because their sons didn't want to join the military? You may think I don't remember much at all, and that's true. I don't recall my time with you or our travels or meeting a tiger or freeing her from a trap. But I do remember losing my family and how my auntie cried at the thought of losing her sons. After losing her sister, my mother, the idea of losing any of her sons sent her to her bed with worry. It was so bad that I was willing to do anything to help."

"That included selling off your inheritance? Your instruments?"

"Yes. At first it was enough."

"And when it wasn't?"

"When it wasn't? I went hunting. That way at least the younger boys could stay home longer."

Now she understood. Veru had been in the meeting when it was decided that citizens with more than two healthy children must either send one to join the military or pay a penalty of increased tax. The size of the penalty increased with the number of children eligible to serve but refusing to enlist. It was a way to ensure that the military would always remain strong. She'd never considered what would happen to a family whose children refused to join. Most everyone volunteered willingly and was proud to serve.

"Danik, I . . ." Veru trailed off, not knowing what to say. She had always assumed Danik had moved in with his aunt's family because he was an orphan, not because they'd needed him to help pay the taxes. She'd known hunting wasn't his first choice, but she'd assumed he'd go back to music when he was ready to strike out on his own. Now it seems he'd always been ready. That Danik was just the type of person to sacrifice himself to help others. Turns out, he was indeed a better man than she deserved.

"Look," he said, rubbing his neck. "It doesn't matter." He turned his back to her, and Veru felt defeated.

She stood there a moment, staring at him, thinking. This wasn't a moment where she could manipulate another person with a winning smile or the wink of an eye, and truthfully, she didn't want to do such a thing with Danik. Her skill with knives wasn't going to help her in this situation either. If only she was as skilled at diplomacy as her mother had been. Taking a deep breath, Veru said, "It does matter. I can't pretend to know all the answers. The easiest thing to do would be to just shrug and say laws are complicated, and leave it at that, but that's a lazy person's justification for doing nothing."

Veru put her hand on his shoulder, and he turned back halfway. "As for my mother's pet programs, I know for a fact that each and every one was put in place because she had a good heart and wanted to help others, not because she intended to cause injury or pain. Not that that's an excuse—I'm just explaining her purpose. Intentions do mean something. Good hearts mean open ears and a willingness to listen to others. I would hope that I'm like her in that regard.

"Unfortunately, I am not well-versed in all the laws regarding taxation, but I can promise you that upon our return, I will look into this one and see about amending it. Do you—would you—that is . . . I wonder if you might be willing to help me and share some of your insights into the matter? I would appreciate your unique perspective."

Danik tilted his head, considering her offer, then nodded. "I will accept your proposal, Tsarevna." Then he lifted a finger. "But don't get any ideas. I'm only agreeing to counsel you. Nothing else."

"Hmm," she said, raising her hands. "I'd never assume otherwise."

Each of them retreated into their own thoughts and wandered out onto the summer porch around sunset, waiting for the black knight to arrive.

"I never doubted it, you know," Danik said quietly when the daylight finally disappeared, and the first stars arrived.

"Doubted what?" Veru replied as she leaned back against the wall of the house, her fingers clasped around one drawn-up knee.

"Your heart."

Veru tried to make out his expression in the dim light coming from the open door of the house, but all she could see was the flash of his eyes. She wished she had her tiger's eyes again. How she missed her cat. Max seemed to sense her loss and twined his body around her leg, purring furiously. She reached down to scratch his ears just as she heard a snap of lightning and thunder, and the clap of hooves hit the ground.

Sparks trailed behind a horse as black as night, with fiery flames shooting from his nostrils. He drew to a stop by the porch, and his rider with black armor and a flowing black cape strode up and bowed.

"Dobryy vecher," he said after removing his helmet. "I am Sumerki."

"Priyatno Poznakomit'sya. It's nice to meet you. I'm Veru, and this is Danik."

"My brothers told me about you. I'm afraid they are becoming hopeful. I wish you hadn't encouraged them. It's much better if they resign themselves to their fate. You should do the same and give up now."

"Give up?" Veru said. "But don't you wish to be free?"

"Of course. But such a thing isn't possible. In the centuries we have been enslaved, none, not a single trapped soul, has gone free. At least not in the sense you mean."

"I don't understand," Veru said.

The knight sighed. "Have you heard farmers call barren fields a 'devil's garden' or 'bare bones'?"

Veru shook her head, but Danik nodded. "I have," he said. "They consider it cursed."

"That's right," the knight replied. "Where a thriving farm, one considered vernant and flourishing, might be what most seek, that's not the case with our mistress. She flouts every rule, sows the tares with the wheat, and breaks ground on Fridays using iron plows. Instead of gardeners, she uses pollincters who practice foul fetidities such as grinding the bones of the dead to use as fertilizer. Because of this, anyone setting foot on the field is at risk of the most despicable chicanery. I fear her intention is to undo the two of you utterly until you are completely riven."

"Why does she want you to hold the sesame seeds?" Veru asked.

"Sesame seeds?"

"Yes. A jar of white and a jar of black."

The knight paced, stroking his short black beard. "I've only seen her harvest once. She sent me away and didn't think I watched, but I hid and saw . . . something."

"What?" Danik asked. "What did you see?"

"She scattered something white. I thought it was rice at the time. Thousands of white mice appeared. I don't know what they did exactly, but when they were done, the tares were gone."

"What happened next?" Veru asked.

"Then it was time for the other stuff. It was dark. Must have been the black sesame seeds. After scattering those, blackbirds came. They gathered the rest. She never had to set foot on the field."

"So she wants us to do the same but without the sesame seeds? How? Why would she even give them to us, then?" Veru asked.

Danik said, "Maybe she thinks the game wouldn't be fair if we didn't have all the pieces to play with."

"Somehow I don't think she'd care," Veru said. Turning to Sumerki, she asked, "Do you know where we could buy more sesame seeds? We do have your brother's mirror. Maybe we can replace them, and she wouldn't notice."

"It might work," the knight agreed. "But I don't think the two of you have the time. She'll be returning tomorrow. My brother has been watching her comings and goings. We need to finish tonight."

"Then it's over," Danik said. "We've lost."

"Perhaps not," the knight said, putting his hand on Danik's arm. "I have heard you know something of music."

Danik nodded. "I do."

"Then perhaps there is hope. Come. We must hurry."

He instructed Danik to climb on the back of his own black stallion, and then he gave Veru a leg up behind him. Once they were in place, he slapped the horse on the rump and a portal opened, taking them to a distant field that grew under a gray moonlit sky. The portal opened again, and the knight soon joined them.

Never had Danik seen such a sickly, stunted field. The wheat looked half dead, and he wondered if there was any to harvest at all.

As if reading his thoughts, the knight assured him, "There is more than enough to fill her purposes, I promise you." After helping Veru down, he opened his saddlebag and produced a pipe. "Here is what I was looking for." He handed it to Danik.

"What am I supposed to do with it?" he asked the knight.

"It is said to contain magic—the ability to summon aid to those who need it. I have never been able to coax the right song from it to do so, but seeing as how you are a musician, I thought perhaps you . . ." He smiled and held it out, gesturing that Danik should try.

"Pipes aren't my strong suit," Danik said.

"It couldn't hurt though, could it?" Veru said.

"Just remember: Don't step on the field," the knight warned. "At best, you'll get sick. And at worst—"

"We'll die," Veru finished. "We understand."

"Okay, here goes," Danik said.

"Wait!" Veru said. "You need to hold these." Veru passed the flasks containing the sesame seeds as well as the containers filled with rice over to the knight. "It's part of the contract. I don't want to leave any part of it undone."

"Very good," the knight said. "I'll hold on to these. You may proceed, then," he said to Danik.

Lifting the pipe to his lips, Danik began playing and closed his eyes. The song was sweet and happy, a bright tune for such an awful place. A little yellow bird arrived and landed at his feet. Then a second one, this one blue, and then a third bird came, this one red and brown. They danced and pecked at the ground around him.

"Good," the knight instructed. "That's very good for a first try. I've never been able to summon so much as a cricket."

"But they aren't white mice. Do you think that matters?" Veru asked.

"I don't think we can spare the time to figure it out," the knight replied. "Now, Danik, tell them to collect the tares."

"How?"

"I don't know. You must instruct them in the music somehow."

Danik piped a new tune, and soon the little birds lifted overhead and began circling. Then, almost as one, they flew out and landed in the field. They started pulling on the tares and eating them, and then, suddenly, they screamed, and one by one, they began exploding in a mass of blood and feathers.

"Danik!" Veru shouted. "Get them out of there!"

"I'm trying!" he spat and played faster. One little bird almost made it out, but it screamed, and its neck broke just before escaping. Its little body rolled and landed near their feet. Veru started crying and bent to pick up the tiny bird, but the knight stopped her.

"It's best if you don't touch him," he said. "You'll have to try again, young man. This time targeting the white mice. Apparently, it matters a great deal which animal enters the field."

Danik shook his head and tried to hand back the pipe. "I can't do it."

"You have to."

"I won't," he insisted. "I won't be responsible for killing any more creatures."

"Then you'll be her slave," the knight said, taking the pipe reluctantly.

"It's a better end than killing others. At least I'll be able to live with myself."

"Perhaps. But think. You're also making this choice for your young woman. Would you have her suffer in this way as well? I promise you, a lifetime of servitude to my mistress will not go well with you. She has a way of, shall we say, extending life, making your vassalage an endless toil."

"Danik?" Veru put her hands on his cheeks. His whole body was trembling. She knew how much he hated killing. "Close your eyes." She waited for him to comply. "Do you remember when you had to catch mice once to feed two very hungry tigers? We were starving, and that's all we had to eat."

"We were in a church barn," he said softly. "It was snowing."

"That's right. You set traps."

"I did." He smiled. "Zakhar was so frightened."

"You remember," she said.

"Pieces come back sometimes."

"You did what was necessary so we could survive. That is the reason you hunted. To help your family. This is not much different. But we will spare them if we can. This time we'll do it intentionally, properly. Focus on only the mice. Tell them you're going to feed them, but they'll need to be very careful. They'll know what to do because they've done it before. Play them a little tune. Tell them there's good food waiting for them. They're hungry. Lots to eat. They'll be safe if they do it like last time. But only the mice. Spare the wheat, take the tares."

"I don't want them to suffer," he said.

"Then they won't. You can do this. Tell them in your song to tread carefully."

He began to hum with his eyes closed. "Only the mice, lots to eat, you'll be safe, just spare the wheat." Lifting the pipe, he pursed his lips and began blowing a little marching tune. Soon the underbrush began moving, and hundreds of tiny white mice scurried out onto the field. Danik played and played until every mouse had eaten their fill and had left, then he collapsed at Veru's feet, his limbs quivering with fatigue, beads of sweat on his brow.

The knight gave him a flask and he drank deeply, then wiped his mouth with the back of his hand. "What now?" he asked.

"Now it's time for the blackbirds," the knight said. "But this time we need them to collect the wheat and bring it to us so we can put it in bags."

Danik mumbled a few lines and then seemed to settle. Before he began, Veru asked, "What are you going to say?"

"Something like, 'Birds of black, collect the wheat, bring it back, stack it neat, fly true and swift, tilt and drift, so we can beat the bitter hag, by stuffing full our little bag.'"

"Good," Veru said, putting her hands on his shoulders. "You can do this. You'll keep them safe, just like the mice. All you need to do is remind them they've done it before. Help them remember."

Danik began to play, and Veru could almost hear the words in her head as he fingered the notes and mouthed them to herself as he did, repeating them over and over. Soon she heard the cry of large blackbirds as they circled overhead, their gleaming eyes peering at them with great intelligence. Like the others, they landed on the ground and tilted their heads, listening to Danik's song at first. Then, one by one, they took off for the field and began harvesting the wheat, but this time, the birds didn't explode.

Sumerki quickly spread out a large piece of canvas, and the birds began dropping shafts of wheat onto it. Veru bent and began binding up the wheat into bundles. Once they were grouped together, she moved them aside and bound the next one and the next. It took several hours, but finally, all the wheat was harvested.

The birds finally left, and Veru collapsed next to Danik.

The knight gave them both water from his own flask. "That was very well done," he said. "Why don't you two take my horse home, and I'll come along behind and bring the wheat with me."

"Are you sure?" Veru said.

"I can handle it," the knight promised. "I'll have all of it there before morning."

"Okay," Danik said. "And thank you for your help." He tried to hand the pipe back to the knight, but he wouldn't take it.

"It's yours," he said. "I've no use for it. Clearly, such a thing was meant for you. Please, keep it with my regards."

"Spasibo," Danik said.

"Pozhaluysta. Safe returns and see you soon."

"You as well," Veru said.

The knight handed them the flasks containing the sesame seeds and the others full of rice, and with a wave of farewell, Danik and Veru galloped through the portal amid a clap of thunder and lightning, hoping they would make it back before Yuga.

CHAPTER 27

One Who Sees the Future Will Still Make the Same Choices

Nik realized at once that the Death Draughtsman's men had gotten there first. His best and only hope was that Pasha and the sisters had managed to escape before they'd arrived. In case anyone had remained to watch for his arrival, he quickly used his tunic to turn invisible again and stole through the suite searching for clues.

Relieved to find no signs of blood, Nik was just about to leave when he caught sight of something small—tiny enough to be overlooked, especially when the room was being tossed over by men. It was a torn piece of Pushka's veil. Picking it up, Nikolai rubbed it between his fingers, and a blurry image of Pasha appeared before him.

"Sorry we had to leave you, kid. Needed to get out in a hurry. No way to communicate our whereabouts and keep it secret like, without using my power on you. When you picked up the veil, it triggered something only you can access. Thing is, I had to give you a wee little curse to make it work. Won't hurt or last too long, but you'll be very thirsty for the next two days. Then your wiz will turn green and sort of pulpy for the next three. It's one of my favorites. Used for those who cheat on their ladies. Always scares 'em straight. Least for a little while. Like I said, not to worry. Nothing permanent, and it won't gum up your works, so to speak.

"Now, while I'm talkin' . . . get out of there. You shouldn't have gone in my place. You probably saved my gal and her sister though. Appreciate it. I *told* him I'd come to him. He's notorious for changing the rules. I should have anticipated that."

Nik kept his fingers pressed to the cloth and made his way out into the hall. Just in time, too, because as he did, four men dashed past his invisible form and barreled into the room, slashing every inch of the space with their swords. Clearly, they'd been told he could hide. The men looked different from the ones he'd seen in the compound. He wondered if the other men had all been hacked up and fed to the tigers. He shivered and carefully made his way back outside, listening to Pasha's instructions.

He was to go to a caravan camp outside the Games on the far side of the mountain and search for a fortune teller named Lyudmila. Once he located her, he was to say he was searching for his brother, Gedeon Volkov. Nik smirked at that. Gedeon Volkov meant "mighty warrior." It was just like Pasha to name himself something like that. Nikolai wondered what *his* secret identity would be. Probably Mr. Danger-Always-Finds-Him, or perhaps Mr. I-Have-A-Target-On-My-Back. Honestly, it was likely more along the lines of "I'm-Already-Down-So-Go-Ahead-And-Kick-Me."

Swallowing, Nik realized his mouth had gone dry. Never in his life had he been so parched. The curse was already at work. Still invisible, he stole two huge mugs of sbiten and drained them immediately, then headed to another stall and took two dippers of water from a barrel. That lasted him until he got outside the walls, where he suddenly had the pressing need to relieve himself, which he did behind a tree.

Thankfully, there was nobody around to hear his scream. "Painless?" he hissed. What came out of him was green all right. It reminded him of the mossy beard the tree spirit, Larix, wore. "That bloody, button-eyed, bitter blister."

He groaned as he adjusted his pants, realizing he was now thirsty again. He could definitely see why this particular punishment was effective for curbing a man's enthusiasm for straying. Nik was extremely uncomfortable. Cursing under his breath, he made his way around from camp to camp, trying and failing to look and act normal and becoming more desperate by the moment to scratch himself. He asked everyone who'd bother talking to him long enough if they knew of Lyudmila, and finally, he found someone who did. When he arrived at the formidable woman's camp, she took one look at his miserable self and clucked her tongue.

Waggling her finger at him, she said, "I do not abide the cheaters. If you are asking me to soften the pain, I will not help you."

"No. It's not that." Nik groaned, longing to clutch his privates. "I'm looking for my brother, Gedeon. Gedeon Volkov? That and a drink, if you have one. Water is fine."

She looked him up and down. The bangles on her arm jingled musically as she put her hands on her wide hips. "Yes. I bet you are thirsty. Thirsty and chafing. No? Come. I give you drink and help you find brother, but that is all. Yes? And don't scratch. Not in my tent. Understand?"

Nik nodded and bit his lip. "Yes. Spasibo."

"Come. You sit here. I bring brother."

Disappearing through a curtain, Nik sat at a table, warming his hands by a small cookstove. Soon the fabric stirred, and a serving girl brought a glass with a pitcher of cold water and set it down beside him. He stared at it greedily, not even waiting for her to leave before gulping down a glass. He'd emptied three more before he heard voices. One sounded familiar.

"But who is it, good lady?"

"You go, see."

"If you're scared, I'll go." This came from a young girl. She was the first one to enter. The girl cast aside the curtain and strode up to Nik, offering her hand as if she were a princess. "Hello," she said.

Before he could shake her hand, the fortune teller called out from behind the curtain, "Don't shake hands with that one, girl. He's stricken with a curse. You would'na want it ta rub off."

"Oh. Sorry," she said and gave him a curtsy instead.

"Don't worry about it," Nik replied. "Dobryy den', to you," he added, inclining his head.

"I'm Zima. Who are you?" the little girl asked boldly.

"I'm—"

Before he could answer, the man strode into the room, gave a shout of delight, and exclaimed, "That, my dear, is Nikolai Novikov! I can't tell you how good it is to see you, Nik. Now what's all this about a curse? Is there something I can do to help?"

Nik rose from his chair and grasped hands with the priest, then quickly stepped back, withdrawing them. "Better not take a risk. I don't think it will rub off on you, but I was also promised it was painless, so you never know. You have no idea how good it is to see you, Zakhar. How have you been? I've got so much to tell you."

"And I, you. I'm so relieved we are reunited at last."

"Yes, but not all of us. We'll get to that. But first, have you seen my friend Pasha? He might be going by the name Gedeon. Gedeon Volkov."

"Oh. I'm a . . ." Zakhar leaned in closer. "I'm afraid Gedeon is *my* watchword."

"Really? Well, that's interesting. How did you come by that, I wonder?"

"It was the little man," Zima said. "He said we needed to be more careful. And hide our balloon too."

"Is that right?" Nik queried Zakhar. "So you have a balloon?"

"Yes. I gave the man our gold. In exchange, he's going to help us rescue Stacia."

"Did this little man happen to have one large eye in the center of his forehead?"

"He did!" Zima exclaimed.

"Ah. That's Pasha."

"At least that's one mystery solved," Zakhar said.

"Yeah. About that. You'd better sit down."

Zakhar and Zima sat, and Nik poured himself another glass of water, downed it, and then peered at the empty pitcher with a scowl.

"Okay, I don't know how much time we have," Nik said, "so I'll just get right to the point. Veru, Stacia, and Iriko have all been captured by the Death Draughtsman."

"What?" Zakhar said in alarm.

"Who is that?" asked Zima.

"Perhaps, before we continue, we need to make sure certain things aren't heard by the w-r-o-n-g sort of people." Nik then asked the little girl, "Who, my dear, are you? And why are you with Zakhar?"

"She's, um . . . she's someone we came across along the way. We offered to take her with us in exchange for help from her aunties," Zakhar explained.

"That's right," Zima said, lowering her delicate eyebrows in a scowl that made her look somehow more adorable. "And I'm not *wrong*. My aunties said so. I was made absolutely correct. Besides, I'm helping you."

"I see," Nik replied. "My apologies, then. And, um, how do you *help*, exactly?"

"I share my gifts."

"Right. And what gifts might those be?"

Zakhar held up a hand. His expression held great alarm, but Nik ignored him. Nothing was more pressing to Nikolai at the moment than his need to urinate, yet he desperately did not want to leave the tent to do so.

"This is one of them," Zima said, pulling an ornate timepiece from a knapsack. "Would you like to know your future? I've been helping Lyudmila with some of her customers."

"Sure," Nik said, hoping indulging her would distract him from his other, baser needs. "Why not?"

He answered her at the exact same moment Zakhar leaned across the table, saying, "Zima, no! Not him!"

The little girl turned to Zakhar and said, "You know I need to share my gift with those I feel is right. This one needs to see."

Wincing, Zakhar reluctantly nodded while Nik glanced between them in confusion. "What is it I need to see, little one?"

"You need to meet Death."

"Meet . . . Death?" Nik raised an eyebrow, glancing between Zakhar and Zima, but neither explained further.

Adjusting the clockwork on the top, the little girl angled the dials toward Nik, twisting them back and forth until she was satisfied, and then, when all was ready, she flipped the device upside down.

Nik stared in fascination as white sand began falling . . . up, mixing with black, twisting and turning in a spiral. Then the particles passed through one another, filling opposite sides of the timepiece.

Quietly, Zakhar took a bottle of ink and a pen from his bag, along with a fresh sheet of paper, and dipped his quill twice. With a flourish, he wrote Nik's full name across the top of the sheet and then slid it over.

"In case you want to write anything down," he said. "I'll leave you to it."

As he rose from his chair, Nik said, "I don't understand. You don't have to leave. What's supposed to be happening?"

"You'll see," Zakhar said softly. His smile was sad and apologetic. "I'm sorry, but I don't like staying for these. I'll return when it's over."

Before Nik could further protest, Zakhar was gone, and he was left alone with the strange little girl. Then, suddenly, Nik realized the two of them weren't alone. Another man had appeared in the room.

"Kak dela, malyshka?" the man said in a smooth voice. "How may I serve you today?" But his dark eyes never left Nik's face.

"I think this one needs to talk to you," Zima said.

"Really? He doesn't appear to be dying at the moment." Then the man cocked his head, and a small smirk appeared. "Though I suppose he is suffering somewhat."

"He isn't dying. It's true," Zima said soberly.

"Then why do you want to burden him, child?"

Zima blinked. "I don't know. I just think he needs it. Or needs to talk to you, anyway."

"Interesting," the man said.

"Who are you?" Nik asked.

"I don't answer questions you already know the answer to."

The room was silent for a moment as Nik studied the other man. His heart began beating fast, and his breathing kicked up like he'd been running.

"You . . . you're a demon?" Nik speculated.

"Not quite."

"A ghost?"

"Guess again." The man studied his fingernails. "You *can* feel it, can't you? The inevitability of me? The one you can't evade, no matter what you do."

Nik stared at him, and he knew. He simply knew. This man had been in Nik's presence before. Many times, in fact. Sometimes Nik had even prayed for him to come, knew he'd been there, lurking in the shadows. And yet he hadn't taken him; he'd left him alive to suffer another day, another week, another month. He'd been there when the knife had slipped between his mother's ribs and her lifeblood had spilled out on the floor of their little home. He'd been there on the hillside as he'd watched their cabin burn to the ground, retrieving the tiny souls of his siblings. Yes. There was no denying—he'd been in the presence of this being before.

"You're Death," Nik said, swallowing.

Grinning, Death said, "Give the man a prize!" He laughed, then shrugged and added, "Just kidding. There's no prize. No trump card that lets you escape my clutches."

"You're a prize to me!" Zima said.

"Thank you, love," Death said. "That's why you'll always be my favorite."

"And why you'll come for me twice."

The little girl grinned, showing a dimple when the dark man smiled at her and touched his finger to her pert nose.

Nik felt sick. No. He felt worse than sick. He was going to vomit. Closing his eyes, he practiced his breathing. In through the nose, out through the mouth. In through the nose, out through the mouth. Then he tried to wet his lips, but his mouth was so, so dry. Nik lifted his glass and got only a few drops. Opening his eyes, he saw Death staring at him. No. Into him. "What . . . what do you want from me?" he asked.

"It's not what *I* want from *you*. I'm here at your behest. What is it you want from me? Zima thinks you need to talk."

Wringing his hands, which had gone cold and numb, Nik shifted in his seat uncomfortably. "What do people usually talk about when visiting with you?" he asked.

"Hmm. Most want to know if it's their time. But I sense you know the answer to that question already. They usually want to know the when. The how. The who."

"And what about the why not?"

"Ah." The man spun a chair around backward and took a seat, folding his arms on the chairback. "I wondered if you'd be brave enough to ask me that one directly."

"Most aren't?"

"No. I frighten most. Not because of anything I've done. Death is as natural as birth, breathing, eating, going for a walk, or planting a tree. It's part of what makes you human. Want to know my theory?"

"Sure."

"I think humankind just doesn't like endings. But without endings, how can you have beginnings? Or middles, for that matter? Personally, I like a good ending. If a story just went on and on without an ending, eventually you'd get bored and quit reading. There's something satisfying in wrapping up a tale. Every river ends somewhere. Each sunrise becomes a sunset. That's just life. The trick is being willing to step into the unknown. Finding out what comes next. But you . . . you weren't afraid of what was next; you were more afraid to live in the now. That made death seem pretty good, didn't it, son?"

Nik lowered his head. "If you know all that, then why?"

"Why didn't I take you, then? Well, the answer to that question is simple but complicated. It wasn't your time. In other words, you still have things to do."

"What things?"

"Ah, that's the complicated part and the piece I can't answer for you. The answer is different for each person. What I can tell you is that just like you knew me, you'll know the answer to that question in your heart if you want to know badly enough. Now, as to the other, more standard questions, the hows, whens, and wheres of your actual demise, I can be pressed upon to share that information. I should warn you, though, that knowing is a burden."

"Yeah. I can see that."

Again, Nik shifted, crossing and uncrossing his legs, trying to find some way to relieve the pain. *Blast that Pasha!* he thought.

The three were silent for a long time. All waited on Nik. With Veru or Stacia, Nik never had to speak first. Any time there was silence, they rushed to fill it, each sister talking over the other one. Nik had learned from the time he was young that there was great protection in being quiet. Not only could you glean information you would otherwise miss out on, but you avoided saying anything that would cause upset in others. Those who traveled with you always assumed you agreed with their opinions.

His mother rarely spoke, especially in the presence of their father, but when she did, she usually said something so profound it stuck with him. One thing she'd said was, "A fool's tongue runs before his feet." She'd always encouraged him to gain experience in a thing before he went on trying to speak about it. Another one, his favorite, was, "A silent man is never conquered."

Nik had quoted that to himself time and again when withstanding his father's blows. It was part of the reason he'd survived. He bore the pain because he told himself he was the victor in the end. But he'd since learned, for whatever reason, that most people didn't think or feel the same way about being still or quiet, or just sitting with their thoughts. He appreciated that the two people in the room with him did. It was rare.

When he finally gathered himself, he said, "I don't care about my own death. When or how it happens, it will happen. I'll accept it, no matter what. Death—or you, I suppose—have passed me by many a time. Now that I know there's a reason for me to keep walking upon this earth, I'm satisfied to continue searching for the why until I find it and accept that my work isn't finished."

Death spun his chair back around and stood as if preparing to leave. "That's an impressive worldview. And fairly healthy, considering your background. Then until we meet again, my dear." He picked up Zima's tiny hand and pressed a kiss on the back, then bowed. The little girl giggled in response and tossed her head back, jiggling her bouncy curls.

"I'll take my leave now. Unless there's something else? Think hard, young man. I won't return for you again until it's your time, so if there's something pressing, best get it out."

"Yes," Nik said. "There is something else."

"Very well. Tell me," Death said. "What is it that itches in your thoughts? If it's not for yourself, then perhaps for another?" he suggested.

Dozens of people he cared about shifted to the forefront of Nik's mind—Veru, Stacia, the tsarina and her husband, each of his siblings, his maternal grandparents, his mother and the unborn babe, Pasha, the ghosts he'd met, even the kikimora grandmother and her tree-spirit leshi husband. Nik thought he might ask after any one of them. Were they happy? Did they suffer? Were they in a better place? Did they forgive him?

But Nik realized the answers to those questions didn't matter. What difference did it make now? Death happened. It was done. There was nothing he could do about it now. He couldn't fix it. There was no going back and undoing the fire or the knife to his mother's belly. Could saying, "I'm sorry. I made a mistake," ever be enough to compensate for the loss of an unborn child and its mother?

So instead of asking Death any of those very valid, yet ultimately pointless questions, Nik asked him the one thing he truly wanted to know.

"Is my father in hell?"

Death blinked once, twice, then straightened. "My, my. Now that is a question, isn't it?"

"Well? Is he?" Nik almost felt desperate to know the answer now.

"I don't get asked that one often. The truth of it is . . . I don't know."

"What? *What?*" Nik asked incredulously. "How do you not *know*?"

"I think you have me confused with Hades or maybe Anubis. I don't manage an afterlife or an underworld. I'm Death. Plain and simple. Once a mortal end has been reached, my work is done. Justice? Punishments and such? Not my bag."

"I think he's getting upset," Zima said.

"I think you're right," Death agreed.

"Look, young man. I can see you're very sincere. You really unearthed some baggage here today. I *can* tell you that your papa died the first time by your hand and the second time, if you can call that half-life living, by your hand as well. That much I do know."

Nik was quiet for several moments. Death and Zima sat patiently, waiting for him to talk. When he finally did, he smiled. "Thank you for your visit. This conversation has been most enlightening," he said.

Death stood and bent over Zima, whispering something in her ear, then called out, "Priest! It is time for you to return. I place the young one in your care until such time as she summons me again."

Zakhar parted the curtain nervously and refused to make eye contact with Death, but the dark-eyed man did glance at Nik once more, who boldly returned his gaze.

After Death melted away, Zakhar retrieved his quill and bottle of ink. "Oh, I see you didn't take any notes yet. Did you want me to wait a bit?" he asked Nik.

"No, spasibo," Nik said. "I've got what I need." He pointed at his temple and smiled. "It's all up here." He slammed his palm down on the table, making everyone jump. "Serving girl!" he shouted. "Bring me more water!"

Zakhar glanced at Zima and then thanked the serving girl, whose hand was shaking when she poured a glass of water. When she spilled some, Zakhar offered to clean it, but Nik insisted she return and clean it herself.

"What's gotten into you?" Zakhar asked Nik.

Waving a hand in dismissal, Nik said, "I'm just having a really, really bad day. Now, tell me everything."

Chapter 28

Don't Throw a Punch When the Fight Is Over

"I cannot submit your eligibility for that fight, miledi."

"Why not?" Stacia insisted. "What difference does it make who I fight?"

"Because even if I did not care about my reputation or have pride in my work, I do not throw away lives without thought. I am to fructify—to make fruitful my choices." He thumped his palm against his head and groaned in frustration. "I won't make you . . . yeda dlya poroshka, food fit for rabbits, or in this case, tigers. It helps no one."

"I beg you. Is there anything I can do to change your mind?"

"No. I'm sorry. Dinner's in an hour or so."

Stacia's guard left her then, and she heard the slamming of not one but three different gates and the sound of keys turning in locks. The noise from the Games carried even to their high location, and without a window to observe or try to pry loose, she had nothing else to do but figure out how to escape her cage. Careful not to nick herself again, she used the blade in the staff to try to open the lock. It didn't work.

Next, she tried to cut through the bolt, but that didn't meet with success either. Nor did trying to pry the hinges off the door. The floor and ceiling were made of concrete, and though something wet dripped down from the corner of the ceiling above, there was no indication that the box they'd put her in had any weaknesses.

Her machinations were interrupted when her jailer brought her a wooden tray with a small, bruised piece of fruit, a slice of bread, some water, and a small pot. She bit into the old apple and winced. As she chewed, she held up the pot and asked through a mouthful of pulpy dinner, "What's this for?"

"To do your business. Go on the floor like some of these other brutes and you go without dinner."

Stacia gagged, catching a whiff of the pot, and set it aside, pushing it away with her boot. "Got it."

He turned to go, and that's when she noticed his slight limp. Taking another bite of her apple, she motioned toward his leg. "Battle wound?" she asked casually.

"Took an axe to the leg when I was young. Never healed properly. Least I still have it. Could have been worse."

Nodding, Stacia said, "Must have sank into the muscle. Lucky you didn't nick a major blood vessel. Lost a good many soldiers in battle before. Axe wounds are brutal. Personally, I'd prefer a nice clean sword through the heart if I'm to go that way. That means whoever fought me looked me in the eye and at least had some style if they beat me. An arrow is a bit cowardly, to my way of thinking. An axe? Don't need to have much skill to wield those."

"Oh? I disagree. True, you need muscle to carry it and to strike, and it may be that only a brute of a man would choose it for a weapon, but to throw it with precision takes talent."

"I suppose that's an accurate assessment."

"Did you bring a sword to fight with, then?"

"Sadly, no. I left my sword at home."

"What do you have?"

Moving aside her coat, she showed him the staff.

"Oh, that's a beauty," he said.

"It is, I agree. A staff has never been my weapon of choice though."

"No?"

"Not really. But I do have something that can help you."

"Help me?"

Reaching into the pocket of her coat, she fished out the coin. He held up his hands. "I already got the red gold from your master. As you can see, it didn't benefit you at all."

"I know. This is different."

She picked up the mug of water and plopped the coin into the cup, swirling it a bit with her finger, then took a sip for effect. "Now you," she said.

"Me, what? You want me to drink?"

"Yes."

"Why?"

"It will help your leg. At least that's what the aunties told me. Couldn't hurt to try, I imagine. Go on," she said, thrusting the mug toward him. "Just swallow some."

He took the mug and sniffed the contents, then narrowed his eyes. "How do I know you aren't drugging me?"

"Because you saw me drink from it too. You can lock me in here first and drink it outside, if you like."

He decided to do just that while Stacia rolled her eyes. Still, she would have done the same thing.

After he swallowed a mouthful, he took another, then passed back the cup with the coin at the bottom. "Don't feel any different," he said.

"Give it some time. Maybe it takes a while," she replied.

He grunted and left, but returned a short time later with a full pitcher of water for her and then began snuffing most of the torches for the night. Stacia rolled herself into her warm pelisse and fell asleep.

The next morning, her keeper unlocking her cell was the sound that woke her. "Hurry," he said. "I can get you in with me to watch the match with your tiger, but that's all I can manage for now."

"Thank you," she murmured, passing him as he closed the cell behind her.

She followed him through dark passages that twisted and turned until they emerged through a door that led out into the cold, bright sunlight of a mountaintop morning. Three fights were already underway. One took place in the water arena. Two large ships were blasting each other with cannons while sailors clashed steel and swung back and forth from ropes. Stacia could also see there were huge, vicious monsters in the water that quickly ripped apart and devoured anyone who fell overboard.

The second looked like a desert with mounds where men climbed and leaped from structure to structure. They fought for dominance atop each narrow space. Below, huge scorpion creatures waited to grab those who fell. The third was a series of boxes with holes and tubes. Warriors had to make their way through them like rats. Weapons and helpful items were littered throughout, but so were deadly dangers, such as snakes and blades that snapped into vulnerable torsos or skulls.

Horns blasted, indicating that a fourth arena was just about to get underway. This was where they were headed. Stacia pulled her cloak tighter around her body and fingered the staff tucked into her pocket. Her jailer had his hand on her arm, escorting her just as he would anyone else, and she noticed him nodding at others from time to time. All the men carried the same look about them. She wondered how many of them there were and how many she and Iriko would have to kill to earn their freedom.

"Your tonic worked," the man said softly when they turned a corner.

"Good," Stacia replied. "I'm glad you're well."

"I'm more than well," he said. "It didn't just cure my leg. The ache in my bones has disappeared, too, and the darkness clouding my vision is gone. You healed me. I-I won't be able to save your man or tiger or whatever he is, but I will try to save you. I aim to add your name to the list on the ship in the first arena. They won't be able to recover all the bodies with those toothy fish in the water. I'll have to wait until the Games are over, but I'll be able to smuggle you out. I'll say you're a woman I won some time with."

"Thank you, but I . . ." Stacia looked into his earnest face and realized what he was risking for her. "Thank you," she finished, patting his arm and not saying what she'd intended. She didn't need to put him in more danger, and having a way out for at least one of them was a step in the right direction.

"Here we are," he said, stopping at a grate. Bending, he pulled it open and indicated she could climb down. There was a metal ladder leading into a dark pit. "I'll need to lock this behind you," he said. "But I'll be back for you when the fight is over. I'm sorry about your man."

"Spasibo," Stacia said, putting her foot on the ladder. She began climbing, descending into the dark, which became even blacker when the small opening above her head was closed, and she heard the snick of a lock. Her heavy cloak swirled around her body, nearly tripping her as she continued. It felt like she'd gone down several flights of stairs before her eyes finally adjusted to the dimness and she could finally make out a bit of her surroundings.

The stairs came to a stop on a grate that circled a dark arena. This was the place where all the lights were attached. The walkway was only about two to three feet wide and at least two floors up from the arena floor. She stepped all the way to the edge, and then she heard a buzz and nearly fell as the whole thing began to move.

A huge dome shifted, opening to the sky, blinding her with its light. Thunderous cheers erupted from the crowd that came into view by the thousands as the arena circled in their direction. Stacia darted behind a spotlight just as it came on and reflexively turned to the scene laid out below. Her mouth fell open. It was a forest, filled with trees, complete with a river that ran down the middle filled by a picturesque waterfall. It was lovely enough to take her breath away.

A beautiful white stag entered the landscape. He bent to drink from the stream, and when he lifted his head, she noticed that his impressive antlers were made of gold. Drums began, and then an announcer spoke. "Damy i gospoda, ladies and gentlemen. For your viewing pleasure, I give you a very special treat. Here we have the rare white stag of the tundra, but not only this—his horns have been dipped in bronze and sharpened to razor points. A more striking and uncommon creature you will never see, except for those who hunt him. For today I bring you not one, not two, but four unusual tigers, each one as unique as the stripes on their bodies. And it appears to me that they are *hungry*."

The crowd erupted at that word.

"That's right!" He laughed. "And are *you hungry* for them? Let's show them we are as we watch the hunt! Five will go in, but only one will come out! Place your bets. Which one will it be? For this arena you can bet on color! A special treat. Your choices are gold, red, silver, and oh, let's call this last one pearl. Or is it fawn? I just can't decide. Such a beauty though. Am I right?"

Stacia watched in horror as four cages were wheeled up to the arena.

The announcer continued, "And for those of you who enjoy bettering on an underdog, you can select white. Who knows? Maybe this stag has a few magical gifts of his own up his sleeve. Better hurry. The doors are opening now. Stakes will raise soon."

Stacia?

She heard Iriko's voice, though he felt far away and . . . and something was different about him. It was almost like he was throwing his emotions onto her. The tiny hairs on the back of her neck raised, as did gooseflesh on her arms and legs. Her heart raced, and she felt a desperate need to pace.

I'm here, she called out in her mind. *Try to calm yourself. We're going to get you out of here.*

It's too much, he said. *Too much pain. They're cast off. Angry. They need a home. I can't provide for them. They hunger. They need . . . they need so much.*

Who hungers? What are you talking about?

Too late. I can't stop them. They'll kill each other if we don't do something. I'm not right. I can't hold them.

Do you mean your captors? The vodnik?

No. Not them. They mean nothing. Sold me and walked away. Help them. Please, Red. What I did was wrong. He didn't deserve it. He didn't mean to do what he did. They can't help themselves.

Just tell me what to do, Iriko.

Oh no. It's too late.

She heard a blast from the horns, and the gates were opened. The stag lifted his head. His nostrils widened as he scented danger. He froze, but only for an instant, then he turned and bound like lightning up the side of the cliff. Higher and higher he climbed, rocks tumbling beneath his hooves until he stood atop the edge of the mountainside, where the water spilled over onto the boulders below in a glorious shower.

Meanwhile, at the edge of the trees, Stacia spied movement. A tawny flash sped through the underbrush. She heard a roar. Bushes shook, and then her eyes spied another large shape. This one, she knew well. The silver-and-black coat was barely visible, but she knew what to look for and she spotted him.

How are you seeing? Stacia asked him as she watched him move carefully in and out of the tree line.

I'm using their eyes, he said simply.

The tawny-white cat pushed in front of him. She was beautiful. Smaller than Iriko, but lithe and lean. Stacia was transfixed, watching her slink in the shadows as she hunted. Iriko trailed behind her. Then, on the opposite side of the arena, she spotted another cat. This one was orange, no, red, and it was bigger than the one hunting with Iriko. It was . . . it seemed . . . familiar.

Stacia's breath caught, and her heart started beating hard in her chest.

No. It can't be!

It is, Iriko said. *She's your cat.*

But how? How did she get here?

I don't know. But she's feral. My cat says if she kills, she'll be broken. Gone. A wild thing forever. There'll be no bringing her back. No taming her.

But what do we do? How do we stop her?

He doesn't know. We've been trying to communicate, but they seem . . . lost. Like they don't know who they are.

The red cat leaped from the trees into the clearing and faced down Iriko. She snarled, baring her teeth in challenge. Then she lowered her head, smelling him and seemed to find him familiar somehow. As if changing her mind, she switched direction and bound the other way, tracking the stag. But right behind her, a golden tiger paced out of the trees. She lifted her head and grimaced, tasting the air.

Ignoring Iriko, she turned and raked her claws down the tree, then snarled viciously at the cream-colored tiger standing behind him before disappearing down the trail after the red tiger. Stacia watched the very familiar animal, her heart hurting for her missing sister.

"Oh, Veru, where are you?" she whispered.

But who is the tiger staying with you? Stacia asked. *Who does she belong to?*

There was a long pause, and then Iriko finally answered. *I guess you could call her my penance.*

I don't understand. What do you mean?

I can't be certain. It's been a long time. But if I'm right, this is the tiger that belonged to my sister. I think—I think I'm meant to return her home.

Stacia took a long look at that cream tiger with the tawny stripes, and she could almost see the proud older sister who'd drowned to save her baby brother. She could also hear in Iriko's voice how desperate he was to save her, or at least her tiger, in return. The tsarevna sucked in a breath. *What do you want me to do?* she asked.

Just help me try to get through to them. At the very least, we can't let them kill the stag, he said. *No matter how hungry they are.*

Okay, Stacia said. She looked around. *No problem. I just need to keep three hungry tigers away from their supper.*

There was no hiding for the beautiful stag. His white coat stood out against the gray mountains. Perhaps if they were covered with snow, she thought, he'd have a better chance of hiding.

Just as she imagined the stag hidden in a winter background, the clouds turned dark, and snow began falling. Lightly at first, and then thicker. Soon the arena was dusted with snow, showing clear pugmarks where the tigers marked their trails.

Right, Stacia thought. *Zima must be watching.* Belting her pelisse tightly, she measured the distance between the scaffold and the cliff peak where the stag hid. If she was careful, she might make it without breaking a leg, but if she mistimed it, she'd be hurting. She was about to jump when there was a stirring in her pocket. "What's that?" she said, wrenching open her coat, only then remembering she had a stowaway who'd been very quiet since she'd disappeared.

"Belizna! Don't want to die with me? I don't blame you. Fine. Hop out. Hopefully, I'll find you later."

The ermine scurried out of the pocket, squeaking as it did, and hopped madly over to a section of scaffolding that had a dangling section of rope. She leaped onto it, grabbing the end in her sharp teeth, and dove over the side into midair.

"Oh no!" Stacia cried.

Wispy clouds obscured her view, so Stacia put her hands on the rope, hoping to pull the little ermine back to safety, but when she tugged, something tugged back. She let go, not knowing what to do, and then tried again a moment later. This time, when she yanked on the rope, it was tighter. She pulled harder and found it was so tight it wouldn't give at all.

"Belizna!" she called softly over the edge of the scaffolding, but she didn't hear a squeak of any kind. She stood back, waiting for the clouds to clear a bit so she could jump, and kept herself occupied by thinking of how she'd apologize to Zakhar and Zima for killing their pet, if she herself should survive, when she saw the rope bouncing wildly. A moment later, the little ermine leaped up onto the scaffold and into Stacia's arms, having climbed the rope on her own.

"You smart girl," Stacia said.

The wispy clouds cleared then, and the tsarevna could see what the ermine had done. The rope had been secured to some rocks below. "Clever beastie," she said. "Why don't you ride down in my pocket, then?"

She put Belizna inside Father Frost's cloak and then lifted one leg and then her second over the rail. Gripping the rope with both hands, she closed her eyes and prayed her sister wasn't doing anything nearly as foolhardy or dangerous; then she leaped, wrapping her legs around the rope and sliding down two stories to the top of a mountain in an arena filled with thousands of spectators, wild tigers, and a stag so frightened he'd probably impale her the moment she came too close.

Thankfully, Belizna had wedged the rope between the mountain and a very large boulder. Unfortunately, what was strong enough to hold an ermine wasn't always strong enough to hold a tsarevna. The rope gave way and came loose when she was just nearing the top. Stacia screamed as she careened out over nothing. Her boots came in contact with a boulder when she swung back, but her hands, which were now raw and blistered from sliding down, threatened to slip off at any second. She bounced and spun out a second time. The third time she was determined to make it meaningful and pushed on the boulder deliberately.

She got enough power behind the push to swing far enough out to kick herself back to safety, but the boulder shifted, and she knew it would fall. Desperately, she dropped the rope and grabbed on to the boulder, finding one handhold but slipping until her boots caught. Quickly, she climbed and leaped just as the boulder tumbled out from beneath her, rolling down the mountainside in a great tumble of rocks and debris.

Stacia! Iriko cried out.

I'm fine, she managed to tell him as she lay in an awkward position, panting. She heard a noise above her and saw the stag, leaping even higher, trying desperately to get away from the newcomer who had just destroyed his ledge of safety.

At least the polar bear fur acts as a nice cushion, she thought as she laid there, trying to assess her body for damage.

Polar bear fur? Iriko said.

I'll tell you later.

She heard a noise and the sound of claws scraping rock. Scrambling to her feet, she whipped open her coat and pulled out the staff, elongating it and pushing the button that exposed the blade.

Twirling the staff, she held it at the ready, just as not one but three very hungry cats leaped onto the ledge. Stacia knew she stood between them and their dinner. A bit further down was Iriko, struggling up the side of the cliff.

Hold on, Red! he called. *I'm coming!*

At first Stacia thought she should try to talk to them, but one look in the tigers' crazed eyes told her there would be no talking. The cream and gold tigers paced, mouths open, saliva dripping, but they didn't pounce like Stacia expected. Instead, they moved aside, allowing the red tiger to approach.

She stalked toward Stacia, head lowered, her mouth wide, fangs exposed. When she growled, Stacia could feel the vibration in her own chest. Though she expected to feel fear at the sight of so monstrous a creature, especially one ready to pounce, one powerful enough to rip her to pieces, Stacia wasn't frightened. Instead, she felt kinship. A sense of loyalty and respect. Much as she would when she worked with her soldiers.

She didn't lower her weapon. Not yet. It was a sign of respect. It showed she knew the tiger was lethal. The other two tigers sat, one on either side. They were watchful. Not relaxed, but not on alert either. This battle was one that needed to be fought between the two of them.

The crowd began chanting, one voice surging into a roar of hundreds, then thousands as they picked up the refrain.

Kill.

Kill.

Kill!

Stacia could almost feel the thrum of bloodlust in the arena. The crowd's appetite had been whetted. Once, when she'd been younger, a giant wild boar had become crazed, killing everything that crossed its path. When the soldiers finally managed to slay the raging animal in the forest outside the palace, they'd discovered it had smothered its own offspring, likely by accident.

She didn't know what triggered most people into becoming brutal, but she'd learned something that day. The line was thin indeed. All it took was a simple push. A loss. A wound. A fear. An illness. Sometimes the only thing holding back the monster threatening to break free was an incredible self-will. One that was more powerful than the beast.

When the red tiger turned, Stacia turned with her, angling her body to mimic her movements. This went on for a few moments. Then, finally, the tiger's fierce growl turned to a softer rumble in her chest, and she sat, keeping her eyes trained on the girl in front of her. Stacia pushed the button, hiding the blade inside the staff.

Finally, she spoke. "It was wrong of me to consider you a curse," Stacia said. "I've missed you. I didn't think that was possible."

The rumble cut off, and the tiger lifted a paw and began licking the pad.

"I've made mistakes. Many of them. And I'm certain I'll make more in the future. But I don't consider you one of them. Iriko's mother said you were blessings for her people. I don't know much about that, but I do know there's nothing a mother or a leader wouldn't do for her children or her people."

Stacia set down the staff as the tiger closely followed her movements.

"Maybe I'll never become as good of tsarina as my mother was or as clever as either of my parents, but perhaps that's why they sent you. To make up for my weaknesses. Will you come back?"

Swallowing, Stacia undid the belt on her coat and took hold of either side, opening it to expose her tunic beneath and the length of her vulnerable throat.

Iriko arrived at the top. *What are you doing, Red? Stop! It's too dangerous!*

Come! Stacia commanded the cat. *It's time for you to come home.*

No! shouted Iriko in her mind.

The red cat snarled, baring her teeth. Then she rose up, crouched on her hind legs, and leaped, her front claws hitting Stacia directly in the chest. The cat's heavy body caused the breath to whoosh out of the tsarevna's body as she was pushed flat on her back. Fangs descended and Stacia closed her eyes thinking, it felt right.

Father Frost's cloak moved of its own accord, enveloping the tiger's body, and just when Stacia thought she was done for, her breath returned. She sucked in frigid air and opened her eyes, and the world shifted. Stacia was still human, but she was also a tiger. She could feel the cat within, and it was home. But their work wasn't finished. Now she needed to save their sisters.

Rising to her feet, feeling feral and stronger than she'd been in a long time, Stacia cried out in her mind, *Come, sisters. I will make a place for you as well.* Opening her coat, she crouched and leaped several feet in the air just as the gold cat sprang for her throat. They wrapped limbs around one another, and soon the golden tiger was absorbed just like the red one had been.

Stacia turned to the cream-and-fawn tiger. Cocking her head, she said, "You too, little one." The tiger snarled and turned to run, but Iriko blocked the way. Stacia jumped on her back, opened the coat, and wrestled the tiger until it disappeared just like the others. She got to her feet and stumbled when she felt three tigers within her struggling for dominance.

"Cease," she said softly. "Be still."

She pressed her fingers into her temples, closing her eyes, and a furry head bumped into her leg.

How are you? Iriko asked.

"I'll be fine," Stacia said. "But we need to get out of here."

Looks like a ride just showed up.

Cracking open her eyes, Stacia realized she stood in a shadow. It was Zakhar and Zima waving to them from the balloon as it descended into the arena. Above them, dragons circled, waiting to take all of them into custody.

"Guess we're going to fight our way out," Stacia said.

My favorite way to escape, Iriko replied.

CHAPTER 29

Don't Boast When You Begin But When You Finish the Journey

Veru and Danik arrived back at the cottage just as dawn broke over the eastern mountains. Max greeted them at the open door, meowing furiously, which they took as a bad omen. He'd never done such a thing before. The moment they dismounted, the black steed galloped away, disappearing in a vortex of lightning and fire, leaving only a trail of rapidly disappearing sparks in his wake.

When they entered the cottage, they found it dark. The fire was unlit, and no food was bubbling in the cauldron, which only meant one thing to them—Yuga would be returning any moment. Quickly, they removed their packs, and while Veru moved the sesame seeds back to their original containers, Danik stowed away the magic gifts they'd been given, wrapping them carefully inside clothing, or stowing them inside the now empty flasks and hiding them in their bags.

By the time they heard the scraping of Yuga's heavy stone bowl as it landed by the door, they were seated in their usual spots, Danik softly strumming his domra and Veru brushing through Max's coat with her fingers, working out all the burrs and chiding him for whatever it was he'd been up to for the last few days.

The door flew open, and Yuga dragged in her newly acquired supplies, along with her mode of transport, ignoring the two of them as she did. She grumble-groaned to herself as she bustled about, tossing items into cupboards and complaining about the ache in her bones and the cold weather that made her nose leak worse than the old pipes in the house.

Finally, she sank into the creaky chair across from Veru. "Well now," she said. "I can tell the two of you are still alive. At least my traitorous cat is still good for something, anyway."

"Yes," Danik said. "Alive and fit. And we've done our packing. We've completed our end of the bargain, and we'd like to be bidding you dos vedanya now."

"Is that so?" she said, glaring in their direction down her very long nose.

"It is," Veru replied, calmly stroking Maxsim. She glanced meaningfully at Danik. "No . . . no rush, of course. You're welcome to examine the wares, if you like. We'll wait until you do. Then we'll expect to be taking what's ours as well as our leave of you." Leaning forward, she slid the contract across the table. "And just in case you forgot, here's the signed contract for your reference. I can reread it for you, if you need it, so your memory will be refreshed. You'll want to take special note of the items you promised us. We're happy to go over them with you again. Item by item."

"Ha! Perabsurdum nugatus." Yuga said, standing up and stabbing a bony finger on the paper. "I'll thank you not to get ahead of yourself, my dear. Let's just taste that water first, shall we?"

The old woman rose and cracked open the water barrel, then located a dipper and swirled it inside. After sniffing it, she caught a few drops between her fingers and rubbed it carefully. Last, she touched a few drops to her tongue, then froze.

"Scaturigenous selynesse magicum. How did you do this?" she demanded. "Tell me."

"I don't believe we have to tell you," Veru said. "That wasn't part of the deal. But I'm assuming by your irritation that we accomplished your task."

"You did," she agreed. "And it's very valuable, I'll give you that."

"Is it really? You called it scaturigenous selynesse magicum. That's . . . let's see . . . if I remember my Latin, that's magic happy drink?"

"Close. It's Magical Fountain of Happy Waters."

"Ah, so you'll be using it to dupe other poor souls like ourselves."

"It's none of your business how or why I use it."

"Very well. It's yours to do with as you wish. As we agreed."

The old woman searched the cottage with her rheumy eyes. "Don't tell me you completed the second task." Her gnarled hands opened and closed as if she were already clutching the bolt of fabric.

"We did," Danik said. He stepped behind a table and brought out the shimmering black fabric.

Though the woman was blind, or at least Veru thought she was, her gaze fixed on the bolt the minute it appeared. "Here, boy!" she said, a definite tone of greed in her voice. "Give it over. Quickly!"

He placed the heavy material in her outstretched arms, and she clutched it to her bosom. "Oh!" she exclaimed. "Oh my. It's more beautiful than I ever imagined. It's perfect. It's . . ." She quickly unrolled the bolt, measuring it against her arm and counting the lengths. "One, two, three . . ." Then she stopped at forty. "Forty and a half. Surely, there's more."

"I'm sorry, Yuga," Danik said. "That's all there is."

"You must make more. You absolutely must."

"I'm afraid you didn't stipulate the length of the bolt in the contract," Veru said.

"Surely this isn't enough to count as a bolt," Yuga replied craftily. "In the marketplace, a bolt would never be sold this small."

Veru interrupted. "Hold on. Before you try to default by arguing semantics, you should know I am well-versed in this particular area, as I've had to sit in judgment over disputes often enough. In the marketplace, a bolt is typically one hundred arshins in length."

"There! You see?" Yuga sat back with a smug expression. "You failed."

Holding up a finger, Veru added, "I said typically. Depending on the type of fabric, it can also be as small as thirty arshins. It may still be defined as a bolt, so long as the type of material meets certain conditions. In this case, the fabric is a woolen, and therefore heavier. This is one common exemption. In addition, it is very difficult to weave and collect. Exemption number two. It is also extremely rare and would therefore be one of the most expensive fabrics ever to be placed on the market. That is exemption three. For these reasons, I would be extremely surprised if a bolt of this particular type was ever sold at more than thirty arshins in length. Therefore, I'd say we met the task. And I'd think you'd be hard-pressed to find an impartial judge in this land or any other who wouldn't agree."

Yuga went still, thinking, obviously trying to come up with another way to trick them into losing, but Veru pressed further. "Obviously, you're unsatisfied with our efforts. I suppose we could simply keep it for ourselves or sell it at the marketplace and see what we could get for it instead."

Veru rose and began rolling the fabric back into a bolt, but Yuga tore it away from her hands. "You will not!" she said. "Those sheep are mine!"

"Perhaps, but the effort was ours. You don't own us . . . yet. We would be compensated for our work. But you are right. You do own the sheep." Veru glanced at Danik and winked. "Very well. We'll sell it, then, and split the profit with you, fifty-fifty."

Yuga seemed almost desperate to stop Veru from taking away the fabric but didn't quite know what to do. Veru rolled up the black material and lifted the bolt from Yuga's lap, but the old woman stopped her and pulled the bolt to her chest and then chuckled awkwardly. "Upon consideration, I'll take it. I suppose it meets the criteria, though I'll have you know I'm being very generous."

"I'm sure you are," Danik said. "Shall I help you carry it somewhere, Babushka?" he offered.

"No. No, boy. I'll take care of it." Once she'd stowed it away and sat back down, she said, "Well, now. It seems the two of you did well. You should be proud of yourselves. It's too bad you didn't finish the final task, but you did much better than anyone else. That's excellent. I've a mind to reward you with a little something for all you did. I'm very pleased with your work. And I'll tell you, that's a rare thing."

"Oh, but, Babushka, we did finish the last task," Danik said.

"You—you did? But where's the wheat?"

"The black knight is stowing it for you as we speak," Veru said, hoping it wasn't a bluff, and she was right. "While he's finishing up, here are your sesame seeds, just as you asked."

Veru placed both jars on the little table between them, and Yuga opened the jars and peered inside them, then ran a finger into each one, feeling to see if they contained the seeds.

When she stoppered them again, she said, "I'd ask how you did it without using the seeds, but I already know you won't tell me."

"That's right," said Danik. "Just like you won't tell us your secrets."

"I'm an old woman. I have no secrets."

"I think we both know that isn't true," Veru said.

"Let's get this over with," Yuga said sharply. "I don't see any wheat, and I think the two of you are stalling." Closing her eyes, she mumbled a few words and then opened her mouth. They heard the crack of thunder and saw lightning flash just outside the window. There was a banging on the door. The old woman flicked her fingers, and standing outside in the snow was the black knight.

"You called, mistress?" Sumerki said after bowing to Yuga.

"Yes. These two tell me you stored wheat for them. Is this true?"

"No, mistress. I stored the wheat according to *your* instructions," the knight said very carefully.

"Is that so?" Yuga turned to Danik and Veru and smiled widely. "I wonder, then, why they seem to be under the impression that you were helping *them*?"

"I wouldn't know."

"It's very strange, I agree."

Danik rose from his seat. "You've betrayed us," he accused, his hands clenched at his side.

"Now, now," Yuga said, still grinning. "I'll not have my servants tussling with one another. Let bygones be bygones, why don't you?"

"Predatel'!" Danik shouted. "Negodyay! Posramit' upon you and your ancestors!"

The black knight simply stood there, taking Danik's insults without even flinching, but Veru recognized defeat when she saw it. She rose and Max jumped from her lap. Putting a hand on Danik's arm, she patted it lightly, trying to still the trembling rage she could feel vibrating through him. Truthfully, it wasn't Sumerki's fault. She was certain he'd been compelled to do what he'd done. Perhaps there was still a way out for them.

"It would appear that congratulations are in order, then," Veru said. "Unfortunately, when it comes to the matter of the wheat, seeing is believing, wouldn't you agree?"

Yuga stopped crowing and narrowed her eyes. "What are you going on about, girl?"

"Well, *we* did harvest the wheat, and if Sumerki did gather it for you, then I would need to see it. What if you're wrong? Perhaps he means to sell it. Perhaps it's missing."

"Of course he didn't steal it. He wouldn't cross me. And the contract clearly states that *you* are to deliver it to me, not my knight."

"Oh, I understand. But I also know that those who double-cross are often double-crossed themselves. When it comes to freedom, there isn't much that most wouldn't do. Perhaps if I could see the wheat, or at least know its location, then I might believe your story."

The black knight spoke, "If I may, according to my mistress's own instructions, the wheat was stored in her granary, not two verts from here. I can show you this myself, if you like."

Yuga waved a hand. "We believe you."

"I don't," Veru said. "I think I need proof before I can accept eternal servitude. You'd ask the same of us, I'd think."

"Bah! Very well," Yuga said huffily. "Come, you stubborn girl."

"Danik, you stay behind, won't you? We won't be too long, I shouldn't think. Of course, if the wheat somehow magically arrives here while we're gone, make sure to stack it up properly so Yuga can see we did our part."

"What are you going on about, girl?" Yuga said as she dragged out her stone bowl and opened the door.

"I'm only saying nothing is proven yet. I still believe the black knight will come through for us."

"Clearly, he didn't," Yuga said, gesturing Veru should climb into the bowl beside her. "He's loyal to me."

"If the wheat is where the two of you say it is, then I'll happily agree with you. But if we return and find it here instead, then it means that we succeeded."

"You stupid girl. It's not here. How could it be here when we return?"

"I have faith."

Yuga shook her head and snapped her fingers.

The black knight bowed and climbed on his waiting steed. "I'll ride on ahead and prepare the way," he said.

"Yes, yes. Off with you." She lifted the heavy stirring wand, and the two of them rose in the night sky. Veru looked back at Danik, who stood at the open door, staring after them. She hoped he understood what she wanted him to do. As she strained to hear the sound of notes coming from the little house, they picked up speed and were soon high above the ice-covered trees. The door slammed shut, locking Danik inside and sealing off the light coming from the house.

The wind was freezing cold. Veru ducked down inside the deep bowl as they journeyed through the sky. She missed the warmth of Danik's arms holding her and looked up at the stars above, making a wish that they could get out of this witchy woman's web. All too soon, they landed, and after Yuga awkwardly climbed out, Veru followed.

The ground was crunchy and hard where she stepped, though there was no snow in the place they'd arrived. Two large silos sat near an open field. A portal opened, and the black knight appeared, pulling up near them.

"All is ready," he said, dismounting and walking them over to the first tank. He pulled a lever and opened it up, and grain spilled out and over their hands, pooling around their feet. Before too much fell, he quickly closed the hatch, sealing it off and locking it once more.

Yuga laughed, holding out handfuls of grain to Veru, and said, "There you are, young woman. Are you satisfied, then?"

"Oh yes. You have a lovely bin full of fine corn."

"That's right," Yuga said. "It's the finest. The best corn . . ." She trailed off. "Wait, what?" She bent down and scooped up a handful and smelled it, then tossed it aside. "You idiot," she said to the knight. "This is the wrong silo. Take us to the other one."

The black knight thumped his head and offered her his arm, but she shoved it away and made her own way, following the sound of his armor. When they were in position again, he pulled on the lever, opening the hatch, but nothing came out. Sumerki frowned and peered inside. "I-I don't understand," he said. "It was all here. All the wheat. It was entirely full just a few hours ago. I promise you."

"You durak! What happened? Can you not follow the simplest of instructions?"

"But I did, mistress! I promise you, I did."

Veru clicked her tongue. "How very vexing and strange. I wonder whatever did happen to the wheat we harvested, then?"

Yuga shook her head. "Come along, girl. I'm tired. We'll play more of your games another time."

"But don't you want to know what happened to the wheat?" Veru asked, trailing behind the woman as she made her way to the stone bowl.

"It's likely still in the field and you never collected it in the first place. Either way, I win. I'll get it myself later. There's time for that another day. As for you," she said to the black knight as she climbed into her bowl, "begone for tonight. I'll think of a fitting punishment for you another day."

Nodding his head, he climbed into the saddle and turned his horse around. As Veru stuck her leg into the bowl and glanced up at the knight, she noticed the tiniest flicker of a smile cross the edge of his lips. She took it for a good sign and kicked off the ground not a moment too soon, because Yuga uttered a spell that caused her bowl to lift up before Veru was even aboard. She fell awkwardly into the basin, bruising her cheek and hip before righting herself.

Yuga was in a terrible mood by the time they arrived back at the little cottage, and it showed by the abuse of the stone basin on the porch. It bounced hard three jaw-shaking times before coming to a stop and took out several boards as it did. The front door blew open with a bang, and she heard a cautious meow come from Max.

Veru poked her head up as Yuga was muttering and climbing out and saw that every corner of the house was filled with sheaves of wheat. She could not only see it but smell it. Danik stood. She hadn't seen him before. His hair was as golden as the wheat. But now her eyes were fixed on him, and Veru realized for the first time how much she'd come to depend on him.

His eyes were tired, his lips were chapped, and his limbs were trembling with exhaustion. She knew how much effort he'd made to get all this wheat moved in the time they'd been gone. It was one sacrifice of dozens—no, hundreds—he'd made on her behalf since she'd met him. Danik was just . . . amazing.

Spasibo, she mouthed to him.

He simply nodded in return.

It was time to put her game face on. Yuga and Veru entered the house, and Veru exclaimed, "Oh! Oh my! Well, look at this. Isn't this just a shocking turn of events?"

Yuga stopped and turned slowly around the room, then lifted a finger and trailed it down a shaft of wheat. Softly, she sighed and sank into her chair.

"Very well. You win. Never let it be said the great Yuga is a bad loser."

Veru snorted.

"Tell me, what is it we agreed to?" Yuga said. "Hurry up, before I change my mind."

"You promised that once our tasks were complete, we will have won our freedom, the promised gift, the freedom of the knights—"

"Yes, yes . . ." She rolled her hand, then looked at the fireplace. "Do you really want to leave me?"

Danik and Veru looked at one another. Veru asked, "Who are you speaking to?"

"Shhh," the old woman said to them and turned back to the fireplace. "We've been together so long. I can't imagine it's been that hard. I know I've been difficult, but I can change."

Finally, she nodded. "The house has agreed to stay with me as long as I agree not to trick you. It will hold me to my side of the bargain. Is that acceptable to you?"

"If the house is okay with it," Danik said.

A fire started at that moment, and Danik smiled.

"Very good," Yuga agreed. "You'll find panniers outside strapped to a sledge. Inside them, you'll find any manner of food, supplies, clothing, money, and a map that will guide you to those you seek. As you stipulated, my knights have been freed. Whether your champions will choose to reveal themselves to you again or not is their prerogative.

"Now, for my stone pot . . . I cannot give you my large one, but you may keep this small one. It has transformative powers. If you meet the knights again, they can explain it to you in more detail. And last . . . Max? Come."

Obediently, the cat paced over to his mistress and leaped onto her lap.

"Maxsim has been my cat for decades. Our relationship is complicated. True, we don't always get on, but I do love him in my own way. I-I would ask you not to take him. Please. As a favor to me."

"Max?" Veru asked. "What do you want?"

The cat looked up at his mistress, then at Veru, and meowed softly. He hopped down from her lap and made as if he wanted to head back to Veru, then stopped and sat and began licking a paw.

"Will you promise to feed him better?" Veru demanded. "No more bones and mice?"

"But he likes mice," the old woman protested.

Veru waited.

"Fine," Yuga said. "He'll be fed whatever he likes."

"Then he can stay with you."

"Spasibo."

"Pozhaluysta."

Veru rose and Danik put his hand on her shoulder to guide her out the door, but the fire in the grate burned blue and hot.

"Wait!" Yuga said. "Your special gift. Max?"

The cat meowed and leaped up on the arm of the chair. From there, it bound into Veru's arms. Max opened his mouth to meow again, but this time Veru heard a distant roar, and Max pounced directly onto her chest, knocking her back into the chair. She toppled to the ground on her hands and knees, her back popping and stretching. Her nose twitched and her vision blurred. She shook out her arms and legs.

"Whoa!" she heard Danik exclaim. "What just happened?"

"She got back what she's been searching for," Yuga explained. "Now it's your turn. Place your hand on the fireplace mantel. The one you so painstakingly cleaned."

Danik cautiously put his hand on the polished wood, and then he closed his eyes. All of a sudden, it was like someone had taken cleaning polish to his mind. The blanket covering his memory disappeared. He remembered everything.

"Veru!" he said, kneeling down beside her. "What have you done to her?" he accused, turning to Yuga.

"I gave her back what she's been looking for. A connection, as it were. It's not there yet. Not precisely, but the possibility exists. She can find it again, if she wishes."

"But she wanted to get rid of it."

"Not truly."

Veru sat up, looking up at him as if dazed.

"It's a part of her," Yuga explained. "Anyway, she can now choose if she will accept the bond or not. She'll need to get used to it again, though she cannot use the tiger's strength or endurance, or change, for that matter. Too bad, since you'll need something to pull the sledge, won't you? I suppose that means the two of you will have to do it yourselves."

The old woman began to cackle.

Danik nodded dumbly as if his mind was still a bit misty as well.

"Best get going now, boy, before my good nature wears off."

Reaching behind the chair, Danik took hold of his bags and patted the mantle a farewell. Just then the secret door popped open, and a wrapped bundle fell out. Danik picked it up and placed it in his satchel. Yuga began to protest, but the fireplace roared, and she settled back in her chair with pursed lips and a sour expression. When Danik walked to the front door, it opened of its own accord. Veru bent and patted Max, then stumbled after Danik. They headed down the rickety steps and were securing their bags on the sledge when the little house rumbled, stretched up on tall, stilt-like boards, and walked over their heads, quickly disappearing into the dark forest.

Just as it did, the sun broke over the eastern mountains, signaling a new beginning. Both Danik and Veru wondered what this new beginning would look like for the two of them.

CHAPTER 30

Befriend the Wolf but Keep the Axe Sharp

"So, we're in agreement?"

"Yes." The powerful man stood with his back turned to the boy who was not as unlike himself as he thought back to who he'd been when he'd first arrived in this strange dreamworld. True, Nikolai Novikov wasn't as clever and didn't possess as many gifts, but he held one very valuable gift that even someone with as many assets as Grigor had amassed in his time couldn't easily come by—knowledge of his future.

Turning, he said, "Tell me again—why would you do this? Betray your friends, the tsarevna you profess to love, all simply in the hope that I will take you on as my protégé? I must confess, I'm afraid I cannot trust your motives."

"Then let's go over it again. When you return, you take me with you. You train me in your ways. Teach me how to bend time like you do. Perhaps you haven't done it yet, but you will. You'll become so powerful that one day you'll be able to reanimate the dead. Then, when all is in place, we're going to stop my father from marrying my mother; either that, or kill him when he's young. Either way, I'll be able to remove the curse of him from my life."

"But won't that mean you'll never be born?"

"Maybe. If so, I don't care."

"How can you not care about such a thing?"

Nik picked up one of the Death Draughtman's books of magic and flipped through the pages boldly. He was no longer frightened about what the man could do to him. Now he was filled with purpose and determination, and there was nothing on earth or in the heavens that could shift him from it. "I had a meeting with Death," Nik replied softly. "He said I was kept alive all these years for a purpose. Now I know what it is."

"Do you?" Grigor Sobol Petrovsky hadn't felt that level of feverish determination in himself for quite some time. Perhaps he should reconsider killing the young man and see if he could indeed help him escape from this prison of the mind he'd found himself a captive of all these years.

"Yes," Nik replied. "I carry the deaths of innocents on my back and shoulders, dragging them like weighted balls, shackles, and anchors that threaten to drown me with each step. It's time I cast off those chains, placing them upon the man who truly deserves them."

"So, what do you intend to do?"

"With your help, I'm going to send my father to hell."

EPILOGUE

It's Better to Turn Back Than to Lose Your Way

"So he betrays his friends? What kind of a coward was he?"

"Lay down again, son. Your fever will return," Kadam chided, rising to wet a towel in the sink, then placed it on Kishan's forehead. "Don't forget how easy it is to judge others when we haven't walked in their shoes. You and your brother had the advantage of being loved and cared for by a wonderful set of parents."

"Even if we hadn't, we also had you for a mentor. This young man did as well."

"I . . . wasn't as hands on with this group as I was with all of you. It's one of many things I have come to regret."

"But surely he made his own choices."

"Yes," Kadam conceded. "All of us do. But you forget how many life paths I went down when exploring our own world. Not all of *your* own life paths were as joyful as the one you ended up selecting."

Kishan grunted. "You mean the one *you* selected."

"Be that as it may, I hope you know that my intent for all of you was only that you find a measure of happiness."

"We all know that."

"Good. Now get some rest."

"But what happens next? Will Nik succeed in banishing his father to hell? Will all of them escape the dreamworld? How will Stacia handle having three tigers inside her? What must *that* be like?"

Kadam chuckled. "Sleep. I'll return in the morning and continue the tale, if you wish. Perhaps, if you're feeling better, I'll tell you of how the sisters were ultimately able to triumph over evil and overcome their trials. Does that suit you?"

Nodding, Kishan closed his eyes, and Kadam stepped outside and took in a deep breath of fresh evening air. All was quiet. The sun had just set. It was the time between, when the things of the day switched to the things of the night. He knew that soon evening predators would be on the prowl, seeking, hunting, searching for anything they could find to assuage their hunger. As he well knew, there were some dark things in his world as well as others, with an appetite so powerful that no matter how much they consumed, they could never be filled.

Anik Kadam glanced up at the wide expanse of the sky and felt small and a bit sad. There was so much dark in the world. It was hard to continue fighting it all the time. But then the first star appeared. Then another, and another. He smiled.

It was a little reminder that light could always be found if one looked.

And light could always defeat darkness.